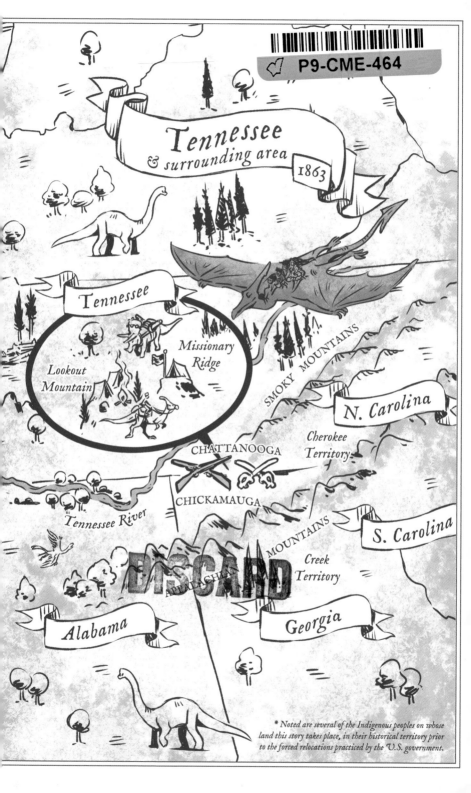

"*Dactyl Hill Squad* has everything a reader could possibly want in a middle-grade book: action, adventure, magic, humor and dinosaurs. Magdalys is the same kind of young, engaging and flawed protagonist as Philip Pullman's Lyra — a character readers can't help but love even when (especially because) she's frustrating. An entertaining and wholly fulfilling series opener." — *Shelf Awareness*

"This book is true fire. It is everything I didn't even know I needed."
— Jacqueline Woodson, National Ambassador
for Young People's Literature

"This is the story that would've made me fall in love
with reading when I was a kid." — Tomi Adeyemi, #1 *New York
Times* bestselling author of *Children of Blood and Bone*

"Older's uprising of sheroes and heroes grips, stomps, and soars from
start to finish." — Rita Williams-Garcia, *New York Times* bestselling
author of *One Crazy Summer*

"*Dactyl Hill Squad* is an engaging, lively adventure with a heroine
I wish I were, in a world I didn't want to leave."
— Jesmyn Ward, two-time National Book Award-winning
author of *Sing, Unburied, Sing*

"This incredible story brings history to life with
power, honesty, and fun."
— Laurie Halse Anderson, *New York Times* bestselling
author of *Chains*

DANIEL JOSÉ OLDER

DACTYL·HILL SQUAD

— BOOK TWO —
FREEDOM FIRE

ARTHUR A. LEVINE BOOKS

AN IMPRINT OF SCHOLASTIC INC.

Library of Congress Cataloging-in-Publication Data available
ISBN 978-1-338-26884-3

10 9 8 7 6 5 4 3 2 1   19 20 21 22 23

Printed in the U.S.A.   23
First edition, May 2019

Book design by Christopher Stengel

FOR KIRA, GABRIEL, AND KAI

TABLE OF CONTENTS

· PART ONE ·

TENNESSEE

CHAPTER ONE
NIGHT FLIGHT

A **GLINT OF LIGHT** flickered in the darkness below. It was late — the sun had sunk behind the trees hours ago, and it seemed to extinguish the whole world of mountains and sky when it went. Magdalys Roca had lost track of how long she and her friends had been flying southward on the back of Stella, the giant pteranodon, but she was pretty sure she'd never get used to that sense of emptiness that closed in whenever night fell across the vast American wilds.

But what was that light?

It had disappeared almost as soon as she'd seen it. A bonfire maybe? A Confederate battle camp? Her heartbeat tha-thumped just a little harder in her ears at the thought. They'd passed the sparkling lights of Washington, DC, a few nights ago, then veered west, and according to Mapper, had

passed into Tennessee yesterday. There were Union outposts throughout the state, but it was still enemy territory.

Stella swooped lower just as Magdalys was craning her neck to see over the huge ptero's wing. Magdalys smiled. She'd started to get used to the fact that dinos and other huge reptiles could understand her inner thoughts and wishes, but with most of them she had to make explicit requests. *Charge*, she'd think, and those hundreds of pounds of scale and muscle would lurch and lumber into action. But Stella seemed to have connected to her on an even deeper level. The ptero knew when Magdalys was tired or afraid, knew, apparently, when she needed to get a better look at something.

There it was — that same sparkle of light in the darkness below. Stella tilted eastward just so as Magdalys grabbed the reins and stood in the saddle, squinting through the night at the dancing splash of brightness.

"Ha," Magdalys said out loud. She looked up, directly above the shimmer to where the almost full moon sat perched on a cloud bank like a queen on her throne.

"The river." Cymbeline Crunk scooched up beside Magdalys with tin cups of cold coffee in her hands. She took a sip from one and passed the other over.

"It's beautiful. Like the moon is keeping an eye on us from above and below. The Mississippi?"

Cymbeline shook her head. "Mm-mm, we're not that far west yet. Probably the Ocoee, an offshoot of the Tennessee River."

Magdalys had never met anyone like Cymbeline before. At just eighteen, she had become a renowned Shakespearean actress along with her brother, Halsey. Plus, she seemed to know everything there was to know about the war and all the messy politics surrounding it. And she was a crack shot with a carbine.

Magdalys had gotten so used to seeing the actress dressed up as princesses and fairies (or sometimes kings and demons), it was still strange to see her in a plain button-down shirt and slacks. Her big wonderful hair was pulled tight against her head, like Magdalys's, and, also like Magdalys's, it then exploded into a big terrific bun just above her neck.

It was Cymbeline who'd insisted they veer west after DC. Tennessee had been the last state to secede, she'd explained, and whole swaths of pro-Union communities still resisted the Confederates in every way they could. And anyway, all the battle lines in Virginia were liable to explode into action at any moment, and the last thing they needed was to get caught up in a major engagement.

Mapper's eyes had gone wide at that — the idea somehow exciting to him — but Two Step, Little Sabeen, and Amaya had all shivered at the thought. Magdalys didn't really care which way they went, as long as it got them to wherever her brother, Montez, was faster. Montez had been wounded in a shoot-out at Milliken's Bend during General Grant's Siege of Vicksburg. One of the other soldiers in his battalion, Private Summers, had sent a letter to Magdalys saying Montez was

still unconscious and they were on their way to New Orleans. All Magdalys knew was that she had to get to him, had to make sure he was okay, be there when he woke up if he hadn't yet, whatever it took.

Montez was the only family Magdalys knew, really. She'd been dropped off at the Colored Orphan Asylum when she was just a baby along with Montez and their two sisters, Celia and Julissa, neither of whom she could remember very well. They'd been whisked off back to Cuba a few years later and then Montez had joined the Union Army, and the Colored Orphan Asylum had been burned down in the Draft Riots right when Magdalys had found out he was wounded.

"I was worried at first," Magdalys said. "When I saw that light below . . ."

Cymbeline nodded, a grim smile crossing her face. "I know. These are the Great Smoky Mountains beneath us. An encampment could be anyone at this point."

"You think they'd have pteros?"

"If they do they're probably not going to be friendly. The only ptero raiders I've heard of are on the Rebel side, unfortunately."

Magdalys glanced back, found the series of dark splotches in the sky behind them. Exhaled.

"The Rearguard still with us?" Cymbeline asked with a hint of laughter in her voice.

Magdalys tilted her head, glanced back at the moonlight dancing in the river below. "Guess they in it for the long haul."

About a dozen dactyls had shown up in the sky behind them just as they'd crossed out of New York City. Magdalys and the squad had been scared at first, but the dactyls were riderless, just a friendly escort out of town, apparently. And then they'd stayed along all through the journey across Pennsylvania and Maryland, heading off on little hunting expeditions and returning with small mammals to cook and for Stella to munch on along the way. Cymbeline had dubbed them the Rearguard and they'd become a source of comfort to Magdalys as they journeyed further and further from home.

The mountain forests opened up suddenly to a long swath of moonlit open fields. At the far end, a pillared mansion with well-trimmed hedges seemed to preside over the clearing.

Magdalys shuddered. She knew exactly who'd been forced to trim those hedges and clear that land. Something churned deep inside her. She wanted to summon all the giant reptiles of the forest around her and smash those mansions into splintered wreckages. Then she'd set fire to the whole thing and those flames would leap from plantation to plantation, reaping devastation and catastrophe like a burning tornado, with a hundred thousand dinos stampeding in its wake to finish the job.

"You alright?" Cymbeline asked.

Magdalys started to nod, knew she must look anything but, and finally shook her head.

"It's okay," Cymbeline said. "Me neither."

"I want to burn it all to the ground," Magdalys said.

Cymbeline nodded. "Same. Maybe one day we will. But not tonight."

Magdalys nodded. She fought to shove that fiery destruction somewhere deep inside herself, realized she was shaking. Blinked a few times, trying to calm herself. She couldn't concentrate through that blinding rage.

Away, she whispered to her own fury. Not now.

The forests rose again and the plantation disappeared into the night behind them but that fire kept rising inside Magdalys. Fire and fear. They were in the South now. The slaver states. Any misstep . . .

Magdalys concentrated harder, fought away the flames inside herself.

Not now. What good did it do her — all that rage?

"Let's bring her down for the night," Cymbeline said, startling Magdalys from her reverie.

The fires seemed to extinguish on their own, washed away by a sudden flash of uncertainty. "What? It's only a little past midnight I think. We still have a ways to go before dawn."

"I know but . . . this is new territory, we have to move cautiously now." A crispness singed the edges of Cymbeline's words. It was that faraway voice she used every now and again since they'd left New York, a sudden sadness that seemed to swallow her whole for a few moments at a time; then she'd recover and act like nothing had happened.

Magdalys wasn't sure how much more cautiously they could move than flying under the cover of darkness and making

camp during the day. And anyway, that plantation wasn't as far enough behind them as she would've liked. But she didn't want to go back and forth about it. "The others asleep?" she asked as Stella glided toward the dark treetops below.

"'Cept Amaya. She's keeping watch. There. That'll work."

Magdalys followed the imaginary line from Cymbeline's finger to a moonlit field amidst the dark maple trees.

"Out in the open? Are you sure that's —"

"Just to land, Magdalys," Cymbeline cut her off. "We can hike in a little to make camp. I'll wake the others." She got up carefully and made her way to the far end of the saddle.

Cymbeline had never interrupted her before. Sure, Magdalys had only really known her a few days, but she'd come to view the older girl as a kind of sister, especially after all they'd been through together.

Stella spun a smooth arc over the treetops, the Rearguard falling into formation behind her, and then launched into a sharp dive as the open field spread long beneath them.

CHAPTER TWO
FROM ACROSS
A MOONLIT FIELD

"**WHERE ARE WE?**" Two Step grumbled, sliding down from Stella's saddle and glancing at the field around them. This was the first time he'd set his feet on land without breaking into one of his signature dance moves, Magdalys realized, watching her friend's wary face.

"A whole bunch of mountainous, forest-filled miles east of Chattanooga," Mapper reported, stretching and helping Sabeen work her way onto the stirrups so she could climb down. "In other words, somewhere near where Tennessee, Georgia, and North Carolina crash into each other."

Behind him, Amaya shook her head. "I don't know how you do it."

"Even while he's asleep," Magdalys said. "It's uncanny." She'd been the first one on solid ground and was scanning the edge of the forest for movement. Cymbeline had hopped down right after her and immediately headed out into the darkness without a word. Probably looking for a spot to camp, Magdalys figured, trying to ignore the roiling uneasiness she felt.

"What kind of dinos do they have down here?" Amaya asked.

"If it's anything like Pennsylvania and Maryland," Two Step said, "not many, and what ones there are will be boring and a nuisance." It was true: Besides some wandering pteros and a few wandering microraptors scavenging for food, they'd barely encountered any reptiles at all since they'd left New York.

"Boring dinos are almost the best kind of dinos," Amaya said. "Second only to no dinos."

Magdalys tried to remember what Dr. Barlow Sloan had written in the Dinoguide about Tennessee species, but all she could come up with was a typically crotchety paragraph about how North American megafauna tended to get weirder and even more mega the further south you went. A good number of the dinos in big cities like New York had been imported from other parts of the country anyway, so everything was all mixed up, as far as Magdalys could tell.

"The forests are empty because of the fighting," Cymbeline said, walking back from the edge of the trees. "Many of the

dinos migrated west to get away from all the explosions. And plenty were captured for use in combat or as cargoluggers. There's a path through the forest up there. We can follow it in some and find a spot to camp." She picked up a rucksack and headed back toward the tree line.

"Remind me again why we stopped in the middle of the night," Amaya said, falling into step beside Magdalys.

Magdalys shrugged. "Cymbeline said since we don't know the terrain as well and we're in enemy territory we have to be more careful."

"I thought we were being careful by flying at night."

Magdalys didn't say she'd been thinking the same thing — she just kept walking toward the trees. "Hey," she said, a few paces later. Behind them, the boys were playing another game of I Spy while Sabeen sang quietly to herself. The Rearguard dactyls spun wide circles in the open sky above them.

"Hey what?" Amaya said.

"You never told me what the letter said."

Now it was Amaya's turn not to say anything. Her father was a white man — some big-time Union general, in fact — and he'd raised her, training her like a soldier since she was a little kid. But then the war had broken out and he'd dumped Amaya at the Colored Orphan Asylum and she hadn't heard anything from him right up until the day the orphanage burned down. A letter had come from the General in the same bundle with Private Summers's message about Montez being wounded, but Amaya hadn't been ready to read it, and one of the matrons

had kept it and then the Draft Riots threw everything into disarray and they'd thought it was gone forever, until another of the matrons showed up with it just before they took off.

"*John Brown's body lies a-moldering in the grave,*" Sabeen sang. "*John Brown's body lies a-moldering in the grave.*"

"That song is so grim," Mapper sighed. "I love it."

"I spyyyyyy with my little eye," Two Step said behind them, "something . . . that starts with *s*."

"*John Brown's body lies a-moldering* — the sky — *in the grave.*"

"This game is impossible!" Two Step complained. "There's only like two things anywhere we go. Stupid trees and stupid sky!"

"*His soul's marching on!*" Sabeen finished.

"I haven't read it," Amaya said flatly.

Magdalys stopped in her tracks. "What?"

Amaya grabbed her arm, shoving her along. "Keep walking!" she whispered. "Do you think I want the whole world bugging me about this? You know they're gonna ask."

"I wasn't bugging you about it," Magdalys said. "I was just —"

"Hey, what you guys whispering about?" Mapper called.

"Nothing!" Magdalys and Amaya said together.

"It's fine," Amaya hissed.

"Oh, wow, okay," Mapper said. "Excuuuse me!"

"I spy," Sabeen said, "with my little eye. Something . . . that starts with *b*."

"Butt!" Two Step yelled, pointing up at the circling dactyls. Everyone stopped and stared at him.

"Get it? Because they're the Rearguard! Rear! Like rear end! Ha! You guys! Wait up!"

"Why didn't you read it?" Magdalys whispered once they'd gotten a little ahead of the others.

"I just . . ." Amaya shook her head, shrugged. "I can't?"

"Bats?" Mapper said. "Do you see bats? Because if you do, they're probably about to be pterofood, so don't get too attached."

"Nope!" Sabeen said.

"I know I seem tough," Amaya said, looking down, her face mostly hidden by the long strands of jet-black hair hanging down to either side. "But the truth is I'm a coward."

Magdalys scoffed. "That's definitely not true."

"Who else but a coward would leave the only letter they've ever gotten from their father unopened for days on end?"

"Blankets?" Two Step tried. "There've gotta be blankets in one of these rucksacks right?"

"Nope!"

A familiar hooting sounded across the sky above them. Everyone stopped in their tracks and looked up. Two long dark shapes stretched up above the treetops ahead of them.

"Brachiosauruses!" Mapper and Two Step yelled at the same time.

Magdalys and Amaya traded a glance. "Does that mean —" Amaya started. She didn't have to finish. Brachys were plains

dinos, according to Dr. Sloan. If one was out in the forest, it probably meant someone had brought it there.

"I dunno," Magdalys said.

"Up here!" Cymbeline called from the forest. "Hurry!"

"Hurry?" Magdalys glanced around. Dark shapes were moving toward them across the field. *"Amaya!"* Magdalys whispered, nudging her friend. They both drew the carbines they had holstered and fanned out to either side as the boys and Sabeen rushed forward.

"What is it?" Two Step asked.

"Something's coming," Magdalys said, backing toward the trees. "Can't make it out." The shapes got closer. There were three of them and they were tall and very fast. "Run! Get to the woods!"

A shot cracked through the night and Magdalys almost crumpled into herself from surprise. It was Amaya, she realized. Out in the field, a dino squealed and someone yelled, "Ho there!"

"Hold your fire," Cymbeline called. "Get into the woods!"

Magdalys and Amaya backed into the shadows of the trees together, guns pointed out at the approaching riders. Cymbeline stepped forward, a lit lantern raised above her head, shotgun in the other hand. "Declare yourselves!" she hollered. "Or get annihilated."

"Whoa, there, whoa," a low voice muttered in a long Tennessee drawl as the riders dismounted and stepped forward. "Almost winged Horace." In the dim lantern light,

Magdalys could make out their faces. All three men sported beards trimmed to line their jaws with no mustaches. And, except for a long scar running down the man in the center's cheek, all three had exactly the same face. Worse than that, they wore the gray uniforms of Confederate cavalrymen. Magdalys gasped.

"Card!" Cymbeline said, shaking her head and laughing. "It's about time! Where have you been?"

CHAPTER THREE
THE MYSTERIOUS
MR. CARD

"**CYMBELINE!**" **THE WHOLE** Dactyl Hill Squad gaped at the same time.

"You . . . you . . ." Magdalys stuttered. On the other side of Cymbeline, Amaya raised the carbine, her face steel.

Cymbeline shook her head. "No, wait, slow down everyone! I see what this looks like, and it's not . . ." She sighed. "They're not Confederates, okay?"

"Then why . . ." Two Step demanded, waving his arms in exasperated, self-explanatory little circles. "Why!"

The man in the middle smirked. "You can see why they might think we were though, Cymbie."

"Card is a Union scout," Cymbeline said. "He goes behind enemy lines to find out their positions and —"

"We know what a scout does," Mapper seethed.

"Then you can understand why he's dressed like that."

Magdalys felt like all the blood in her body was rushing into her brain. This whole situation was rotten, from the moment Cymbeline had said they should land onward. "What I want to know is, how did they know where we were going to be and why were you expecting them?"

Cymbeline looked at her, brows raised, eyes wide, mouth slightly open. The only other time she'd seen her make that face was when the Zanzibar Savannah Theater, where she lived and worked, had gone up in flames right in front of her. "It was . . ." Cymbeline started. Her voice trailed off.

"Not to interrupt the moment," one of the other men said, "but there's a secesh raiding party not far away and now that we've found you, we need to get you safely back to the Union camp so you can report to General Sheridan immediately."

"Report?" Amaya said. Cymbeline whirled to face her.

"What's secesh mean?" Sabeen asked.

"It's short for secessionist, lil' darlin'," one of the men said. "Confederates. The baddies."

"Why do you guys all look exactly the same?" Two Step demanded.

"Like, literally identical," Mapper added.

Card tilted his head. "This here's my older brother, Card. And that" — he nodded to the other rider — "that's my younger brother, Card."

"And you youngens must be the crew from Dactyl Hill. Pleased to meet ya!" the younger Card said. "We've heard great things."

"Heard?" Magdalys hissed at Cymbeline.

"Great things?" Amaya finished for her.

Cymbeline glanced back and forth between them.

The older Card doffed his gray cap. "Indeed. But my brother's correct. We gotta get a-movin', folks." He shot a worried glance at the moonlit sky.

"How far to the camp?" Cymbeline asked.

"Far enough that we'll need you to hop on the back of our paras if we're gonna make it safely."

Magdalys had been so busy glaring at Cymbeline, she hadn't bothered getting a better look at the mounts.

The parasaurolophus, Dr. Sloan wrote in the Dinoguide, *is among the most noble and versatile of all dinomounts. With their elegant crest stretching like a plume behind their head, they strike an impressive visage on four legs or two. They are equally at home grazing amidst the swaying North American grasslands or trundling amorously through the deciduous forest mountains of the middle states.* (What, Magdalys had tried not to wonder, did it mean to trundle amorously?) *What's more, the parasaurolophus makes a whimsical, intelligent companion whether one plans a long journey, is preparing for battle, or simply wants a gentle beast of burden nearby who can perform menial tasks and act as a loyal coconspirator in gentle pranks and assorted shenanigans.*

("Dr. Sloan is a weirdo," Two Step had said, reading over Magdalys's shoulder in the orphanage library.)

The Cards' three paras stepped (or trundled amorously, Magdalys supposed) into the lamplight. She'd never seen one before. They were shaped a little like their cousin dinos, the iguanodons, which could be seen promenading the streets of Manhattan and the Crest beneath their wealthy masters. The paras had those same thick hind legs and wide hips that curved forward into arched backs and smaller torsos, with long, arm-like forelegs extending toward the ground. Those bony crests that Dr. Sloan called elegant reached up and back from their short snouts, and their sunken-in eyes blinked at the world with an irritated, skeptical squint.

"What about Stella?" Magdalys said. "And the others?"

"Stella?" one of the Cards asked, raising a bushy blond eyebrow.

"Our pteranodon," Mapper said proudly.

"Oh, that's what that big ol' ptero y'all flew in on is?"

"I'm sure General Sheridan would love to have a look at that one," the older Card said.

"Mm-hmm," the middle Card agreed.

Magdalys wasn't sure if she was more upset at herself for bringing up Stella in the first place or Mapper for spilling the beans. More than anything though, she was furious with Cymbeline for keeping so many secrets. Everything was happening faster than she could keep track of and none of it was bringing her any closer to Montez.

Out in the field, Stella stirred. There was no telling what would happen if the Union Army got their hands on her.

Go! Magdalys commanded. Stella looked up sharply. Magdalys felt the raw power of her glare, the huge creature's unwillingness to leave her side. *Fly. Stay away from any signs of humans. We'll be . . . we'll be alright.*

In a single, fluid leap, Stella crouched low and then hurled herself into the air, sending a flush of wind across the field with her enormous wings.

Cymbeline shot Magdalys a look. Magdalys watched the huge shadow disappear into the moonlit night. The dactyls must've scattered to scavenge for dinner; the sky was empty.

Except.

A flutter of movement over the far end of the field caught Magdalys's eye just as an eerie howl sounded over the breeze and chirping crickets.

"What was —" Mapper said.

"Confederate Air Cavalry!" Card yelled. "No time to argue. Everyone get on a para. We gotta move out."

Shadowy shapes flitted across the sky toward them as more howling sounded and then a series of flashes erupted from above amidst the crackle of gunfire.

"Let's go!" Card yelled.

CHAPTER FOUR
THROUGH THE WOODS AND AWAY

DARK TREES RUSHED past on either side as the para galumphed along in a wild, dip-and-divey gallop beneath Magdalys. She'd hopped on the nearest, Young Card's mount, as gunfire thudded into the dirt around her and shattered branches overhead. Two Step had jumped on behind her and then Card had yelled "Heeyah!" and the para had leaned all the way forward onto all fours, making Magdalys feel like she might tumble off at any second, and away they'd gone.

Up above, the Confederate dactylriders yelled back and forth to each other and let out their triumphant howls, occasionally swooping down beneath the tree line to hurl a shot or two into the darkness. Older Card had galloped ahead with

Amaya and Cymbeline, while Middle Card's para thundered along a few paces over to the side with Sabeen and Mapper.

"Can you get a shot?" Young Card yelled.

"Probably not," his brother called back. "Looks like they're just a small scouting expedition, not the full unit. Still . . . the others won't be far behind."

"Uh-huh."

Blam! Another shot rang out from above and smashed into a nearby tree.

"Ragged Randy Run!" the Card up front called.

All three brothers pulled their reins back and forth in sharp turns as their paras grunted and adjusted their forward charges into a zigzagging kind of dance.

"That oughta keep 'em confused," Young Card snickered. A few more shots hurtled down around them.

Magdalys closed her eyes. Where were her Brooklyn dactyls? *Come through*, she called silently. *We need you.*

The sound of the panting, snorting paras and their heavy footfall filled the air as the Confederates above held their fire.

Magdalys gulped. Once again, someone was taking potshots at her and her friends. And to top it off, she was being carried along like some defenseless damsel in distress by strange men. Strange men wearing Confederate gray no less!

A sharp caw sounded and more flapping from above, then yells of confusion from the air cavalry.

The dactyls! The birch branches jumbled into a trembling

dark haze with each bound from the para, but Magdalys thought she could make out a group of shapes flash into the crew of dactylriders and scatter them.

Then more gunfire sounded.

Swing low for me, Magdalys thought, and within seconds a whooshing sound blitzed through the woods toward them, branches snapping and leaves fluttering as one of the dactyls dove through the trees and fell into a smooth glide alongside the para.

"What in the —" Card yelled, but Magdalys had already stood in the saddle, steadying herself with both hands on his shoulders. "Girl, what are you —"

Magdalys leapt, grasping the neck of the dactyl just as it swooped into a steady climb back toward the treetops.

"Now, how in the —" she heard from below just before the dactyl burst through the branches and out into the moonlit sky.

"Magdalys, no!" Cymbeline yelled, but Magdalys didn't care what Cymbeline said anymore. She had lied to them, in one way or another, like so many adults before her, and now she couldn't be trusted. And anyway, Magdalys had had it with being dragged around places. She willed the dactyl to spin around and caught her breath.

The four Confederate air cavalrymen were flapping off on their steeds, routed by the sudden onslaught from her Brooklyn dactyls, who were giving chase with hoots and screeches. But it was what they were heading toward that stopped Magdalys

short: Out above the open field they'd just come from, at least two dozen more mounted dactyls flapped toward her, the howls of their riders rising in the night.

"Ten-hut!" a stern voice cried over the wind. "Slow your steeds and take aim boys! On my mark, knock those pteros out of the sky!"

Magdalys's eyes went wide. *Scatter!* she pleaded. *Get away!*

"And fire!"

The first crackling barrage burst out from the Rebel Air Cavalry just as the Brooklyn dactyls were launching out in all directions like a slow-motion ptero explosion.

A horrible shrieking filled the air. Magdalys saw three dactyls blasted out of the sky outright as two others spiraled in dizzy loops into the treetops.

"And fire!"

Another explosion. Something whizzed past Magdalys's head. A bullet. Then the dactyl she was riding screeched and they both tumbled downward as the darkness of the forest suddenly engulfed them.

CHAPTER FIVE
RACE TO THE UNION LINE

EASY, MAGDALYS COOED to the tumbling dactyl beneath her. Time seemed to slow as branches scraped across her face and more gunfire crackled overhead.

Easy, big fella, shhh . . .

The dactyl's mind was a muddle of terrified screeches and hoots of pain, but she felt him trying to regain some bit of control as he flapped fiercely to slow their plummet.

One of his rear legs had been hit; she could see it dangling limply. Another shot must've passed through one of his wings, which was bleeding freely through a ragged hole.

Landing would not be an easy thing.

Slow, buddy, slowww, Magdalys insisted, and the dactyl seemed to quiet his panic some in response as they slid closer and closer to the forest floor. *Easy fella, easy.*

When she could make out a patch of moonlit dirt and grass below, Magdalys leapt down, still grasping her hands around the dactyl's neck, and pulled them into a messy somersault tumble.

The ptero let out a squeal of pain and pulled himself out of her grasp, hopping a few limping steps away on shaky wings before falling to a heap.

Magdalys stood. Her whole body ached and about a thousand little cuts probably crisscrossed her face and arms, but she was alright otherwise.

"Mag-D!" Two Step yelled from not far away. "She's over there! Come on!"

Up above, the head of that air cavalry unit let out another bellow and another volley burst out. Magdalys prayed at least some of her dactyls were okay, but there was nothing she could do.

A shape rushed toward her through the trees: one of the Cards on top of that para, galloping forward in that strange, seesaw gait. Then she saw the man's stern face, that carefully trimmed jawline beard and furrowed brow, his arm reaching out and scooping her up and placing her on the saddle in front of Two Step.

"The dactyl!" Magdalys yelled. "We have to bring him! He saved my life!"

"There's no —"

"He's wounded and he saved my life," Magdalys yelled. "He's right there!" She pointed to the panting heap where the dactyl had collapsed in the shadows a few feet away. "Please!"

Card sighed, swinging his mount around and pulling it beside the ptero. "I don't even know how we're going to —"

"I'll do it," Magdalys said, climbing down from the para with Two Step close behind.

C'mon, boy, she thought, pulling the dactyl to his feet as Two Step helped him from the other side. *This the only way you gonna make it.*

The ptero wheezed, dark blood splattering Magdalys's face, but finally heaved himself upright and then clambered over the top of the para, which stomped its feet a few times with impatient grunts but otherwise behaved.

More gunfire crackled above.

"Kids . . ." Card warned. A few shots thunked the trees and soil nearby.

"He's on!" Two Step yelled, pulling himself up as he steadied the dactyl.

Magdalys climbed on behind him. "Go! Go!"

They surged forward, more shots ringing out around them and the foliage overhead rustling with sound of the Confederate Air Cavalry dactyls on hunt.

"This way!" one of the Cards up ahead called as all three paras bounded down a rocky hill and then flushed forward between towering birch trees toward a shadowy grove.

Magdalys and Two Step's para lumbered along at the back,

barely able to keep up with the extra weight it was lugging. Up above, the Confederate Air Cavalry swooped and hollered, occasionally taking potshots through the trees, but the moon had slid behind a cloud and the riders couldn't seem to get much of a view of the forest below.

"Ho there!" a stern voice yelled as the lead para pulled up to a halt before some trees. "Password or we light you up."

Card muttered something Magdalys couldn't make out over the pants and stomps of the para beneath her.

"Open the gates, then," the sentry said. "Ah, the Cards, of course!" A creaking groan erupted from the trees and the darkness seemed to give way around them as a wooden door Magdalys hadn't even noticed swung open, revealing a torchlit campsite.

"Tighten the lines and ready the howitzers," the older Card said as his para rumbled through the gates. "There's a Rebel Air Cavalry unit in pursuit, and we don't know how many are with 'em."

"We'll let the commanding officer know," the sentry called as Magdalys's para thumped past. A few more scattered shots rang out behind them, but then the night grew still. The Cards slowed their paras to a brisk march as they maneuvered through row after row of tents and crackling campfires. Some men sat perched on logs around the fires in their mud-stained blue uniforms, sipping from tin cups and muttering to each other.

Magdalys felt a tug on her arm. "Hey," Two Step whispered. "You okay?"

Was she? Magdalys wasn't even sure what okay meant anymore. Somehow being shot at again didn't seem half as horrible as the sinking feeling that Cymbeline had deceived them. She met Two Step's eyes, still trying to figure out what to say, and realized he'd been crying.

"Two Step," she said, touching his shoulder.

He rubbed his eyes. "No, no, I was really asking you. I'm . . . I'm okay, Mags."

"You don't look okay." Back in Dactyl Hill, Two Step had shot a member of the notorious Kidnapping Club who was charging at them on a triceratops. He'd saved Mapper's and Magdalys's lives, not to mention his own, but killing that man seemed like it had broken something inside of Two Step. He still hadn't quite lost that faraway look in his eyes. And this had been their first time amidst gunfire again since that night. "Talk to me," she said when he looked away at the fire-speckled rows of bivouacs.

Out beyond the tents, Magdalys could just make out the dark shadows of the Union combat and supply dinos, those long sauropod necks and the bulky, shadowed bodies of trikes stirring in their pens.

"Two Step?"

He shook his head, his face now steeled as he looked back at her. "Nothing. No, I don't. There's nothing to . . . no."

"Riders, dismount!" one of the Cards called. The paras pulled to a halt and Magdalys watched Two Step slide down, careful not to let the wounded dactyl fall. He was just a kid,

Magdalys thought. All of them were. Just twelve and thirteen. Sabeen was still ten. And the world had already demanded so much of them. She shook her head, slid down from the saddle, and helped Two Step ease the dactyl down.

The ptero let out a soft moan as they eased it onto the dirt floor and then it rolled over, limp.

Two Step shuddered. "Is he . . . ?"

Magdalys knelt beside the dactyl, closed her eyes. The soft murmur of life reached her, just a faint, trembling kind of hum. She shook her head. "Not yet. But he's not good." She ran her hand along the dactyl's long neck and rubbed his belly. The bleeding had stopped, at least.

A pair of dusty boots came to a stop in front of Magdalys. "What we should do," said the solemn voice attached to those boots, "is put a bullet in its head."

Magdalys looked up and directly into the eyes of one of the Cards — the middle one, she thought. "You won't."

"You almost got my little brother killed stopping to save this dino."

"He's a ptero, not a dino," Magdalys said. "And he saved me."

"So did my little brother, if I recall correctly. Just count yourself lucky you didn't get him killed. That's all I'm saying." He turned around and walked away.

Magdalys narrowed her eyes, but no snappy comeback came. Too much had happened too fast. And the man wasn't all that wrong either — it had been reckless, what she'd done. He just didn't have to be a jerk about it.

"Sorry bout my brother," Young Card said, smiling awkwardly. "He means well. He's just real protective and, you know . . . to some folks, dinos, er — pteros too, I guess — are just another beast. Mind you, if anyone hurt ol' Horace he'd have an absolute fit."

Magdalys managed to smile.

"Anyway, pay him no mind. Get yourselves settled and we'll have the dinomedics look at your friend there."

"Thank you," Magdalys said.

"Magdalys," Cymbeline said, walking up beside Card.

"Don't say a wo—" Magdalys started, but a sharp voice cut her off.

"Agent Crunk," someone called from the entrance to a large torchlit tent, "General Sheridan requests your report forthwith."

Cymbeline blinked, then sighed, rubbing a hand over her eyes.

"*Agent?*" Magdalys said.

"Come with me," Cymbeline said.

CHAPTER SIX
THE VOCIFEROUS GENERAL SHERIDAN

AN OFFICER WITH an altogether much too pristine dress suit and aggressive handlebar mustache stood at attention by the tent entrance. This had to be the major general's adjutant, Magdalys thought. The newspapers were full of stories about upper-class Northerners with cushy military jobs.

Cymbeline offered him a smile that hinted unambiguously at murder. "I'd appreciate it, Corporal Buford," she growled, "if you would not alert the entire state of Tennessee of my clandestine designation in the future."

Buford snapped a salute. "Official designations are to be used in campsites at all times, Agent Crunk."

Cymbeline's salute caused him to duck out of the way.

Magdalys smirked to herself. She was still mad at Cymbeline, but it was always good to see her one-up someone.

"I'm afraid unattended Negro children aren't permitted in the general's presence. Is this a contraband?"

Contraband was the word the US Army used for people who had escaped slavery and made it safely to their lines. Everyone was always talking in the streets about how no one knew what to do with them, even after Lincoln's Emancipation Proclamation, although this year many of them had finally been granted the right to be soldiers.

Magdalys felt the full glare of Corporal Buford settle on her. She suddenly felt very tiny and filthy.

"She's not dressed like a contraband, is she?" he mused. "No rags and such, that is."

"Corporal Buford," Cymbeline seethed.

The officer didn't take his curious eyes from Magdalys, so she met his glare full on with one of her own. That seemed to shake him. He glanced up at Cymbeline. "Hm?"

"Miss Roca is part of a clandestine program ordered at the highest levels of the War Department. Secretary Stanton granted me deputizing powers to create an espionage network with the blessings of General Grant himself."

"Well, I certainly —" Buford sputtered.

"You haven't heard about it because it is above your rank to know of its existence."

"That's simply —"

"I only included you in the secret because I'm feeling magnanimous today, Corporal Buford. You're welcome to wire the War Secretary yourself for confirmation if you'd like."

"I most certainly will do that immediately!"

"Outstanding. Send him my warmest regards. Good evening, Corporal Buford."

Cymbeline grabbed Magdalys's hand and hurried her into the tent.

"Ah, Miss Crunk!" a jaunty voice called from the far end of the tent as Cymbeline snapped a salute. "Card here has just been regaling me with tales of your adventures!"

Major General Sheridan was a wisp of a man, probably only a little taller than Magdalys, and he looked even tinier beside Card, who had to crook his neck to the side to keep from scratching his head on the top of the tent. Sheridan strode forward in long, bouncy strides and shook Cymbeline's outstretched hand excitedly. He was wearing blue trousers and a simple white shirt, like he'd been roused suddenly from sleep and hadn't bothered putting his full uniform on. A tightly trimmed goatee framed his sharp face. "You brought me pteros, I hear!"

"No," Magdalys and Cymbeline said together.

Sheridan blinked at them. Behind him, Card rubbed his face and sighed.

"Card my good man," General Sheridan said without looking away from Cymbeline. "I could've absolutely sworn you told me Agent Crunk here had arrived on pteroback."

"That is accurate, sir."

"With due respect, General," Cymbeline said, "the pteros are not mine to turn over to you, sir. Further, we're not sure where they are currently, as they were scattered during an engagement with the enemy air cavalry on our approach to the camp, sir."

"Mmm, so I've been told, so I've been told." Sheridan raised his eyebrows and squinted, as if the brief skirmish was playing out in front of him somehow. "Card?"

"At least one survived, but is wounded. The girl brought it back to camp."

No thanks to you, Magdalys thought.

"We must see to it that ptero receives every bit of medical attention."

"Card already brought it to the medic tent," Cymbeline said. "Uh, the other Card."

"And what of the other pteros?"

"Based on what I saw, sir," Card said, "I believe the girl here could summon them back at will, if any survived."

Sheridan whirled around. "Did you say *summon*?"

Magdalys felt all the blood rush to her face. She had barely gotten used to being able to communicate with dinos, and had hoped to keep it a secret as much as possible. Back in Brooklyn, her friend Redd had told her not to be ashamed of her power,

to proclaim it to the world. And it had seemed so simple for a moment. But now she was in the middle of war and she didn't know who to trust anymore. Everyone seemed to be putting her under a microscope as soon as she met them.

"Summon a dino?" Sheridan marveled.

"A ptero, sir, technically," Card pointed out.

Magdalys glared at him. He glared back.

"And you saw this happen, you say?"

"On our way here, sir. I've never seen anyone ride a dactyl like that."

"Major General," Cymbeline cut in.

"Also, sir, they have a pteranodon."

Sheridan gasped. "A live pteranodon?"

"They landed in Druid Field on it."

The general stepped up directly in front of Magdalys and leaned forward, his hands on his knees. "What's your name, child?" he said with a friendly smile.

"Magdalys Roca, sir."

"Is what my man Card says true?"

Magdalys felt Cymbeline's stare, had no idea what it meant. She wished she could turn to the older girl for help, find some hint of what to do. But Cymbeline had lied to her, was a whole other person than who she'd thought her to be. Magdalys couldn't trust anyone, except the Dactyl Hill Squad. That's all there was to it.

"It's true," she finally said. "I can communicate with them. They do . . . they do what I ask them to."

"Magnificent," Sheridan whispered. "Like the legendary dinoriders of old." He straightened up. "This changes everything."

"Sir," Cymbeline said. "If I may —"

"Do you know, Agent Crunk, how long I've been trying to convince those old fusspots in the War Department to authorize a federal air cavalry? Why, you saw yourself how the Confederates had the run on us tonight, didn't you?"

"We —"

Sheridan pounded his fist into his palm. "We could smash them across the skies and then wreak havoc on their ground troops from above!"

"She's a child," Cymbeline said.

"Wondrous. To think, the whole victory or defeat of the Army of the Cumberland, perhaps the Union itself, could rest on such tiny shoulders" — Sheridan shook his head, eyebrows raised — "and Negro shoulders at that."

"Sir!" Cymbeline said. "That's not fair."

Sheridan blinked, shaken from his reverie. "Fair, Agent Crunk? What on earth gave you the idea that anything about war is fair? A man's head was shot off by an artillery shell not five feet from where I stood the other day. Was that fair, Agent Crunk? That it should've been him instead of me? We who find ourselves in war's all-encompassing theater don't have the luxury of worrying about these existential questions. We have to worry about victory, and not getting destroyed. That is all.

And that includes you, Agent Crunk, and, unfortunately, it includes your small friend here, Magda — what was it, dear?"

"Magdalys," Magdalys said, imagining mortars hurling out from her eyes as she stared at the general. "And I'm just . . . I'm only here because my brother, Montez, he was . . ." The words wouldn't come. Three sets of eyes stared at Magdalys: Card's cold, inscrutable stare; Sheridan's curious, concerned one; and Cymbeline, who looked like she might cry.

"He's with the Louisiana 9th, sir," Cymbeline finally said, "and was wounded at the Battle of Milliken's Bend."

"Ah, of course," Sheridan said quietly.

"Last we heard he was being transported to New Orleans along with the other wounded for recovery. Unconscious."

Magdalys saw Card's gaze soften ever so slightly. "All I want," she said, "the only reason I'm here at all, is to find my brother and make sure he's alright."

Sheridan blinked a few times, then nodded kindly. "May I show you something, Magdelis?" he asked, butchering her name.

"Um, okay."

"Xavier!" Sheridan hollered, startling everyone except Card, who rolled his eyes. A few moments passed; Cymbeline and Magdalys traded uncomfortable glances. Sheridan scrunched up his face and yelled again, "Xavier!," this time stomping one booted foot for emphasis.

"I believe he's sleeping, sir," Card offered tightly.

"What good is a mobile table if he's constantly nodding off on the job?" Sheridan snapped at no one in particular. "Wake him up then!"

Card nudged his foot at something under a table that stood in front of him. And then Magdalys realized it *was* the table: the whole surface wobbled and an unimpressed grunting sounded as Sheridan stood waiting, eyes squinted with irritation. Then a sleepy-looking tortoise's face poked out from under the tablecloth and blinked languidly around the room. Finally, Xavier shuffled into an exquisitely slow rumble across the floor and came to rest beside Sheridan.

The general shook his head. "I'm quite sure the table tortoises of the Army of the Potomac are not nearly so lugubrious in their duties, Xavier."

The tortoise seemed to consider that with a slow nod and a few blinks, then sighed and retracted his big head back beneath the tarp.

On the surface of the table, a crinkled, coffee-stained map was spread out beneath tin cups, quills, and blue-and-gray wooden figurines. It looked like some mad genius had gotten drunk and tried to reinvent chess without the squares. She tried to make sense of it, recognize some landmark she'd seen along their flight, but came up empty.

"This is us." Sheridan lifted a little blue raptor in the middle of a chaos of lines, some straight (state borders?), some swirling (rivers? Mountains? Supply lines?), some notched (railroads!). "These fellows here" — he pointed at several gray trike and

raptor figurines — "are General Braxton Bragg's Confederate divisions."

"There are a lot of them," Magdalys said.

"Indeed. There are a lot of us too, but see here?" The handful of other blue dinos were scattered around the mountains; most had Confederate divisions between them and the rest. "We pushed Bragg's men out of Chattanooga a few weeks ago and had them on the run. But in our zeal, we've been scattered. And now are in the gravest of danger, I'm afraid. The tides may be turning as we speak. And here." He pointed further down the map, where a straight line of gray trikes was arrayed along a railroad track. "General Longstreet's riders on their way by train to reinforce Bragg. That is, according to what Card here has learned from his most recent foray."

Card nodded once.

"But of course, this could all be wrong. And tomorrow, will look completely different. And perhaps worst of all? This." He picked up a small gray piece in the shape of a dactyl. "General Forrest's air cavalry. I believe you met some of them tonight."

Magdalys nodded, the echoes of their rifle fire still ringing through her mind.

"These flying maniacs can keep track of our every move. They can attack from almost any angle, set up ambushes and then rain down withering fire upon our men and dinos. We are flailing around like fools in the darkness hunting Bragg's men while our own prey closes in on us from all sides.

If one division is attacked, will we even know? Will we be able to reach them in time? This" — he pointed at a dot on the map with the word *Chattanooga* scrawled beside it — "is where we'll have to retreat to if things go sour, the only safe zone in hundreds of miles."

Card grunted and shook his head.

"So you see, we are currently in a predicament, Magadis. And what we need is a way out. Do you understand?"

Magdalys felt like she only barely understood, but she nodded anyway.

"Go rest," Sheridan said. "You've had a long day. We'll see what news the morning brings, and discuss further then."

For a moment, Magdalys and General Sheridan just stared at each other. Then he smiled, snapped a salute, and said, "Dismissed!"

CHAPTER SEVEN
CAMPFIRE SHENANIGANS

"**W**AIT!" CYMBELINE SAID, hurrying out of the tent.

Magdalys whirled around in the muddy pathway between rows of tents and campfires. "Don't speak to me."

"Please," Cymbeline said.

Magdalys just shook her head and turned, squinting and blinking away the tears. Up ahead, she recognized Amaya's tall, lanky frame standing beside a few other people near one of the fires. She quickened her pace, praying Cymbeline would have the decency not to follow her.

"Hey," Magdalys said, coming up beside Amaya.

Amaya put a finger to her smiling lips. "Shh! They're coming up on the good part."

"Good part of wha — oh!" Magdalys looked around. All the men around them were black and wearing Union blues. A division of the US Colored Troops! Immediately she thought of Montez, but of course, he was probably already in New Orleans. Still, there was a certain comfort in being around men who may have served with him. They'd formed a semi-circle around the bonfire, where Sabeen sat on the shoulders of a lanky brown-skinned man in his mid-twenties wearing a white undershirt and blue trousers. "Brahhh!" the man yelled, leaning forward and placing both hands on his forehead, pointer fingers sticking out like horns.

"Um . . ." Magdalys said. "Is this what I think it is?"

"Your trike impression is garbage, Octave," said a boy who looked a year or two younger than Cymbeline. "Let Big Jack do it. His dino impressions second to none, my man."

"Nobody asked for your opinion, Hannibal," the man named Octave snapped back. "And it's Corporal Cailloux who told me to be the trike, talk to him."

A middle-aged guy with a dashing mustache shook his head. "Stop breaking character, Octave. And anyway, we need Jack for the tyrannous. Didn't you kids say there was a tyrannous there?"

"GRAWRAWRAWRAR!!" a huge bald-headed man with bulging muscles yelled, jumping out of the crowd with Mapper on his scar-lined back. Everyone gasped and then burst into hoots and hollers.

"Too good," Cailloux said. "He's too good at this."

"Could put a shirt on though, is all I'm saying," Hannibal said.

"Tyrannouses ain't wear no shirts," Big Jack growled.

Everyone laughed.

"Get back into character!" Cailloux yelled.

"Did they wear pants that were five sizes too small for them?" Octave asked.

Big Jack stomped toward him. "If they were in the Union Army they probably did, yeah."

More raucous laughter.

"Um, guys," Mapper said, "can we get back to the action? This is the cool part."

Big Jack spun back around and leapt at Octave and Sabeen with another terrific roar.

"Aren't you one of those sniveling little orphan brats from the asylum I burned down in the Draft Riots?" Mapper crowed in what was actually a pretty good impression of Magistrate Riker, the man who had tried to kidnap Magdalys and all her friends and sell them into slavery.

"Charge!" Sabeen yelled, making her usually squeaky voice a little deeper and plastering an exaggerated scowl on her face.

Magdalys smacked her forehead. "I can't believe this is happening."

"Relax, champ," Amaya said with a chuckle. "You're a hero."

Octave gave another sorry growl and lurched forward, almost toppling Sabeen. He smashed into Big Jack but only came up to the man's midsection. Big Jack chuckled.

"And then," Two Step said, stepping out in front of them, "a huge shadow fell over the prison yard."

"What was it?" a scrawny soldier with a goatee yelled.

"Shut up for five seconds, Sol," someone else called, "and we might find out."

Two Step stretched his hands all the way out to either side, his eyes blinking with the passion of the moment. "A HUGE PTERANODON!!"

"How huge?" Cailloux asked.

"Like, twelve times bigger than the tyrannous!"

"Whoa!" the whole crowd exclaimed.

"Wait," Cailloux said. "We ain't got nobody bigger than Big Jack."

"A person bigger than Big Jack don't exist," someone pointed out.

"I just mean from a theatrical standpoint," Cailloux said, shaking his head, "how we gonna —"

"CAROOO!!" Hannibal yelled from on top of another man's shoulders. They wobbled into the middle of the semicircle.

"Do pteranodons say *caroo*?" someone wondered out loud.

"They still ain't as tall as Jack," someone else pointed out.

"Whatever, just keep going," Cailloux said. "We'll work with it."

"Arr!" Mapper exclaimed, wisely drawing everyone's attention back to himself before saying his line. "Aren't you that girl

Margaret Rocheford who can talk to dinos with your special mental powers like the dinoriding warriors of old?"

Magdalys shook her head. "If I hear that phrase one more time," she whispered. "What does 'of old' even mean?"

"Old-timey," Amaya whispered back. "Shush!"

"Was this guy Riker a pirate?" Sol asked. "Why he saying *arr*?"

"Quiet, Sol!" about five different people yelled.

"My name," Sabeen said defiantly, "is Magdalys Roca!" Then she slo-mo punched Mapper, who fell limp on top of Big Jack with an elaborate "Oof!"

Everyone cheered.

"Then the giant pteranodon swooped down," Two Step exclaimed, eyes wide, hands gesticulating wildly, "and snatched up the tyrannous in her beak!"

"Uh," Hannibal said. "That might be difficult."

"Did you say 'her beak'?" the guy beneath him asked.

"Yeah," Two Step said. "Stella."

"Aw, man!" the guy moaned, putting Hannibal down a little too quickly. "I can't play no girl dino!" He stormed off.

"Bradsbee will play the bottom half of a giant dino but it's the fact that it's a girl he has a problem with," Cailloux sighed. Everyone guffawed.

"Pteranodons are actually pteros," Sol pointed out as groans erupted around him.

"I'll take his place," Cymbeline said, stepping into the circle.

Magdalys tensed. Everyone got very quiet. "But I'll have to ask the good Private Hannibal if he'll switch places and take the bottom half, as I'm not sure I can support his weight."

"It's a lady," someone whispered.

"Put a shirt on, Jack!" someone else yelled.

Big Jack just blinked at Cymbeline.

"That really won't be necessary," she laughed.

"Wait," Cailloux said, stepping forward. "Are you Cymbeline Crunk? The Shakespeare actress they talk about in the colored papers?"

She bowed elaborately. "The same."

"Fellas, we are performing our sad little spectacle in the presence of theater royalty!"

Various *oohs* and *well hey nows* erupted from the crowd.

"Why, it's not sad at all," Cymbeline said. "Although, while me and the young folks were all there to witness, you might want to consult with the young lady who was actually at the center of it all." She nodded toward Magdalys, who was already shaking her head as the crowd peeled off to either side around her with an awed gasp.

"Uh, no . . . I . . ."

"Magda Lee the Rock!" Big Jack yelled.

"It's Magda*lys*," Sabeen said, but Magdalys was pretty sure no one heard her.

Cailloux shook his head. "Well, well, well."

"Tell us what happened!" Octave called.

Magdalys felt tiny. All these eyes on her, each with a

different expectation and idea of who she was, all based on some goofy story the others had told them. Ridiculous! And terrifying. Even if the story was pretty much true. "I . . ." She shook her head, no words forming. "I just . . ."

"Don't be shy!" Cailloux said.

"It was all Stella really," Magdalys said. "She's the one that ate Riker."

"Ohh!!" everyone yelled amidst wild applause.

"And my friends," Magdalys said. "These guys were fighting it out in the prison the whole time while I faced off with the magistrate." She nudged Amaya beside her, then looked at Sabeen (who still sat on Octave's shoulders), Mapper (who'd gotten down from Jack's), Two Step, and finally, grudgingly, Cymbeline, whose eyes were sad behind her bright smile. "I'd be dead if it wasn't for them."

"Can you really talk to dinos?" Hannibal asked.

Magdalys raised one shoulder all the way to her ear without meaning to. "I mean I —"

"TEN-HUT!" a booming voice called, and all the men snapped to attention, backs straight, chins up, arms at their sides. Magdalys blinked. It had happened in seconds: They'd formed perfectly ordered rows from an unruly crowd without even a word exchanged. "Do you know what time it is, soldiers?" Corporal Buford strutted in front of them, his eyes narrowed. The fire behind him lit a shimmering line to the edges of his otherwise shadowed form, and Magdalys had the distinct impression that he had done that on purpose.

"Half past two in the morning," Mapper said.

Magdalys groaned inwardly. Why could that boy never let a question slide by unanswered?

Buford whirled on him. "Are you a member of the Louisiana Native Guard Mounted Artillery Unit of the Union Army, young man?"

Louisiana Native Guard? Magdalys almost yelped. Montez had been assigned the Louisiana 9th. They *had* to have crossed paths!

"Not that I am aware of, sir!" Mapper said, dropping his voice a few decibels and straightening his back like the others.

A few of the troops snorted back laughter.

Buford looked like he didn't know who to curse out first. "Perhaps," he finally said, eyeing Mapper, "you would like to be."

"Perhaps so, sir. They seem like pretty cool fellas."

"Aay!" a few soldiers crooned appreciatively.

Buford spun around. "That's quite enough! Soldiers, you were supposed to turn in hours ago, unless this young man is incorrect in his timekeeping skills." He paused, letting the crackle of the bonfire and a far-off dinohoot fill the night for a few moments. "Which I highly doubt!" he finally said, as if he'd just wrapped up a stunning prosecution and the case was closed. "This is a military bivouac, not a cheap saloon for revelry and shenanigans. Also," he added with a sly look on his face, "your payments have come in, and I expect you'll be eager to receive them?"

"Sir, no sir!" the troops hollered as one.

Buford shook his head. This seemed like a routine they'd been through before. "I can't promise the Senate will approve an equal pay measure any time soon, men."

No one stirred.

"I'm sure you have wives and families that need any help they can get. . . ."

Silence.

Buford seemed to sag. "Very well. Get to your quarters immediately. Dismissed."

He turned to Magdalys and the others as the men hurried off into the darkness of the camp. "If you will follow me, children, I will escort you to your sleeping quarters."

CHAPTER EIGHT
THE DINO QUAD

"**I HOPE THIS WILL** be suitable," Corporal Buford said, standing outside a large tent and ushering them forward.

"Whoa!" Two Step said, stepping inside.

"Definitely beats the cold hard ground," Mapper agreed, following him.

"Blankets!" Sabeen yelled.

"Thank you, Corporal," Cymbeline said, giving him a salute.

"You are most welcome, Agen —"

Cymbeline cut him a sharp look.

"Ah," Buford corrected himself. "Young lady."

Cymbeline shook her head but smiled and then ducked into the tent. Buford turned to Magdalys. "The major general

would like to see you in the morning, young lady." Then he nodded and headed off into the night.

"What was that about?" Amaya asked.

Sabeen came back through the flaps and shot Magdalys a concerned look. "What was what about?"

Magdalys shook her head. "Long story. You guys want to take a walk? I gotta see if we can find the dino quad so I can check on that dactyl."

"Sure," Amaya said.

Sabeen motioned toward the tent. "Why don't we ask —"

Magdalys shook her head before Sabeen could finish the thought. "Just come on," she said. "I think it's over this way. And if nothing else, we can just follow our noses."

Combined with that mulchy forest scent from the surrounding trees, the crisp campfire freshness almost, *almost* covered the undodgeable assault of dinopoop stench. Magdalys knew it well. It came on like a fast-moving wall of foulness, overran any attempt to block it, seemed to dive directly into her very pores in a relentless deluge. "Guh," she muttered, waving at the air in front of her nose. "Over here."

"Ooh yeah," Sabeen said. "I noticed."

They made their way along the outer row of tents toward an open area where large shapes shifted in the shadows.

"I like those guys," Sabeen said.

"Who, the soldiers? Me too." Magdalys smiled.

"I don't think any of 'em are Native," Amaya said. "So I don't know why they're the Native Guard, but I like them too."

"They remind me of David and the folks at the Bochinche," Magdalys said. When they'd escaped the riots in Manhattan, Cymbeline had taken them to a small bar in Dactyl Hill, Brooklyn. There, they'd been taken in by Miss Bernice, David Ballantine, and Louis Napoleon — members of the Vigilance Committee, a group that helped rescue black New Yorkers from the clutches of Magistrate Riker's Kidnappers Club.

In the short time Magdalys and her friends had spent in Dactyl Hill, the Vigilance Committee had become like a family to them.

"Yeah," Sabeen said. "But scary as things got in Brooklyn, it's wild to think that where we are now, we could just get overrun at any moment by an army of people who think we don't even deserve to live."

"Girl . . ." Magdalys told the other two about the dire situation Sheridan had laid out for her earlier that night. They were surrounded and cut off from the rest of the Union forces: a total catastrophe waiting to happen.

"Are you gonna help them?" Sabeen asked, and Magdalys appreciated that her friend seemed to put no weight in the question, no pressure or guilt. It was just a question.

"I guess I gotta," Magdalys said, feeling tears start to well up in her eyes without warning. "I just . . ."

"I know," Amaya said. "You didn't come here for this and you don't like being pressured into things."

"Exactly!" Magdalys said, sniffling and feeling a little better already, just on the strength of someone understanding without her having to explain herself. "And I hate that Cymbeline . . . that . . ."

"You gotta talk to her about that," Amaya said. "Otherwise the anger'll eat you up from the inside."

"You guys aren't mad?"

Sabeen shook her head.

Amaya shrugged. "I kinda figured something like that was going on, and . . ." Her voice trailed off but she didn't have to finish. Her father, the great General Cuthbert Trent, had been letting her down and keeping things from her for Amaya's whole life. She still hadn't opened that letter from him, but Magdalys wasn't about to press her on it twice in the same night.

"Who goes there?" a surly voice called out from the shadows.

"It's uh . . . we're . . ."

Amaya saluted. "Members of the Dactyl Hill Mounted Regiment, sir!" she barked. "Here to check on one of our mounts that was brought in earlier."

Magdalys tried not to let her eyes go wide. Amaya had spat that lie out like a pro.

"Oh," the soldier said, stepping into the torchlight. He was a tall, slender fellow with bushy, bright red sideburns and a

dirt-spackled uniform. On second thought, Magdalys realized, that probably wasn't dirt, considering where they stood. "Of course! How lovely! The Dactyl Hill Mounted Regiment, you say? I haven't heard of that one, but goodness knows we need some air cavalry support these days. I'm Lieutenant Knack. You three seem a bit young and er . . . female . . . to be in the corps, you know."

"Oh, we don't serve in battle, of course," Amaya said without missing a beat. "We travel with the menfolk and take care of the mounts. You know, women's work."

"Right, right," Knack said, nodding. "Come this way, my dears."

Magdalys nudged Amaya as they fell into step behind the lieutenant. "How did you do that?"

Amaya smiled and wiggled her eyebrows. "If you talk like them, you can say almost anything you want and they'll go along with it. Trust me, half of these guys don't listen to anything anyone's saying; they throw in a word or two that was said to make it sound like they were paying attention and then do whatever they were planning to do anyway."

"What's that?" Knack asked without looking back.

"Sir, nothing, sir," Magdalys said in her best impression of a gruff, military voice. "We were just discussing the lovely smell of dinopoop."

"Dinopoop, you say? Ah, yes, lovely, lovely."

They followed the lieutenant past a few makeshift paddocks. Magdalys thought she recognized the wide barrel

chests and long horns of triceratopses, and beyond that the tall, shield-covered backs of stegosaurs. The raptors and other carnivores were probably housed in a separate area to keep them from munching on these guys. Grunts, growls, and squeals rose in the night around them.

"Ah, here we are." He stopped at the edge of a large tent. "You know, the strangest thing happened earlier tonight."

Magdalys barely heard him. Her whole mind had filled with a different sound: the gentle, concerned *fubba-fubba-fubba* of a whole squad of pterodactyls.

CHAPTER NINE
SQUAD!

MAGDALYS BLINKED, BOTH her eyebrows raised.

Before her, nine of the dactyls that had left New York with them perched on metal bars around a wooden table. Under the dactyls' watchful gaze, four black men in aprons labored away with scalpels and bandages at something large behind a bloodied sheet hanging in front of the table.

"I believe this is the fellow you're looking for," Knack said. "Although you'll notice several of the others are suffering from various minor injuries. They showed up a few hours ago and refused to accept treatment until our surgeons stabilized the worst off of them, I'm afraid. Which seems to be what's happening just now. Isn't that right, Dr. Pennbroker?"

"Right indeed!" one of the men called back. "Then maybe we can get these old boys on out of the operating room."

One of the dactyls squawked at him and Dr. Pennbroker went back to what he was doing. "They're sort of . . . persistent," the surgeon said with a chuckle.

Magdalys felt like someone had lit a candle inside of her. Her friends had survived, most of them anyway. And they'd come to look out for the one that had saved her life! What noble, loyal animals they were. A few looked up and seemed to acknowledge her with those inscrutable squinting eyes before turning their attention back to the surgery in progress.

On top of that, they were being cared for by black surgeons! "I didn't know . . ." she started.

"That the Union Army had black surgeons? Ha!" The doctor shook his head. "Nobody does, it seems. Technically, they only let us operate on the Negro soldiers and the dinos . . ."

"Technically," the other three doctors echoed, rolling their eyes.

"Right," Dr. Pennbroker amended. "When push comes to shove and the broken bodies are pouring in faster than anyone can work on them, all those rules go out the window, of course. You want to see your friend here?"

Magdalys stepped forward and peered around the sheet. The injured dactyl lurched his big head around and locked eyes with her, letting out a long, heavy breath. He was alive

and awake. *Dizz,* Magdalys thought. *I'll call him Dizz.* "He's going to make it?" she asked.

"Oh he'll be up and ready to go in no time," Dr. Pennbroker said. "Took quite a scrapping though — pulled two slugs out of him and a third went right through his left wing. But you know, as Dr. Sloan always says: The dactyl is a ptero of unimpeachable character."

"Whatever that means," another surgeon scoffed.

"Yeah, I've never figured that one out either, to be honest."

"You know Dr. Sloan?" Magdalys asked. "I . . . I've read his book so many times."

"Heh, you could say he's a good friend," Dr. Pennbroker said. "Though we do have our disputes on anatomy and physiology. He's serving with the Army of the Potomac now, over in the eastern theater."

"I didn't know he'd enlisted. I didn't even know he was still alive!"

"Oh, lord, very much alive," Dr. Pennbroker said. "Alive and stubborn as ever, I'm afraid."

"Thanks for taking care of our dactyl," Magdalys said, waving at the squad and surgeons alike as she joined Amaya and Sabeen at the far end of the tent.

"I gotta say," Amaya whispered, "I'm reevaluating my dislike of giant reptiles based on this experience alone."

"I've been trying to tell you," Magdalys said.

"And Stella, of course."

Magdalys nodded. "Stella the top dog."

"The best ptero in the whole world," Sabeen said.

"Stella the indomitable," Magdalys added.

"Stella who puts up with Two Step and Mapper's singing all night," Amaya said.

"We can't all be Sabeen."

"Aw," Sabeen said, blinking. "I don't really . . . I just . . ."

"You have a beautiful voice," Magdalys said.

Knack peered over at the girls. "What's that now?"

"We were saying we're pleased to see our loyal mounts are in such good hands, sir!" Magdalys yelled. A few of the dactyls cast what may have been incredulous gazes at her, which she ignored, smiling inwardly. "We'll be returning to our sleeping quarters now, sir!" She and Amaya saluted. The surgeons, their hands busy, nodded their goodbyes, and Knack opened the tent flap for them to leave through.

CHAPTER TEN
A LETTER, FINALLY

AN OFF-KEY SYMPHONY of crickets took over the night, rising even over Sabeen's enthusiastic snoring and broken only by occasional grunts and hoots from the dino quad. Magdalys rolled over and blinked at the tent drooping over her head.

The whole victory or defeat of the Army of the Cumberland, Sheridan's voice said over and over, *perhaps the Union itself, could rest on such tiny shoulders.*

She clenched her teeth, a blurry flash of anger rising in her chest. Who was Sheridan to put so much pressure on her? He knew exactly what he was doing, being at the head of an army that executed its own soldiers for deserting. He knew the power he wielded. Didn't even have to say it. The implicit threat was there, and even if he couldn't do as much to her as long as she

was a civilian, he'd made sure to let the weight of that burden sit as heavily as possible on her. Suddenly, Magdalys couldn't breathe, like the war itself was sitting on her chest, laughing in her face. She sat up, pulling in as much of the thick Tennessee night air as she could.

She stood, trying to keep her panting as quiet as possible.

For a few moments, she kept perfectly still, let her breath return to normal, her pulse simmer back down. The crickets screamed their song on and on; the snores around her rose and fell.

Cymbeline had lied; Sheridan wanted to coerce her into fighting a war she barely understood, and he would never let her go, that much was clear. Somewhere far away, her mom and dad had gone on with their lives, and her sisters too. Maybe they'd already forgotten about her. She'd never felt so tiny: just a dot amidst all these sleeping soldiers and dinos, the world and its battlefronts spinning endless circles around her. She needed someone to tell her what was right, someone who knew her deep down, but the only person she could think of was wounded and en route to New Orleans.

Hopefully.

Or maybe Montez was dead.

She blinked away tears, her breath coming fast again; the air seemed to escape her lungs before she could catch it. She'd been telling herself this whole journey was to keep him safe, but really it was Magdalys that needed him. Who was she kidding?

Without thinking about it, she slung her satchel over her shoulder and hurried as quietly as possible out of the tent, where she found herself staring directly into Amaya's face.

The older girl shook her head. "You can't stop running away, huh?"

"I . . ." Magdalys started. All her silly lies just floated away into the night before she could pick one that might work.

"Don't bother," Amaya said. "I get it."

"You do?"

"I get the impulse. If you keep going though, we have a problem."

Magdalys stuck the toe of her boot into the dirt and looked away. The torches around them crackled in the night. Soldiers and dinos snored and crickets droned on and on.

"They put a lot of pressure on you," Amaya said. "And that's not fair. And I would want to run away too."

Magdalys nodded, still looking away. "I'm scared."

"Me too. Thing is, and I know this doesn't make it any easier: We need you too. And you don't necessarily owe them anything, but we came here with you. For you."

Magdalys met Amaya's eyes. "I know and —"

"Let me finish. More than that: *I* need you. Right now."

"Huh?"

She held an envelope out to Magdalys.

"What do you want me to do with that?"

"Read it."

Magdalys took the gram, shoved her finger into the

opening, and pulled along the top, tearing the envelope open. "Out loud?"

"No, just to yourself. Of course out loud, Mags. Why else would I — never mind. Yes, out loud. Please."

"Sheesh, I was just asking."

They stopped beneath one of the perimeter torches and Magdalys squinted at the ornate handwriting.

Dearest Daughter Amaya,

I write you with incredible news, more incredible than I can even share within the confines of this letter, in fact, so I suppose what I mean to say is, I write to tell you that there is incredible news, but sadly, I must see you in person to let you know. I can say that all of my hard work and dedication to this noble country has finally come to fruition, and Dr. Lassiter has provided me with the technology I need to complete my life's work.

You must come at once. I have instructed the matrons to provide you with train fare to Galveston. Your destiny awaits, my daughter, as does that of your two sisters —

"Sisters?" Magdalys said, cocking an eyebrow. "You never —"

"*Half* sisters," Amaya corrected. "They're . . ." She shook her head with distaste.

"Ah, say no more."

— Iphigenia and Mary Claire —

"Iphigenia?" Magdalys said. "Does she live in a tower and only wear ballroom gowns?"

"Keep reading please."

"I'm just saying."

— who will also be arriving shortly. All three of you will soon find out the true extent of our family's fortune and important role in the future of this great nation.

Come quickly, daughter! Greatness awaits! All that you have worked toward, all that I have worked toward, all that is yet to come awaits! And this Union rests its tired hopes upon us, my daughter, but such is the burden of greatness.

Your father,
Major General Cuthbert Trent

Magdalys lowered the gram. "Wow."

Amaya just shook her head.

"I guess we both bear the burden of greatness now, huh?"

"I don't even know what to say."

"Neither would I. Are you . . . what are you . . ."

"I don't know."

"Oh, wait, there's more." Magdalys turned the paper over, where a few more lines were scrawled.

PS Perhaps you already have heard, but I am unwell, dear daughter. The doctors are at a loss and have hooked me up to

various infernal devices without much success. You must come quickly, I'm afraid, in order to inherit your destiny.

Amaya scoffed and sniffled at the same time. "Just like the old man," she said quietly. "Everything is amazing, come blah blah blah destiny, oh yeah by the way I'm dying, okay bye." She closed her eyes for a few seconds then blinked them open, shaking her head.

"That was a whole lot," Magdalys said.

Amaya took the gram and, without so much as a glance, held it up to a nearby torch. The parchment turned brown as fire snarled and snapped away at its edges, then it crinkled and was whisked away in sparkling ashes into the Tennessee night.

CHAPTER ELEVEN
ROLLING OUT

DINOS SCATTERED ACROSS an open plain as the whole world trembled. There were brachys and diplos; a flock of microdactyls skittered between the stomping legs of an allosaurus, as a whole rumbling trike herd thundered past. The ground shook and shivered, maybe from the dinos themselves or maybe that's what was making them run. Some had sprouted feathers from strange places; others had one limb or another covered in thick, matted fur.

In the distance, boulders tumbled down the side of a huge mountain.

Magdalys watched it all, her mouth hanging open, and wondered why she didn't get trampled in the mad stampede. Something shoved her from behind and she thought, *There it*

is, my death has come and then she opened her eyes and Two Step was smiling down at her, wearing his pajamas, his fro pointing every which way but down.

Magdalys blinked. "You're not Death."

Two Step looked himself over. "Doesn't seem like it, no. You coming?"

A great hubbub filled the air outside their tent. Metal clanged and hammers pounded over the rustle of many bodies moving at once. Somewhere further away, the hoots and growls of dinos mingled with various sternly given commands. "Where we going?"

"We're rolling out!" Mapper called from across the tent in his best drill-sergeant baritone.

Two Step broke into a smooth shoulder dip and then spun, landing back facing Magdalys with two finger guns pointed her way. "Rolllllling out!"

"Why are you two so hype?" Magdalys grumbled, pulling the covers off and stretching.

"US Army coffee!" Mapper said, taking a sip from a tin cup. "America's finest!"

"Is it really?" Magdalys asked.

"Absolutely not," Two Step said. "But it's strong. We got up early and some guys in the next tent gave us theirs. Said they drank tea! Can you imagine?"

"Gimme some," Magdalys said.

Mapper dutifully passed the cup to Two Step, who handed

it down to Magdalys. It was still hot and sure, not that great, but definitely packed just the right punch. Magdalys closed her eyes.

"The cats from last night said we can roll with them today," Mapper said. "They're so cool!"

"And they're an artillery unit," Two Step said, "so their trikes and stegos have howitzers mounted on 'em."

The Louisiana Native Guard, Magdalys thought. She'd ask them about Montez. She hopped up. "Well, what are we waiting for, boys? Let's roll out!"

The dark green forest-covered mountains rose to either side as the Louisiana Native Guard Mounted Artillery Unit rumbled along a well-worn path with the rest of General Sheridan's division. Fanners — soldiers who carried fans at the ends of long sticks — marched at regular intervals on either side of the caravan, swooshing away the billowing clouds of dust so they wouldn't leave an obvious imprint of where they were going across the Tennessee sky. The mid-morning sun blazed down at them from a near cloudless sky and the strains of a single trumpet reached Magdalys over the stomps and clinking metal and grunts of armored triceratops.

She looked up from the trike saddle she shared with Mapper, the young soldier named Hannibal, and the big muscled one, Jack Jackson. The blue-clad, mud-covered army and

their ironclad dinos stretched all through the valley and disappeared around a bend up ahead. Behind them, another armored unit, the Tennessee 7th, picked up the rear along with a few battalions of foot soldiers and a single squad of raptor riders. Magdalys could see those sharp, birdlike snouts bobbing along over the heads of the men at the very end of the procession.

The trumpet's song, at first just howling a series of sad, rasping notes into the blue sky, suddenly resolved into a melody: "John Brown's Body," and the whole regiment immediately began singing along. The lyrics were different though.

". . . *where the flag is waving bright!*" everyone sang together.

A glint of sunlight caught Magdalys's eye and then she spotted the trumpet player.

"*We are going out of slavery, we are bound for freedom's light!*"

Octave Rey — the one whose trike impression Hannibal had called garbage (not without cause, Magdalys had to admit).

"*We mean to show Jeff Davis how the Africans can fight!*"

He stood up on the saddle he was riding on as cheers and raucous laughter rose around him, and led the soldiers into the final bar of the verse.

"*As we go marching on!*" they sang, and then fell into an even louder rendition of the chorus: "*Glory, glory, hallelujah! Glory, glory, hallelujah!*"

When they finished, Octave sat back down and sent the song into more spiraling, melancholy melodies, like he was having a conversation with the sparkling sun and mountain paths around him.

"Hey," Magdalys said, making her way to the front of the trike saddle where Hannibal and Jack were sitting.

"Hey yourself," Hannibal said with a mischievous smile.

"Did you guys ever serve with the Louisiana 9th?"

Jack Jackson perked up. "The 9th? Mounted Trike Division right?"

"Yes!" Magdalys nearly yelped, trying to quell the thrill of possibility rising inside her. "My —"

"Weren't they with us at Milliken's Bend?" Hannibal said.

"Yes!" Magdalys yelled again. "That's right!"

Jack nodded. "Gave them Rebels a beatin'." A moment passed. "Took a beating too." He craned his neck to one side, showing a long, barely healed scar running from his jaw and around down one shoulder. "That's where I got this. And a few others too. Barely made it outta there alive."

"Won the day though," Hannibal put in.

"And helped Grant sack Vicksburg soon after," Jack added proudly.

"Did you meet a soldier named Montez? Montez Roca."

Jack and Hannibal looked at each other. "Don't recall one with that name," Jack said.

Hannibal shook his head. "I'd remember a name like Montez."

Magdalys felt her whole heart sag. Had he not really been there? Maybe Private Summers's letter had been wrong about which battle they'd been in. But that didn't seem right — Summers had been there too. "Oh," she said in a

voice so far away it made both men turn and look her over carefully.

"What's he look like?" Jack asked.

"He looks like her but with glasses and a shade lighter and even skinnier," Mapper offered. "Real bookish." He shook his head. "Always in a book."

Jack and Hannibal studied Magdalys for another few seconds, then looked at each other and yelled, "RAZORCLAW JONES!"

Magdalys's jaw dropped open. From behind her, Mapper made an incredulous gurgling noise.

"Come again?" Magdalys said.

"That's your brother?" Hannibal gaped.

Jack punched his shoulder, possibly shattering it. "Of course it is, man! Look at her! They're practically the same person, but what the little map dude said: glasses, lighter skinned, a little skinnier. I *knew* Magda Lee looked familiar!"

Hannibal shook his head and rubbed his injured shoulder. "I just . . . wow."

"Wait, slow down," Magdalys said. "What did you call him?"

"Razorclaw Jones," Jack and Hannibal said again, both chuckling and turning back to the front.

"But . . . why?"

"Razorclaw is army talk for a sharpshooter," Jack explained. "A sniper."

"Your brother could write his name in bullet holes on a tin can from fifty feet away," Hannibal bragged.

Jack tipped his head. "Well, I dunno about that, but —"

"Plus, y'all from New York, right?" Hannibal asked.

Magdalys nodded, still trying to take in the revelation that her brother could actually shoot, let alone well. "Yeah, but —"

"And the famous Raptor Claw neighborhood's there, so I guess someone just put two and two together."

"And threw in a Jones for good measure," Jack said.

Hannibal shrugged. "As we do."

"We're not even from that part of New York!" Magdalys yelled, overwhelmed with all the many impossible things happening at once. "And Montez is named Montez, not Razorclaw Whatever!"

"Jones," Mapper said helpfully.

"And he can't shoot guns! He hates guns!"

Jack and Hannibal traded a wry glance. "Oh, guess it was someone else then," Jack said.

"Yeah, it totally had to be a *different* kid from New York who looks just like you but with glasses. Got it."

"YOU GUYS!" Magdalys exploded. She climbed into the saddle between them. "You guys! That was . . . I mean . . ." She waved her hands around, trying to snatch the words that wouldn't come out of thin air. "I just . . ."

"Come to think of it," Jack said, "he did say he was Cuban. You Cuban?"

"Mentioned he had a sister too," Hannibal added. "Three, now that I think about it."

From behind them, Mapper let out a sigh.

"It's just," Magdalys said, and then, before she could even try to get another word out, she was crying. The tears didn't give her any warning and when they showed up she didn't even bother trying to stop them; she just leaned against Big Jack's big arm and sobbed into it as Hannibal patted her shoulder.

"She okay?" Mapper said, poking his head up.

"Sorry, little lady," Jack said. "We didn't mean to get you worked up."

"It's okay," Magdalys sniffled. "I didn't see it coming either." Something yellow appeared in front of her face — a handkerchief. Hannibal was holding it out to her. She took it and unloaded a whole nasty ton of snot into it. "Thank you."

"We got separated right after the battle," Hannibal said. He gingerly accepted his sullied handkerchief back, inspected it, and then just tossed it into the wilderness with a shake of his head. "Our crew got loaded onto the two ironclads that had shown up to shell the enemy for us. Didn't get a chance to see what happened to the boys from the 9th but I know it was a rough one for 'em."

"He was wounded," Magdalys said, sitting up. "Knocked unconscious with a rifle butt. Another soldier sent me a gram saying they were being transported down to New Orleans for treatment but . . . that's the last I heard."

"That's why we're here," Mapper said. "We're trying to get to him and make sure he's alright."

For a few minutes, the sounds of creaks of metal dinoarmor and heavy trod of a dozen trikes filled the air. Somewhere out

in the forest, birds twittered and squawked at each other, and the sun cast dazzling lightworks along a tiny stream meandering beside the dusty road.

"Wow," Hannibal said. "We'd all been wondering what a bunch of kids was doing out here in the middle of the war. I mean . . . I'm a kid, but you guys are *kid* kids."

"And y'all came all the way out here," Big Jack added, "knowing at any moment you could be captured, killed, or enslaved, all to make sure your brother's okay."

It hadn't really felt like a choice, Magdalys realized, and certainly not heroic — just the most obvious thing to do. But when he put it like that, it did sound pretty wild.

"I hope you find him," Jack said, as something out in the woods started rustling toward them.

Jack and Hannibal pulled carbines from their saddle holsters. Magdalys stood, her mind already casting around for some sense of an approaching dino. Before she could figure it out, the proudly crested head of a parasaurolophus emerged from the trees, followed by Card's stern, scarred face.

"Air cavalry," he yelled, pulling his mount into a quick canter alongside them. "Haven't had time to alert the officers yet. Don't wait for orders. They'll be on us any minute." He galloped on ahead. "Get into battle formation. Now!"

CHAPTER TWELVE
AIR ATTACK

"**LOAD THE BULL** pups!" Big Jack hollered as Hannibal yanked on the reins, pulling the trike into a sharp turn so it blocked the dirt road. The squeals of dinos and iron clanking into place rose around them.

Magdalys couldn't be sure, but it looked like some of the other mounts had pulled into position without anyone guiding them. She wondered if they'd been trained to follow what the other dinos did around them or . . .

"Sol, we need shells and powder!" Jack yelled. "Mason, get ready to mount these up. Someone pass word to the back that things are about to get hot."

"What can I do?" Magdalys asked.

"Take cover," Hannibal said, hopping down onto the road

and rummaging through one of the saddlebags. "Stay alive so you can find your brother."

Magdalys didn't like that answer, but he had a point: The dinos had all been wrangled and there was no way she or Mapper could help set anything up. Plus, the Native Guard clearly had that under control. They moved with sparkling efficiency, barely saying a word between them as they fell into action, each soldier playing his part.

"Shells!" Sol pulled up beside them on a long, low to the ground creature with a huge fin cresting along its scaly back. *A dimetrodon*, Magdalys realized. She'd never seen one before. Munitions cases had been slung along its flanks with leather straps, and Sol hopped off and immediately began heaving them up on the trike with some effort.

"Where's that bull pup?" Big Jack yelled, easily grasping one of the cases in a single hand.

"Here!" another soldier yelled, riding up on another fin-back, this one with a cannon strapped to either side of it. "Sorry, this one didn't want to get moving."

Big Jack and Hannibal hopped down and unstrapped one of the cannons.

"Bull pups?" Magdalys asked, trying to stay out of the way.

"Mountain howitzers," Hannibal said as he and Jack lifted one. "Oof! That's just what we call 'em."

"Shouldn't you be taking cover?" Big Jack asked, grabbing up the other cannon in his free hand while he helped Hannibal with the first one.

"I told her to!" Hannibal said between pants.

"Aim for the sun, boys!" Jack called. Around them, troops were mounting the howitzers on either side of their trikes' iron armor plates.

"Why the sun?" Mapper asked.

"Take cover, we said!" Jack snapped.

"Because," Hannibal said, heaving one of the cannons into position on the trike's armor and securing it in with a series of clicks and clacks, "air cavalry always try to attack from wherever the sun is, that way they get a clear shot and we have the sun in our eyes."

"Smart," Mapper said.

"DACTYL HILL SQUAD!" a voice thundered. "TAKE COVER IN THE SURROUNDING FOREST IMME-DIATELY!" It was Cailloux, the middle-aged corporal with the excellent mustache who had been calling the shots at the campfire the night before. He stood on a saddle a few trikes away and bellowed into a megaphone cone as Two Step, Amaya, and Sabeen dashed toward Magdalys and Mapper.

"We better get moving," Mapper said, pulling Magdalys toward the woods.

"We said to take cover how many times?" Big Jack grumbled, securing the second howitzer.

"You didn't call 'em out by their squad name," Hannibal pointed out with a grin.

Magdalys was just backing to the tree line when she saw the first shadow flicker over the troops. She was safely beneath

the forest canopy a moment later when the second and third shadows passed, but Amaya, Sabeen, and Two Step were still sprinting toward her. "Run!" Magdalys yelled, but her voice was swallowed up by a rising murmur of commands and then the urgent *pop-pop-pop* of muskets all around her.

Sabeen reached the trees first, then Amaya. Two Step seemed to be running in slow motion, but Magdalys knew he was doing his best. Behind him, Hannibal swung the trike into position while Sol placed an iron ball into the mouth of the cannon and shoved it home with a ramrod.

Musket fire plinked against the iron trike armor and thunked into the dirt around Two Step as he ran. Up above, a half dozen dactyls flapped in an unruly cluster in front of the sun. Magdalys tried not to imagine Two Step getting hit, but the image kept coming anyway, his wounded body dropping just shy of the tree line, Magdalys helpless to do anything without getting torn up by enemy fire herself.

"Made it!" Two Step yelled, bursting into the woods past Magdalys and collapsing in a panting, sweaty heap just as Cailloux screamed "FIRE!" and the Louisiana Native Guard's bull pups burst to life one by one.

A series of deep booms sounded from down the road and then Magdalys saw Big Jack turn away from his cannon as he whipped a cord away from it and *ka-FWOOMbraaahhh!!* So much smoke poured out around him that at first Magdalys wasn't sure if he'd fired or been hit. Then the wind swept away most of it, and there was Big Jack, already setting up his next

shot as Hannibal swabbed the inside of the cannon with a rag on a long stick.

"Sol!" a soldier called from the next trike up. "We need another round!" Sol was already back on his dimetrodon and guiding it gingerly along the dirt road.

The dactylriders had dispersed above them but were already swooping back into formation as they sent random bursts of musket fire in all directions. Most of them didn't seem to have much control over their mounts, Magdalys realized. Now that she could see them in the daylight, the Confederate Air Cavalry seemed like a desperate, chaotic mishmash of untrained riders, with only a few exceptions.

Magdalys closed her eyes, reaching out, and immediately a wave of frantic, irritated *fubba-fubbas* rolled over her. These were the enemy dactyls, but Magdalys could sense her own too, and they were coming up fast from somewhere nearby.

More gunfire erupted from above and Cailloux yelled "FIRE!" again and the cannons shredded the sky, sending dactyls tumbling and screeching away.

Except one, Magdalys noted. One rider seemed to know exactly what he was doing, and he maneuvered his dactyl deftly out of the way and then swung back over the Native Guard, firing shot after shot. The first three ricocheted off a trike's armor but the fourth and fifth hit the dirt near where Sol's finback was hauling the munitions cases.

The munitions cases! Magdalys realized. Panicked, she cast her mind out for the dactyl's and for the first time since she'd

learned she could connect to these giant reptiles, she found herself rebuffed. No *fubba-fubba*, nothing at all. Magdalys stood, fists clenched, and watched in horror as the rider let off two more shots and then a sharp blast went off and with an ear-shattering *kaTHWOOM*, the whole world seemed to rip apart at the seams.

CHAPTER THIRTEEN
UP AND OVER

MAGDALYS LOOKED UP, the blast still echoing like a ghost cackling through a canyon in her ears. A charred crater smoldered in the road where Sol and his dimetrodon had been. The nearest trike had been knocked over by the blast, but it looked to be otherwise unhurt. Soldiers were staggering to their feet, shaking their heads and wiping dust out of their eyes.

"You guys okay?" Magdalys asked, looking around. Amaya, Sabeen, Two Step, and Mapper all nodded solemnly.

"Solomon?" Sabeen asked, peering past Magdalys.

She shook her head. "Don't look."

"There's nothing to even . . . see," Mapper blurted out, tears welling up. "There's nothing left."

Sabeen hugged Amaya, who just patted her head and frowned.

Magdalys glanced at Two Step. That look on his face — the wide-open broken one he'd had when he'd shot that trikerider back at the Penitentiary — it was nowhere to be seen. Instead, Two Step's brow was creased, his eyes narrowed to furious, fast-blinking slits.

"Easy," Magdalys said, putting her hands on his shoulders as they heaved up and down with each breath. "Easy, man."

More shots rang out. Disaster had struck and the battle wasn't even over. Magdalys whirled around just as another *ka-FWOOMshaaa* burst out from Hannibal and Jack's cannon. The smoke cleared, revealing them, covered in cuts and bruises, their blue uniforms in tatters as they frantically worked to clear the cannon mouth and reload it.

Then more shadows rippled over the trikes and troops and bullet-battered road: the Dactyl Hill dactyls. Magdalys gave a shout of joy and looked up just in time to see them smashing into what was left of the enemy cavalry, scattering them every which way.

"I want to . . ." Two Step seethed. Magdalys turned back to him. Tears streamed down his face. "I just want to . . ." He shook his head and she closed with him, pulling him into a hug that he didn't return. "I just . . ."

"I know," she said, although he hadn't finished his sentence. It was all over his face: Two Step wanted to kill. He had gone from a scared little boy, heartbroken at having been forced

to take a life, to . . . this: an overflowing volcano of rage. She squeezed him harder as his shoulders heaved with silent sobs.

"They're dispersing," Card yelled, riding up on his para. He didn't sound happy about it though.

"Keep firing, men," Cailloux hollered. "We can't let them get away!"

"What is it?" Sabeen asked, stepping out of the woods. "What's happening?"

Magdalys squeezed Two Step one more time and then took his hand and walked out toward the road with him behind Amaya and Mapper.

"They've learned our position," Card said, pulling his mount to a halt. "If one gets back to Braxton Bragg's camp they'll hurl the full weight of his army at us."

"And the way we're spread out over the next twelve miles," Cailloux said as he hopped down from his trike, "it'll be nothing for him to outflank and smash us." Magdalys saw him glance at the crater where Sol and the finback had been and shake his head, eyes closed.

"I can . . ." Magdalys said, already quickening her pace as the *fubba-fubba-fooo* sound of the Brooklyn dactyls diving grew louder inside her. "Let me take a dactyl. Put a gunner on the back and we'll catch them."

Card swung his para around and squinted at her, his face somehow sharp and forlorn. He traded a glance with Cailloux, nodded. "Corporal Cailloux, send a squad into the woods beneath them to capture any survivors." Then he leaned

forward and yelled, "Heeyah!" urging his mount off the road and back into the woods.

"Where are you going?" Cailloux yelled.

"Scout out the enemy position," Card called over his shoulder. "So we can smash them instead!" And then he was gone.

Magdalys watched him disappear into the trees and then turned to Cailloux as the others came up behind her. "Amaya," she said, "stay with Sabeen and Two Step."

Dactyls landed on the trikes nearby: one, two, three.

"I can —" Two Step started, but Magdalys spun on him.

"No. You have to stay," she said. "Don't fight me on this." Some kind of fire flashed in Two Step's eyes — a look Magdalys had never seen in him before, and for a second she thought he might lash out and take a swing. Then he seemed to crumple into himself as Amaya swooped in with her long arms and he put his face into her shoulder.

"Mapper," Magdalys said, breaking into a run toward the trikes. "You take the tall gray one."

"On it."

"Private Hannibal," Cailloux said, "go with Magda Lee. Private Rey!"

"Sir!" Octave Rey ran up from the still-downed trike and saluted just as Hannibal dusted himself off and headed toward Magdalys.

"Ride with the one they call Mapper. Stop those dactylriders!"

"Sir yes sir!" the two men shouted as Magdalys grasped the shoulder of the smaller blue dactyl and heaved herself onto its back.

"The one they call Mapper," Mapper said. "I like that."

This would be just like hopping rooftop to rooftop back in Dactyl Hill . . . except with no rooftops . . . and Rebel Air Cavalry trying to snipe them down . . . and nowhere safe to go if they got separated and stranded. Hannibal climbed on behind her just as the dactyl stretched to full height, flapping her wings and letting out a fierce caw.

"Go!" Hannibal yelled, already loading cartridges into his carbine. The dactyl began to climb. "Go!" Magdalys leaned forward, felt the dactyl's mind sharpen along with her own toward their singular purpose. And then they lifted into the air above the miles of marching troops and hurtled out over the treetops.

CHAPTER FOURTEEN
AIR CHASE

GRAPPLER, MAGDALYS DECIDED to call her new mount.

Up Grappler, she thought, clenching her jaw and leaning forward. *Up!*

The dactyl cawed and flapped once and then again with her long, graceful wings, taking them higher and higher in an arc so steep they were almost vertical to the ground. The Confederates wouldn't be expecting any pursuit by air. Magdalys wanted to see what she was up against before they had a chance to get away. In the corner of her eye, she saw Mapper following close behind them and a little off to the side as Octave prepped his weapon.

"Alright, I get it!" Hannibal yelled against the shrieking

wind. "You're one of those dinotalking freaks from the days of old or whatever!"

Magdalys growled. "Oh, we're freaks, are we?" Grappler steepened her climb even more.

"I mean! In a good way!"

Magdalys allowed herself a slight chuckle and kept climbing. "Don't tell me you're scared, Private Hannibal."

"Never, Miss Roca!"

Up they sped.

"Okay, maybe occasionally," Hannibal allowed, but Magdalys was already tilting Grappler back into an open soar. Below, Mapper had leveled out too and was scanning the treetops for enemy flyers.

There.

Three pteros flapped in a triangle formation off to one side while two more fled in the opposite direction. Magdalys recognized the one she'd seen wield his mount better than all the others to take out Sol. She grimaced at the memory — the shredding, impossible boom of that blast; the crater — then tried to shake it away. "Mapper!" she called, then pointed three fingers at the retreating trio. He nodded, veered his mount after them.

"Why give them all the glory of taking out three?" Hannibal said as Magdalys took Grappler into a long-ranging dive toward the other two cavalrymen.

"This all a game to you, huh?" she said, still fighting back

the sheer, impossible emptiness of the space Sol had once been in. Sure, the men they were talking about probably killing would kill them first in a heartbeat but . . . she didn't know how he could be so lighthearted about it.

Hannibal was quiet for a few moments, and all Magdalys heard were the clicks and clacks of metal over the whispering wind as he unfolded a portable shaft and placed it on Grappler's back to steady his aim.

"No," he finally said quietly. "None of it is. It's life and death, but when that's all there is, every day, and maybe all there ever will be, the only thing you can do to keep going is make peace with it or it'll eat you alive."

Magdalys didn't know what to say. She wasn't being fair and she knew it; who was she to judge how a soldier did his job? The first dead body she'd seen had been Mr. Calloway, the caretaker at the orphanage, who'd been hanged by a mob the night of the riots, and that hadn't been that long ago. Hannibal had probably already lost track of the death that had piled up around him.

"Bring us into a glide behind them," Hannibal said. "I don't expect you to understand it, sis. I don't even understand it, and I been in the thick of it for the past year. But I know I gotta keep moving, no matter what — we all do — and I'ma keep doing whatever I have to do to do that. Duck, please."

Up ahead, the two flyers had widened the gap between each other, almost to the point that they were flying in different directions.

"The green-and-gray one," Magdalys said. "That's the reason we're going after these two and not the other three. If you have to get one and not the other, get —"

She was interrupted by two shots exploding over her head in quick succession. Up ahead, *both* dactyls shrieked and spun out of control, one of them throwing its rider into the trees below with a yelp.

"Forgot to mention that I taught your brother everything he knows," Hannibal said with what Magdalys was sure was a smirk.

"Not bad," she said, "but that one's still going."

The green-and-gray dactyl had pulled back into a lopsided flutter, its rider frantically pulling himself into the saddle. The other flapped crookedly downward and disappeared beneath the canopy of leaves.

Magdalys gazed down, urging Grappler after them. *Had the man died?* From the way his dactyl tumbled out of sight, it looked like the bullet had winged it, probably without hitting the rider. But a fall like that could surely kill someone, right?

Blam! The Confederate cavalryman's pistol sang out over the wind. They hadn't been hit — that dactyl was flying too erratically to get any kind of steady shot — but it snapped Magdalys back into focus.

"You with me, Mags?" Hannibal said, positioning his carbine again.

She nodded, swooping them a little lower so they could come up at the rider from below.

"What's so special about this guy anyway?"

"He's a freak like m—" Magdalys started to say, but then the dactyl executed an impressive roll just as Hannibal let off another shot, swooping out the way and then diving suddenly into the trees.

"That!" Magdalys growled.

"How in the —"

"Dive!" yelled Magdalys, and Grappler's ecstatic *fuuuuuu* lanced through her mind as the forest raced up to greet them.

CHAPTER FIFTEEN
BENEATH THE CANOPY

BRANCHES RAKED SHARPLY against Magdalys's face for the second time in as many days, but at least it was daylight and her dactyl hadn't been shot from under her.

Not yet, anyway. A few more cracks rang out from the woods ahead of them, one smashing loudly into a tree barely a foot away.

"Yikes," Hannibal said dryly. "This guy won't quit. Can you bring us a little lower so I don't get my eyes gouged out?"

"Working on it," Magdalys grunted. She dipped Grappler down further, below the thickest cluster of branches, swung into a hard roll to avoid a maple tree and then swooped between two bifurcating trunks. Another shot whizzed past, shattering a twig to her right, and then she caught movement

up ahead. The rider had perched his dactyl on a sturdy branch and dismounted to take potshots, and now he was clambering back on.

"No, you don't," Magdalys whispered, urging Grappler straight for them.

"What'd you say?" Hannibal said. "Oh my —"

Grappler whipped to the side of another tree, pulling her wings tight to her body at the last second, and then flicked them out and back again in a sudden flap that sent them bursting through a thick mesh of foliage. She ducked her head just as they emerged and rammed the bony crest on her forehead straight into the enemy dactyl before it could take off.

The dactyl flung forward in a messy tangle of wings and claws and the rider went tumbling through the underbrush with a yell, crashed through snapping branches and twigs all the way down, and then thudded heavily on the forest floor below.

"Down," Magdalys said to Grappler just as Hannibal folded up the carbine stabilizer and yelled, "After him!"

They swooshed into a dive, Grappler arching her rear legs beneath her and slowing with a tilt of her wings as they approached the writhing soldier.

"Get back!" the man yelled, and Magdalys spotted the glint of light on the barrel of his raised pistol. Grappler had come up on him fast though; she landed with a claw pinning each of his arms to the ground.

Ka-BLAM!! The pistol went off, sending a bullet crackling through the woods off to the side. Hannibal slid out of the saddle and snatched the gun out of the man's hand. Magdalys climbed down and signaled Grappler that she could step back.

A scraggly goatee framed the Confederate's long face. He wore a dirty gray uniform with two bars on the sleeve that Magdalys was pretty sure meant he was an officer of some kind. One leg lay twisted beneath him at an unfortunate angle. His bright blue eyes blinked up at Magdalys and Hannibal and his breath came in short, desperate pants. "Shoulda figured I'd be captured by two —"

Hannibal cut the man off with the sound of his own six-shooter cocking a round into the chamber. "I'm guessing you don't want to finish that sentence," Hannibal said, leveling the pistol between the Confederate's suddenly wide eyes.

"Never did like the dang Confederacy anyway," he grumbled. "Dunno how I ended up in this ol' mess."

"Oh yeah," Hannibal sighed. "All y'all just *hate* the Confederacy once you end up on the wrong end of a pistol. That was the fastest tune change I've heard yet though. Mags, search him."

Magdalys blinked for a second, then nodded and gingerly started patting down the man's pockets and supply belt for anything that felt like a gun or knife.

"Name and rank," Hannibal demanded.

"Lieutenant Hardy L. Hewpat."

"You one of Bragg's men?"

Hewpat snorted up something nasty and blood-tinged and hocked it into the grass. "That demented hack! Never! I'm with General Forrest's Tennessee Air Cavalry, 3rd Division, the Smokys' Fighting Finest!"

"Alright, alright," Hannibal snapped. "Didn't ask for all that. Got anything, Mags?"

She stood and shook her head, then stared Hewpat in his laughing eyes. "How do you know how to dinowrangle so well?"

"Heh," Hewpat chuckled. "We're the finest flyers this side of the Missi —"

"No," Magdalys said. "You. How do *you* know? These others weren't as good."

He smirked. "I mean, that's mighty kind of you, but . . ."

"Answer the question," Hannibal growled. "You don't have much choice, in case you hadn't noticed."

"Don't I?" Hewpat closed his eyes and took a deep breath.

"What happened?" Hannibal said. "He dying?"

Magdalys squinted at him. The high-pitched *fuuu* sounded like it was coming from a hundred miles away but closing fast. A twig snapped from somewhere up above and then a vision of what was about to happen exploded like a firework in her mind. There wasn't time to explain to Hannibal. She shoved him out of the way, pulling his bayonet blade out of its sheath as she passed him and then swinging it with both hands in a

wide upward arc across her body as the Confederate dactyl came screeching down at her.

The blade sheared a bright red gash across its belly and the dactyl yelped and hurled itself off to the side, slashing Magdalys's arm as it went. It crashed into the dirt a few feet away and scrambled to its feet, blood weeping freely from the bayonet wound. The dactyl let out a fierce caw and lurched toward Magdalys, snapping with its armor-plated beak.

Magdalys took one step back, bayonet raised, and then a blue-and-gray blur blasted out of the woods and slammed full force into the dactyl, lifting it clear into the air.

"Grappler!" Magdalys yelled. Grappler held the enemy dactyl in her claws just long enough to send it barreling into a tree trunk with a mighty *THUNK!* The dactyl slid to the ground and landed in a pile of broken limbs sticking out in all the wrong directions.

"Lil' Calhoun, baby! No!" Hewpat gasped. "My baby!"

Grappler flapped to a sturdy branch above them and gazed serenely off into the distance.

"You killed Lil' Calhoun!"

Magdalys realized Hannibal was staring at her. "You . . . saved my life."

She shook her head, held up his bayonet with the point facing herself. "Grappler saved us both. Here."

He took it and nodded his thanks, still blinking like the sun had just risen in the middle of the night.

"Y'all savages gonna kill me already or what?" Hewpat said between pants. "Might as well, seeing as how you murdered poor Lil' Calhoun."

Hannibal sheathed the bayonet. "Stop talking. And no, we're not going to kill you. We're bringing you back to Major General Sheridan so you two can have a long talk about what you know."

CHAPTER SIXTEEN
WHOA BEANS

SOMEONE ELSE LIKE *me*, Magdalys thought as they flew just beneath the foliage with Lieutenant Hewpat trussed up and slung over the back of Grappler. There was no other explanation: the cavalryman had been wrangling his ptero just like Magdalys did. That was why she couldn't even reach out to his mount as he was attacking Sol. That was why he flew so much better than the others, and how he'd had Lil' Calhoun attack them right when he needed help.

She shook her head. There were others like her. Who knew how many? What if . . . the image of an unstoppable surge of Confederate raptors and pteroriders came billowing into her mind.

"There!" Hannibal yelled, pointing down at a perfectly still lump of gray and pink down below.

"Rosworth!" Hewpat yelled, writhing against his bindings. "Aw, Rosworth! You murderers! You killed Rosworth!"

Rosworth was indeed dead, Magdalys realized as they glided slowly over his contorted body and empty eyes. She shuddered.

"He had two children," Hewpat moaned. "And a pretty young wife, Sarahbelle."

Magdalys tried not to imagine them, but the vision surfaced anyway: a gram delivered by minidactyl; a white woman in a fancy pink dress with curly hair opening it, two squirming kids by her side, their little faces contorting as they found out their daddy wouldn't be coming home.

Their daddy who would've killed Magdalys in a heartbeat and was fighting to keep her people enslaved. The whole world seemed to spin and tilt around her and she felt like she might hurl up the hardtack they'd had for breakfast over the side.

"Quiet," Hannibal ordered, and Magdalys silently repeated the command to her own troubled mind. "All it takes is one tip of this ptero and you will have a sudden reunion with the ground, Hewbert."

"Hewpat!"

"What's that?" Hannibal said, rocking Grappler back and forth a few times. "I didn't hear you over the sound of me being about to toss you over the side."

"Nothing!"

Less than an hour ago, Magdalys thought, they'd all been singing a battle hymn along with Octave's coronet, marching

through the sunlight on trikeback. Solomon had been alive. So had Rosworth. And now . . . the world seemed to spin faster and faster around her.

"What happens now?" she asked, guiding Grappler back up through the canopy of leaves into the open sky.

"Ol' boy will get interrogated," Hannibal said, "and sent to a prison camp and probably released in a few months for political reasons or some nonsense and be back taking potshots at us from the air."

"That's messed up," Magdalys said, "but I meant . . ." She shrugged and gazed down at the peaks and valleys sprawling beneath them.

"Oh, Private Solomon?"

She nodded, relieved at not having to explain herself. The long stretch of bright blue sky seemed to slow the spin of the world. Magdalys took a deep breath.

"He's dead. There's nothing to bury, from what I could tell, so we'll just hold a ceremony tonight by the campfire and that'll be that."

"I mean . . ."

"If we was back in New Orleans, we'd throw him a big ol' marching band funeral — a second line, it's called — and Octave and the boys would play some of the finest music you ever heard. Not that straight-laced military band nonsense, I mean *real* music, and everyone would come out from their houses and join the party, cuz it *would* be a party. And it'd feel like the whole world was there, celebrating, and even the trikes

and stegos would be decorated and covered in sparkly outfits and streamers as they hauled that empty casket all along the avenue to the cemetery."

"Sounds beautiful," Magdalys said, breathing deeply again, letting the world slow back down even more.

"That's what I was trying to say earlier, Mags. That's how we do death down there. My folks anyway. My family's been part of the Mardi Gras Indians for ages —"

"The what?"

"Hard to explain. It's like a club, you know? We make these beautiful feathered outfits and we know how to make a funeral right. It's a celebration, not because they died but because they lived, whoever they were. And that's how we gotta do it here in the war too. Solomon lived. He was a pain in the butt sometimes, but he had a girlfriend on Iberville who'll be sad he's gone, and a married white society lady who'll probably be even more sad he's gone, but that's another story —"

"Wait . . ."

"And he had the best handwriting of all of us and folks in the Guard would dictate letters back home to him." Hannibal shrugged. "If we stopped to mourn each death, we'd be the next one to die, and what good would that do poor Sol? So we just gotta keep moving."

Magdalys nodded, breathed, nodded. "I'm sorry about what I said before. I made it sound like you don't care about what you do and that's not fair. I . . . I really don't know what I'm talking about."

"It's arright," Hannibal said, his Louisiana drawl growing longer with thoughts of home. "You made up for it by saving my life, so we even now."

Up ahead, two dactyls swooped out of the trees. Magdalys squinted at them, but Hannibal had already pulled out his spyglass. "That's Octave on one." He chuckled. "Looks like he lassoed himself a Rebel. Got him trussed up on the back just like ours. Guess he still getting the hang of riding that thing though."

"Is Mapper on the other?" Magdalys asked, trying not to sound desperate. In all the commotion, she had forgotten her friend was off having his own adventures.

"Yeah, your little buddy's alright. He got himself a Rebel too! Wonder where the third one is. . . ."

"Probably reaching our lines right now!" Hewpat yelled from behind them.

"Quiet, Hewbert!" Hannibal yelled. "When we're curious about your opinion we'll drop you over the side and ask whatever's left on the ground."

"Ayyy!" Magdalys called, urging Grappler forward behind the other two dactyls. Hannibal was right about Octave — his mount swooped and scuttled in that ungainly way they had when they knew a rider had no idea what they were doing.

Mapper glanced back and a wide smile broke out on his face. "Mag-D!" he yelled, waving, and the dactyl he was riding swerved sharply to the side, nearly tossing him. "Whoa! Easy, Beans!" He wrapped both arms around its neck and clung on as his mount glided back into position.

He named the dactyl Beans? Magdalys just stared at him wide-eyed. "Mapper, careful, man!" she yelled.

"Good hunting, Private Hannibal?" Octave asked, rearing his dactyl back some so it flew neck and neck with Grappler. On the back, a kid about Hannibal's age, all in Confederate grays, lay unconscious, his hands and feet expertly bound up and a shiny blue lump rising on his face.

"Excellent, Private Rey," Hannibal said. "One captured; one didn't survive the fall."

"Mags!" Mapper said, pulling Beans along the other side of them. "Octave has a lasso! And he straight up just lassoed a dude! Two dudes!"

"Told ya," Hannibal said.

"And one other dude tried to get away and fell so like, he didn't make it, but Octave lassoed the other two like . . . Whew! Like cattle, Mags! And then he like, reeled 'em in and trussed 'em up and —"

Mapper's dactyl lurched suddenly upward, throwing Mapper backward on top of the tied-up Confederate. "Whoa!" Mapper yelled. "Be cool, Beans! Be cool!"

"What's happening?" Magdalys called, sending Grappler after them. "Mapper!"

Beans surged forward; Magdalys could see Mapper still trying to untangle himself and find something to grab on to, his hands flailing as the Confederate struggled and cursed. Then the dactyl squawked and spun into a barrel roll, sending them both over the side.

CHAPTER SEVENTEEN
TRIP, TANGLE, TRUSS

"**GRAB ANYTHING!**" **MAGDALYS** yelled as Mapper's feet flew out from under him and he tumbled off the dactyl.

"Gah!" the Confederate yelled. Octave had secured his hands to the saddle and now he dangled by his wrists in midair, Mapper grasping on to his waist for dear life. "Let go of me, kid!"

"Hold tight!" Magdalys yelled. "We're coming!" Beans had lurched off again, flushing down and then back up in a messy zigzag through the sky. Magdalys sent Grappler racing after them as Octave spurred his mount on behind.

"If I could just . . ." Magdalys said out loud as they came up behind Beans. She concentrated as hard as she could, reaching out for Beans's mind, grasping for any hint of his thoughts or even a single *fubba* to let her know she was on the right track.

Nothing.

She was blocked out just like she'd been from Lieutenant Hewpat's dactyl earlier.

Of course!

"Hewpat!" the Confederate dangling from Beans yelled. "That you, Lieutenant? Can you . . . can you right us, sir?"

Magdalys pulled Grappler directly below Mapper and the Confederate. "Mapper! Drop!"

"Are you su—" Mapper started to say and then Beans spiraled into a steep dive. "AAAAAAAAAAAH!!"

"Hewpaaaaaat!" the Confederate yelled.

He knows the lieutenant can control dinos, Magdalys thought, sending Grappler after them again. "Private Hannibal," she said, "what's Hewpat doing?"

The air rushed past as Grappler swooped over the trees and came swinging down alongside Beans again.

"He's got his eyes closed and his brow furrowed," Hannibal reported.

"You have to —" Magdalys paused as she noticed Octave's dactyl gliding straight toward them and Beans. "You have to break his concentration somehow! Distract him! He's controlling that dactyl!"

"AAAAAAAAH!!" Mapper yelled.

"HEWPAAAAAT!" the Confederate yelled.

Octave was doing something with his hands that she couldn't quite make out. His dactyl made straight for Beans, then swung to the side at the last second, and something long

and black whipped through the air from below and tightened around Mapper.

"Yow!" Magdalys yelled, raising herself on the saddle to see better as Mapper was yanked away from Beans and went hurtling through the air with a wild yelp on the end of Octave's lasso.

From behind her, a heavy thunk sounded. Beans flipped right side up and shook his head, blinking like he'd just woken up from a pleasurable nap.

Octave reeled Mapper in, hand-over-handing it as Mapper giggled uncontrollably.

Magdalys glanced back. Hewpat sat slumped over, a nasty lump growing shiny on his left temple. Hannibal turned to Magdalys; he had the lieutenant's six-shooter by the muzzle, grip out.

"You pistol-whipped him?" Magdalys asked, blinking.

Hannibal shrugged. "You said distract him."

"I said break his concentration, not his forehead!"

"I mean . . . it worked."

"Mags!" Mapper yelled as Octave flew up beside them, shaking his head. "Mags! Oh my god! Did you see that?"

"Did I ever," she sighed, reaching out for Beans in her mind. The familiar *fubba-fubba* sounded, if a little tentative and confused now. She nodded at the others and one by one they sped through the air back to the Union lines.

· PART TWO ·

CHICKAMAUGA

CHAPTER EIGHTEEN
BACK AT THE LINES

"**M**AGS." **HANNIBAL'S HAND** wrapped around her forearm. It wasn't too tight, but between his sudden grip and that quiet, urgent voice, almost a whisper, she knew something had finally broken that cocky exterior. His brow furrowed, eyes squinting like he could sense the answer to all that was troubling somewhere off in the distance but couldn't make it out.

"What is it?"

The procession's easygoing stride from that morning had ratcheted up into a fierce quickstep since the attack. Around them, soldiers and dinos alike glanced to either side and skyward as they marched along the dirt path between the southern Appalachian peaks. No one cracked jokes; no one sang. The only sounds to be heard were the endless stomps and shuffles

of dinos beneath the chimes of their clanking armor, and, from some far-off, peaceful part of the forest, birds singing back and forth to each other in the trees.

"It's true then, isn't it?" Hannibal said, his face a tight fist, waiting for a blow.

They fell into stride with the ongoing river of troops. Magdalys cocked her head at him. They'd handed the prisoners over to Young Card, who'd called for a medic to cart off the still-unconscious Hewpat and escorted the other two to General Sheridan for interrogation. Octave had gone along to give his report, and Magdalys figured she'd be summoned soon, but she'd wanted to take a moment to get herself together before facing Sheridan again.

Clearly, that wasn't going to happen. "What's true?" There were so many things he could've been referring to. So many possibilities dancing through the air, most of them terrible.

"You're a . . . you can . . ."

Ah, that. Magdalys's face hardened. "That I'm a freak, you mean?"

Her friend Redd's words always echoed through her head at moments like these: *Girl, say it loud. Otherwise how you gonna get even better at it?* It still wasn't easy, but she was trying. Even with the crew having already talked her powers up and Hannibal having had a pretty clear demonstration of them just now — there was no telling how someone would react. He *had* called her a freak, after all, though she could tell there wasn't much conviction behind it.

Hannibal cringed. "I was . . . I just . . ."

She smiled. "It's alright. I didn't take it too personally."

He seemed to deflate some. *"Too?"*

"And anyway, yes."

A look flashed across Hannibal's face, something between fear and awe, Magdalys thought, then acceptance as it resolved back into that determined frown he'd started with.

"And that's why we went after Hewpat." A statement, not a question. Good. He wasn't wasting time or going all mushy about it.

She nodded, waiting for him to put the rest of it together.

"And he's . . . too?"

"That's what it looks like. . . ." She shook her head. There wasn't time to second-guess anymore. "He is. I first noticed cuz I tried to reach his dactyl to stop them from attacking Sol but . . . I couldn't."

A wave of emotion sizzled through her — some vicious cocktail of regret, sorrow, helplessness, and rage. She let it rise and then pass, then wondered if she was already becoming more like these men and boys who'd lived with carnage as their daily bread for so many months.

Hannibal nodded, still squinting, and she almost could see the gears turning in his mind.

"And then he got to the dactyl Mapper was riding. And the worst part is —"

"The other Reb knew he could do it," Hannibal finished for her.

"Exactly!" Magdalys yelled.

"Which means . . ."

"The Confederates might be developing other dino-wranglers with the same ability."

Hannibal froze in his tracks, and soldiers peeled to either side of him, grumbling. He searched the dinobacks around them, then called out: "Corporal Cailloux, sir!"

Cailloux peered over from his trike, nodded at Hannibal. "Yes, Private?"

"Permission to advance to the front of the regiment for a word with the major general, sir?"

Cailloux nodded, barked, "Granted!" and the two traded a salute.

"C'mon," Hannibal said, grabbing Magdalys's hand and shoving his way through the soldiers he'd just made pass him.

"What are we doing?" Magdalys asked.

"They'll be interrogating the captives," Hannibal said. "I gotta let them know what we may be up against."

There was really no way to grasp the full giganticness of an army from inside its camp, Magdalys realized. It just felt like a big ol' cluster of folks and tents and bonfires. But make your way through the miles and miles of marching men and clomping dinos? This was just a single division and it seemed to go on forever.

Up ahead, the afternoon sun had started to slide through the sky, throwing the soldiers' shadows behind them like long, dancing spirits. If they were marching toward the setting sun, Magdalys figured, that meant they were heading west. West toward the Mississippi, which went straight down to New Orleans where Montez was. Maybe. It all seemed so slow and impossible and hopeless.

"So, you're with us, then, right?" Hannibal said as they passed a group of stegosauruses hauling wagons full of dinofeed amidst a sea of blue-uniformed troops.

"Huh?"

"I'm sure the major general asked you to join up. Everyone knows he's been champing at the bit to get Washington to give him permission to start an air cavalry. And you have dactyls *and* that mystical skill of yours. . . ."

Magdalys frowned, shook her head. "I . . ." She shrugged, knowing that wasn't explanation enough.

"Mags, we —"

"Yes, you need me," she snapped. "He gave me the whole shpiel. I just . . ." Cymbeline's worried face crossed her mind. "I'm just a kid, Hannibal."

"So am I," he pointed out.

"And look: You had to ask someone permission just to walk forward in the line. You can't go anywhere they don't tell you to go, do anything they don't tell you to do. They *own* you, Hannibal."

Shock flashed across his face and then he shook his head.

"It's not the same thing if you're the one who chooses to take part in it."

"I just don't . . . If I muster in . . ."

"How will you run off and save your brother?"

Magdalys looked away, a twist of shame gnawing at her.

"Mags, we all got brothers and sisters in danger."

She thought about David Ballantine in Dactyl Hill, who organized with the Vigilance Committee and had told her just before she left that he'd lost a younger brother. He hadn't elaborated, but he didn't need to — the never-ending ache was right there in his eyes. And Cymbeline's brother, Halsey Crunk, who was probably wondering if she was safe too. "You . . . you got a sibling?"

Hannibal laughed sadly, shaking his head. "Yeah, but that's not what I meant, girl. This thing bigger than you or me. It's not just we, the army, who need you. We," he said again slowly this time, "*all* got brothers and sisters in danger right now, Mags. They need your help."

Those scars crisscrossing Big Jack's back. The plantation they'd flown over the night before. Magdalys sighed, feeling those embers within crackle. *Not now*, she thought, dampening the flames. Without meaning to, she'd shoved the truth of slavery as far back in her mind as she could, if nothing else because the enormity of it felt like it would knock her over if she thought about it too much, like she'd never be able to make it through the day or even get out of bed if she really sat and pondered all the human beings in bondage. And the truth was

it made her feel guilty, on top of everything else. Why should she be free when so many of her people were enslaved?

She nodded. Hannibal was right, she just didn't know what to do with that truth. "I know," she finally said, the words woefully inadequate beside the hugeness of how she felt. "I just . . . I don't trust these guys either." They'd passed the stegos and moved into a battalion of paras, stomping along in that smooth, wavy gait of theirs as the riders eyed the surrounding forest. "They're not fighting for us, Hannibal. It wasn't long ago these same folks owned our people themselves. And they don't even pay y'all equal wages!" At the orphanage, Mr. Calloway had told them stories about growing up in bondage on a provisional farm in upstate New York. She still had nightmares about it sometimes. Then again, he never stopped talking about how proud he was that his only son was serving in the Army of the Potomac.

"I know that," Hannibal said. "We all know that. And we don't trust 'em. Well, Octave and I don't. Cailloux probably don't either but he's an officer so he keeps his mouth shut. And sure, Big Jack thinks the Union Army's the best thing to happen since Moses, but they freed him from a plantation outside Baton Rouge, so he can feel however he wants about 'em, far as I can tell."

"Were you . . ." Magdalys's voice trailed off. None of the words seemed right somehow.

"Nah," Hannibal said. "But being who we is, where we are? Might wake up free, find yourself in chains when the sun sets.

I dunno why these cats fighting, Mags." He nodded at the all-white battalion of parariders. "But that's why *I* fight."

The ongoing thunder and clank of hundreds of armored dinos on the march seemed to coalesce into a single steady pulse that Magdalys could feel rattle up her spine.

"Whoa," Magdalys said as they came up on the back end of a huge sauropod plodding along with mounted trikeriders on either side. "I didn't know y'all rolled with a diplodocus!"

She felt the earth shudder with each clomp of the huge dino's armored feet. The diplo was even more gigantic than the brachiosaurus she'd ridden the night of the Manhattan riots, basically running the length of two city blocks. In the Dinoguide, Dr. Barlow Sloan talked about it with undisguised awe and said it was one of the biggest animals to ever live.

"Yeah, that's one of the command dinos. They have to make sure he stay low when we're trying to keep our moves a little undercover though." He pointed to where the diplo's neck stretched straight ahead instead of up into the air. Magdalys spotted a fabric-wrapped chain slung around it just below the head and connecting to the saddle of a trike marching along beneath it.

She scowled. "Can't be comfortable."

"Actually," Hannibal pointed out, "that's the natural position for a diplo. They're more long than tall. It's brachys that like to have their necks sticking straight up."

Made sense that the New York fire brigades would use brachys then, Magdalys thought, to be able to reach high-up

windows. Plus, a diplo probably wouldn't fit in the Manhattan streets.

"That's just there to keep them from poking up now and then when they get curious. Can't give the Rebs any more chance to spot us, can we?"

"You know a lot about dinos, huh?"

He shrugged. "I'm in a mounted artillery division. Kinda have to."

Hannibal saluted the guards and led Magdalys up into the saddle. There, Cymbeline stood, shotgun in hand, eyes darting from tree to tree. Behind her, a group of officers gathered around someone slumped over in the chair he'd been tied to.

"Wait here," Hannibal said. "I'll go talk to the major general." He nodded at Cymbeline and walked away.

"Hey," Cymbeline said.

Magdalys pursed her lips.

CHAPTER NINETEEN
BATTLEFIELD SISTERHOOD

"**Y**EAH, WELL . . .**"** All the sharp retorts she'd been cultivating for this moment fell away. Instead Magdalys just wrapped the older girl in a hug. The boom that ended Sol echoed through her once again as she saw that Confederate falling to his death and the made-up version of his wife and kids sobbing.

"I'm so sorry," Cymbeline whispered.

"You lied to us," Magdalys said, the heat of that betrayal suddenly rising in her again. She stepped back, wiped her eyes.

"I just didn't —"

Magdalys cut her off with a look.

Cymbeline sagged. "I know. I'm sorry. I . . ." She shook her head.

"But?"

"Not but: and."

"Huh?"

"Look," Cymbeline said, one hand landing on her hip, her eyes sharpening. "I *am* sorry I lied, and yes, coming along without telling you I was in contact with the Union Army was a lie, *and* I want, no: I *need* you to understand that I had to."

"*Had* to?" Magdalys's voice stayed just below a yell. The last thing they needed was a bunch of people gaping at them arguing in the middle of a war zone.

"Yes. It's not because I don't trust you, or care about you. Of course I do. *And* I swore an oath *and* me being what I am puts everyone in danger —"

"ALL THE MORE REASON WE NEEDED TO KNOW THAT!" Magdalys exploded, onlookers suddenly unimportant.

"Except that what puts everyone in even more danger than me *being* a spy," Cymbeline growled in a whisper, "is everyone *knowing* I'm a spy. Don't you see, Magdalys? If we were captured, and they somehow figured out what I am, and *you* knew too, they'd then try to get information out of you, out of you all . . . they'd . . ." She blinked away some tears, took a deep breath. "They'd torture you, Magdalys. All of you."

"Then why come at all?" Magdalys demanded, blinking her own tears away. "Why bother?"

"Because you were about to fly into the most danger-ous war zone on the planet all by yourselves and you're only twelve!"

"I . . ."

"And not only that, you want to fly *all the way across* it to the single Union-occupied city in the South — a city entirely surrounded by armies that want you and me dead or in chains. I came because I love you and care about you, Magdalys, and I don't want you to get killed. And I also have my duty and the oath I swore, and that includes not revealing my identity to *anyone*. Sometimes what you love and what you have to do don't get along. If I could've told you, I would've." She put her hand over her eyes and shook her head. "I'm sorry."

Magdalys watched the trikes trodding along below, the graceful swoosh of the duster fans herding those ghostly clouds out into the forest around them on either side, the weary sol-diers. *Sometimes what you love and what you have to do don't get along.* This was *exactly* what she'd been trying to tell Hannibal about why she didn't want to sign her life away. She felt the steady thud of the diplo rumble beneath her. "Does Halsey know?" she finally asked.

"Only because he mustered in with me." Cymbeline wiped her eyes one last time and looked down at Magdalys. "The whole thing was his idea actually. 'We're actors!' he said." She smiled sadly. "'We'll make great spies!' Turns out acting and lying use two different muscles. He's a genius onstage. When

there's life and limb on the line — not so much. Plus, they made him pose as someone's slave."

"Oof," Magdalys said.

"Yeah, it was a whole lot. He didn't. . . . It didn't work out too well for him. Kinda messed him up, actually. So he got himself evaluated and they put him on medical leave."

Magdalys thought about Halsey — the smell of alcohol that seemed to stay on him like a cologne, the way he kept sobbing and couldn't pull it together the night of the riots. They'd burned his life's work to the ground right in front of him, so it made sense, but still. . . . He had only sharpened again when he started performing Shakespeare at the Bochinche bar in Dactyl Hill. "But they could call him back in anytime they want," Cymbeline said. "If they decide he's okay enough to be made not okay again."

Without thinking about it, Magdalys found herself hugging Cymbeline. They were even more alike than she'd thought, she realized, taking in her friend's flowery scent and feeling those arms wrap around her. They'd both had brothers wounded by the war and ended up in the battlefield themselves.

"I hate this war," Magdalys whispered.

"I know," Cymbeline said. "Me too. But I hate the world that was before it even more."

Magdalys nodded into her friend's shirt.

"Agent Crunk," Corporal Buford's voice blared out behind them.

Magdalys whirled on him. "How many times does she have to tell you not to broadcast that information across god's creation?"

Buford blinked at her, mouth hanging slightly open. "I ah . . . you, erm, are both requested, your presence, that is, in the major general . . . 's presence." He creased his brow. "Forthwith."

CHAPTER TWENTY
WAR COUNCIL

A TALL, GRIM-FACED SOLDIER passed Magdalys and Cymbeline as they made their way toward Sheridan; the Confederate who had almost toppled off Beans was slung over one of his shoulders, sputtering tearful apologies to no one in particular.

"Yikes," Magdalys said, glancing back, and then all five feet four inches of Major General Sheridan seemed to materialize in a fast-talking blur before them, his eyes all a-twinkle with whatever intrigue was at hand.

"My good young Magadis," he chattered with a head nod, then ran a fast circle around them, appearing in front of Cymbeline before Magdalys could even correct him on her name. "And the renowned young thespian." He kissed her hand with a dashing bow. Sheridan was all decked out in his

double-breasted dress jacket. "The battle is anon, my ladies, come this way at once!"

"What battle?" Cymbeline asked.

"That remains to be seen, I'm afraid. But I'm sure we'll find out soon enough." Sheridan led them to a table where several of his commanders stood glowering at each other. The gentle rise and fall of the diplo's thunderous stride had been disorienting at first, Magdalys thought, but already she could feel herself getting used to it; something like the rocking of a boat at sea. None of the officers seemed to notice that their strategy table kept going up and down as they glared at it. Octave and Hannibal stood a little to the back.

"What'd you find out from the prisoner?" Magdalys asked. "Did you ask him about —"

"We'll deal with that presently, my dear," Sheridan cut her off. "First, I'd like you both to be here to hear this report from one of General Thomas's scouts. Go ahead, sir."

"General Thomas leads another division of the Army of the Cumberland," Cymbeline whispered.

A white man in civilian clothes and a wide-rimmed hat stepped forward from behind some of the officers, saluted, and then cleared his throat. "The noble Major General Thomas sends his regards to the great Ma —"

"Yes, yes, get on with it, man," Sheridan snapped. "We're at war, not a royal banquet. And use the map, won't you? Save everybody time."

"Right," the scout said, startled. "We've entrenched on the

banks of the Chickamauga River. Here." He picked up the metal piece tagged *Gen Thomas* and placed it beside a curvy blue line a little ways from where Sheridan's piece was and a few miles below the carved city that represented Chattanooga.

"The enemy has divisions here, here, here, and, according to our other scouts, here." He placed trike and raptor figurines in a tight semicircle wrapping all along the southern front of Thomas's regiment and looping up along the western side. Then he glanced nervously at the worried expressions of the officers around him.

"Sweet mercy," Sheridan said softly.

"What is it?" Magdalys whispered.

Cymbeline shook her head, brow furrowed. "Wait."

"With Longstreet's Confederate trikeriders still on their way by rail, due in some time tonight." He placed a gray triceratops on the railroad symbol between Sheridan's position and Thomas's.

"Card!" Sheridan suddenly yelled, still staring at the map table. "Where's Card? And our other divisions?"

"He's not back from his scouting mission," someone reported.

Sheridan tore his eyes from the map and glared at him. "What did you say?"

"He's not —"

"I heard what you said, you cad. Where's the other Card?"

"He went with him, sir."

"No! The younger one!" Sheridan looked ready to shred

a man with his bare hands. "Do these men have no first names?"

"No one knows them, sir."

"Find Young Card! Immediately!"

"Sir, yes sir!"

"And find me Old Mother Card so I can ask her why she didn't bother naming her children!"

"Right away, sir!"

"It was a joke!" Sheridan called after the departing officer. He shook his head. "Now, where were we?"

The scout had arranged a series of dark blue dino pieces in a scattered mess near Thomas. "The Union positions, sir."

Sheridan shook his head.

"Sir?"

"They're trying to turn Thomas's right flank," Sheridan said, his eyes narrowed.

"Yes, sir."

"If they do, they'll cut us off from Chattanooga and force the whole Army of the Cumberland south. General Braxton Bragg is no longer in retreat."

"He's in full attack," the scout said.

"And if he outflanks us from the north we'll be facing utter annihilation."

"That," Cymbeline whispered.

"We must make a fast dash for Chattanooga," one of the officers offered. "If we move quickly we could make it there before Longstreet arrives to reinforce Bragg. With fortifications

set up on Missionary Ridge and Lookout Mountain, we'll be unassailable within the city."

"And abandon Thomas to certain destruction?" Sheridan said. "Never."

"We could implore him to retreat as well! Surely the major general will see the —"

"WHERE IS CARD?" Sheridan bellowed.

"Here, sir," the youngest Card said, appearing behind Magdalys and Cymbeline. "I was just with the prisoner that Private Hannibal, ah, handled."

"Has he woken?"

Card tipped his head, eyebrows raised. "Ah, no, sir."

"What did you do to that man, Private Hannibal?" Sheridan demanded.

"A brother in arms was in danger, sir," Hannibal said.

Young Card cleared his throat. "But I did do a search of his person and retrieved something that may be of interest."

Sheridan nodded, seeming to turn inward again as his eyes scanned the various statuettes scattered across the map. "Officers, alert your men: We're to march double-time to the Chickamauga. Thomas will be needing reinforcements. By god's grace we'll get there before the battle begins."

"Double-time?" one of the officers gasped. "The men and mounts are already tired from marching all day, sir, we won't —"

"Then they'll be left behind and shot for insubordination, Corporal. The fate of this entire army hangs in the balance. You have your orders. Dismissed, all of you."

The men began to disperse, some of them muttering beneath their mustaches.

"You stay, Miss Cymbeline," Sheridan ordered. "And you, young Magdalys." He softened, his tense face suddenly growing sad. "If you will. And Privates Hannibal and Rey, remain. Mr. Card, show us what you found."

"It's a medallion, sir." Card pulled a fold of cloth from his jacket and opened it, revealing a golden coin.

Magdalys caught her breath.

On it, the words *K of the G. C.* were inscribed around the image of a roaring tyrannosaurus with rays of lights bursting out from it.

She'd seen that image once before. It was stamped all over the papers of Mr. Harrison Weed, the man who'd taken her out of Cuba when she was a baby and dropped her off at the Colored Orphan Asylum.

Card flipped the coin over; it read *Lieutenant Hardy Luther Hewpat, Class III Dinomaster.*

"K of the G. C.," Sheridan puzzled. "What the deuce does that mean?"

"Knights of the Golden Circle," Magdalys said. "The people who tried to sell the other orphans into slavery."

CHAPTER TWENTY-ONE
MAKE MOVES

"**A**RE THOSE DEVILS still causing trouble?" Sheridan shook his head, inspecting the coin carefully.

Harrison Weed and Richard Riker, along with other Knights of the Golden Circle, were actively snatching black New Yorkers off the streets and shipping them south, then selling them off to slavers. At least, they were until the Dactyl Hill Squad teamed up with the Vigilance Committee. Now Weed's Manhattan headquarters was a pile of ashes and Riker was probably scattered all along the eastern seaboard in the form of Stella the pteranodon's pteropoops.

But the paperwork Magdalys and Mapper had stolen from Weed's office spoke of a huge network, a global organization dedicated to creating a whole new country, the so-called

Golden Circle, spanning South America and the fledgling Confederacy: an empire built on the slave trade.

And now it turned out a Confederate officer who could control dinos was part of the Knights too. The medallion caught the sunlight and flashed across Magdalys's vision as Sheridan held it up. *Class III Dinomaster.*

She shook her head. Of course the secret society was recruiting members who had the same special abilities she did to fight for the Confederacy. And of course they called themselves "masters." When she rode a dino, most of the time it felt like they were having a conversation, like they were agreeing together to do something. She could feel the great reptile's reluctance or excitement, could move accordingly and figure out how to do something the right way. Sure, if it was an enemy mount, the wrangling might involve a little more coercion, but she certainly didn't consider herself the master of any dino. That seemed absurd.

"Did you find out anything from the prisoner you were interrogating just now?" Magdalys asked.

"Just the same sob story they've been told to feed us about how demoralized and hungry their armies are and how they're all about to surrender," Sheridan said with disdain. "They've been fake defecting to our camp for weeks trying to goad us into attacking with that nonsense."

"Uh, sir," Hannibal said. "Permission to speak?"

Permission to speak, Magdalys thought, growling inside

herself. How was she supposed to dedicate her life to a group that demanded such dramatic comeliness?

"Go ahead, Private."

"The prisoner did mention that he was aware Lieutenant Hewpat was a part of a specially designated elite force of dinoriders."

"He meant Forrest's squad, I'm sure," Sheridan snorted. "The fighting finest or whatever they call themselves."

"I believe he meant that Hewpat is what's indicated on this medallion, sir. A dinomaster."

"Hannibal's right," Magdalys blurted out. Everyone turned to stare at her. "Er . . . Private Hannibal. That man managed to take full of possession of Mapper's dactyl and almost killed Mapper in the process. And he flies better than any of the other air cavalry guys. And I couldn't reach his mount to try to keep them from . . ." Her words trailed off as images of the explosion once again flashed through her mind. She rallied herself, feeling the weight of all those eyes on her. ". . . from killing Sol."

Sheridan glared at her for what felt like a very long time. Had she made a mistake, speaking out like that? She had no idea how all these things worked, chain of command and asking for permission to speak.

"You're positing," Sheridan said, very slowly, "that this secret society — the Knights of the Golden Circle — is recruiting an army of dinowranglers with your special skills to help the Confederacy destroy us?"

Magdalys nodded. "That's exactly what I'm saying . . . er, positing."

"Why this is treason of the highest order!" Sheridan snarled. "We must . . ." He paused, turned his sharp glare back to Magdalys. "Does this mean you'll join us, young lady? You see the urgency of the situation now, do you not? It's not just that they have an air cavalry and we don't — the Confederates have superiority in their dinowranglers across the board. And, well . . . if Bragg succeeds in turning Thomas's flank and cuts us off from Chattanooga, we'll be crushed and scattered within days. The entire western theater will be wide open for Confederate expansion, the gains made at Vicksburg and Gettysburg nullified, the Emperor Maximilian will invade from Mexico, and the European powers may well throw their support behind the enemy, tilting the entire balance of the war. Add to that this secret society's elite dinomaster force and the fact that we still have no air cavalry or reconnaissance. . . ."

Magdalys felt Cymbeline's hand land gently on her shoulder — support she hadn't realized she needed as the major general rattled off their dire circumstances and she felt the full weight of the responsibility he was placing on her. She took a step back, shaking her head, said, "What do you need?" in a choked whisper.

"What we need is someone with your abilities to train an elite corps of dinowranglers and their steeds. It's no longer enough to just have a force in the air. We need . . . you." He shook his head. "But even more urgently: We need eyes

in the skies!" Sheridan exclaimed as if he'd been waiting his whole life for this moment. "We are running blind through the woods toward a battleground we barely understand. Our ground scouts can barely keep up with the constant movement — you saw we had to rely on another regiment's scouts for information just now, and —"

"Wait," Young Card interrupted.

Sheridan blinked at him, astonished at the breach of protocol.

"My brothers haven't returned yet?" Card's reddish face had paled. "I . . . I thought they'd come back."

"No," Sheridan said quietly. "We're still waiting for their report."

Magdalys looked at Card. He was blinking like it would somehow change what he'd just heard, and she could tell their report was the least of his concerns. "They should've gotten back by now."

The middle Card had headed off to check on the enemy position, Magdalys remembered. That must've been the last time he'd been seen.

Sheridan nodded gravely. "I agree." Magdalys imagined the temptation would be to spew some nonsense about how everything would be alright, and she was glad the major general didn't bother with that obvious lie. Instead he put a hand on the younger man's shoulder. "Your brothers know these woods better than any man alive," he said.

Card looked into Sheridan's eyes, finally stopped blinking.

"Except me." He straightened, seemed to grow several inches as his once-stricken face hardened into a look of grim determination. "Permission to ride out and find my older brothers, sir?"

Sheridan nodded curtly. "But be careful, Card. I can't afford to lose any of you, let alone all three. Bring them back to us alive. Is that clear?"

"Sir, yes sir!" Card yelled with a salute.

Magdalys watched him grapple partway down the saddle and then leap onto his waiting para below and gallop off in a cloud of dust. A deep hunger rattled through her chest, something like longing. Card was doing exactly what she'd been trying to do all this time, but his brothers were so much closer. And it had seemed so simple! Ask permission, off you go. Of course, the Cards had proved themselves invaluable to the Union time and again, that much was clear, and who was Montez Roca to the Grand Army of the Republic? Just another black soldier: good for digging ditches or throwing into the line of fire to hopefully prove his worth in death.

She looked up at Sheridan, who was staring at her. "Permission to speak?" The words felt sour coming out of her, like a lie.

Sheridan smiled wryly. "By all means, young Magdadis."

"It's Mag-da-*lys*, Major General, sir. And I'll help you," she said, and Sheridan's grin widened. "But I'm not mustering in. I'll help scout out the enemy positions at Chickamauga and that's all I can promise." She frowned, then reluctantly added, "Right now."

CHAPTER TWENTY-TWO
FLIGHT PREPARATIONS

"**ALRIGHT, LOOK,**" **MAGDALYS** said, glancing at the four familiar faces of her friends. "We have a mission."

She'd thought they might be excited to do something again, but she hadn't anticipated the wild cheer that went up. Amaya yelled "Finally!" and high-fived Two Step. Mapper hugged Sabeen, who giggled and swatted him.

"Wait, wait, slow down," Magdalys said. "You haven't even heard the plan yet!"

"Don't matter," Mapper said with a shrug. "We in."

"Yeah," Amaya agreed. "Everyone's tired of marching along on trikeback forever and ever."

A fresh buzz of excitement whirred through Magdalys's mind since Sheridan had ordered a faster march. The drudgery of a march to nowhere had given way to a fresh urgency;

there was a battle afoot and the dinos could feel it; they tittered and grunted about it as they rumbled along.

But only Magdalys could sense them. To everyone else, they were just moving somewhat faster, and the endless procession still felt like when the orphanage's old triceratops, Varney, would get stuck in a traffic jam lugging their wagon back through the busy Manhattan streets. The trike beneath them plodded on at a steady jog, but blue-clad troops and armored dinos streamed on and on behind and in front of them, while it seemed like the same mountains and trees passed in an endless cycle on either side.

"What's the plan?" Two Step asked, and Magdalys felt a pang of guilt for what she was about to say.

"It's a scouting mission, and we need an armed escort with us: Hannibal, Octave, and Corporal Cailloux from the Native Guard will act as gunners, plus three riders: myself, Amaya, and Mapper."

"But —" Two Step started.

"We'll take Stella," Magdalys went on. "And then make short distance runs on the dactyls, using Stella as a mother ship. There's a creek up ahead, the Chickamauga."

"Chickamauga!" Mapper exclaimed. "That used to be Cherokee territory."

"Until the army we're about to help out forced them off their land," Amaya said. Everyone got quiet for a few moments. Magdalys didn't know how to respond.

"Both armies are gathering there, but we don't know how many are on either side or what the field is looking like, and . . ."

"Amaya doesn't even like riding dinos!" Two Step said. "Or pteros."

"I kinda do now," Amaya said.

Sabeen put a hand on Two Step's shoulder. "It's okay, man. We'll just —"

"Stop," Two Step said. "Don't . . ."

Magdalys stood. "I'm going to check on Dizz," she said, working her way down the saddle. She stopped, looked at Two Step, her best friend, with the face that wouldn't take no for an answer. "Come with me."

"What do you mean I can't go?" Two Step demanded.

"I didn't say you *can't* go," Magdalys sighed. They were walking along the endless procession of soldiers toward the medical unit. She'd hoped talking it out one-on-one would be better, just in case he—

"What's even the point of my being here if I can't go along with you when you're doing dangerous stuff?"

—lost his cool.

"I just think it would probably be better," Magdalys said, "if you—"

"You're benching me!" Two Stop yelled, his eyebrows

inching closer together as his nostrils flared. "You're benching me because I'm not good enough!"

Soldiers and dinos alike were glancing over with concern now.

Magdalys shushed him and immediately regretted it. "That's not it," she tried to say soothingly.

"Don't shush me, Magdalys Roca!" Two Step yelled. "You don't get to shush me! And who made you the boss of us anyway? Just because we came to help you find your brother doesn't mean you get to just decide what happens to everybody!"

"I'm not bossing you around," Magdalys said, stopping. "I'm worried about you, Two Step!"

He spun around, finger out. "Well, don't!"

"Two Step, you haven't . . ." She shook her head. Any way she could think of to say it, it sounded like she was calling him weak, or saying that he wasn't good enough, but that was the opposite of what she wanted to say.

"Go head," he goaded. "Say it."

"You haven't been the same since what happened that night in the Penitentiary."

They stood face-to-face now, but Two Step looked like the wind was knocked out of him, his eyes glaring at Magdalys's shoes, his shoulders heaving up and down with each labored breath. "Say it," he whispered. "Say what I did."

"Two Step . . ."

"Say it, Magdalys."

"You saved my life."

"I killed someone, Magdalys."

"You saved your own life."

"He's still dead though."

Magdalys shook her head.

"He is. And now you think I'm not good enough to fly."

"No!" Magdalys yelled, taking him by the shoulders. "Listen to me: I love that . . ." No, that definitely wasn't right. She shook her head, tried again, forcing herself to slow down. "I think it's . . . right . . . that it's hard for you. You're not weak, Two Step. You're human. I mean, I don't want you to be hurting and torn up about it, but it would be weird if you were just cool about it too. Nothing is right, none of this makes sense. There is no *right* way to deal with what we've been through, what *you've* been through. And it's even harder because everything just keeps" — she flailed around at the never-ending march of war streaming past — "everything keeps happening! It's only happening more now, in fact! And none of us can catch our breath. But none of us did what you did. And I'm not . . . I won't let you . . . I know I'm not your boss, but I'm not putting you back into a situation where you might go through it all again when you haven't even . . . when you're still dealing with what you've been through."

He stared at her.

"With killing someone," she finally said. "To save my life and yours," she added quickly. "And Mapper's."

"But it's like you said," Two Step sighed. "It's all happening around us whether we like it or not. Look around, Mags. Do you really think you can *stop* me from being in that situation

again, at this point? And it's not just because we're here. I mean, it happened in Dactyl Hill, of all places. The one part of this messed-up world where we're supposed to be safe." He shook his head. "And anyway, ever since it happened, all I've done is replay it over and over in my head and wonder if I could've done something differently or should've done something different and all I can think is the only way to find out is to be there again, with a gun in my hand and our lives on the line. And then a day like today happens and part of me just wants to . . ." He clenched his fists and his words trailed off.

"I understand," Magdalys said. "Kind of."

"Hey, the dactyls from Brooklyn girl!" a voice said from behind them. "You looking for your friend?" It was Dr. Pennbroker, now out of his surgeon's coat and wearing a regular dark blue Union Army uniform. They'd walked right past the medical caravan without realizing it.

"Am I ever," Magdalys mumbled.

The surgeon waved them over. "He's right over here. Should be good to go!"

Two Step cocked his head, still in the middle of his storm of emotions, and then stumbled after Magdalys with a curious pout on his face.

Dr. Pennbroker was a tall, thin man with well-trimmed sideburns and an elegant goatee. He flashed a wide smile at Magdalys and Two Step as he ushered them forward amidst the marching dinos. "This is Dr. Pennbroker, the surgeon

who was taking care of my dactyl," Magdalys said. "And Dr. Pennbroker, this is my friend Two Step."

"Whoa!" Two Step said, all traces of anger gone. "A black US Army surgeon!"

Dr. Pennbroker chuckled. "Yeah, I get a lot of that. There are about eight of us total; four here with the Army of the Cumberland alone."

"They only let them work on dinos and black soldiers," Magdalys said.

"Technically," she and Dr. Pennbroker added together, both smirking.

"Whoa whoa whoa," Two Step said as his eyes kept getting wider and wider. "I had no idea!"

"Join the club," Magdalys said. "*And* he knows Dr. Sloan."

Two Step looked like his head might explode. "WHAT? The Dinoguide guy? You *know* him?!"

"You could say we go way back," Dr. Pennbroker snickered. "Anyway, here's your dactyl, good as new." He nodded at a wagon being dragged behind a grumbling stego. The dactyl's light blue snout poked up over the side of the wagon, then his whole head. His eyes widened at Magdalys and then Dizz flapped up into the air, landing unsteadily on top of the stego's back.

"Dizz!" Magdalys yelled, running over.

The stego gave a howl of disapproval and reared up. Dizz hopped from leg to leg a few times with what almost sounded like a snicker and then jumped off as the stego's front legs

came back down. The dactyl landed in front of Magdalys. He crouched forward toward her, snapping playfully, and she wrapped her arms around his slender neck and squeezed. Around them, Dr. Pennbroker and Two Step chatted and the stomp of soldiers and dinos churned on. "I'm so glad you're okay," she whispered. "Thank you for saving my life."

Dizz unfurled his wings and straightened, lifting Magdalys off the ground. She laughed and pulled herself over his shoulder so she straddled his back as he flapped once, twice, then perched on a wagon next to Dr. Pennbroker.

"Hey, big guy," the surgeon said, amiably stepping out of snapping range. "Tell you what, how bout we do a switch-off, Miss Magdalys? You get your dactyl back, and me and the fellas need another set of hands in the medical tent, and your friend here just volunteered to help out. Sound like a plan?"

Magdalys blinked at Two Step. He nodded, his gaze still on the surgeon.

"Sounds like an excellent plan," Magdalys said.

"Be careful out there," Dr. Pennbroker said.

Two Step glanced at her, anger roiling beneath his tight face, then looked away.

Magdalys opened her mouth but realized she didn't know what to say.

Dizz swung his head around, squawked once, and then hunched low on his knees, preparing to take off. "You be careful too," Magdalys called as Two Step and Dr. Pennbroker and the medical caravan got smaller and smaller beneath her.

CHAPTER TWENTY-THREE
RECONNAISSANCE RUN

MAGDALYS SHOOK OFF the recurring image of Two Step's parting scowl as she surged over the Appalachian treetops on Dizz, Hannibal laughing and howling in the wind behind her and holding on for dear life.

Another haunting to add to her ghost collection. It consisted of both the living and the dead, a nonstop carousel of the missing, the wounded, the silent, the murdered; it was always available to trouble her idle moments or sleepless nights.

Still: the setting sun splashed sharp orange streaks across the comely magentas and darkening blues of the western sky ahead of them, and sent the long shadows of the four dactyls rippling along the dark green forest below.

"I see the joy of flying hasn't worn off yet," Magdalys said

when Hannibal paused to catch his breath. They'd rustled up some saddles from the mounted raptor units and adjusted them to fit the dactyls, and it did make flying much more comfortable.

"Man!" he panted. "And I hope it never will! This is the most amazing thing I've ever done!"

"Miss Roca," Corporal Cailloux called as Amaya pulled their mount alongside Dizz. "Would you kindly inform Private Hannibal that we are on a reconnaissance mission and thus under orders to *not* alert the entire Confederacy to our presence?"

Hannibal straightened up. "Duly noted, sir!"

Beans flew up on the other side, apparently just so Octave and Mapper could make sure everyone heard them snickering. Grappler soared up ahead, her long beak moving back and forth slowly as she scanned the horizon for trouble.

"How exactly are we supposed to ascertain the whereabouts of this pteranodon?" Cailloux asked. His voice sounded skeptical but not unkind.

"Magdalys," Hannibal said. "She can do anything."

It was a small statement — just four words! — but it was one of the best things anyone had ever said about her. *She can do anything.* Magdalys wanted to make a talisman of it to dangle around her neck and repeat the words in Hannibal's laughing voice whenever she was afraid. Maybe that would ward off the carousel of ghosts.

"I want you to know, Miss Roca," Cailloux said, "Private

Hannibal rarely has a kind word for anyone, so, though he is a troublemaker, his endorsement carries some weight."

"I take umbrage, Corporal!" Hannibal said. "But you have a point."

And maybe Hannibal was right. The gathering storm of Stella's sweet and lowdown song kept getting louder and fiercer inside Magdalys. Finding her was simply a matter of following the trail of her call. It seemed second nature to Magdalys, but trailing a giant pterosaur through enemy territory would've been daunting to pretty much anyone else.

Maybe she *could* do anything.

"There!" Mapper cried, just as the wail inside Magdalys crescendoed. Something huge crested the mountaintop up ahead, blotting out the sun.

"STELLA GIRL!" Magdalys yelled, and Hannibal let out a wild laugh behind her.

"Remember General Sheridan's orders," Corporal Cailloux said as Magdalys veered Stella south and clicks and clacks of the soldiers preparing their weapons filled the air amidst the caterwauling songbirds below. "We're not to engage the enemy. We're not to fly directly over the battlefield. We're *definitely* not to get shot down. Clear?"

"Sir, yes sir!" Octave, Hannibal, and Mapper yelled in unison. Amaya just nodded.

"Everyone have their security belts secured to both themselves and the saddle?" Cailloux yelled.

"Sir, yes sir!" everyone responded. The corporal had insisted on some security measure in case Stella tipped suddenly, and Magdalys had been glad they'd had the belts handy, although they'd given up sleeping with them attached a couple days out from Brooklyn.

"The Chickamauga heads away from the Tennessee River just north of Chattanooga," said Mapper. Magdalys felt a momentary panic: Mapper was just some kid to these soldiers, not the geographic wunderkind she knew him to be. Who was he to lecture them about geography? But no one chided him or cut him off; they just nodded and waited for him to go on. She breathed a tiny sigh of relief and turned back to the rising and falling peaks around them.

"It runs along the side of Missionary Ridge," Mapper went on, "which should be that high up plateau up ahead."

"So we're in Georgia?" Cailloux asked.

"Probably just crossed into it, yeah," Mapper said, squinting at the imaginary maps imprinted across his brain and then nodding.

"This kid's good to have around," Octave said.

"How do you think we've made it this far," Amaya said with a giggle. Magdalys peeked back again. Amaya never giggled.

"Uh, thanks," Mapper said, looking wildly uncomfortable, the goofiness of his grin turned all the way up to ten.

"I hate to break up the lovefest," Hannibal said, and at the sound of worry in his voice, Magdalys immediately scanned the tree line ahead for signs of trouble, "but y'all hear that?"

Everyone got quiet. Then she saw it: A plume of smoke rose above the trees into the darkening sky.

"I don't hear no—" Mapper started to say, but a low rumble cut him off, then light flashed across the clouds up ahead and a crack ripped out, followed by a ghostly, shuddering afterblast that seemed to flush across the valley toward them.

"Artillery," Octave said. "The battle's already begun."

A gnawing, sinking feeling crept over Magdalys from the inside. They were too late; that was all she could think. But for what, she didn't know. It's not like they had any ability to stop the fighting or turn the tide. Sheridan was already marching as fast as his men and dinos could travel for the battlefront. There was nothing more to do except find out whatever they could, and maybe that was the worst part.

"Stay low," Cailloux said, snapping Magdalys out of her thoughts. "We don't need any of their air cavalry spotting us." More lights flashed across the sky as the rumbling continued at a steady drone, and then the sharp reports of each bursting shell reached them. The sound of death raining down from above, Magdalys thought, veering Stella into a smooth glide just over the treetops.

"Octave, Hannibal," Cailloux ordered. "Hop on dactyls with one of the kids and head in opposite directions. See if you

can get the scope of the battlefield and a sense of the enemy numbers."

"Yes, sir!" the two men hollered with a salute. Beans and Grappler were already flapping on either side of Stella; with a quick thought from Magdalys they swung beneath her huge wings. Amaya and Mapper turned to her, and it struck her again that without meaning to or even so much as a vote of confidence, she'd somehow become the commanding officer of this strange, tiny army they'd formed back in Dactyl Hill, Brooklyn. She nodded her approval and Mapper climbed on Beans, Amaya on Grappler, the soldiers mounting up behind them, and they swooshed silently off into the war-torn skies.

CHAPTER TWENTY-FOUR
THE BATTLE BELOW

"**IT'S TERRIFYING, ISN'T** it?" Corporal Cailloux said.
Magdalys realized he was watching her as she stared
off after the dactyls. She shook her head, somehow smiled.
"Which part?"

Cailloux chuckled. "I mean, all of it, of course, but especially this part. Sending men off to what may be their death. Or kids, in this case. Even worse."

Magdalys nodded. It didn't matter that she hadn't given the order and didn't hold any rank to speak of; he'd seen the mark of leadership, the deference they paid her, and he knew what it meant, that it mattered more than any chain of command. If something bad should happen to any of them, Magdalys would carry it with her. "How do you . . . how do you deal with it?"

Cailloux scowled, eyebrows raised, and made a vague circle with one hand. "I remind myself that this is what they came here for, that this is what we fought for, in fact, and what we're still fighting for: to be able to fight, and maybe die, for a cause we believe in." He paused, his mouth still shoved all the way to one side of his face in a lopsided frown. "Freedom."

For a few moments, they watched the shells paint sudden bursts across the violet-streaked sky. Then Cailloux shouted in a hoarse whisper: "Veer left!"

Magdalys ducked without knowing why and pulled Stella into a sharp curve. "What?" she asked quietly.

"There's a camp right below us," Cailloux said. "Can't tell if it's ours or theirs but I just saw the fires between the trees. Keep veering and take us around closer to the fighting; I don't think they spotted us or we'd have heard shooting by now."

Either side would probably start taking potshots at them, Magdalys realized — there was nothing to mark them as being on one side or the other from below, and anything flying directly above an encampment would probably be presumed an enemy.

Musket fire crackled from the battlefield now, an ongoing barrage that meant countless men were crumbling beneath its onslaught on either side. Magdalys saw the trees light up ahead and more artillery shells crashed through the night.

"We're close," Cailloux whispered, more to himself than Magdalys. "Very close." Then sharply: "Left!" as the whole raging battlefield suddenly opened up beneath them. Men

burst out of the trees amidst the muskets' never-ending pop and crackle. Other men charged forward toward them; it was too dark to make out what color anyone's uniform was. Men screamed, crumpled, muskets cracked, artillery boomed. Torches and bonfires punctuated the otherwise dark field.

"Those are the skirmishers," Cailloux explained as they veered low along the edge of the woods. "Infantry. Each side is testing the strength of the other's front lines."

Testing. It seemed like such a sad thing to die in the service of: a test. But Magdalys knew much bigger stakes loomed behind each tiny movement.

"When they find a weak spot, that's when you'll see . . . there!" A low rumble sounded now, even deeper than the artillery cannons: trikes on the move. Many, many trikes, Magdalys realized, gazing at the sudden rush of movement below. The dinoriders guided their mounts in a thundering charge straight into a collected mass of foot soldiers. It would be a massacre, Magdalys thought, but the infantry fell away in perfect unison just before the trikes reached them, and it was a snarling brigade of raptor riders that took their place.

"Those are our boys," Cailloux said with pride. "General Thomas's 7th Mounted Raptor Squad."

The raptors leapt as one, landing directly in the thick of the trike charge, and then everything became a muddled mass of howls, musket shots, and dinosnarls.

"How can anyone make sense of this?" Magdalys asked.

Cailloux shook his head. "You can't. War doesn't make

sense. Everyone who tries, loses. All you can do is fight as hard as you can and do your best to keep a cool head in the storm."

Artillery bursts rumbled out nearby and then explosions shattered the melee of trikes, raptors, and men.

"Who's shelling them?" Magdalys yelled. "They're hitting everyone!"

"I don't know," Cailloux admitted. "Could be us, could be them. Could be a horrible mistake, could be some terrible strategy at play."

Screams rose from below now as fighting seemed to fade amidst the carnage of the artillery attack, and a thick cloud of dust and smoke covered the battlefield.

"Can you tell . . . if anyone's winning?"

"Not yet," Cailloux said. "Swing further along the edge, I want to see if . . . ah." The field stretched long beneath them, illuminated by the fires of many, many campsites. It seemed to cover the night, that never-ending army in the shadows, and keep going through the mountains and into the sky above.

"Is that the . . . the enemy?"

"Braxton Bragg must've consolidated his whole army. And Longstreet's trikeriders have arrived too."

The darkness itself seemed to writhe with them, and then Magdalys realized why. They were on the march, surging forward into battle.

CHAPTER TWENTY-FIVE
RUMBLE AND CAW

"**W**HAT DO WE do?" Magdalys asked.

"See what they have to say," Corporal Cailloux said, nodding to where both the mounted dactyls could be seen gliding over the treetops toward where they'd perched Stella. "And then send a message back to General Sheridan to let him know what we've seen. Although I'm sure he's already heard the artillery and is rushing his men toward it."

Magdalys glanced back at the approaching dactyls. Night had fully fallen now, the moon just barely peeking out from behind a cloud bank. Something seemed to flicker up into the sky behind where Mapper and Amaya were flying at full speed. Magdalys squinted. Their fourth, unmounted dactyl was gliding a smooth circle nearby, keeping watch, so what . . .

More fluttering shapes resolved and vanished in the darkness. They seemed small, or maybe one huge creature with many moving parts? Magdalys couldn't tell. And then all at once the shapes coalesced into a single, ever-shifting snake that whipped out through the sky; the fires below illuminated a hundred flapping, feathered wings.

Magdalys gasped. The clouds cleared, and the moon revealed a sudden splash of rainbow: brilliant greens, sharp reds, hazy magentas, and stark royal blues all flashed and spun in the air, the breathtaking plumage of these crow-sized creatures on full display.

Archaeopteryx! Magdalys thought, catching sight of those long snouted reptilian heads stretching out from the feathered bodies. All those razor-sharp teeth glinted in the moonlight as nearly four dozen mouths opened at once. *Although small,* Dr. Barlow Sloan noted about the archaeops, *and deceptively beautiful in their plumage (if not their hideous faces and wide, eager eyes), these little fellows are some of the fiercest and smartest dinos known to man! Beware!*

With a hissing squawk, the snaking limb of archaeops dispersed and they seemed to cover the whole sky behind Beans and Grappler.

"FLY!" Magdalys yelled, her hoarse cry almost buried by another eruption of gunfire below.

Amaya leaned forward, urging her mount into a mad scramble, but Mapper glanced back just as the archaeops

converged again, now into two whiplike shapes. Both curled up into the sky and then dove.

Someone was controlling those dinos, Magdalys realized. And whoever was doing it was really, really good. There had to be almost fifty of them, all wielded in perfect unison as a single, unstoppable weapon. But where was the wrangler? She scanned the treetops and skies, but barely had time to look before the two attacking archaeops streams bore down on Amaya and Mapper.

Shots rang out — Hannibal and Octave letting loose from each dactylback, surely. Winged shapes screeched and were flung backward and then down with each shot, but there were more than anyone could hope to take out one by one.

"What are those things?" Corporal Cailloux asked, constructing some kind of contraption on Stella's saddle.

"Archaeops," Magdalys said. "Hold tight to whatever you're setting up. We're about to fly."

"Hang on," Cailloux said through gritted teeth. "Let me just . . ." He heaved a long, fierce-looking gun with several long barrels onto his contraption.

"Hurry," Magdalys said. "They're almost on them."

Grappler had surged ahead but the attackers were closing on Mapper.

With a click and snap, Cailloux growled, "Okay, go!" and at a signal from Magdalys, Stella unfurled her forty-foot wings to either side and launched into the air.

"Roll up on 'em and then swing her to the side," Cailloux commanded as Grappler came barreling forward full speed. The caws of the pursuing archaeops grew louder. Amaya and Hannibal jumped off Grappler and landed on the saddle. Magdalys sent Stella directly at the approaching swarm. "Now!" Cailloux yelled, and she spun Stella off to the right. An earsplitting barrage burst out behind her: *BRADAGA-DADAGA-BRADADAGA-DAGAGA!!* and Magdalys found herself grasping the huge pteranodon's neck as the bonfires and battles veered past below. For a second, she thought she'd been hit herself, the gunfire rattled so viciously through her core.

But no: Up ahead, the archaeops swarm had been decimated — limp, bullet-riddled dino bodies tumbled from the sky and a passing breeze carried hundreds of multi-colored feathers out over the trees. Magdalys gasped. Sure, those creatures were bent on attacking them, but . . . that *machine* had seemed to tear apart the sky and sweep them away by the dozens in a matter of seconds. Wholesale slaughter. She should've been celebrating, but those creatures had clearly been wrangled — it wasn't their fault some Confederate dinomaster snatched them up and hurled them into battle.

There wasn't time to mourn though — Hannibal was right.

"What *is* that thing?" Magdalys demanded as she picked herself up.

"It's a Gatling," Amaya said, gazing over Cailloux's

shoulder with a glint in her eye. "I've never seen one in action before."

"HELP!" Mapper's voice carried to them over the wind. Magdalys swung Stella around just in time to see the other swarm descend on Beans, enveloping him, Mapper, and Octave in a bright and lethal rainbow.

"No!" Magdalys gasped as Stella swung into a turn so sharp it almost tipped them all over the side, and then surged forward. In a matter of seconds, she'd gone from feeling bad at the archaeops being slaughtered to wanting them all destroyed to save her friends. And even worse, now they couldn't be without making everything worse.

The swarm screeched and cawed and three gunshots from within sent a couple archaeops spiraling away. Then a long gray beak appeared, followed by Beans's face, his eyes narrowed with determination. One of his wings broke free, blood flowing freely from gashes the smaller dinos had torn in it, and then the other. Finally, Beans merged fully from the swarm, Mapper and Hannibal crouching with their faces covered on his back.

"Mapper!" Magdalys and Amaya cried at the same time. Beans flapped unsteadily — cuts lined his whole body, Magdalys now saw — and then fell into a wobbly glide toward them.

BRIGAAWWWW!!!! came a wretched, high-pitched screech from somewhere below.

Cailloux swung his Gatling toward the treetops a moment

too late: a brilliant flash of color leapt up into the sky between Stella and Beans.

It was shaped like the other archaeops — same shimmering plumage and bare reptilian head, same wide, wild eyes and sharp pupils — but this thing was much, much larger. On its back, a pale woman — no, she was a *girl* — sat riding sidesaddle in a full ball gown. She didn't look much older than Magdalys, maybe sixteen. Another swarm of smaller archaeops fluttered up into the sky around the huge one. The girl's face curved into a triumphant grin. *This* was who'd been commanding those legions of archaeops?

Cailloux swung his Gatling up toward her.

"Don't shoot," Amaya said. "You'll hit Mapper and Hannibal!"

"I won't," Octave said, lifting his rifle, but the girl had already kicked the spurs on her pink-and-white raptorskin boots, sending the giant archaeop into a swooping charge. "On, Rathbane! Attack!" she shrieked. The two swarms surged forward around her.

Even with their heavy firepower, a pteranodon and three dactyls could never best that many archaeops, especially with that huge one leading the pack. They were outnumbered and probably doomed, but trying to escape would be a disaster: The dactyls they had were already worn out and wounded, and Magdalys wasn't sure Stella could outfly that feathered monstrosity.

Fine. She narrowed her eyes and urged Stella straight

ahead into the oncoming assault. Behind her, the clicks and clacks of Hannibal, Octave, and Cailloux preparing their weapons sounded. A shape rose in the sky beside them, then another. Magdalys glanced over.

Dactyls!

They weren't the Brooklyn squad Magdalys knew, these were other ones. Was there a Union wrangler helping them out from below? More likely her own crew had somehow recruited these local ones. Either way, she didn't have time to worry about it — they were on her side, that much was clear, and that was all that mattered. They stood a fighting chance after all.

Rifle shots sang out from behind her. Archaeops fell from the sky to either side but there were too many. And then, with a calamitous rumble and caw, the two sky giants smashed full into each other as the dactyls and archaeops clashed in the air around them. Stella went right for the archaeop's neck, just missing it as the smaller creature dug all four of its claws into Stella's neck. A clutch of smaller archaeops followed suit, each cutting long red gashes along her hide.

Stella let out a howl that must've reverberated across the valley, but the deeper one shuddered inside Magdalys. It was the first time she'd felt panic from her humongous friend. Rathbane had latched on to a part of the pteranodon's chest that she couldn't reach with her huge claws.

Magdalys climbed up Stella's neck. Gunfire burst around her as Mapper, Amaya, and the soldiers fought off the attack.

In the sky just ahead, a small clutch of archaeops swarmed one of the new dactyls and slashed its wings, sending the creature into a shrieking plummet toward the trees. Magdalys shuddered — the poor thing had come to save her and now . . .

She blinked away tears, shook her head, and peered over the pteranodon's shoulder. The girl stared up with a defiant grin. "So you're the Union's new dinomaster. Just a child, I see. And a Negress at that." She shook her head pityingly. "I guess they're determined to prove to the world how pathetic their sham ideas about equality are."

Magdalys had no idea what to say to that. All she knew was that people and dinos were being massacred all around her, and blood was pouring out of the creature that had saved her life. Another desperate caw rose inside Magdalys and Stella heaved suddenly to the side.

"Whoa!" Hannibal yelled behind Magdalys.

"I'm about to destroy your pitiful air cavalry," the girl said, pulling out a chain with a grappling hook at the end and sending it into a swing over her head, "but you can be comforted in knowing you were defeated by the greatest dinomaster that ever lived, Elizabeth Crawbell. I'm sure you've read about my exploits."

"I haven't," Magdalys said. "I have no idea who you are." Stella had swung them away from the battlefield, and now the dark Appalachian forests filled the world below them.

Elizabeth looked a little put out, then just shrugged and sent her grappling hook flying up toward Stella's crest. With

all the others busy fighting off the archaeops, there was only one way to dislodge this arrogant girl and her beast.

Dive! Magdalys commanded. The last cohesive thought Magdalys had before the terror of a sheer plummet took hold was that she hoped the others had remembered to secure themselves to the saddle.

CHAPTER TWENTY-SIX
DIVE

MAGDALYS WAS PRETTY sure she was screaming. Someone definitely was. Or maybe many someones. Or maybe it was the wind, shrieking the sound of Magdalys's panic as the line where the earth met the sky steepened.

Stella's urgent caw slid into a grittier, more determined growl and the giant ptero sped at full velocity toward the treetops.

Elizabeth's chain-hook had swung wide and then dropped uselessly to the side at the sudden change of trajectory, and now the Confederate dinomaster was clinging desperately to the neck of her mount, teeth clenched. "It won't work, you fool!" she howled over the wind.

Magdalys glanced back. Mapper and Amaya had both grasped Hannibal and were holding each of his hands as his

legs flew out in the wind behind. Cailloux and Octave had been thrown to the back of the saddle but then managed to secure themselves. Archaeops and dactyls still grappled above them.

Back on Stella's chest, Elizabeth was peering nervously at the fast-approaching treetops. Finally, just as the dark leaves began to take shape behind her, she snarled and spurred Rathbane to release. The giant archaeop swooped away, tearing a few new gashes in Stella's hide as he went, and Stella evened out into a smooth glide over the forest.

BRADAGA-BRAGADA-BRAGADA-BRAGADA Cailloux's Gatling sang, but when Magdalys turned, it was Amaya behind the turret. Out in the sky behind them, Elizabeth swung Rathbane into a dazzling series of evasive maneuvers and then, when Amaya's barrage didn't let up, simply turned tail and sped off into the night followed by what was left of the fluttering archaeop swarm.

Magdalys exhaled, then glanced over Stella's shoulder at the still bleeding gashes.

Come on, girl, she thought, *let's get you on the ground.*

"What . . . was that?" Mapper gasped once they'd found a clearing and brought Stella down for a bumpy, lopsided landing.

Magdalys, already on the ground and approaching Stella's wounded hide with caution, shook her head. She'd been

thinking the same thing, over and over, since the wrangler behind that impressive archaeops swarm had revealed herself. There had to be at least thirty dinos flying in perfect coordination at one time, Magdalys thought. People were impressed with Magdalys summoning a dactyl here or there, but that was all cute parlor games next to what this girl could do. "Elizabeth Crawbell, she said her name was."

"Ugh," Hannibal said. "The one and only. If I hadn't been busy fighting off her little beasties, I'd have gotten a shot off and Abe Lincoln himself woulda pinned me with the Medal of Honor for ridding the world of that traitor."

Six large claw cuts formed a spiraling bright red crescent from Stella's jaw to the top of her wide chest. They didn't seem to be bleeding anymore, so that was good, and hopefully meant they weren't too deep. The pteranodon, settled into a precarious squat that reminded Magdalys of a nesting hen, gave a feeble caw and shook her massive head. "I know, baby girl," Magdalys said, rubbing small circles on her smooth hide. "She seemed to think I should've heard of her — Elizabeth, that is."

"Yeah, the papers have been covering some of her so-called exploits," Octave said, sliding down from the saddle. "Oop, hang on." He stepped a few feet away and then ralphed a full day's worth of hardtack into some bushes. "Man . . . I gotta get used to this flying thing."

Hannibal chuckled. "You good, Private Rey?"

Octave waved him off. "I'll be alright. That was some fast shooting, Amaya."

Amaya nodded her head, conceding the compliment without a word, and went over to stand beside Magdalys.

"She got you for your Gatling, Corp," Hannibal laughed.

"She did indeed," Cailloux acknowledged. "Where'd you learn to do that, young lady?"

Mapper piped up, "Her dad's a super-famous commander in the a —"

"Mapper!" Magdalys snapped as Amaya's hand wrapped around hers and squeezed. "Shut it."

Mapper's eyes went wide. "Oh. I thought —"

"You thought wrong," Magdalys said.

The soldiers traded glances, then shrugged and went back to checking their equipment.

"You okay?"

Amaya shrugged, still holding Magdalys's hand in a death grip. "Let's get these wounds cleaned up."

"Anyway," Hannibal said, "the young Miss Crawbell ain't even a Southerner. She from Connecticut or something."

"DC," Octave corrected him.

"Whatever," Hannibal said. "Ain't the South. But she wanna be Southern so bad. Well, Confederate Southern, that is. Not us Southern, obviously."

"And her daddy's a big-deal secessionist politician," Octave added. "The Pinkertons arrested him for aiding and abetting the enemy a couple times but the charges never stick."

"She's part of the reason General Sheridan's so pressed about having an air cavalry of our own," Cailloux explained.

"And he ain't wrong," Hannibal said, with a pointed look at Magdalys.

A familiar cawing cut the night, and then Beans, Grappler, and Dizz flapped out of the sky followed by a handful of those new dactyls. Magdalys caught her breath. "You guys alright?" she called, running over as they landed.

The three from Brooklyn seemed to be, besides some cuts and bruises (Beans had been slashed pretty badly when they'd surrounded him, and he looked extra ready to get back out there and whup more archaeops). But one of the Tennessee dactyls came in for a calamitous landing and then just lay there, barely breathing. The others gathered around, nudging him with their beaks.

Everyone stopped what they were doing and watched. For a few moments, they kept murmuring to each other and poking their fallen brethren; then a quiet understanding seemed to descend on them. The wounded dactyl's body stopped rising and falling; he lay still. The others bowed their heads; one swept a single wing over the body and then they all turned away sadly.

Magdalys watched in horror. It was just one life, and a dactyl at that, and the cannons and rifle fire still boomed across the valley around them as many hundreds of human lives were snatched from existence, but . . . that dactyl had shown up in the nick of time to help, and now he was dead. They all had. Sure, she hadn't summoned them, but they'd still come and she definitely would be summoning more before this was all

over. In her mind, she saw the dozens of bloodied archaeops cascading from the sky amidst Cailloux's withering Gatling fire. And how many more people and dinos would die around her? Because of her?

"Breathe," Amaya's voice whispered in her ear, and Magdalys realized she hadn't been.

She blinked, exhaled, tried to pull in air but it was like there was none. She'd been bested. Elizabeth Crawbell was still out there, and now she'd be looking for Magdalys. And she had whole battalions of archaeops ready to strike at her command.

"Breathe," Amaya said again.

Magdalys nodded, pulling harder. Around them, everyone had shaken their heads sadly and gone back to what they were doing. The world kept turning. Life flickered out and all there was to do was keep moving, keep moving, headlong into more destruction.

"Breathe," Amaya commanded quietly.

Magdalys nodded. Let a shaky breath out and pulled in another. She couldn't keep throwing dinos to their doom. And what would happen when it was one of her friends who was hurt or killed? If it was this hard with a dactyl she'd never even met before.

Beans, Grappler, and Dizz hopped over to Stella, who gave an appreciative coo, nuzzling each of them with her big head, and then settled back into having her wounds cleaned.

They were okay. They were more okay than Magdalys,

from the look of it. She exhaled a shivering chuckle and Amaya eyed her. "Just . . . sad. About all this," Magdalys said.

Amaya nodded.

"Can they fly?" Corporal Cailloux asked, stepping up to where the other dactyls had now gathered around Stella.

"Seems like they're okay," Magdalys said.

"Good. We have to get back out there. Sheridan's column will be entering the fray anytime now, if they haven't already. Can you guys fly?"

The soldiers had already finished gearing up and dusting themselves off. They'd just been through the worst smashup Magdalys had seen yet — she'd barely caught her breath — and they were ready to jump back into the thick of it. She glanced at Mapper and Amaya, found they were looking at her expectantly. They were already clicking into the relentless rhythm of war, she realized. But she wasn't sure if that was a good thing or not.

She nodded to them, and they started gearing up.

"What about Stella?" Amaya asked.

Magdalys looked over the towering pteranodon. For a few moments back there, she really thought they might both be destroyed by that horrible girl and her beast. Hearing that giant yelp of panic inside of herself had been terrifying. But more than that, the existence of Elizabeth Crawbell meant more than ever that the Union was vastly outmaneuvered in the one area Magdalys had the power to help.

She looked up at Stella, who was lashing her long tongue

along her freshly cleaned wounds. "How bout it, girl — you ready to get back in there?"

Stella shot her such a fierce and brittle glare, Magdalys didn't have to wait for the roar to erupt within her to know how the ptero felt.

Ready.

She only wished she could say the same about herself.

CHAPTER TWENTY-SEVEN
A ROUT AND A RUN

MAGDALYS WASN'T SURE if it was that it was
her second time, or that the field had been brightened by
even more torches, but as Stella approached the raging calam-
ity of soldiers and dinos below, it all seemed so much clearer
than it had earlier that night.

There were the skirmishers up at the front of both armies.
Foot soldiers and raptor riders both rushed forward in quick,
desperate pushes toward each other's lines and then fell back
suddenly, or sometimes just seemed to shatter where they stood
and be swept away by the ravenous tide of battle. Row after
row of trikeriders and stegos stretched away from the front
lines in either direction, occasionally punctuated by the long
body and swooping neck of a command sauropod; these were

the reserve units, waiting for a break in the line or the need for reinforcements.

And there, out in the dark woods at the far end of the corpse-strewn battlefield, the moonlight caught the momentous dust cloud rising around General Sheridan's weary soldiers as they surged forward toward the fight.

"Can you tell how it's going?" Magdalys asked, taking Stella in a wide arc around the edge of the woods and staying low. Surely their fight earlier had attracted some unwanted attention, which meant they'd be on the lookout now, and the air cavalry would probably be lurking somewhere nearby, if not Elizabeth Crawbell and her archaeops. She didn't seem like the type to sit and nurse her wounds for very long, if she'd even gotten any.

Hannibal shrugged. "Could go either way. Think they've got us outnumbered now that Longstreet's trikeriders showed up, but not by much. And Sheridan will help even it out some more. But if they turn that right flank" — he pointed to the far edge of the fighting, where smoke hung over the battlefield like a huge angry ghost — "it might well ripple all the way down our lines and then they'll get behind us and block our retreat to Chattanooga."

Magdalys shuddered. She didn't plan on staying in Tennessee much longer, but the thought of the whole Army of the Cumberland being cut off from their supply line and any hope of escaping north . . . they wouldn't stand a chance.

"That's why the Confederates are trying to build up on that end. But Thomas won't let 'em, see?" He nodded toward a small plateau in the center where a battalion of blue-clad soldiers on paraback were launching attack after attack on the Confederate line. "He keeps hitting 'em over here so they can't mass their forces over there. Wait, something's happening . . ."

Magdalys brought Stella even lower, felt the cool wind against her face as her heartbeat triple-timed against her ears. "What is it?"

"The Ohio 7th is advancing!" Corporal Cailloux yelled further back on the saddle, where he'd set up a spyglass. "They're pushing away that stego unit."

"That's the right flank!" Hannibal said just as they came around from behind a tall row of pines and glimpsed the full battlefield. The Confederate resistance was indeed falling away as the Union fighters pushed forward, but it wasn't in disarray. Instead, it looked like they were gathering at the center of their line.

"Uh-oh," Amaya said.

One of the Union battalions near where Thomas was fighting was in motion too, but instead of rallying around the embattled soldiers on the plateau they headed the opposite direction, toward a far flank.

"What's happening?" Magdalys yelled, trying to quell the panic rising in her.

"I don't know," Hannibal said. "It's impossible to tell from outside the fray, really."

"And even harder from inside," Octave said, shaking his head.

There was a terrible pause, like the night itself just needed to stop and take a deep breath away from the ever-mounting carnage. That gaping hole in the Union line glared up at Magdalys — it must've been glaring out at the Confederate generals too. The whole world seemed suddenly so quiet, and Magdalys imagined that maybe they'd all just realized how futile this whole thing was and decided to call it quits.

Then a terrible howl rose — the Rebel yell — and the whole mass of gray lurched forward as one, its focus right on that opening in the lines.

Another sound rose up now, but it wasn't the desperate yells of men in battle or the grunts of combat. This was something far worse, Magdalys realized as the blue army seemed to scatter like blown dust in the night: the cry of retreat.

CHAPTER TWENTY-EIGHT
CATCH AND CARRY

ONE REGIMENT REMAINED.

It had all happened so fast. After so much back and forth, hours and hours of death and destruction but no real gains one way or the other, virtually the whole army had simply vanished in a matter of moments.

Magdalys blinked at the rush of men across the battle-field as the last retreating Union soldiers disappeared into the woods toward Chattanooga. She'd read that nearly as many men died getting stampeded by fleeing dinos during a retreat as did in actual battle. Already, trees were collapsing through-out the forest amidst the rumbling escape.

She took in a gulp of that crisp mountain air.

One regiment remained: General Thomas's men, still on

that plateau that had once been the center point of a whole sprawling army, now alone in a sea of gray.

She narrowed her eyes on the position.

Thomas had spread his men out just enough to block the main escape route the others had taken. A few squads of trike-riders had slipped past and were in hot pursuit through the woods, but the rest of the army seemed to be kept back by these few men holding their lines.

They had remained so the others could get away.

The Confederate advance checked, they now hurled squad after squad of raptor riders crashing against the rapidly thinning Union lines.

For the second time that night, Magdalys sent Stella into a headlong dive that she wasn't at all sure they'd make it out of alive. Her heart thundered away as the wind rose to a shriek and the blasting of muskets grew louder.

"Incoming!" Octave yelled from behind her, and then the smell of gunpowder filled the night and shots erupted around her. "Air cavalry!"

More blasts rang out — the others returning fire probably — and then the Gatling's ear-shattering staccato song.

"There's too many of 'em!" Hannibal yelled.

The shooting got even hotter now as Stella swooped low over the colliding armies and then something high-pitched whistled over Magdalys's head and exploded behind them.

Artillery.

She glanced up and almost burst out laughing. There was Big Jack standing tall atop his trike, the howitzer still smoking. They'd pulled up behind the crumbling Union lines and immediately jumped into action.

"Nice shot!" Hannibal yelled. "Scattered 'em!"

"WOOHOO!" the men below yelled as Magdalys swung Stella into a half moon over their heads and more artillery shells screeched up into the night.

Already, the Confederate cannons grew louder as the growls of their mounted raptor units rose up over the celebrating troops. Sheridan's column may have arrived just in time to reinforce Thomas's beleaguered last stand, but they were still vastly outnumbered.

"Those trikeriders are getting ready for another charge," Cailloux said. "Set her down in that clearing, Magdalys."

Musket balls whistled through the air around them — the skirmishers had probably caught their breath long enough to take some potshots. Magdalys eased Stella into a landing on a trampled-down open area behind the Union line and squinted out at the dust cloud of combat nearby.

It was impossible to tell what was going on; all she could make out was a rustling sea of blue uniforms pressed together between the back ends of trikes and stegos. Every once in a while the sea would push back and then surge forward as shouts, gunshots, and dinogrowls filled the air.

"Major General!" Cailloux said, sliding down from Stella and snapping to attention.

Sheridan rode up on paraback as his men streamed past him in a steady flow into the fray. He saluted Cailloux and then his eyes went wide as they traced from Stella's humongous claws up past her folded wings to where Magdalys sat near her neck. "My heavens! Is that the . . ." He shook his head, the grim rictus of battle momentarily lifted from his open face. "She's a wonder."

Magdalys smiled and patted Stella.

"Sir," one of the officers nearby said, and then he nodded at something approaching in the darkness above. Sheridan held out his arm for a tiny flapping minidact, which landed on it and held out a roll of parchment in its beak. The general unraveled it and squinted at the writing, shook his head. "Heavy fighting on Missionary Ridge and Lookout Mountain, but they'll hold out. Those positions are well fortified. These lines, on the other hand, won't last much longer." He looked at the entourage of scouts and officers around him. "Tell General Thomas we have arrived and await his counsel." A uniformed man saluted and scurried off and Sheridan turned to Cailloux. "Report, Corporal."

"Aerial surveillance revealed a pretty evenly matched fight for most of the evening. The air cavalry has been out, including Miss Elizabeth Crawbell, who we had quite a scrap with. Just now though, the enemy charged our center as an opening was created, causing both flanks to collapse. General Thomas's men have been holding out to provide cover for the retreating men."

Sheridan shook his head, one hand idly stroking his goatee. "It's what I feared. Still . . ." One eyebrow rose, and Magdalys imagined this was the face he made every time he was about to leap into action. "We'll have to pull back to Chattanooga. From there, we'll regroup, and with coverage from Lookout Mountain and Missionary Ridge we'll be able to make forays into the valley and push Bragg's men back once more."

"Sir." A ragged voice came from the other side of the steady stream of soldiers still pouring toward the battle. Magdalys looked up just as a few of them cleared out of the way for a limping parasaurolophus.

"Card," she gasped.

It was the middle brother, and the older Card rode up just behind him. Both wore bloodstained clothes, their faces even more sullen than usual.

"Good god, man," Sheridan exclaimed. "Where have you been? I sent . . ."

Card silenced him with a shake of his head.

"Oh no," Sheridan said.

"Partisan guerrillas caught him over by Bellham's farm," the eldest brother said. "Hanged him from the tree outside our daddy's house."

"We're going to . . ." Middle Card said in a choked whisper that sent chills up and down Magdalys's spine. He cleared his throat, sent his deathly glare at the ground. "We're going to kill them all. Every last one. I've already put out the word."

The war had snatched someone else's loved one. Once

again, Magdalys was struck by the heartbreaking absurdity of caring so much about one life when hundreds and hundreds were being vanquished just feet away from them, but she had met Young Card. He'd been kind to her, saved her in fact. And anyway, nothing made sense. Not in the world, and especially not at war. She blinked away tears that she didn't even fully understand and the battle seemed to close in around her, around them all, the whole terrible war. One death amidst so many. . . . She shook her head.

"Card," Sheridan said firmly. "I know you have to do what you have to do, but . . . we need you. We're about to get run off this battlefield entirely and it's a miracle we weren't pressed into enemy territory. We're barely scraping by, man. I must . . . I must command you to put off your revenge until *this* fight, which you have sworn an oath to see out, is finished."

Card looked slowly up at the general with all the cool ferocity of a raptor about to make a kill.

"And by order," Sheridan added, meeting his scout's glare with a firm one of his own, "I mean, ask you, as a friend."

The older Card put a firm hand on his brother's shoulder. They exchanged a look, the slightest of nods. "We will honor our oath," he said. "And then we will do what must be done when this wretched war is over."

Sheridan closed his eyes. "I thank you."

"General!" A voice rose from the fighting. "General Sheridan!"

What now? Magdalys thought. A thickly framed man with

a short beard and harried scowl hurried over amidst a small gaggle of attendants.

"Thomas!" Sheridan said, dismounting and rushing over to him. "What news, man?"

General Thomas shook his head. "We've held as long as we can. We must pull back. They've overrun our positions on Lookout Mountain and Missionary Ridge!"

Sheridan boggled. "What?"

"I just got word. If we don't move now, we'll be cut off from the rest of the army."

Bugles erupted around them — the signal for retreat. Magdalys looked on in terror as the ocean of blue began drifting toward them. But it wasn't an ocean at all, she realized, just a very thin dam, and it was barely holding off the real ocean of gray that raged just on the other side. She gulped down a wave of panic, looked to Cailloux, who yelled to Sheridan, "Sir! We need to get you out of here. Now!"

CHAPTER TWENTY-NINE
FLIGHT

"**TAKE HEART, MEN!**" Sheridan yelled into the wind as Magdalys brought Stella low over the heads of the retreating soldiers. They stumbled along in a bedraggled, shambling shadow of the glorious parade they'd been just a few hours ago. Men limped and dragged each other; some all-out ran as cannon fire erupted behind them. A few straightened up and cheered when they heard Sheridan's voice, then gaped at the humongous pteranodon he rode on. Others just kept shuffling, heads bowed.

"Sir," Corporal Buford urged nervously. "I'm not sure you should be hanging quite so far over the edge of the saddle like that."

"Nonsense," Sheridan scoffed, leaning even further to prove his point. "How else will the men see me? And anyway,

I'm quite secured by these straps. Magdalys, take us around again, dear."

"You want to go *back*?" Buford gaped. "Back toward the advancing Confederate Army that just smashed us to bits? General . . ."

"That's quite enough, Corporal. If you don't like it, you're welcome to get out and walk, you know."

Magdalys wasn't wild about the idea of getting anywhere near the advancing Rebel lines, but she smirked to herself at Buford getting put in his place yet again. "C'mon, girl," she whispered, steering Stella up over the tree line and then into a wide turn back toward the rearguard of the retreating army.

Sheridan had insisted on taking a ride to encourage his men and wouldn't be swayed by the other officers urging him to use the opportunity to remove himself from the battle-field. Mapper and Amaya had stayed on board, and Hannibal and Octave trained their weapons to either side in case of an ambush. Cymbeline rode up front with Magdalys.

"I was worried about you," she said.

Behind them, Sheridan was encouraging Buford to shout his own heartening words to the troops below. It wasn't going well.

"I was worried about you too. I've lost track of all the people I'm worried about," Magdalys said with a frown. "People keep . . . people keep dying. And dinos too."

Cymbeline grimaced. "I know. This is . . . it's been bad the whole war, but I guess . . . after Gettysburg and Vicksburg, I thought things had turned around. This . . . this is really bad."

"Good job, men troops!" Buford yelled shakily. "Er . . . troop troops! Soldiers! Keep . . . keep at it! Excellent retreat!"

"What happens now?"

"That," Sheridan said, startling both of them, "is precisely why I joined you on this magnificent creature." He'd somehow made his way up front without either of them noticing.

"Stealthy, aren't you, sir," Cymbeline said wryly.

He leaned back and yelled over his shoulder, "Keep going, Buford, you're doing great!" then leaned forward conspiratorially and whispered, "He's not."

"You have a plan?" Magdalys asked.

Sheridan shook his head and the brave, unflappable veneer came suddenly crashing down as his face creased into an anguished frown. "I . . . There is no plan. All I know is this: We need General Grant. Without those two mountain outposts, we'll be starved out of Chattanooga in a matter of days. And then we'll be crushed. Grant has an army at his disposal and he's the only general with the tactical genius to get us out of this."

Cymbeline looked stricken. "Isn't Grant in —"

"New Orleans," Sheridan said, leveling a look at Magdalys.

Her eyes went wide, but Sheridan quelled the yelp she was about to release with a raised hand and a solemn shake of his head. "What is it?" she asked.

"Of course, I would rejoice at this seeming coinciding of our needs and yours, but . . ."

Magdalys's heart sank. The US Army needed an air cavalry

now even more than ever, and without someone who could connect directly to pteros, what good would they be against a wrangler like Elizabeth Crawbell?

From not too far away, the booms of artillery shells concussed the night. The battle was still raging even as the Union Army did everything it could to escape. If the Confederates decided to pursue them it could be an all-out massacre.

Magdalys closed her eyes. "I . . ."

"This pteranodon is the only way we can get someone to Grant fast enough," Sheridan said.

"I know," Magdalys said, eyes still shut. A mounted dactyl would have to keep stopping for breaks and risk capture every time. A minidact would probably never make it. And traveling by land through that much enemy territory was far too dangerous.

"But without someone who can reach the dinos the way you do . . ."

"There is someone," a voice said.

Stella let out a bellow that Magdalys was pretty sure was triumphant.

Magdalys's eyes sprang open. Dactyls rose in the air all around them. Not just the Brooklyn dactyls — the Tennessee ones who'd helped them out earlier against Crawbell too. They glided silently up from the dark forest below, their eyes narrowed with determined intent.

"I can do it," Hannibal said.

"What?" Magdalys, Sheridan, and Cymbeline all burst out at the same time.

"This . . . you're doing this," Magdalys said, waving at the squad surging around them. "And that was you who called them to help us earlier!"

"Remarkable!" Sheridan exclaimed.

Hannibal smiled but his eyes were sad. "That was the first time I'd actually got up the courage to try it. Every other time, it's just sort of . . . happened. I . . . I've always known. I just didn't have it in me to admit it. Not to anyone. I was afraid. I mean . . . I'd never met anyone else who could do that. And sure there were stories, legends really, but even knowing what I could do, I still didn't believe it could be me . . . like, why me? I'm just some street kid from Tremé, you know? I thought I had just lost my mind, even though I knew I hadn't. And then . . . and then I met Magdalys."

Magdalys just stared at him, understanding where this was going but unsure how to take it in.

"And you," Hannibal said, shaking his head and blinking away tears. "You're just so . . . you know who you are, you know your power. And you embrace it. I . . . I want to be like that. I want to be like you, Magdalys. Or maybe I should say: I *am* like you, Magdalys, and for the first time, I know that's something to be proud of."

"Remarkable," Sheridan said again, this time in an awed whisper.

Cannons boomed below them, and artillery tore the sky, its ragged echoes shuddering across the valley.

"Thank you," Hannibal said, his eyes meeting Magdalys's.

She grinned. "Anytime, freak."

"In that case," Sheridan yelped, "we have not a moment to lose! Cymbeline!"

"Sir?"

"You will accompany Miss Magdalys. Borrow a uniform from one of the men. You will pose as a Union soldier now, my dear. Can't have you that deep in enemy territory as a woman. You are to cut your hair and find a man's name. Is that clear?"

She nodded, eyes wide. "Actually, Cymbeline *is* a —"

"Never mind all that," Sheridan said. "I'm sure it can be done! Why, just last week, we discovered not one but *two* of our men bathing in the Tennessee River, and do you know it turned out they weren't men at all!"

"That's not what I was —"

"Indeed!" Sheridan yelled. "Apparently it's quite common. Now, Private Rey!"

Octave looked up from his position scanning the battle-field below. "Sir!"

"You are to accompany Cymbeline and Magdalys on their mission to retrieve General Grant. Keep them safe at all costs and alert the general to our present circumstances. He'll know what to do. Is that clear?"

"Sir, yes sir!"

"And give him this." Sheridan passed Octave a sealed envelope. "It's my report. Already vastly out of date by the sudden turn of events, of course, so you'll have to fill him in on the rest yourself."

"Very good, sir."

"Magdalys!" Sheridan barked. "You are not one of my men, er, girls, ah, you know what I mean. I humbly ask that you fly this pteranodon to New Orleans to help us retrieve General Grant."

Yes! Everything in Magdalys yelled. But the thought shattered almost immediately: Sabeen and Two Step were down there somewhere, running for their lives. "Is there any way . . . the rest of my friends . . ."

"There's no time for that, I'm afraid," Sheridan said, and Magdalys felt a tiny shattering feeling in her chest. She'd known there was a good chance that would happen, that any time they separated it might be for good, but . . . it still hurt more than she'd thought it would. "These two may go along, of course," Sheridan added, "but that's all. You must trust that your other friends are in the best of hands and we'll do everything in our power to keep them safe."

Two Step's hurt, furious face flashed through her mind again. What if that was the last time they saw each other? She shook away the thought.

"Will you accept the mission, Magdadis?"

Sure she'd been about to take off on her own just the night before but . . . some part of her hadn't really thought through

what it would feel like to actually be separated from her squad for real. It hurt. Magdalys gulped back the sadness. Then she stood and saluted as best she could. "Sir, yes sir!"

"And," he added with a sly wink, "I sincerely hope you find your brother while you're down there."

The grin that crossed Magdalys's face rose from a place deep inside her.

"Now!" Sheridan spun around, facing Hannibal. "Young man! Why don't you use some of these special powers you've been concealing to get us safely out of here so these folks can set off on their mission, yes?"

Hannibal flashed his cockiest smile. "I've been waiting my whole life to do that, sir!"

CHAPTER THIRTY
DARKNESS OVER THE DEEP

TINY, SHINING GLIMMERS of light danced in the darkness below — the moon again, winking at them by way of the Mississippi River to let them know that even as the stifling night closed in around them, they traveled the right path.

"I don't trust him," Amaya said, clipping another strand of Cymbeline's hair.

"Who?" Magdalys asked. She had the comb held out but Amaya didn't seem to need it.

"Sheridan."

Instinctively, all three of them looked to the front of the saddle, where Private Octave Rey sat scanning the dark horizon beside Mapper, rifle ready.

They'd passed through Georgia mostly in silence, with the exception of Mapper's occasional notes pointing out where this or that land had once belonged to the Cherokee or Creek. To Magdalys it seemed like the echoes of mortar blasts and those endless barrages of musket fire only got louder as the thrill of battle fell away and left behind only that rumbling, roiling dread. *What would happen now? Where were Two Step and Sabeen?* At sunset on the second day, Magdalys had looked out across the treetops and glimpsed what Mapper explained must be the faraway lights of Atlanta shimmering in the sky, and she'd realized they'd witnessed firsthand the army of a nation bent on enslaving them crush the army of a nation that wanted to free them. Or at least it claimed to. But even that nation had once enslaved them too. And it didn't even seem so enthusiastic about freedom so much as it was about preserving its precious union. She'd shaken her head, turned away from the illuminated sky, back toward the gathering night, and let out a deep, exhausted breath as the cannons and muskets boomed through her memory once again.

Now, two days later, Magdalys watched Amaya chop away at Cymbeline's thick hair and wondered: If all that had happened in just a few short hours, how much more had already happened since they'd left? And would Two Step ever forgive her for leaving him behind? It seemed like no matter what Magdalys did, she was letting someone down.

"You shouldn't," Cymbeline said with a sniffle. "You shouldn't trust any of them."

Magdalys looked at the older girl, caught a flash of moonlight reflected in the two streams that slid down her face. "Cymbeline . . . what's wrong?"

Cymbeline shook her head, ran a hand beneath her nose and snorted.

"It's the hair," Amaya said. "We carry it with us everywhere we go for so long, and then suddenly it's gone. Like losing our own shadow. My mom told me once we cut our hair when we're mourning or during times of great change. So . . . makes sense, I guess."

Cymbeline nodded, sniffled again, then shrugged. "Right. It's a good kind of sadness. I feel . . . lighter somehow. Like I just threw away a big suitcase I've been lugging around for ages. But also, I . . . I love my hair." She cradled some of the curls Amaya had let fall in her lap and then threw them up into the air for the wind to take. "Loved."

"It'll grow back," Magdalys said, knowing that wasn't much help.

"It's also that . . . I'm scared. For all of us. Why don't you trust Sheridan, Amaya?"

Amaya scowled, handed Magdalys the scissors, and pulled out her bowie knife. "Hold still. Because I grew up around those types."

Cymbeline scoffed. "Overexcited short men in uniform who will promise the stars and sky then turn their backs on you in the blink of an eye?"

"Pretty much just described my dad," Amaya said. "Except

he's six three. But yeah. And I get it: Winning the war is top priority, but that's just it. Everything else is expendable."

"Including us," Magdalys said.

"You guys are black and I'm Apache," Amaya said. "I don't think they know how to see us as anything but expendable." She sliced away some errant clumps of hair, then tilted Cymbeline's head to the side to get a better angle.

"Whether there's a war going on or not," Cymbeline agreed.

"Exactly, and anyway, there's a whole other war going on that nobody wants to talk about it. A perpetual one. The beloved savior Lincoln hanged thirty-eight Dakotas in a single day at the end of last year, and that's not even to mention the ones who were massacred in the run-up to that."

Cymbeline nodded sadly.

"I . . . I didn't know," Magdalys said. She tried to reconcile the gnawing sense of doom and betrayal with the beautiful world around her. The evergreen and pine forests of Georgia had given way to Louisiana's murky swamplands below, and now the shimmering moonlight danced not just through the wide river but sudden stretches of lake and bayou amidst the trees.

And still, dactyls plummeted over and over again through the sky in her mind, as hundreds and hundreds of men collapsed beneath thundering cascades of rifle fire. She couldn't keep dragging dinos and pteros into this bloody horror show. She wouldn't.

She clenched both fists, watching the forest slide by below. She would get to New Orleans and find her brother and then together they'd run off to somewhere safe. Cuba maybe, or even further safe. Somewhere with no cannons or troops marching to their death, where she wouldn't have to call upon giant reptiles for anything more dangerous than a grocery run.

Yes.

"And you're done," Amaya said, brushing away the last couple of strands from Cymbeline's shaved head. "Did you come up with a boy name yet?"

"That's what I was trying to tell the general," she said, standing and wiping herself off. "Cymbeline *is* a boy's name. He was a king in a Shakespeare play."

"Alright, Private King Cymbie," Amaya said, saluting with a wry smile. "Dismissed."

Cymbeline rolled her eyes, returned the salute, and headed over to the front of the saddle.

Magdalys and Amaya sat beside each other in silence for a few minutes as Octave admired Cymbeline's haircut and Mapper explained to her how she should walk to seem more like a man.

Amaya scoffed. "As if Cymbie needs acting lessons from that clown."

"You know," Magdalys said, and then the full hugeness of Amaya's life and strange father seemed to materialize in a heavy cloud around Magdalys and she didn't know what to say.

195

Amaya looked at her. "What?"

Magdalys dragged a hand down her face and realized how tired she was. "I just . . . we're already scattered. You should . . . when we get to New Orleans . . . you should go."

"Oh."

"Find him, I mean. See what it is he's going on about."

They both turned back to the front, where Cymbeline was pulling one of Octave's blue army jackets on.

"She was a cook at the Citadel," Amaya said so softly Magdalys barely heard her over the wind. "My mom."

Magdalys nodded very slightly, eyes still ahead. Off to the side, Grappler, Dizz, and Beans squawked and swooped back into formation from a hunting run.

"She used to take me aside late at night and tell me about what it was like back home, in Apache Country. About her family . . . *our* family. My older brother from her first husband, and all my cousins. The elders. She smelled like dish soap and a faraway flower and she said every word in English so carefully, like it was a fragile object she didn't want to mishandle." Amaya smiled; tears glistened at the edges of her eyes. "Mama tried to teach me some Lipan — that's our language — but . . ." She shook her head, shrugged.

I'm sorry, Magdalys wanted to say, but what sense did it make? Words were so useless. She didn't have any memories of her own mom, who was still somewhere in Cuba probably. She'd find her one day though. She would.

"One night," Amaya said, "when I went to look for her in the kitchen after hours, she had tears in her eyes. She hugged me extra tight and when I asked what was wrong she just shook her head and told me to do what my father asked of me, *everything*, and to learn everything I could, and in time I would understand. Then she said the name of a place, an important place, she said, but it wasn't that I was supposed to go there, not right away anyway, just that I should know it. Like" — she shook her head — "like one day I'd understand, I guess? But if she's there . . ." Tears welled up. Amaya brushed them away. Magdalys wrapped an arm around her and squeezed. "If she's there, I just want to go there, whenever we get out of this mess. I don't want to go see my dad. But I also know that's what my mom wanted me to do. She said if I wanted to help her, to help us, she said, I'd do what my father asked of me, even if it didn't seem to make sense."

Magdalys didn't need her to say it to know that was the last time Amaya had seen her mom.

"And it wasn't just her telling me to be obedient. There's a lot I don't know about my mom, but I know she was about more than just accepting the lot she was given. I mean . . . it felt like she was planning something. For me, I mean. Like, I was part of her grand plan somehow. But . . . that's all. Then she hugged me tight and sent me to my room. And all I was left with was an order to do what the General says and a name of somewhere I've never heard of." She scowled, wiped a few more tears away.

"So I did what she said. I became the best at everything there was to get good at. Practiced every move I saw them learning in combat class for hours and hours. Aced every test, memorized the ins and outs of each weapon I could get my hands on. But . . . I still don't even know what I'm supposed to understand, and now . . ."

And now the war has broken up the squad, Magdalys thought, watching the swaying swamp trees below and wondering where Two Step and Sabeen were and if they were okay.

Amaya threw her hands up. "I don't trust him. I don't think I love him, even though he's my dad. I don't know what I'm supposed to do."

She put her head on Magdalys's shoulder and day broke slowly across the Southern skies around them.

· PART THREE ·

LOUISIANA

CHAPTER THIRTY-ONE
CRESCENT CITY

A **LOW, RASPY DRONE** sounded and a thousand paras galloped in their strange halting gait across a sun-streaked field as brittle, yellowish hills rose from the ground around them. The paras poured forward, trampling everything in their path. Magdalys swooped closer; she could hear them speaking — not that inner voice that let her know a dino's thoughts — no, these were human voices, discussing the weather, the state of the war and the world, some indecipherable coming crisis . . . and beneath it all, that strange buzz droned on and on, rose and fell, simmered and then suddenly lifted into a startling, urgent shriek just as Magdalys realized those yellow hills were made from hundreds and hundreds of bones.

"Mags!"

Magdalys woke with Mapper's face way too close to hers, his eyes worried as he shook her.

"What happened?" The dream lingered; the buzzy drone still sounded all around her. Thick warm air clung to her as she shoved Mapper away and sat up. "Where are we?"

"Nothing, it's just . . ."

To the east, a pinkish haze swept away the dark blue sky. Below water stretched out to either direction. Stella was gliding low, just over the surface of the lapping waves. "We're over the ocean?" Magdalys blurted out. "We've gone too far!"

"No," Mapper said, and she could tell it was taking all he had not to get snappy with her. "That's Pontchartrain. The *lake*. We made it."

The others were up front, all gazing at the horizon ahead.

Magdalys blinked. "We . . . what?" A surge of something — was it sadness? — rose up in her and she gulped it back, shaking her head. "We're . . . here?"

"New Orleans sits between a curve in the Mississippi River — that's why they call it the Crescent City — and a huge lake called Pontchartrain. In fact, it was founded by —"

"There it is!" Amaya yelled from up front.

Mapper gasped and ran over, and Magdalys stumbled after him. She put her hands on Amaya's and Cymbeline's shoulders and squeezed in between them, gazing out at the stretch of water ahead of them.

"Home sweet home," Octave sighed. "Ain't no place like it."

Rooftops lined the far shore. They mostly just looked like dark lumps from this far away in the half-light of dawn, but they were definitely the beginnings of a city. New Orleans.

They'd made it.

Everyone cheered. Magdalys exhaled a breath that she felt like she must've been holding for months. Cymbeline and Amaya squeezed her into a tight hug as Mapper tried to teach Octave one of his overcomplicated handshakes.

"What is it?" Amaya asked, finally letting go of their hug and taking in Magdalys's solemn face.

Montez was here somewhere, probably. They crossed onto the shore and suddenly tiled rooftops and spiraling Victorian mansions and busted old shacks rushed past beneath them.

"I guess I just . . ." She shook her head. "I don't think I really thought we'd ever get here somehow."

New Orleans meant she would finally have an answer, one way or another, and she wasn't totally sure, even after all they'd been through, that she was ready for that. Even with the riots and the prison yard scuffle with the Kidnapping Club, the world had seemed much simpler in New York, more stable somehow. Sure, people were trying to kill and capture them at every turn, and even their well-meaning organizations meant to protect them were mostly criminally inept, but still . . . newspapers crowed about the US Army's sweeping victories and all those towering buildings offered at least the illusion of some kind of invincibility, however corrupt and unfriendly.

Tennessee and the Battle of Chickamauga had taught Magdalys that the world was just a tinderbox waiting to catch fire, and any life could be snuffed out by a bullet or bomb in fractions of a second. She'd seen it happen up close and then over and over again from above.

The possibility that Montez hadn't survived had seemed to grow large and long while she wasn't looking, a silent, towering shadow. And now, soon, she would have her answer.

Cymbeline squeezed Magdalys's shoulder, catching her eye. "Hey," she said. "We're with you."

Magdalys nodded.

"So, I figured we'd head to the Saint Charles Hotel," Octave said, looking out across the rooftops to where the winding coils of the Mississippi curved through the heart of the city. "That's where General Grant is staying while he's here. From what I've heard about the general, he'll probably be wherever the troops are, but at least the hotel could probably let us know where that is."

"Alternately," Mapper said in a voice that made it clear a Mapper-Knows-All moment was in the pipes, "we could follow the masses of Union troops gathering below."

"Huh?" Octave said, and they all glanced down to the streets below, where blue-coated soldiers worked their way past scowling old ladies and kids playing in the street toward one of the main tree-lined throughways.

Magdalys banked Stella to the side so they could catch a better view. All along the promenade, Union soldiers stood at

attention beneath the long, wandering oak branches. Another group moved along slowly from the far end of the avenue, and Magdalys heard the distant strains of trumpets rising over the incessantly buzzing drone.

"A PARADE!" Mapper yelled.

CHAPTER THIRTY-TWO
AMBUSH MUSIC

MAGDALYS WATCHED AS Cymbeline and Amaya mounted up on Grappler and then went swooping away from Stella over the rooftops. Up ahead, Mapper and Octave were already bringing Beans down for a bumpy landing on the bell tower of an elaborate stone church.

"Get somewhere safe, Stella," Magdalys whispered, wrapping her arms around the huge pteranodon's neck. "Thank you for carrying us all this way." Stella snorted and grunted her acknowledgment and Magdalys felt a loving sadness inside that she knew belonged to both her and the ptero. "I know, girl. I know." She patted that smooth, sun-soaked hide one time and then stood.

Dizz stood in the middle of the saddle, his head cocked to one side, and lifted one foot then the other impatiently.

"Alright, buddy, I'm coming," Magdalys said. Music was rising from below, a sweet, wild, and relentless march that made her miss Two Step. She crossed the saddle at a run and leapt onto Dizz, then felt the air whip around them as he carried them off Stella and away. Magdalys glanced back, caught a final nod from her huge friend as the pteranodon banked off toward Lake Pontchartrain.

Other pteros and flying dinos speckled the thick warm air over New Orleans. They glided and tumbled, flitted around playfully and swooped in long arcs across the city, some paired up, others in massive flocks, many by themselves. A few had that determined look that minidactyls get when they're on a mission, but most just seemed to be wandering free. That was different. New York was a way bigger city, with taller buildings and everything packed tightly together, like it had been shoved into a jar it didn't quite fit. But there weren't nearly as many reptiles flying through the air, and the ones that were usually looked like they were on the way somewhere, not just idly flapping about.

New Orleans looked more like it had been splattered outward from the riverbanks, with low houses speckling the outskirts and tighter clusters along the avenues downtown. None stretched so violently into the sky as those New York monstrosities though, Magdalys thought as several sauropods lifted their long graceful necks over the rooftops nearby and started munching on the leaves of a palm tree.

"It's beautiful," she said, and Dizz's *fubba-fubba* reply seemed to be in agreement. A warm, wet breeze tickled her

face and the thick swampy air seemed to hug her somehow, keep her afloat. She closed her eyes, allowed herself a few moments to take it all in. That music rose around her — those soaring trumpet notes calling back and forth to each other like sauropods and the heavy thump of the bass drums speckled with a ferocious *brat-da-tat-tat* of the snares — and Magdalys smiled. Somewhere down there, Montez might be marching. He was a new person now, a sharpshooter apparently, and maybe, just maybe, they'd get out of this mess together and make it home alive.

Magdalys opened her eyes and sent Dizz into a spiraling dive toward the church tower.

Paramounted soldiers paraded down the wide stretch of Saint Charles Avenue, followed by a trike unit and two huge brachys, each carrying elaborate officer's quarters. Folks had gathered on either side of the block, Magdalys noticed, but none of them were cheering. Most just watched in stony silence; a few jeered and threw things.

"Occupation," Octave said, passing his spyglass to Magdalys. "The Confederate garrison emptied out as soon as our gunboats showed up on the Mississippi two years ago. Gave up the city without a shot fired. Now it's just an uneasy type of truce here. At least between the white New Orleanians and the US soldiers. Our folks though, heh, well, see for yourself."

Octave pointed further down Saint Charles, where the marching band approached behind three brightly colored . . . were those dancing archaeops? Rainbow feathers covered the figures, sprouting down their long wings and along those tall necks. But they were stomping and shimmying in time to the music and marching on two feet like humans. Magdalys had seen stagedinos before — Cymbeline and Halsey used them in their Shakespeare shows all the time — but they usually just functioned as clowns or elaborate parts of the scenery, and couldn't be trained to do much more than come and go on cue or play fight. They'd certainly never danced.

"What on earth?" Mapper said, taking the spyglass Magdalys was holding out to him and squinting through it for a better look. "What kind of boogie-down dinos are those?"

Octave laughed. "They're not. Those are Mardi Gras Indians. It's regalia."

Amaya perked up. "Indians? Gimme the spyglass. Do you know what tribe?"

"Well," Octave said, "I'm not sure it's really that they're with a particular tribe. They're more like paying tribute to the Indians that helped some of our folks get free from slavery at different times, and the cultures kind of combined into something new."

"Oh," Amaya said, not sounding *too* disappointed. "They're beautiful."

The music got louder as the band marched past. Magdalys could make out the thick, shimmering coils of a tuba wrapped

around a tall black man as the driving *oompah–oompah* rounded out the swirl of trumpet and trombone calls. It sounded like they'd taken a regular military tune and thrown it up into the air so all the notes suddenly landed in different places, but you could somehow feel the melody moving along underneath. Magdalys had never heard anything like it — this brand-new swing with those rasping, soaring trumpets, this rumbling, weeping, caterwauling song that was both sad and happy at the same time, that made her want to cry and break into a shimmy.

"There go the Native Guard!" Octave yelled, his voice brimming with pride. "That's my boys!" Amaya passed him the spyglass.

"Wonder if the Louisiana 9th is with 'em," Magdalys said, squinting down at row after row of blue-clad soldiers marching in formation.

"And there's General Grant!" Octave said.

The general sat astride a tall, aging dino that looked like a tyrannosaurus but with small spikes lining its snout. An allosaurus, Magdalys realized, and a bright red one at that. It strutted proudly along, slightly hunched over and squinting impassively at the crowd like it had seen all this before. General Grant wore a tattered blue jacket and busted brown hat with a wide rim. A cigar stuck out from his bearded face and he seemed to regard the whole world somewhat like his steed did, with a kind of weary acceptance. A feisty-looking microdactyl sat on his shoulder and cast a sharp glare at the buildings around them.

A flutter of black from a rooftop across the avenue caught Magdalys's eye.

"*That's* the general that the whole US Army is resting its hopes on?" Mapper asked. "He looks kinda over it. Lemme see the spyglass."

Crows. They'd been perched along the balcony rail of a pillared mansion and suddenly took flight in a splash of dark feathers.

Something had spooked them.

Magdalys squinted at the balcony, then the rooftop. A figure, tall and feathery, rose; then another.

Those weren't the Mardi Gras Indians though. Those were mounted lizards. She could see the sun glinting off the rifle barrel of one of the riders. They wore hooded cloaks, just like the Kidnappers Club members back in New York.

"It's an attack," Magdalys said, already making a dash for Dizz. "We need to —"

A sharp crack ripped through the air, its echo rumbling like thunder across the city of New Orleans.

CHAPTER THIRTY-THREE
ATTACK!

MAGDALYS BARELY PAUSED as the shock of the blast rumbled through her. Montez might be down there, and even if he wasn't, the general definitely was, and whoever those attackers were they were probably gunning for him. Dizz was already extending his long wings and crouching down, ready for flight. Magdalys grabbed his neck and heaved herself onto his back.

"Go!" she yelled, and the church tower fell away beneath them.

Soldiers and civilians scattered through the streets below. Smoke rose from the sidewalk in front of the mansion those mounted riders had appeared in. But where were they? And where was the general? Magdalys pulled Dizz into a steep climb and then circled back down toward Saint Charles.

There! That tired ol' allosaurus still had plenty of fight in it, she realized. The dino had charged down the avenue full throttle, using those front horns to smash any obstacle — a small parade vehicle, an ice cream stand, a fallen tree — out of its way. General Grant had both reins in hand and was bouncing up and down in the saddle but didn't appear especially bothered or afraid.

Two trikes rumbled along in their wake, each mounted by a cadre of frantic-looking blue coats — the general's guard detail, Magdalys assumed.

Another flicker of movement caught her eye and the two flying dinos burst into the air from a nearby rooftop, spread their brown, gray, and black feathered wings and soared toward the street below. Sinornithosaurs. Those things could kill with one bite because of the venom hidden in their razor-sharp teeth. Magdalys launched after them. The trikeriders had their eyes on the surrounding streets, totally oblivious to the attack careening down from above.

"Look out!" Magdalys screamed.

Their faces all turned skyward at once and their rifles followed suit. Magdalys gasped and swung Dizz into a barrel roll out of the way as the bullets blasted past. One of the sinorniths screeched and tumbled, sending its rider screaming toward the ground; the other swung deftly out of the way. Magdalys glanced back. The rider who hadn't fallen landed his mount on a nearby balcony and was prepping his rifle. Across the street, Cymbeline burst into the air on Grappler's back. Octave rode

in the saddle behind her, already hurling shot after shot at the attacker.

So that was handled. Magdalys turned back toward the general. She swooped low past the trikes and was about to swing skyward when something slammed into Dizz from the side with a growl and the world did a somersault. Gravelly pavement scraped her arms as she skidded off to the side amidst flailing dactylwings and snapping jaws, and then she was up, not too hurt, and backing away from a snarling green raptor.

It scrambled to its feet with a growl, dust flying up around them, and then lowered that long snout, eyes wide, and took a slow step toward them. Dizz had tumbled a few feet behind her and was still trying to get himself together, and Magdalys had sworn she wouldn't drag any more dinos into this war on her behalf, she'd *sworn* it! But this one, although riderless, was clearly already involved. And anyway, he was about to eat her. She reached out with her mind and . . . nothing.

Blocked again!

That meant that somewhere out there, another Confederate dinomaster was lurking, watching, controlling things.

The raptor rose up, and then swung his head low again, sniffing loudly, eyes narrowing. One razor-sharp claw scratched a line into the gravel.

Magdalys backed another step away. If she ran, it would simply snatch her up. She reached for her pistol but knew there wouldn't be time to load it before the raptor pounced.

A bright flash of color suddenly took over the world in front of her. A whole rainbow seemed to parade before her wide eyes now. The Mardi Gras Indians!

"HA!" they yelled in one resounding voice amidst a shimmer of tambourine bells and deeper drum hits.

The raptor recoiled.

"HA!" Louder now. And again: "HA!" And they advanced as one, their feet gliding across the pavement in smooth circles. The raptor backed up uneasily, glancing to either side at these strange new opponents. They stepped forward.

Magdalys gaped at them. They weren't in the raptor's head — there was no way. They were just collectively wrangling it away from her, with nothing but drumbeats and the sound of their voices. She'd never seen anything like it.

"Th-thanks!" she said, probably not loud enough for them to hear. Then Dizz gave a startled caw just as Magdalys felt the ground rumble. She looked up just in time to see one of the security trikes barreling toward her, now with only a single rider on top. He wore a US Army uniform and had a long red goatee. He was glaring at Grant. The rest of the soldiers who'd been on it lay scattered on the ground, looking stunned.

The Confederate dinomaster! It had to be!

She dove out of the way as the trike thundered past, was already running as she rose and then leapt onto Dizz's back and they took off after it.

CHAPTER THIRTY-FOUR

THROUGH THESE BROKEN STREETS

GENERAL GRANT HAD his sidearm out and was glancing around wearily, oblivious to the trike charging from the rear.

"General Grant!" Magdalys yelled. "Behind you!"

He spun around, face clenched and eyebrows arched, with the trike just a few steps away and closing fast. That red allosaurus sidestepped just enough so the trike's long horn scratched along its haunch instead of impaling it clean through. The beast roared and swung its head around, chomping a nice chunk out of the trike's upper thigh as it passed.

"Whoa!" Magdalys yelled.

The trike shrieked and swung hard to the left, bustling down a side street as Grant let off a series of pistol shots after

it. "Go, Samantha! After them!" he hollered in a gravelly voice, and the allosaurus lurched forward in a lopsided canter.

Magdalys blinked, veering Dizz into a wide turn behind the general. "I didn't see *that* coming," she said.

Fubba-fub, Dizz agreed.

Up ahead, the trike crashed down a ragged mud-strewn street beneath winding oak branches and palm fronds. It was definitely favoring the side that hadn't been chomped, but the beast had still managed to reach an impressive gallop. Samantha wasn't far behind though, and she wasn't letting up. Grant leaned forward in the saddle, both hands on the reins now.

Something stirred in the shadows of an alleyway and then a finback hustled out into the street from behind a shotgun shack. What was it doing? That tall sail along its spine rocked back and forth as the dimetrodon stopped just in front of Grant's charging allosaurus.

The dinomaster, Magdalys realized. He was wrangling anything he could get his mind on and sending them in Grant's path.

Samantha didn't even pause, just sent the finback tumbling out of her way with a sharp kick and kept it moving. The finback rolled a few times and then got up, shook itself off and headed back to the alleyway, dazed.

But now a whole pack of long-necked, slender-bodied dinos fell into stride on either side of Samantha. They pranced along on their back two legs, snapping at her with long snouts

and squealing. *Struthiomimus*, Magdalys thought. *The ostriches of the dinoworld*, Dr. Sloan called them, *in form, attitude, and general demeanor.* They posed no threat to a huge beast like Samantha, of course, but they might slow her down.

Magdalys swooped Dizz into a long dive and came up fast behind them, knocking the skinny running dinos to either side with ease.

Grant urged his mount on, barely noticing, and pulled out his service revolver again as he got closer.

Up ahead, the red-bearded rider glanced back, face wide with fear, and snarled, turning just in time to see the tremendous pothole in the street ahead of him. "Aiigh!" the dinomaster yelled, and the trike seemed to crumple beneath him as it stumbled, then crashed with a tremendous explosion of dust into the broken concrete disaster area. The Confederate catapulted forward, tumbling a few times, and then sprung to his feet. "Up, fool!" he screeched, but the trike couldn't right itself.

Magdalys urged Dizz up and forward, hoping to swoop down on him from above, but Grant was already lobbing shot after shot at the man, as Samantha lowered her horned snout and broke into a full-on charge.

"No!" he yelled, stumbling back a few steps and then dashing into a nearby alley as gunfire thudded into the street on either side of him.

Samantha skidded to a halt beside the downed trike just as two more mounted sinorniths launched skyward from another

mansion rooftop. The sinorniths had begun their dive, but Grant was still squinting toward where the Confederate had disappeared into the alley. "General Grant!" Magdalys called, spurring Dizz into a dive. "Behind you!"

He cocked his head at her, blinking, then spun just as the first sinornith leveled into a straightforward glide-charge down the street toward him. A single shot sang out and the rider went flying backward with a scream as the sinornith veered suddenly away. Magdalys hadn't even seen Grant raise his pistol.

The second attacker was still coming fast and now a third leapt from a nearby rooftop, glide-diving toward Grant with a shrill caw.

He would never be able to fend them both off.

One snap from those jaws and the general on whom the Union's hopes rested would be a dead man.

"C'mon!" Magdalys grunted into Dizz's ear, and he flapped harder, surging forward as the ornate mansions and twisting oak trees became a blur on either side. Grant fired again but the shot went wide, and then they were rushing up from behind and the sinornith riders swept toward them.

Magdalys leapt from Dizz's saddle, crashing into General Grant from the back and throwing them both out of the way as the allosaurus roared and snapped at the sinornith in front of her, grasping one wing in her mighty jaws and wrenching him from the sky.

Magdalys felt the wind rush out of her body as she landed

on the uneven cobblestones with a nasty thwack. The whole world flashed bright white and then grew hazy. Magdalys was pretty sure she saw the other sinornith land on that bright red allosaurus neck with a terrifying screech, its jaws opened wide, all those glistening, lethal teeth on full display. Then General Grant heaved himself into a squat beside her, raising his pistol so it was almost point blank against the sinornith's chest, and a single shot cracked out just as everything became nothing at all.

CHAPTER THIRTY-FIVE
THE SAINT CHARLES HOTEL

THAT BUZZ.

Or was it a growl?

Either way, those paras were stampeding again, loping along with desperate, thundering strides across the valley, hills made of yellowed bone on either side.

They hooted and barked, and then they spoke in quiet, concerned tones to one another about politics and military strategy, and even from way up above them where she soared, Magdalys could somehow tell that their hands were human hands, pink and brown and long-fingered, and their lips were human lips.

And then the growling buzzing droning murmur grew louder and louder and suddenly the ground itself seemed to open in a gaping maw and the stampeding paras slipped in by

the hundreds, their voices, unperturbed, warbling on and on as they tumbled into the darkness.

Magdalys flew higher, glanced down, gasped in awe as the earth and grass peeled away from either side of the brand-new crater to reveal a gigantic set of very human teeth.

The hole kept getting bigger — or was she falling toward it? Either way, soon the world was in darkness and all she heard was that dissonant, chirping murmur until, ever so slowly, the twittering song of a morning bird accompanied a gentle breeze and the smell of magnolias and jasmine.

Magdalys blinked.

An ornate ceiling came into focus, all flowery plaster motifs and elaborate paisley wallpaper. New Orleans. She could already recognize that warm, swampy air and the hooting calls of so many dinos passing by on foot and overhead.

And beneath it all that never-ending murmur, which Magdalys had come to think of as a song unto itself. She didn't know if it should frighten or comfort her, but whatever it was, it wasn't going anywhere.

She was in a bed, and a dull ache pulsed through her, and by the soft gray light she guessed it was very early in the day. A brass frame rose above her and there was a shape clutching it, no, a figure, she realized, squinting through her aching, blurred vision. A microdact, its little claws grasping the crossbar, its wide eyes glaring into her own.

"Gah!" Magdalys yelled, wishing the thing gone, and with a screech the tiny beast flung across the room, bashed into

the far wall and then fluttered with a squawk to the top of a dresser, where it perched and eyed her angrily.

"So it's true then," a gruff voice rasped from the window.

Magdalys sat up.

General Ulysses S. Grant sat at a small desk, plume poised over a messy stack of papers. One of his legs had been swathed in bandages and was resting on a fancy pink ottoman that seemed utterly out of place beside the general's rumpled blue slacks and off-white button-down shirt.

"Good morning? Sir?" she said. "I'm . . ."

"Magdalys Roca," Grant finished for her, more or less nailing the pronunciation. He spoke with the long, matter-of-fact sigh that she'd come to expect from folks from the Midwestern states like Ohio and Illinois. His gruff face widened into a magnificent grin that then quickly vanished again behind that shabby brown beard. "I've heard all about you already. Mind if I smoke?"

"Uh, no. And what's true?"

He struck a match and lifted it to the cigar already perched between his lips. "I can't even get Giuseppe to fetch me a newspaper from the chair beside me."

"Giuseppe?"

Grant cocked an eyebrow and nodded at his microdact, who still scowled at Magdalys from atop the dresser. "You sent him across the room without moving a muscle."

Magdalys furrowed her brow. He was right — she hadn't even meant to, or realized she'd done it, but the creature had

startled her so much, the shock must've translated into a command that he had . . . been forced to obey. The idea gave her a chill. This was what those Confederate dinowranglers were doing, of course: mastering and dominating their mounts, making them servants instead of partners. That's not what Magdalys wanted to do.

Still.

She threw her legs over the side of the bed and stood. "Yes, it's true." It wasn't a bad skill to have handy in a bind. "What . . . what happened?"

"Well, for one thing," Grant said, letting a gigantic musty mountain of smoke out, "you saved my life, young lady."

"I . . . I did?"

"And Samantha's too, for which I'm eternally grateful, of course. Made my security detail look a touch incompetent though, so they may be a bit salty with you. But that was the Bog Marauders' play, it seems."

"Who?"

"The Bog Marauders are a paramilitary group of Confederate supporters who patrol the swamplands across southern Louisiana. They've been giving our troops a whole lot of trouble out in the wilds, but they hadn't been bold enough to strike within New Orleans." He twisted his mouth and sighed. "Until yesterday that is. That fellow we were chasing was Earl Shamus Dawson Drek."

"What a name," Magdalys said.

Grant nodded. "Indeed. We'd been tracking his moves as best we could for the past year, but what we didn't know until your intel came through was that he's a Knight of the Golden Circle. What they call a Class II Dinomaster."

Magdalys sat up very straight.

"Seems these Knights have been traveling to different hot zones, bolstering the combat troops or partisan guerrillas as needed by the Rebs. Causing political trouble in places like Kansas and Kentucky." He scowled. "Bad business. I was hoping to wing him at least and then bring him in for questioning."

"But?"

"That area of the Garden District he escaped into is well-to-do and white, I'm afraid, so when our boys got there for pursuit, nobody had seen anything." The general rolled his eyes. "Perils of a Union-controlled city in Confederate territory, you know. Drek has protection and he's probably back out in the Atchafalaya Swamplands by now." He looked up. "Anyway, they were certainly trying to kill me. And they would've too, if it hadn't been for you."

"Oh," Magdalys said. "I . . ."

Grant waved her wordlessness away. "That's alright, Magdalys, I never know what to say to people either. Wouldn't mind if folks just left me alone altogether, if we're being honest. But by the look of things, that's not going to happen anytime soon."

Magdalys shook her head. "No, it's probably not."

"Sheridan sent a letter along, you know," Grant said. "An excitable little fellow, that one, but he's not an easy man to impress."

Magdalys still didn't know what to say. She reached over to the tray of breakfast food someone had left on the bedside table and held one of the rolls out to Giuseppe, taking care not to accidentally demand he come to her. "I . . . I just want to find my brother."

Giuseppe eyed her suspiciously for a few moments, then flapped down to the foot of the bed.

"Yes," Grant drawled, "he mentioned that. I've sent my man Parker to make some inquiries about the Louisiana 9th."

Magdalys looked up, her heart racing, and Giuseppe took the opportunity to hop over and snatch the roll from her hand, then flap back to his perch on the bedframe.

"Quite a regiment," Grant continued. "They really came through for us at Milliken's Bend. Took a serious beating too. Up to that point, I hadn't been sure if . . ." His cigar-stained voice trailed off. If Negro troops would be of any use in battle, the rest of the sentence went. He didn't have to say it. "Well, you know."

"Did . . . do you . . ." Magdalys stuttered.

"Don't know anything yet, but I'll let you know as soon as I do." The general adjusted himself on the chair to face her more directly, cringing slightly as he moved. "But listen, Magdalys, if I may . . ."

"Yes, sir?"

"I've also been updated about the situation at Chattanooga."

Magdalys nodded and tried not to look away. She knew where this was going.

"I'm not going to lie and say the US government is fighting this war just to free your people," Grant said matter-of-factly. "In fact, there are a good number of folks up north who would just as well call it quits right now and let the South keep their slaves, as I'm sure you know."

She nodded, staring at him.

"And to be plain, at one time it seemed like the path to victory might include such a concession, and I was all for it if that's what it took to win this war." He frowned, shaking his head. "I'm not a savior, nor a liberator. Not an abolitionist, although I think the whole matter of slavery is a cursed endeavor."

Giuseppe flapped across the room and perched on Grant's shoulder, glancing uneasily out the window and then around the room.

"But that's no longer a possibility, and as many lives as it's cost, I do think the world will be a better place for it in the long run. We need to crush the South to end this rebellion, and that includes ending slavery. And we need your help to do it. All of you . . ." He waved his cigar in little circles, searching for the word. "Your people. But especially you, Magdalys."

She tightened her lips.

"I know it's not fair, to put that burden on one so young. Especially one who has already been through so much. I won't

pretend any of this is fair, or noble, or glorious. It's war, and it's ugly, and it'll snatch your whole soul away if you let it. And it's the world we've inherited, and I intend to make this place a better one than it was when I got here, and if you can help me do it, well, it'll be that much easier, is what I'm trying to say." He exhaled, seemed to deflate some now that he'd gotten that off his chest. "You've had a run-in with Miss Crawbell and her archaeops, I heard?"

Magdalys nodded.

"Then you know what we're up against. If the Knights of the Golden Circle are as well organized as your friends and the Pinkertons have told us, this whole war could be won or lost on their whim. I don't plan on letting that happen, and for that I need all the dinowranglers I can get to help me."

Magdalys felt a lump gather in her throat — the damp, heavy weight of disappointing yet another person who was doing everything they could to win this war. "I'm not..." She'd promised herself. She wouldn't drag any more lives into this sinking pit of a war with her. She wouldn't. And if she wasn't willing to wrangle dinos, what good was she to the Union cause? She was just some kid, was all. And anyway: She had to find her brother. And as soon as she signed up, she'd have to do whatever they told her. "I'm sorry, sir," she said in what sounded like a tiny, faraway whisper. "I just —"

"You're worried about having to do what you're told, aren't you?"

"Well..."

"That you'll never see your friends again, or your brother, because once you sign up you'll be beholden to whatever order your given, on pain of death."

"That's definitely part of it, yeah," Magdalys admitted. It was nice to have someone else say it for her, even if it kinda sounded like a threat. And anyway, what good did it do? The general understanding her predicament didn't change it.

Grant leaned forward, winced, then squinted directly into Magdalys's eyes. On his shoulder, Giuseppe did the same. "What if I were to tell you that you could be in charge of your own special regiment of dinowarriors."

Magdalys blinked at him.

"A team that you could put together yourself and have total authority over, answering only to me. Let's call it a counterbalance to the Knights of the Golden Circle. Heck, you can even name it if you want. I'm sure you'd think of something better than anything I could come up with."

"Is that even . . . possible?" Magdalys managed. "I mean, do you . . . can . . ." There was no way to ask the question without sounding like it was undercutting the president's favorite fighting general.

Grant leaned back, chuckled. Giuseppe kept squinting at Magdalys, but she thought just maybe he was smiling now. "You mean" — he pulled on his cigar — "how could I possibly have the authority to do such an audacious maneuver?"

"I . . ."

He smiled and shook his head. "It's a good question. As it

happens, the president has seen fit to name me commander in chief of this entire army." The general looked uncharacteristically pleased with himself. "A brand-new position, in fact, with unprecedented powers. Just went through Congress. Probably hasn't even hit the wires yet."

"Whoa," Magdalys said. "Congrats."

"Heh." He nodded his acknowledgment, long crow's feet stretching away from his smiling eyes. Then his face grew serious again. "I don't like it, mind you. I don't mean the position — that's fine. I don't like young people being in the line of fire. Not now, not ever. But when I accepted the position I told the president I'd do whatever it takes to win, that I'd meet any force they brought to bear on us with an even greater fire that would smash them into submission, and that's exactly what I intend to do. Now, we may have another dinowarrior of your skill within the ranks of this army, but if we do I'm not aware of it and we simply don't have the luxury of being able to go looking for him right now."

Giuseppe squawked and flew over to land on Magdalys's shoulder.

"Or her," Grant said. "And anyway, I imagine you in more of an administrative capacity. Overseeing and training and such."

A moment passed.

"So, what do you say, Magdalys?" the general said. "How would you like to have the full weight of the US Army at your back so we can stop these Rebels in their tracks?"

"I don't know what to say," Magdalys said.

Grant nodded. "Good. It's a big decision. You shouldn't rush it. Giuseppe."

The microdact squeezed Magdalys's shoulder once and then stuttered across the room, snatched a sealed envelope off the desk, and delivered it to Magdalys.

"See," Grant said. "Exactly what I wanted him to do. That never happens. He's trying to impress you."

"What's this?" Magdalys asked.

"A document stating exactly what I just said to you in no uncertain terms. If you should decide to join us, just show it to the nearest commanding officer and they'll sort you out. All I ask is that you don't tear it up. Could come in handy."

A knock came at the door and then some scuffling noises. Magdalys pocketed the envelope. "Ah, sir?" someone called from the other side. "There are some, ah, people . . . here."

"Come in," Grant said gruffly.

The door flew open and Mapper and Cymbeline rushed in, followed by Octave and a tall, stout officer with light brown skin and a wispy goatee. "Magdalys!" Mapper yelled. "You're alright!" He rushed over and threw his arms around her while Cymbeline stood by, her expression sad.

That wasn't like Mapper.

"What is it?" Magdalys asked. "Where's Amaya?"

"She's gone," Mapper said, and squeezed her even tighter.

CHAPTER THIRTY-SIX
PLANS AND PARTINGS

"**AND THEN SHE** just..." Mapper shook his head, staring at his hands. "...just...." He shrugged. "She gave me a big hug and said she was sorry and walked out the door. That was it."

They stood on either side of Amaya's empty bed. In the other room, Cymbeline, Grant, and the officer, Colonel Ely Parker, conferred quietly.

"You gonna open it or do I have to do it for you?" Mapper said, nodding at a crisp envelope on the pillow with Magdalys's name written on it.

She scrunched up her face, somehow dreading what she'd find. The scrap of paper inside just had three words:

Tamaulipas — Esmeralda Crusher

"What's that mean?" Mapper demanded. He'd hurried over to where Magdalys was standing and was reading over her shoulder. "Is that a name? Sounds like a name kinda."

"I have no idea," she said. Was it the place Amaya's mother had whispered to her before she'd disappeared? Had Amaya gone there instead of off to find her father? The information felt sacred somehow, something she wasn't even supposed to tell Mapper. Not yet anyway. And she had no idea what to make of Esmeralda Crusher.

"Tamaulipas looks Spanish," Mapper said, his voice harried. "You speak Spanish, right, Mags?"

She shook her head. "Yeah, but . . . not perfectly and it's nothing I recognize. I . . . look, whatever the word means, what this really means is she's gone." The Dactyl Hill Squad was truly in the wind now, scattered like seeds across the battle-torn country. Magdalys sniffled. Everything they'd built with each other — this war had just shredded it to pieces.

"We gotta . . ." Mapper threw his hands up. "We gotta go look for her. She might be —"

"No," Magdalys said. "She wasn't snatched off the street, Mapper. She left."

"I know." He hugged Magdalys. "I get it. But . . . why?"

"She . . . she's doing what her mom wanted her to," Magdalys said. "Something she has to do. And it won't be easy, whatever it is. But we can't go after her, Mapper. I . . . I'm sorry." She put a hand on his shoulder and he hung his head and covered his eyes.

"We're all over the place," Mapper sighed. "I didn't think this would happen. Not this fast, anyway."

"I know," Magdalys said. "Me neither." She knew she'd told Amaya to go, but it still hurt. Way more than she'd thought it would. She tucked the note in her pocket. She'd have to figure out whatever it was Amaya was trying to tell her later.

Mapper looked up. "Are you okay, though? We were worried about you."

Cymbeline came in and sat on the bed beside her. "We were really worried. You were . . ." — the actress's eyebrows rose and then she tipped her head — "*very* brave."

Magdalys shrugged. "I'm alright. Aches and pains."

"They said you might have a concussion," Cymbeline said.

Now Grant limped in on a crutch, his finger fidgeting endlessly with the buttons on the jacket he'd just pulled on, Colonel Parker just behind him. "Ah, young people?"

Magdalys stood, because she wasn't sure what else to do with herself. "What is it?"

"We . . ." Words seemed to fail him again, and Magdalys was about to yell at him to spit it out when he managed to do just that. "Your brother's medical convoy was attacked while they were en route to New Orleans."

Magdalys gulped and her legs seemed to give out from under her. She felt Cymbeline's steadying hand on her shoulder, felt the bed beneath her, felt a wide, impossible emptiness stretch out inside her.

"He and his fellow soldiers have been declared missing in action, but . . ."

"We have to go find him!" Magdalys blurted out.

"The area where they went missing," Colonel Parker said, stepping up beside the general, "the Atchafalaya Swamplands, is a vast, almost impossible terrain that is completely under the control of the Bog Marauders."

"That's where you said Earl Shamus Dawson Drek probably escaped to," Magdalys said.

Grant nodded. "Indeed. And . . ." He looked around, flustered. "It is said to be haunted by the phantoms of long-dead dinosaurs. But that's just silliness, of course."

"And the convoy was lost over a week ago, I'm afraid." Parker shook his head. "I don't think —"

"I don't care what you think," Magdalys snapped. She was standing again, her finger raised, aimed directly at Parker. Cymbeline's hand stayed on her shoulder, and Magdalys felt like without it she might just float away on a torrent of her own wrath. "It doesn't matter how many Marauders there are or what the terrain is, we *have* to —"

"No," General Grant said, not unkindly. "I'm sorry, Magdalys. I can't authorize a rescue mission into the swamplands. I've ordered Sherman to march overland for Chattanooga and bring all available corps from the Army of the Mississippi."

"But . . ."

"And Emperor Maximilian is massing troops at Matamoros

on the Mexican border and they'll tilt things toward the Rebels if they have a chance, so General Banks has already marched out with whatever units he has left to deal with that and the mosasaurus-riding blockade runners." He shook his head. "I'm sorry," he said again, his sad eyes meeting hers.

She turned. Shrugged. Shook her head. She wouldn't cry. This wasn't the time for that. She had a mission to prepare for. "Doesn't matter," she said, heading for the door. "You may need my help to get the job done" — she shot Grant a long, sharp glare — "but I don't need yours."

The door slammed on a cacophony of yells and questions behind her.

The churches, mansions, and run-down shacks of the Garden District stretched to either side of her. The buildings got taller and fancier and then slid back into dilapidated one-stories, on and on throughout the city.

The sun had risen on a muggy purplish morning as huge tortoises lumbered up and down Saint Charles Avenue with dark green streetcars hitched to their harnesses. They stopped every few blocks to let off and collect passengers; nodded solemnly as they passed one another.

A bakery opened its doors on the far side of the block, and the smell of fresh bread reached all the way up to where Magdalys stood on the hotel roof with Dizz, Beans, and

Grappler perched on either side of her. She thought she'd come up here to cry, but no tears had come. Maybe she didn't have any left; all that was left inside her was fire — that never-ending flame she'd first felt flying over that Tennessee plantation.

But even the fire had been reduced to a quiet, crackling sizzle. She'd told it to cool and it had, tamped down by the shock of Cymbeline's lies and then the confusion of all that army protocol and tough decisions and the suddenness of battle. And with no tears and barely any fire, all Magdalys felt was empty.

Sol had been killed before her very eyes. There was nothing even left of him, no body to send home or bury. The youngest Card had died that same day, and countless others. Sabeen and Two Step were trapped in a strange city, surrounded by enemies who wanted to kill or enslave them. Amaya had run off to find out what twisted destiny her father had in mind for her, and how it all fit into her missing mother's plan.

The US Army was on the verge of total destruction, it seemed. And Montez . . . Montez was lost in the Atchafalaya Swamplands, probably dead.

Magdalys shook her head. She'd come all this way, crossed the whole country from north to south just about, only to find that he was still gone, just gone.

And no one would go look for him except her.

She heard the rooftop door creak open and then slam closed — someone coming to convince her it was alright somehow, that she should just give up and go along with Grant to Chattanooga.

"Magdalys," Cymbeline said from behind her.

Magdalys shook her head. "I'm not going."

"I know," Cymbeline said. "I'm not asking you to go. The general knows you're not going too."

She raised her eyebrows. "He does?"

Cymbeline came up beside her; Grappler edged a few inches over to make room. "He's no fool, Magdalys. And neither am I, by the way. I don't think you should go out there by yourself, but I know I can't stop you. I don't think anyone could stop you from doing anything you've set your mind to, Magdalys Roca. And I'm not totally sure that's a good thing."

Magdalys acknowledged the point with a surly shrug.

"I don't know what you're going to do," Cymbeline said, "or how you think you're going to do it. But I know what I have to do. I have to help this army win this war."

Magdalys wished it could feel so simple for her, and the wish tasted bitter, wrong somehow. Because it wasn't simple for Cymbeline either, or Hannibal, or any of them. And still — the feeling remained, worming its way through her thoughts without permission. "They're taking you with them back to Tennessee?"

"I have orders, Magdalys. New ones. I'll be taking the general to Tennessee, yes, and then I have to head back up north from there. There's an operative in New York they need me to . . . handle."

Magdalys wanted to scream but instead she just leaned against Cymbeline and put her head on her shoulder.

Cymbeline wrapped an arm around her. "I'm sorry," she whispered.

"Don't be," Magdalys said. "I understand, just like you understand me."

"Yeah. Doesn't make it any easier, does it?"

Magdalys shook her head, sniffed. "Nope."

A moment passed, that never-ending murmur rising and falling amidst the sounds of the city waking up for another day. Magdalys reached out with her mind, past the clutter of commuters and beggars, the snorts of giant tortoises and grumbling dinos.

There.

She turned to Cymbeline. "Listen," she said, found herself smiling. Somehow, the path was clear. She didn't know what it meant or why, but she knew what to do. At least in this moment, if no other. This must've been what Hannibal had felt like, carrying that secret and then suddenly seeing how he could put it to work.

"What?" Cymbeline asked.

"I have something for you."

Then yells erupted from below and a huge shadow passed over them. Cymbeline gazed up, mouth open.

Magdalys's smile grew bigger. "Some*one*, I should say."

"Stella," Cymbeline gasped as the magnificent pteranodon landed with a thud on the rooftop and looked around languidly. The three dactyls squawked a joyful song and waddled over to nuzzle her.

"How else were you going to make it back there in time to save Chattanooga?" Magdalys said.

"But —"

Magdalys cut her off. "These guys are all I'll need."

"You mean all *we'll* need," Mapper said from the doorway.

"Wait," Magdalys said. "What?"

'I'm coming with you, Mags." He was lugging a whole bunch of saddlebags. "Did you really think I'd just let you run off to save the day on your own? I said I had your back from the beginning and I meant it. Now give me a hand with these ammo cases General Grant asked us to hold on to for him while he's away!"

CHAPTER THIRTY-SEVEN
INTO THE SWAMPLANDS

THE DARK GREEN and murky brown forest swamps blurred past beneath Magdalys and Mapper. New Orleans had become a scattering of cabins and occasional clustered tents as they flew west, and eventually the wilderness became the world and sparkling bayous snaked through vast oak and pine forests.

"Atchafalaya," Mapper said, but Magdalys could tell his usual excitement was dimmed some.

"Go on," she said, after a few moments passed of just the whistling wind and burps, chirps, and yelps of swamp life around them. "I'm listening."

"It's a Choctaw word. But there are tons of different nations besides the Choctaw that were and are on this part of the state: the Houma, the Chitimacha. . . ."

"How —"

"Books, Magdalys." Mapper's voice wasn't cold exactly, but it certainly wasn't warm either. "We had a whole library at the orphanage, remember? And sometimes the newspapers report on different nations around the country."

"Gotya."

That murmur only grew louder the further they got from the city: a deep, chortling burble that sometimes swung upward into an all-out wail. Magdalys had just gotten used to it. The sound was either the collected calls of the many, many dinos of the Louisiana bayou country or it was . . . she shuddered. Grant had said the Atchafalaya was haunted, but he was right: that was silliness.

Still.

The swamp gave way suddenly to an expanse of trimmed grass and hedges. A few busted shacks speckled the edge of the property and two grandiose pillared mansions faced each other from either end.

Magdalys shuddered, felt that familiar rage start to build up in her again, but this time when she told it to go it listened right away, eased back to a sparkly simmer and then dispersed entirely, leaving only sadness in its wake.

"I know," Mapper said, watching her face go from clenched to resigned. "Me too."

She glanced across the open sky to her friend.

It had been a while since she'd really taken the time to look at Mapper, or anyone for that matter — everything kept

happening so fast, pausing seemed like a luxury. But no one was shooting at them right now; in fact, no one was around at all. Besides the never-ending murmur and the hoots and caws of swamp dinos below, they were alone. The world was theirs, and, of course, very much not at the same time.

Mapper smiled a sad smile. His face looked older somehow, more solid. The past few weeks had shoved them all much closer to being grown women and men than Magdalys wanted to think about.

"You really . . ." she started, then just sighed. She would say he didn't have to come and he would say of course he did. What was the point? "Thank you," she finally settled on. "I'm not sure what I'd do without you, Mapper."

He tipped the Union cap that Octave had given him before they left. "Anytime, Mags. We should probably give them a rest soon, huh?"

"Yeah." She'd been about to suggest that anyway. Grappler's weariness had begun tugging at her and she knew they'd all need to be careful of the dactyls' flagging energy if they wanted to get out of this alive. Or be ready for an attack.

"What's the . . . ah, plan, by the way?" Mapper asked as they circled toward the treetops.

Magdalys laughed ruefully. "Ah, Mapper. Always with the plans." She shook her head. "We fly around till we find my brother and then we get him and leave."

"And the other soldiers he's with? We gonna leave them behind?"

"I . . ."

Mapper sighed. "Ah, Mag-D. Never with the plans." They brought Beans and Grappler down on a sturdy branch and Dizz flapped down with the saddlebags a few moments later.

Magdalys started unstrapping the bags so Dizz could rest. "Ugh! You have one, don't you? See — this is why no one comes up with plans around you, Mapper. Because why bother? You're just going to come up with one anyway. This is just like in Manhattan. . . ."

"When I saved you and Miss Du Monde *and* made sure that evil guy's fancy office got a generous helping of pteropoop?"

"Well . . ."

"Greatest plan ever, honestly. You're welcome."

Magdalys rolled her eyes. "Alright, alright, what you got, man?"

"Actually, not much. But I figure, wherever they are, they're probably gonna need ammo and supplies, right? So we got those. And there is a rail line not too far outside the Atchafalaya Swamplands, buuut it's Confederate controlled right now, so that might get sticky. I figure the best way to get a bunch of people back through Rebel territory to New Orleans is on the water. A lot of these bayous lead to major riverways. And then there's the ocean, or gulf technically. If we travel overland we could make it to the coast in a few days and then . . . er, we'd have to figure out something from there, but with your mad dinowrangling skills . . . Mags?"

A plume of smoke rose over the canopy of trees up ahead. It didn't look like an explosion, and Magdalys hadn't heard anything. But then what was it? Magdalys started loading the saddlebags onto Grappler.

"What are you doing?" Mapper demanded.

"That could be him . . . them," Magdalys said. "We gotta —"

Mapper's hand wrapped around Magdalys's wrist and she swung around, her mouth already curled into a growl.

"Don't even think of telling me off," Mapper snapped, and the words caught in Magdalys's throat. "It's one thing to get all righteous with a Union officer and then storm away in a huff. But I'm your friend and I've come all this way with you and . . ." Tears filled his eyes; he wiped them away angrily. "And I'm not about to let you run headlong into what might be a whole nest of Bog Marauders on a worn-out dactyl with no escape plan."

Magdalys blinked at him. He was right. She knew he was right. Still, her whole body thrummed with that ravenous hunger to do something. Anything to make this whole mess be over so she could get her brother and get out of there. And hopefully not have to get any more dinos or people killed in the process.

"He could be . . ." she whispered, then closed her eyes and let her fists unclench, her snarl simmer away, her frenzy disperse.

"I know," Mapper sniffled. "Slow down. Take a breath."

She did — a long deep one that eased her aching mind some.

"Sit."

"So bossy," Magdalys grumbled, but she did it anyway, easing herself down beside Grappler on the winding oak tree branch. Spanish moss dangled in wispy beards around them, swaying slightly in the thick marshy breeze.

Mapper sat next to her, put his head on her shoulder. "Do you think she'll be alright?" he asked after a moment.

The snarls and hoots of swamp dinos filled the air over that sweet breeze and the still-churning murmur.

"I don't know," Magdalys said.

ATCHAFALAYA TIROTEO

THE SUN SAT smack in the middle of an almost cloudless sky as Magdalys and Mapper soared over the swamplands toward the billowing smoke.

Magdalys tried to slow her racing heart, failed over and over. It was Grappler's turn to carry the supplies. Magdalys had let Mapper stay on Beans, since they seemed to understand each other better than anyone else understood either of them, and she rode Dizz.

Mapper had insisted they have their carbines out and ready, but the thing just felt like a heavy, awkward burden in her hand. Magdalys hated guns. She'd been pretty ambivalent about them for most of her life, and during the riots, Cymbeline's shotty had saved their butts more than a few times. But after hearing that barrage after barrage of musket

fire during Chickamauga and seeing what happened to Sol . . . she couldn't stand the feel of firepower against her skin.

Still, she wouldn't turn Mapper down, not after all he'd done for her. And anyway, he was probably right. Again.

Mapper waved at her from up ahead and then veered off suddenly to the side.

She urged Dizz forward and took in the view below.

A group of wooden houses stood on stilts over the murky water of the bayou. On a nearby island, several men wearing brown and gray conferred quietly on sinorniths beside a smoking pile of trash and foliage. The Bog Marauders. Magdalys and Mapper skirted the edge of the clearing, but one of the sinorniths let out a shrill caw and all the men looked up. "Hey!" one of them yelled. "Come back here!"

The shrieks of pursuing dinos filled the air. *The sinornith is a glider*, Dr. Barlow Sloan had written in the Dinoguide. (Sloan reminded her of that surgeon who knew him, Pennbroker, who reminded her of Two Step, who she prayed was okay and didn't hate her, but there was no time for that now!) *They launch high into the air and then come sailing down on unsuspecting prey, immobilizing and killing them with a single venom-filled bite that causes slow agonizing death. Although essentially obedient, sinorniths are incredibly stupid and make terrible pets.*

She looked over at Mapper. His brow creased low over his eyes and his fists clenched the reins. They could outrun these things for a little while, sure, but soon they'd have to stop and let the dactyls rest. He turned to her, nodded, then raised

his carbine, balancing his elbow on one of his knees the way Octave did, and started shooting.

Magdalys glared into Beans's wide eyes. *Stay steady, B,* she thought toward him. *You too, Dizz.* She sent Grappler flying low and out of the way.

Cr-crack!! sang Mapper's carbine.

Then she scooched back in the saddle and turned herself around, breath coming faster with each passing second, raised one knee in front of her and placed her own elbow on it, leveling the carbine at the riders surging toward them across the open sky.

One let out a scream and tumbled into the forest below as his mount flapped in a lopsided spiral. The other four had drawn their own weapons, old muskets from the look of them, and now muzzles flashed amidst the crackle of return fire.

Mapper shot again, missing, and then again, and another Bog Marauder was flung backward and into the trees.

A bullet screamed past Magdalys. She felt its horrible whispering whistle as it went, just inches from her face.

And then she was pulling the trigger again and again as the whole sky caught fire around her and the world became an endless succession of bangs and billowing smoke.

Up ahead, a rider screamed and fell and Mapper was shooting too and then one of the sinorniths screeched, its wing shredded by several shots, and plummeted toward the trees.

Magdalys blinked through the smoke. Something was burning her hands. The carbine. She threw it down on the

saddle, almost leaping backward away from it. Had she been hit? She glanced down at her body. No. Of course not. She would've known if she'd been shot, wouldn't she? She had no idea.

Another crack sounded from across the sky. She'd thought they were all gone. The last Bog Marauder had let off a final, parting shot and was turning his mount around, guiding it into a smooth glide back into the forest.

She was alive. She'd taken life. Probably. She glanced over at Mapper. He nodded toward a nearby oak tree that spread over the other trees like a huge multiheaded sauropod.

Yes. Somewhere to rest. Good idea. But he was alive. He hadn't been hit. They had made it, this far at least. She guided Dizz to the closest branch, her hands still trembling, her breath finally slowing, and set him down. Mapper perched Beans alongside her and Grappler flew up from behind them.

Magdalys slid off the saddle and stood on the thick branch, blinking.

"Hey," Mapper said, climbing down next to her and putting a hand on her shoulder. "Hey."

Magdalys nodded. She was okay. Sort of. She would be. She knew that, somehow.

She knew this moment would come; it had to. And she'd wondered if she'd even survive it, and she had. She had. She looked up at Mapper, trying to get her hands to stop trembling.

"It's alright," he said. "You're alright. You did what you had to do."

Magdalys let out a sad, jittery chuckle. "Pretty sure I said the exact same thing to Two Step when he was all messed up after he shot that guy in Dactyl Hill."

Mapper nodded. "I believe I was asleep at that particular moment. I did thank him later though. Thought it might help him cope a little better, but it just made it worse to bring it up again."

"Yeah," Magdalys said, relieved to be talking about something else, anything else. "Wait, why are you so calm after your first time taking a life?"

Mapper raised his eyebrows. "What makes you think that was my first time?"

Magdalys opened her mouth but nothing came out except a soft gurgle. "What?" she finally managed.

Mapper shrugged and looked away. "I came up on the streets, Mags. The streets of New York. I was born in the Raptor Claw. I wasn't out there robbing random citizens or nothing — I was fighting for my life. Where I'm from, you don't get to be the one who walks away alive without some blood on your hands. I'm not saying I'm cool with it, or that I don't think about it a lot. But I did what I had to do to survive."

"I . . ."

"Why do you think I always have to know exactly where I am? Did you think it was just a random cool skill I developed for fun?"

Magdalys just stood there. That was *exactly* what she had thought.

Mapper laughed. "When people get lost in the Raptor Claw they get found the next morning as a body. That's it. So I swore I'd always know where I was. And turned out the habit was hard to kick, even when I was safe and sound in the orphanage."

"I . . . I don't really know what to say," Magdalys said.

Mapper smiled. "Then don't say anything. It'd probably be corny anyway. I know how you feel; that's what matters." His face got serious again. "The real question is: Why didn't you do your dinomagic back there and just make them all fall off like ol' boy almost did to me back in Tennessee?"

"I . . ." Magdalys faltered. Truth was: It hadn't even occurred to her to wrangle them. She'd already managed to put her own skills so far out of her mind. And anyway, she'd promised herself. "I'm trying not to?" she said, but it didn't come out right at all.

Mapper cocked his head. "Trying not to use the one skill you have that might keep us alive?"

"No, it's just . . . I . . . That night of the battle . . . Elizabeth Crawbell and . . . I've never been bested before." She shook her head. "I don't know if . . . and . . ."

Mapper tensed, then softened, shook his head. "Sometimes I forget you're just a kid like the rest of us."

"What's that supposed to mean?"

He fixed her with a stern look. "It's not losing you're afraid of."

"What's *that* supposed to mean?" she demanded.

Gunfire erupted from out in the swamplands ahead. Magdalys looked up, heart thundering. A few scattered musket shots became a cascade of blasts rippling over the trees. Mapper was already climbing onto Beans, scanning the horizon with a concerned frown. Magdalys grabbed Dizz's reins and heaved herself up. She thought it was coming from somewhere beyond a series of jungly hills rising out of the bayou water.

"That way!" Magdalys yelled. They zoomed out across the treetops.

CHAPTER THIRTY-NINE
JUH

FAR UP AHEAD, the shooting tapered off and then started up again.

Montez. Why else would there be a firefight out here in the middle of nowhere? And if not Montez, at least what was left of the Louisiana 9th. It *had* to be. She was so close!

Beneath them, the hills rose and fell like a giant forest-covered tide that had been frozen in place.

Magdalys took Dizz higher until the whole of Atchafalaya seemed to spread beneath her. The hills went on and on and right up to the edge of a lake, and there, on the far side, a crowd of figures surrounded a decrepit pink mansion. Another series of shots rang out and Magdalys saw smoke rise into the air. "I see it!" she yelled. "Come on!"

Montez. The 9th had survived the ambush somehow, and they'd made their way through the wilderness and found shelter in that big busted old house. And now they were hemmed in by the Marauders, fighting for their lives. It made sense!

"Our friends are back," Mapper called, nodding behind them. "And there are more of 'em." A full two dozen sinornith riders glided toward them, screaming that Rebel howl. They were a good ways back but approaching fast. Magdalys shook her head and urged Dizz onward.

Montez. His name a pulse within her, matched only by that buzzing murmur that seemed to rise around them the deeper they flew into the swamplands. They banked sideways to avoid an especially tall hill and then swooped over a swampy field and headed toward the lake. Microdacts fluttered here and there, some of them probably carrying messages between the Marauders.

"There!" someone yelled from below. "Stop them!"

Magdalys barely had time to look before gunshots ripped through the air around them. Grappler squealed and fell into a swirling dive up ahead. "No!" Magdalys yelled, sending Dizz into a swerve after her.

Montez. She was so close. She wouldn't fail him. Not when she'd come so far.

"Mapper!" Magdalys yelled. "Head for that hill!" Grappler had steadied her dive some but still careened listlessly downward at an ever-sharpening angle. Magdalys swung Dizz

underneath her, his tummy just grazing the tops of the trees below, and pulled Grappler onto the saddle. The dactyl collapsed against her with a sigh. "Okay, girl," Magdalys whispered. "I got you." Dizz wouldn't be able to carry them both for much longer.

"I'm coming!" Mapper called from behind. A few more shots burst out and whizzed past her into the sky. The tangled underbrush sloped upward, became forest and then a towering hill. Still clutching Grappler, Magdalys brought Dizz down through the canopy and they landed in a mulchy grove beside a winding bayou.

"Is she alright?" Mapper said, bringing Beans down nearby and running over as Magdalys eased Grappler to the ground.

"I don't know," she said. A bullet had passed through her right shoulder near where the wing connected and burst out the other side. The holes weren't too big and the bleeding wasn't bad, but that didn't mean she'd be okay. "I don't know," Magdalys said again.

Mapper bit his lip. "We gotta . . ." He looked around, drawing his carbine.

"I know," Magdalys said. "I just don't . . . I don't know what to do."

Juhjuhjuhjuhjuhjuhjuhjuhjuhjuhjuhjuhjuhjuhjuhjuh went the never-ending murmur in her ears. *Montez*, sang her broken heart. Both siren songs had grown even louder and clearer once they'd touched down on the swamplands, and Magdalys could barely think straight.

"What is it?" Mapper asked.

Magdalys shook her head, squinting through the rising and falling tide of noise within her. "Some dino . . . chatter . . . might just be that the ones out here are . . . louder."

Mapper frowned. "Whoever shot us down will be —"

"I know," Magdalys said. What Mapper had left unspoken boomed through her: She would need to wrangle some help if they were going to get out of there alive. "Maybe Grappler and Beans will have to take turns . . ."

JUHjuhjuhjuhjuhjuhjuhjuhjuhjuhJUHjuhjuhjuhjuhJUHjuhjuh

It sounded like some cruel swamp god was mocking her.

"Uh-oh," Mapper said. Magdalys followed his pointing finger. A single, rippled semicircle cut the dark bayou water. It was headed their way. Another fin emerged beside it. Then another. They were striated with shades of brown and dark green and topped with sharp notches.

Mapper took a step back from the edge of the water. "We gotta get Grappler loaded back up on —"

"Already on it," Magdalys said, heaving the inert dactyl on top of Beans and strapping her in with one of the cords. When she turned back, the fins were closer and there were what looked like bamboo shoots gliding along through the water behind each one. "What are those?"

"I don't know," Mapper said, "but let's fly."

A caw sounded above them and the dark shapes of sinorniths crisscrossed the sky overhead.

Something way too close to her growled and then a long

toothy snout and two beady yellow eyes emerged from the water in front of that fin, followed by a spiny neck and three-fingered claws. Another head emerged beside it, then a third, and all three lifted up out of the bayou, revealing their thick bodies and the tall sail-like fin stretching across their backs. Spinosaurs.

Each wore a metal collar with a chain leading into the water. With a splash, three soaking-wet men rose from the swamp. They'd been clutching those bamboo shoots in their mouths, breathing through them.

JuhjuhjuhJUHjuhjuhjuhjuh the forest caterwauled within her, but it wasn't any louder now than it had been, so it couldn't be these foul creatures.

"Well, well, well," one of the men said, shaking his head.

"Run!" Mapper yelled, and then a shot rang out and the man who'd spoken flew backward with a shocked look on his face and splashed into the swamp. The spinosaur he'd had on the chain launched forward and Magdalys tensed her face, reaching out ever so slightly.

Locked and blocked. Someone was manipulating these dinos. Earl Shamus Dawson Drek. It had to be. She took another step back, glancing around. Sinorniths landed in the branches above, but she couldn't make out if any had riders through the branches and glaring sunlight.

The spinosaur lunged, snapping. Mapper shot again, blasting it in the leg, and then again as Magdalys and the dactyls backed away up the sloping hill.

"Mapper!" Magdalys yelled over the gunfire. "Come on!"

He let off two more shots. The spinosaurs had splashed out of the way and two of the men were simply gone, swallowed by the swamp, while the third hid behind a tree rising out of the water.

"Mapper!" she yelled again.

Mapper shot once more, the bullet smashing into the tree, and then turned and ran.

"Where do we go?" he yelled.

Magdalys didn't know. She had no answers, only sheer terror and the never-ending *juhJUHjuh* of the swamp around her and the sheer magnetic force of her brother's name, tugging at her from closer than it had been since she'd seen him last. "Up," she gasped. At least from there they'd get a view of what was going on and maybe see somewhere they could take shelter.

The crackling of branches sounded from somewhere above and behind them — those sinorniths getting ready to attack, surely. She pulled out her carbine, hating it, needing it, hating to need it, and fired up at the trees.

Mapper reached her and glanced back too. The dactyls scrambled ahead. "Keep climbing," he said as the hill grew steeper. "We can see what things look like from the top."

One of the spinosaurs snarled, already clambering after them, and Magdalys heard the splashing of several more emerging from the water and angry hoots and growls calling back and forth. They were coming. Drek was orchestrating a

whole deadly symphony of dinos to close in around them. And he was doing it all from some safe hiding place. The coward!

Magdalys seethed at the thought. This Confederate, this self-anointed Knight, would destroy them without even lifting a finger or having to show himself.

No.

The sizzling embers popped and snarled inside her.

Montez.

Below, the foliage rustled.

JUHjuhjuhjuhJUHjuhjuhJUHjuhjuhJUHjuhjuhJUHjuhJUH juhJUHjuhJUH. It was getting louder now. Magdalys and Mapper reached the top of the hill, shoving through a grove of bushes and dangling vines behind the dactyls, and stopped to catch their breath.

Up ahead was the lake, and beyond it that decrepit pink mansion where she was sure her brother was holed up with his comrades, he had to be! There were a lot more Bog Marauders surrounding it than she'd thought though — had to be at least a hundred of 'em. She could hear the crackle of the muskets and see an occasional muzzle flash from the broken windows of the mansion. She tried not to imagine Montez in there somewhere, taking cover as bullets blasted around him through those old wooden walls.

A crowd of shapes filled the air above the lake though: sinorniths. The Marauders around the mansion must've sent their mounts to help Drek finish her and Mapper off. The dinos hurled skyward, wings spread, and then sailed down,

landing on small islands in the lake and launching up again, closer and closer.

Somewhere nearby, Drek lurked.

Just a little down the hill, the spinosaur snarls grew louder.

Magdalys glanced around, fear rising up within her amidst the sizzle of a newly birthed flame.

JUHjuhJUHjuhJUHjuhJUHjuhJUHjuhJUH

Images of her own death, of Mapper's, flashed through her mind. She tried to shake them away but it was all she could see. Those sinorniths, their gnashing teeth and glinting eyes — all it would take was one bite. And they had almost reached the hill where Magdalys stood now; she could make out the striations along their dank feathered wings, those claws. They would all be under Drek's powerful dinomastery by now — it was no use trying to get at them.

But maybe . . . if she could reach some other dino.

Beyond the panic, a sorrow rose up in her. She'd barely been able to keep her promise more than a couple days.

It came to survival. That was all there was to it, really. They'd forced her hand. She passed Mapper her carbine. "Just try and buy me a little time," she said, and he nodded, face tense, frown severe. As she closed her eyes, the last thing she saw was Mapper turning both barrels toward the sky.

KaBLAM kaBLAM!! Blam! Blamblamblam!

With everything she had, Magdalys reached. She imagined hundreds and hundreds of reptiles clambering through the woods toward them.

*JUHJUHJUHJUHJUHJUHJUHJUHJUHJUHJUHJUH
JUHJUHJUH*

More dinos than she could even grasp. She reached out
even further with her mind than she had before, linking with
that ever-rising murmur that had been growing inside her
since they'd approached New Orleans.

And then she reached further, felt herself coming unmoored
from her own body as the *JUHJUHJUH*s rose around her,
within her, and then the soil itself seemed to take a breath and
cede away, welcoming the tendrils of her mind that burrowed
through them, uprooting ancient, forgotten relics and impossible shapes amidst the churn of swamp water and tree roots
and all that life . . .

*JUHJUHJUHJUHJUHJUHJUHJUHJUHJUHJUHJUH
JUHJUH*

It became everything: sight sound feel smell.

All that power — there had to be dinos all around them,
surely. And they'd poke their heads between the trees and then
flush down the hillside and out into the sky and overwhelm
the spinosaurs below and sinorniths above.

But when she opened her eyes, the surrounding forest was
still empty. They were all alone.

Then the ground beneath them began to shake.

CHAPTER FORTY
FIRE

JUHJUHJUHJUHJUHJUHJUHJUHJUHJUH
The murmur grew to a yell; it seemed to open up inside her, carve a whole new sparkling expanse within her.

"What's happening?" Mapper yelled.

JUHJUHJUHJUHJUHJUHJUHJUHJUH

Magdalys tried to steady herself against a tree but the whole thing uprooted and went crashing down the hillside. The sinorniths pulled back in a scattered panic, suddenly without a safe landing area.

Beans and Dizz were huddled together while Grappler, still strapped to Dizz's back, glanced around nervously. Great chunks of soil dislodged themselves on either side of them and cascaded off the hill, taking trees and bushes down with them

and splashing into the bayou along with a rumbling pile of boulders.

"Hold on!" Magdalys called, finding another, larger tree and pulling Mapper over to it. A family of herons took flight, shrieking as they lifted off. Then the whole front part of the hill gave way before them and Magdalys and Mapper stared out at the open sky.

JUH!!!!

The murmuring burst into a sudden fierce blast that seemed to echo out across the swamp around them.

"Uh, Mags," Mapper said.

Magdalys looked around. "I think . . ." The hill had taken on a moist, dark green shine where the soil had fallen away. It sloped down around them in lumpy, shining mounds. "I think this isn't a hill," she finally blurted out.

Two enormous yellow eyes opened on either side of where they stood.

"No kidding!" Mapper yelled. "What tipped you off?"

JUH!!!! the gigantic toad insisted inside Magdalys. From far away, another call responded: *juhjuhjuhjuh*

"Whatever it is," Magdalys said, "there are more of them."

"Look!" Mapper called. The next hill over wasn't a hill either — the swamp water churned beneath it as trees and soil billowed off to reveal a huge mouth and two long folded-up legs. Slime-covered vines and tendrils dangled from its dripping neck folds.

JuhJUHjuhJUHjuhJUHjuhJUH

In the sky above, the sinorniths were already regrouping. Magdalys spied a figure riding a crimson dactyl of all things, that long red beard visible from the hill where Magdalys stood. Drek waved his hands around him, directing the sinos like a frenzied flying conductor.

"Are you . . ." Mapper asked. "I mean, can you . . . ?"

"I . . . I think so," Magdalys said.

JuhJUHjuhJUHjuhJUHjuhJUH

"You should probably do it now, if you can," Mapper said. "Those guys are coming our way again." Drek was browbeating the sinorniths into a tight formation up above.

Attack! she thought to the toad. *Smash them!*

juhJUHjuhjuhjuhJUHjuhjuhJUH came the warbled reply.

"Mags . . ."

"I know," she growled. "And I don't know . . . I don't know what's happening!"

juhjuhjuhJUHjuhjuhJUHjuhjuh

"STOP JUHING AND DO SOMETHING!" Magdalys yelled. The toad nodded its head slightly but otherwise: nothing. Despair curled around her heart. She had done *everything* — broken her own promise even — and they were still there, trapped and doomed on top of some giant warty amphibian in the middle of a swamp. The growls of the spinosaurs sounded in the forest around them.

JUH!!! A resounding call, a wide-open space within her.

Magdalys hurled a desperate plea at the toad: *We need your help!* And in the stillness that followed, Hannibal's words

echoed back to her: *They need your help*. Magdalys blinked. Montez needed her, if he was still alive even, but it wasn't just about Montez anymore. *We all got brothers and sisters in danger right now*, he'd said. And he was right: They needed her help. And she had wanted, still wanted, with everything inside of her just to run away. But she couldn't. There was no away to run to, not really. She was bound to the destiny of her people, no matter what she did or where she went. And her people were in chains. And the whole Confederacy was to blame. As long as it existed, was armed and organized, she would never be safe.

The Confederacy must fall, she thought, stomping her foot, and the idea seemed to ricochet through that cavern inside her and then, suddenly, explode.

Fire.

She had suppressed it, that fire. Shoved it away. Back in Tennessee, flying over that plantation. Then again and again since. The worry she felt every time she thought about what might've happened to Montez. Big Jack's torn back.

FIRE.

These horrible, jeering men closing in on her and Mapper. On the mansion across the lake. On Chattanooga, where Two Step and Sabeen were probably preparing for another onslaught with the Native Guard, with Hannibal, waiting for General Grant.

The flames roared to life within her, crackled and shrieked and rose.

How would you like the full weight of the US Army at your back? The general's words rumbled through her. Alone, she could rain down some havoc and probably get destroyed in the process. But with an army . . . with an army, she could win, crush the Confederacy forever.

FIRE.

She could win. The thought was terrifying somehow — what that would really mean, the destruction it would entail. She'd forced it away from her mind. Refused to even consider it. Mapper was right: She hadn't just been afraid of losing. It was winning she feared most, her own strength. The true ferocity of her power unleashed.

But no more.

"Give me your knife," Magdalys said.

Mapper passed it over handle first without a word.

She reached back, grabbed her bun with one hand, pulled the blade hard along her head just where the hair was tied, felt the whole thing come free and whoosh away in the wind.

Fire.

"Mags!" Mapper yelled, and then his carbine burst to life again and a sinornith went careening out of the sky with a sharp caw.

As the spinosaur growls drew nearer around them and Mapper let off shot after shot at the sinorniths above, she narrowed her eyes and reached outward with her mind. Men and dinos would die. But she would not.

She found the spinos — there were four — felt that

now-familiar shield that had kept her out of their minds. She shook her head, reached further. Resistance, resistance, the pressure built within her, but the fire raged stronger.

She grunted as sweat broke out across her forehead, glimpsed the four long snouts emerge from the underbrush around them. That fire: she released it, felt it hurl along the pathways she'd opened, shred through the blocks that had been holding her back and then with a snap, all four spinosaurs stood at attention, blinking rapidly.

Awaiting her command.

She waved her arm once and they turned and fled.

"What the — ?" Mapper gasped.

Magdalys didn't have time to explain. She whirled around, faced the army of sinorniths descending from above. Magdalys held up one open hand as Mapper's carbine blasts picked off a few here and there.

Fire.

She stretched her mind across the length of that plummeting horde, felt the grim determination, the need to bite, to kill, that Drek had driven into them. She clenched her fist, obliterating it all, and the horde scattered, sinos spinning off course, bumping into each other with caws and squawks, suddenly confounded and lost.

Fire.

Magdalys let out a long breath of air and stepped back. Mapper blinked at her, then they both glanced upward: Many

of the sinos had fled, but plenty remained and the Marauders who'd been approaching from behind weren't far off now.

JuhjuhjuhJUHjuhJUHjuhjuhjuhJUH, the toad sang.

Magdalys was out of breath but she wasn't done yet.

"Impressive," a voice yelled from above. Drek. He was a ways up, the coward, and further than she'd ever been able to reach with her mind, but maybe . . . "But you can't keep breaking through all of my mastered dinos, girl."

"Watch me," Magdalys whispered, but already she felt her energy waning.

"We have you surrounded, you know. And we'll give you a chance to be taken alive, whoever you are."

Something big thrashed in the underbrush to Magdalys's right. She spun around, arms and mind outstretched just as an alligator the size of a train car lumbered forward, jaws open.

No! she thought, pinpricks of fire exploding inside. The gator's mouth slammed shut and it looked around, confused. Breaking Drek's hold on dinos was getting easier and easier, but still, she couldn't hold out forever.

"Up above!" Mapper yelled, letting off one shot then another. The sky had darkened; twenty more sinorniths converged above them and dove.

She unleashed, sending the imaginary sword of her mind dancing in wild loops across the sky, smashing easily through Drek's hold on them as dinos scattered and spiraled away in confusion.

That crimson dactyl.

Magdalys reached her burning thoughts toward it, but the rebuff was stronger than with the others. It wasn't just Drek's dinomastery that was driving that creature: The thing was there by choice. It was his companion.

JuhJUHjuhJUHjuhJUHjuhJUH

The woods around them rustled again and a bristling, screeching pack of microraptors leapt out of the underbrush. Magdalys sent a few scrambling and Dizz and Beans snapped and whacked away the rest with their wings.

Up above, another pack of sinorniths clouded out the sun, preparing to dive.

Out across the lake, a sudden barrage of musket fire erupted.

Montez! The pulse of his name clamored suddenly louder, ferocious amidst all those flames within her. His face flashed through her, squinting even with glasses, reading his books late into the night by candlelight. Everything that had happened to him since he left. He *had* to still be alive.

And she had to get to that mansion before it was too late.

With a roar of her own, Magdalys sent half of the sinos colliding into the other half, causing enough confusion to throw off the attack for at least a few moments. Then she directed her mind back to the humongous toad beneath them.

juhjuhjuhjuhjuhjuhjuh

This thing was very, very old. It wasn't like any dino she'd ever made contact with. That croaking murmur within her felt

like a murky bottomless pit, something slippery and almost beyond this world. But it had heard her when she reached out, had answered her call, even if it had then ignored her when she needed it most. And now . . . now she'd opened up something new inside herself. If she could break through Drek's control, maybe she could get through to this humongous beast.

juhjuhJUHjuhJUHjuhjuhjuhJUHjuhJUH

She knelt. Placed her hands on its slimy, lumpy skin. Reached. Felt the tendrils of her thoughts slide into that dank and gargantuan consciousness below, felt its ambivalence and beneath that, a grudging curiosity, felt that curiosity grow as the toad recognized the fire she wielded her thoughts with. And then Magdalys felt the full, ragged attention of the ancient creature focus on her.

Help us, Magdalys thought, hearing again the echo of Hannibal's plea to her a few days earlier.

A pause, then a murmured reply: *Juh.*

Take us across the lake. Smash their armies.

Something inside the toad seemed to light up.

For my brother. For all our brothers and sisters.

The *juh*s resolved into a deep, burbling growl.

"Might wanna hold on to someth —" Magdalys started to say, but the toad cut her off with a final, ferocious *JUH!!!*

And then it leapt.

CHAPTER FORTY-ONE
EARTHSHAKER

THE WIND WHIPPED through Magdalys so suddenly she didn't even realize they'd launched into the air until she caught her breath and saw the swamp recede and the lake passing beneath them.

JUHHH!!!!

For a moment the whole world seemed silent.

Then gunfire rang out up ahead, and Magdalys could make out the tiny flashes from the muzzles and then, as she sped closer, the terrified expressions of the Bog Marauders.

"AAAAAAAAAAAAAAAAAAAAAAAAAAAAAAAAA AAAAAAAHHH!!!" Mapper yelled.

"Brace for impact!" Magdalys called as the ground rushed up to meet them.

KAFWOOOM!!! They landed at the far shore of the lake with a tremendous boom, sending dust and debris and a few Marauders flying to either side.

"Rally!" someone yelled from below as Rebel yells shrieked into the sky. "Take down that thing!"

Magdalys and Mapper peered over the edge of the toad's gigantic mouth. The Marauders swarmed over the now demolished shoreline, taking up positions with their backs to the mansion and aiming their muskets at the toad.

"Get down!" Mapper yelled, but then the sound of breaking glass sounded from one of the high-up windows.

A voice called out: "Hit 'em with everything ya got, boys!" and the whole front of the house seemed to burst with flashing muzzles.

The Marauders didn't know where to turn. Several screamed and collapsed; others turned their guns back toward the mansion; a few took potshots up toward where Magdalys and Mapper watched in awe.

A dactyl caw sounded from behind them. Drek.

Do something, Magdalys insisted again to the toad as she stood and whirled around. The sinoriding Marauders had caught up with the free-flying ones now, and the whole swarm of them were just reaching the far side of the lake. Drek fluttered along on his crimson dactyl in their midst. Magdalys ran between the two bony, wart-covered ridges over the toad's eyes to its lumpy back.

But those two other toads were still there, staring expectantly at Magdalys from across the lake. Their immense bellies pulsed, sending ripples of dark water out around them.

She narrowed her eyes.

Break them.

One of the toads seemed to cock its head slightly, then looked away. The other glanced once at the pack of smaller dinos screeching past, then leaned forward and opened its humongous mouth. Something pink unfurled and flashed out across the sky, sending the cloud of sinos scattering. It was gone again in barely a second's time: slurping back into the toad's gaping jaws with a squawking sino in its grasp.

The other toad looked up now, blinked, and released its tongue with a croak, blasting two sinos out of the sky and snagging a third for a meal.

Magdalys gaped, then nodded her thanks and ran back between the eye ridges to where Mapper was crouched, aiming his carbine at the fighting below. She peered over his shoulder. "How we looking?"

"Getting there," Mapper said. Caught between a giant toad and an onslaught of fire from the mansion, the Marauders had all but dispersed entirely. Only a small group remained holed up behind a makeshift trench, and it looked like they were setting up some kind of cannon. "But they'll be regrouping before long."

He was right, and those toads behind them had probably

only put a small dent in the sino brigade. Plus, Drek was still out there somewhere.

Magdalys growled at the massive creature beneath them. "Can you just for once —" she started to say out loud, but then the toad lurched forward, knocking her and Mapper on their butts. That giant tongue flitted out, shattered the trench, and sent the cannon hurtling through the air in an explosion of dirt and debris.

"Aiiii!" the last Marauders yelled as they booked it triple-time into the underbrush.

"Whoa!" Magdalys and Mapper said at the same time. Then they looked up as the dust cloud cleared. Faces appeared in the smashed windows of the dilapidated old mansion. Most of them were various shades of brown and wore blue caps. One had a mustache and an eyepatch and a wide grin. "Ahoy! Who goes there?" the man yelled with a chuckle. "I'm Corporal Wolfgang Hands, commanding officer of the Louisiana 9th, Mounted Triceratops Division, United States Army, although we're fresh out of trikes I'm afraid, and ammo too, after that last barrage. And whoever you are, we owe you some whiskey and a night on the town!"

"Uh . . . hi," Magdalys called back. "I'm looking for —"

"MAGDALYS!" someone yelled directly across from where she stood.

She knew that voice.

Magdalys looked up, tears already welling in her eyes. The

attic window was open and Montez Roca's long, bespectacled face was poking out of it with the biggest smile she'd ever seen.

"What are you doing here?" he called. Then his eyes narrowed. "And what'd you do to your hair?"

He was alive. Montez was alive. And she'd found him.

All her memories of who he'd been came crashing into the sudden vision of who he'd become: a soldier. Hardened by battle, sure, but still somehow glowing with that excitement for life she knew so well. It wasn't just that she feared he'd been killed, she realized; she didn't know who he'd be after all that had happened, even if she could reach him.

A feeling swelled in Magdalys: waves of sadness and joy seemed to have smashed into each other and were rising.

She didn't know how to meet Montez's gaze, this bookworm turned sniper who was her brother, like somehow if she locked eyes with him the whole moment would go up in smoke, become another fever dream of bone hills and gaping maws in the earth. She'd fought so hard to get here and still, none of it seemed possible. But there he was, alive and in the flesh. One of the lenses in Montez's glasses was cracked and he had a bruise on his forehead, but otherwise, he looked pretty okay.

"We came to get you out of here," Magdalys said, as more faces emerged from the darkness behind shattered windows. "All of you."

"Hey, Montez," Mapper yelled.

The caws of approaching sinorniths came from not far away,

and from even closer, more shouts from the Bog Marauders, already regrouping.

"Did General Grant send you?" Wolfgang asked. "Are you with the Union Army?"

Magdalys shrugged. "We weren't when we started out, but somewhere along the way, I think we may have mustered in." She looked over at Mapper. He nodded enthusiastically. "I have a letter from the general that'll explain everything."

"Excellent!" the corporal yelled as a cheer rose up from the mansion. "There should be a division of General Banks's army heading west from New Orleans to dislodge some Confederate blockade runners in Brownsville, Texas, and spook Emperor Maxwell's forces out of Matamoros, across the border. We were hoping to link up with them. Of course, we gotta bust out of here first, and to do that we'll need all the help we can get, but especially the kind that comes sauntering into battle on the back of a giant toad!"

"Now that that's settled," Magdalys said, finally meeting her long-lost-could've-been-dead-apparently-a-sharpshooter brother's eyes, "let's fight our way out of this swamp together."

A NOTE ON THE PEOPLE, PLACES & DINOS OF THE DACTYL HILL SQUAD

Once again, let me get this out of the way right off the bat: **There were no dinosaurs during the Civil War era!** In fact, there were no dinosaurs at any point in time during human history. The Dactyl Hill Squad series is historical fantasy. That means it's based on an actual time and place, events that actually happened, but I also get to make up awesome stuff, like that there were dinosaurs running around. So some of the people, places, and events are based on real historical facts, some are inspired by real historical facts, and some are just totally made up. Throughout this note, I've given some recommendations on books that helped me pull all this together; some of them were written for adult readers, so make sure they're the right ones for you before diving in.

PEOPLE!

Magdalys Roca and the other orphans are not based on any specific people, but there was indeed a Colored Orphan Asylum, and their records speak of a family of kids mysteriously dropped off from Cuba without much explanation. That was part of the inspiration behind this book. You can read those stories and more about the Colored Orphan Asylum in Leslie Harris's book *In the Shadow of Slavery*.

Cymbeline Crunk and her brother, Halsey, are inspired by Ira Aldridge and James Hewlett, two early black Shakespearean actors who performed in New York City. Hewlett cofounded the African Grove Theater, the first all-black Shakespearean troupe in the United States. Halsey and Cymbeline Crunk are entirely made-up characters. You can read more about Hewlett in Shane White's book *Stories of Freedom in Black New York* and more about Ira in *Ira's Shakespeare Dream*, by Glenda Armand and Floyd Cooper.

General Philip Sheridan was a famous Union general known for his charisma and aggressive military tactics. He would go on to lead the cavalry division of the Army of the Potomac in the last year of the war. He wrote about his life and his time in the Civil War in the autobiography *Personal Memoirs of P. H. Sheridan*.

The Card brothers were real scouts under General Sheridan who proved crucial assets during the Tennessee campaigns of the Army of the Cumberland. Much of what happens to them in the book is taken from real-life events, although it has been condensed and the dates moved around.

General Ulysses S. Grant was the leading commander of the US Army by the end of the Civil War and went on to become president of the United States. During the war, he quickly became one of President Lincoln's favorite generals for his unwavering

commitment to victory and determination under fire. While he was never known to have an allosaurus named Samantha or a microdactyl named Giuseppe, he did spend time in New Orleans just after the fall of Vicksburg and suffered a riding accident while reviewing troops that left him bed-bound and in a cast at the Saint Charles Hotel for several days.

Big Jack Jackson was a real US soldier who was liberated from slavery by the Union Army and fought valiantly at the Battle of Milliken's Bend, where he was killed in action.

Both the **Louisiana 9th** and the **Louisiana Native Guard** were all-black divisions of the US army. The Native Guard didn't fight at Milliken's Bend but were involved in a famous assault at Port Hudson. While the soldiers we meet here are entirely made up, many of their names are taken from actual soldiers who fought in those units, including Cailloux, Octave Rey, Hannibal, and Solomon.

In the case of the Louisiana Native Guard, the word Native refers to natives of Louisiana, not Native Americans, as Amaya at first thinks. It's unclear when the word Native became commonly used for Indigenous people. At this time in American history, the US Government was fighting a war of extermination against the many Indigenous nations, many of whom they'd already forced to relocate during the Trail of Tears a few decades earlier.

You can read about the Native Guard in the *Louisiana Native Guards: The Black Military Experience During the Civil War* by James G. Hollandsworth Jr.

While **Dr. Pennbroker** is a fictional character, over a dozen black surgeons served in the US Army during the Civil War, including Dr. Anderson Ruffin Abbot and Dr. Alexander T. Augusta.

General Ely Samuel Parker was a real-life Seneca lawyer, engineer, and diplomat. Both Harvard University and the New York Bar Association refused him entry because of his race. He eventually went on to become a key engineer and general during the Civil War and one of General Grant's right hand men. After the war, he went on to be the first Native person to hold the position of Commissioner of Indian Affairs.

Allan Pinkerton founded the Pinkerton National Detective Agency in 1850, and the organization went on to serve as President Lincoln's bodyguard and intelligence service during the Civil War. It later became the largest private law enforcement agency in the world, and was notorious for violently disrupting the Labor Movement.

Elizabeth Crawbell is entirely made up, though she was inspired by two real-life Confederate spies: Belle Boyd, a teenager who became a famed courier and secret agent, and the widow Rose O'Neal Greenhow, who monitored Union troop buildups and

coordinated spies from her Washington, DC, residence. Both were captured by the Pinkertons. You can read more about them and two women who worked for the Union side, Emma Edmonds and Elizabeth Van Lew, in Karen Abbott's *Liar, Temptress, Soldier, Spy: Four Women Undercover in the Civil War.*

Corporal Buford, Lieutenant Hardy L. Hewpat, Earl Shamus Dawson Drek, and his crimson dactyl are totally made up.

PLACES & EVENTS

Dactyl Hill is based on a real historical neighborhood in Brooklyn called Crow Hill (modern-day Crown Heights), which, along with Weeksville and several others, became a safe haven for black New Yorkers escaping the racist violence of Manhattan. You can find out more about Weeksville at the Weeksville Historical Society and in Judith Wellman's book *Brooklyn's Promised Land.*

The **Colored Orphan Asylum** was on Fifth Avenue between Forty-Second and Forty-Third Streets in Manhattan. It was burned down in the New York Draft Riots. All the orphans except one escaped, and the organization relocated to another building.

By the second half of 1863, when this book takes place, the Union Army had just achieved two major and decisive victories

after two and a half years of **the Civil War**. At Gettysburg, the newly promoted General Meade repelled General Lee's Army of Northern Virginia, effectively ending the Confederate invasion of Pennsylvania; and in Mississippi, General Grant sacked the fortress city of Vicksburg after a prolonged siege. Starting earlier that same year, the US government finally allowed black soldiers to be mustered into service, although they insisted on paying them significantly less than their white counterparts. From Maine to the Midwest all the way down to Louisiana, many thousands answered the call anyway. Besides fighting valiantly in combat, they agitated successfully for equal pay, and eventually made up 10 percent of the Union Army. You can read more about the famed Massachusetts 54th and 55th regiments in *Thunder at the Gates* by Douglas R. Egerton and *Now or Never! Fifty-Fourth Massachusetts Infantry's War to End Slavery* by Ray Anthony Shepard. *A History of the Negro Troops in the War of the Rebellion, 1861–1865* is also a fascinating historical overview written twenty years after the war by a former soldier and one of the first African American historians, George Washington Williams. There are numerous other books about the Civil War, but one of the best is *Battle Cry of Freedom* by James McPherson.

The Battle of Chickamauga took place over several days (not one like it does here), just south of Chattanooga, Tennessee. While some of the details depicted are made up, a few major

parts really did happen that way, including the wider strategic questions the Army of the Cumberland faced once they'd chased General Bragg's Confederate forces out of Tennessee. After a vicious back and forth, the near-stalemate was broken when a miscommunication on the Union side led to one regiment being moved out of the way just as the Confederates charged, which then divided the Federal forces in half and collapsed their front lines. General Thomas famously held out, covering the retreat of the other units, a feat that earned him the nickname "The Rock of Chickamauga." General Sheridan's division was cut off from the rest of the army during the rout, and then regrouped and made their way back to try to reinforce Thomas as night was falling, although it's unclear how much help they were able to provide.

The Battle of Milliken's Bend, which Montez was wounded in, was indeed an important moment in the victory at Vicksburg, as the 9th Louisiana Regiment of African Descent and others repelled an attempt by the Confederates to reinforce their besieged troops.

The song that Sabeen sings, **"John Brown's Body,"** was a popular Civil War marching tune in the US Army. John Brown was an abolitionist who led a raid against Harper's Ferry in 1859. The original melody comes from an old folk hymn called "Say, Brothers, Will You Meet Us." Soldiers in the black regiments

sang a version too — the one Magdalys hears them sing while marching through Tennessee. Julia Ward Howe wrote the most famous rendition of the song — "The Battle Hymn of the Republic" — after visiting Union soldiers in 1861.

The **Knights of the Golden Circle** were composed of various pro-slavery advocates throughout the Americas who were dedicated to bringing an expansion of the slave states into the Caribbean and Central and South America that they dubbed "the Golden Circle."

Federal naval forces led by General Farragut took over **New Orleans** very early on in the war and the city remained in Union control the whole time. A city known for delicious food and a mix of cultures, New Orleans is considered the birthplace of jazz, which grew in part out of the second-line funeral tradition that Hannibal tells Magdalys about.

The Mardi Gras Indians are a New Orleans cultural tradition dating back to the nineteenth century, when black Americans wanted to honor the Native Americans who had helped them out during slavery. To this day, the different Krewes create brightly colored, feather-adorned regalia and parade through the streets of New Orleans on certain days of the year.

DINOS, PTEROS & OTHER ASSORTED -SAURIA

Of course, a lot less is known about dinosaurs than about the Civil War–era United States. Because of this, and because this is a fantasy novel, I took more liberties with the creation of the dinosaurs in this story than I did with the history. Experts can make intelligent guesses based on the fossil data, but we don't really know exactly what prehistoric animals looked like, smelled like, or how they acted. In the world of Dactyl Hill Squad, the dinos never went extinct, but humans did subdue and domesticate them as beasts of burden and war.

The **brachiosaurus** was a humongous herbivorous (meaning it ate plants) quadruped (meaning it walked on four legs). Its long neck allowed it to eat leaves from the tallest trees. It lived during the Late Jurassic Period and probably didn't hoot the way the ones in the Dactyl Hill world do.

Sauropod is a general term for the gigantic quadrupedal dinosaurs with long necks, long tails, and relatively small heads. In the Dactyl Hill Squad world, they are used for transportation, cargo carrying, and construction.

As Magdalys points out, **pterodactyls** weren't dinosaurs, they were pterosaurs, flying reptiles closely related to birds. They flew

through Jurassic-era skies munching on insects, fish, and small reptiles. Generally about the size of seagulls, they weren't really large enough to carry a person. A group of pterodactyls is not called a squad (although maybe it should be!) and scientists don't suspect them to have been pack dependent as described in the book. But who knows?

Raptors were a group of very intelligent, bipedal (meaning they walked on two feet) carnivores (meaning they ate meat). They had rod-straight tails and a giant claw on each foot, and they hunted in packs during the Late Cretaceous Period.

Triceratopses were herbivorous quadrupeds about the size of an ice cream truck that roamed the earth during the Late Cretaceous Period. They had three horns: one protruding from the snout and two longer ones that stuck out from a wide shield over their eyes that stretched out over its neck.

The **diplodocus** was one of the longest known sauropods and it roamed the North American plains toward the end of the Jurassic Period. It was over ninety feet long! Basically the size of a nine-story building turned on its side.

Pteranodons were large, mostly toothless pterosaurs without long tails. In fact, their name means "toothless lizard." Quetzalcoatlus, the largest of pterosaurs, was big as a fighter

plane — forty-five feet long. They ruled the skies of the Late Cretaceous Period.

Archaeopteryx, which means "Old Wing," are considered to be the oldest form of bird. About the size of a raven, these Jurassic-era dinosaurs had sharp teeth, a long bony tail, and hyperextensible second toes called "killing claws." Yikes!

Sinornithosaurs were Cretaceous Period birdlike dinos once believed to have a venomous bite, although experts now don't believe that to be the case. They glided and hunted through the skies of what we now call China, and their name means "Chinese bird lizard."

The **parasaurolophus** were Late Cretaceous Period plant eaters that walked on both four and two legs. They had a long bony crest that extended from the backs of their heads.

Dimetrodons, also known as finbacks, were short, four-legged synapsids (creatures that roamed the earth forty million years *before* the dinosaurs) that were recognizable for the tall sails protruding from their spines. They are related to modern mammals.

Spinosauruses were large theropods that hunted the wetland areas of the Cretaceous Period. They had long, crocodile-like snouts, and the boney spines extending from their vertebrae were probably connected by skin to give a sail-like look.

A NOTE ON WEAPONS

In this messy, broken time of mass shootings and state violence, it's important to note that guns almost always create more problems than they solve. More than that: Young people suffer with trauma from those problems in increasing and heartbreaking numbers. This is an adventure story, and it takes place during a war, in an era when folks were being kidnapped and sold into slavery and an invading rebel army threatened the nation's capital. Guns are one of the parts of life in that time that I chose to include in this story, but I hope that a) the dangers, both physical and emotional, of gun violence ring loud and clear on the page, and b) we one day live in a time when gun violence doesn't exist anymore at all.

Rifled muskets are enhanced versions of the old Revolutionary War firearms. The rifled muzzles gave these weapons greater precision, and their caplock mechanisms made them easier to load and fire than their flintlock ancestors. Rifled muskets, both Enfields and Springfields, were the most commonly issued guns on both sides of the Civil War.

Many rifled muskets were armed with a **bayonet,** a sharpened sword attached to the muzzle that could be used to stab an attacker.

The **carbine** is smaller and lighter than the rifled musket, with a shorter barrel. Because they are breach-loading, meaning you insert the bullets at the middle of the gun instead of into the muzzle, they are easier to shoot from horseback (or dinoback) and thus were favored by cavalry (mounted) units.

The **Gatling** is a multibarreled rapid-fire gun invented by Richard Gatling, a North Carolinian who, horrified that more soldiers died of disease than from combat during warfare, decided to invent a weapon that would "supersede the necessity of large armies." Which doesn't totally make that much sense and definitely didn't work out that way, but hey . . . He sold his new weapon exclusively to the US Army, but it didn't see too much action during the Civil War as it had only just been invented.

The **howitzer** is a short-barreled smoothbore mobile artillery cannon that could fire shells of twelve, twenty-four, and thirty-two pounds in a high trajectory. They were used as defensive weapons and to flush enemies out of their entrenched hiding places.

ACKNOWLEDGMENTS

I am deeply grateful to Nick Thomas and Weslie Turner — we did it again!

Thank you to the whole team at Scholastic, who have been amazing throughout this process, especially Arthur A. Levine, Lizette Serrano, Emily Heddleson, Tracy van Straaten, Rachel Feld, Isa Caban, and Erik Ryle.

Thanks to Erika Scipione, Gavin Brown, and Fay Koh who created the online Dactyl Hill Squad game, Rescue Run. It! Is! So! Awesome!

Nilah Magruder has once again brought Magdalys and the crew to life and it's always such a breathtaking wonder to see her translate my words into images. Thank you, Nilah! And a huge thank you to Afu Chan for the terrific Dactyl Hill Squad logo and to Christopher Stengel for bringing it all together with such grace and precision.

To Eddie Schneider and Joshua Bilmes and the whole team at JABberwocky Lit: you are wonderful. Thank you.

Many thanks to Leslie Shipman at The Shipman Agency and Lia Chan at ICM.

Leigh Bardugo talked me through a key plot point on speaker phone as I drove in circles through the foggy streets of New Orleans late one night, and for that I am forever grateful. And Brittany Nicole Williams came through in the clutch and caught me trying to squeeze in an unearned reveal. Thank youuuu!

Dr. Debbie Reese was terrifically generous with her time and wisdom and analysis. She gave detailed notes after reading both this and Book One, and I'm deeply grateful. Her work at American Indians in Children's Lit is always a crucial resource and necessary reading.

Thanks to Mark Norell and Derek Frisby! All incorrect historical or dinofactual matter is my own fault and it's probably on purpose, unless it's in the appendix and then it's totally my bad.

Thanks to the kind clerks at James H. Cohen & Sons Inc, a rare antique weapons shop on Royal Street in the French Quarter, who were extremely helpful when this writer came in asking about which Civil War-era guns would be best shot from dinoback.

Thanks always to my amazing family, Dora, Marc, Malka, Lou, Calyx and Paz. Thanks to Iya Lisa and Iya Ramona and Iyalocha Tima, Patrice, Emani, Darrell, April, and my

whole Ile Omi Toki family for their support; also thanks to Oba Nelson "Poppy" Rodriguez, Baba Malik, Mama Akissi, Mama Joan, Sam, Tina, and Jud and all the wonderful folks of Ile Ase. And thank you, Brittany, for everything.

Baba Craig Ramos: we miss you and love you and carry you with us everywhere we go. Rest easy, Tío. Ibae bayen tonu.

I give thanks to all those who came before us and lit the way. I give thanks to all my ancestors; to Yemonja, Mother of Waters; gbogbo Orisa, and Olodumare.

ABOUT THE AUTHOR

Daniel José Older has always loved monsters, whether historical, prehistorical, or imaginary. He is the *New York Times* bestselling author of numerous books for readers of all ages: For middle grade, the Dactyl Hill Squad series, the first book of which was named to the *New York Times* Notable Book, *NPR*, and *Washington Post* Best Books of the Year lists; for young adults, the acclaimed Shadowshaper Cypher, winner of the International Latino Book Award; and for adults, *Star Wars: Last Shot*, the Bone Street Rumba urban fantasy series, and *The Book of Lost Saints*. He has worked as a bike messenger, a waiter, and a teacher, and was a New York City paramedic for ten years. Daniel splits his time between Brooklyn and New Orleans.

You can find out more about him at danieljoseolder.net.

This book was edited by
Nick Thomas and Weslie Turner and
designed by Christopher Stengel. The production
was supervised by Melissa Schirmer. The text was set
in Adobe Caslon Pro, with display type set in Brothers.
The book was printed and bound at LSC Communications
in Crawfordsville, Indiana. The manufacturing
was supervised by Angelique Browne.

ODESSA
AGAIN

Dana Reinhardt

ODESSA
AGAIN

Illustrated by Susan Reagan

WENDY
LAMB
BOOKS

Text copyright © 2013 by Dana Reinhardt
Jacket art and interior illustrations copyright © 2013 by Susan Reagan

All rights reserved. Published in the United States by Wendy Lamb Books,
an imprint of Random House Children's Books,
a division of Random House, Inc., New York.

Wendy Lamb Books and the colophon are trademarks of Random House, Inc.

Visit us on the Web! randomhouse.com/kids

Educators and librarians, for a variety of teaching tools, visit us at
RHTeachersLibrarians.com

Library of Congress Cataloging-in-Publication Data
Reinhardt, Dana.
Odessa again / Dana Reinhardt. — 1st ed.
p. cm.
Summary: When nine-year-old Odessa Green-Light stomps out her frustration at
being sent to her room after shoving her annoying little brother,
one particularly big stomp sends Odessa flying through the floorboards
and mysteriously twenty-four hours back in time.
ISBN 978-0-385-73956-6 (hardcover) — ISBN 978-0-385-90793-4 (lib. bdg.)
ISBN 978-0-375-89788-7 (ebook)
[1. Time travel—Fiction. 2. Remarriage—Fiction.] I. Title.
PZ7.R2758Od 2013
[Fic]—dc23
2012008231

The text of this book is set in 12-point Goudy Old Style.
The illustrations were rendered digitally.
Book design by Trish Parcell

Printed in the United States of America

10 9 8 7 6 5 4 3 2 1

First Edition

To Noa, who was kind enough to let me steal many of her ideas.

And to Zoe and the rest of Johnny Galang's class at Live Oak School, thank you for being this book's first readers.

The New House

There comes a day in the life of every big sister when it's simply no longer suitable to share a bedroom with your toad of a little brother.

For Odessa Green-Light, that day was a Tuesday.

They'd only been living in the new house a few months. Odessa and Oliver shared a room, like they had in the old house, and like they did in Dad's apartment. This new house, of which Odessa was not particularly fond, had one redeeming feature that the old house she missed so much did not.

It had an attic.

From the first time the landlady gave them the tour— with someone else's scribbles on the kitchen wall, and someone else's stickers stuck to the dryer that had dried

someone else's clothes, and the narrow wooden staircase scuffed from someone else's shoes—Odessa had her eye on that attic.

"You'll love it here," the old lady barked at Odessa, as if this were an order and not a wish.

Odessa doubted very much that she would love it there, but she did think that she might love living in the attic, a full flight of stairs removed from Oliver.

She asked, but of course her mother said no. If there was one thing Odessa could count on, it was Mom saying no to the things Odessa wanted most.

So a few months back, on move-in day, a day Mom tried to make cheery by blasting old-fashioned music and singing into a broom handle, Odessa unpacked her stuff into one half of a too-small bedroom while Oliver the Toad unpacked into the other.

And each day since, or at least every weeknight and every other weekend, which were the nights she spent at her mother's, Odessa had begged to move into that attic, but it hadn't worked.

Begging rarely did.

She'd also tried cajoling, bamboozling, and hood-winking.

"Not a chance," Mom said.

Sometimes, however, victory is found in unlikely places.

Oliver discovered the field mouse that delivered this

victory in the backyard. Oliver didn't seem to know how to get along with real live people: his terrible shyness got in the way. But there was no denying he had a way with rodents.

It was a Tuesday, which meant the next day was a Wednesday, word-study day, and Odessa had set her mind to moving into word group N, which required some studying.

The fourth-grade class was divided into word groups L, M, and N, and although Mr. Rausche chose letters from smack-dab in the middle of the alphabet, Odessa knew that as an M, she was only a second-level word-study student.

Smack-dab in the middle.

Odessa loved words. And she always tried her best to use the ones that other people too often ignored. But loving words and knowing how to spell them were two different things, and Odessa knew she would never make the move to group N without mastering the illogical rules of spelling, which was nearly impossible to do with Oliver crashing around her too-small room.

So she told him to get lost, not having any idea that this would lead him to their new backyard, where he'd find a field mouse sniffing around a chew toy that someone else's dog had left in the grass. Nor did she guess that Oliver would sing softly to this mouse until it wandered into his outstretched palm, at which point he would carry it

into their bedroom and drop it down the back of Odessa's pink T-shirt with the turquoise stripes.

Well.

Odessa did what any reasonable person would do. She shrieked, ran to find her mother in the kitchen, and threatened to sue in a court of law if she couldn't move into the attic.

From her mother's lips sprang these three beautiful words:

"I. Give. Up."

And so Odessa found herself tucked in bed by 7:45 that Tuesday night under the quilt Mom pulled from one of the attic's boxes. A quilt sewn as a gift for the darling baby Oliver, who had grown up to be a pesky toad.

*

Odessa had been sleeping in the attic for exactly three nights before it happened.

24 Hours

One of the reasons Odessa did not love the new house was that she'd seen it for the first time the day after Dad told her that he was getting remarried.

To *re* something means to do it all over again, so *re*-marrying should have meant he'd be getting married to Mom again, not getting married to someone else.

But Odessa didn't say this to Dad as they sat in a booth at Pizzicato and he made his announcement. Odessa and Oliver loved Pizzicato. Dad hated it. That he'd taken them there without any begging should have been the first warning sign.

The second was when he clinked his glass with his fork and said he had *big news*.

Odessa preferred small news. Big news was never good.

She'd cried that night, and Mom had held her.

"I don't want to be de-hyphenated!" she wailed. She'd never much liked the name Green-Light. If you were a woman named Green, and you met a man named Light, wouldn't you run as fast as you could in the opposite direction? Probably. But her parents didn't. They fell in love and got married and had kids whose names they hyphenated, and then fell out of love and got divorced, and now the most important thing in the world to Odessa was to hold on to the name Green-Light.

"Nobody is taking away your hyphen," Mom said, stroking her hair. "You will always be Odessa Green-Light, for better or for worse."

That night, it definitely felt *for worse*.

The next day Mom took her to see the new house they'd be renting because they'd finally sold the old house that Dad had moved out of the year before.

So Odessa had disliked the house from day one, but now that she'd moved to the attic, that had started to change.

Oliver's behavior didn't change, however.

It started with him mimicking her ("Oliver, have you seen my pencil case?" *"Oliver, have you seen my pencil case?"*) and refusing to stop ("You're so annoying!" *"You're so annoying!"*), and it ended with the comment he made under his breath about how she *like*-liked Theo Summers, something she had only just admitted to her best friend, Sofia, that afternoon.

6

Sofia had called, as she always did, just after Odessa finished her snack.

Sofia had been eying Odessa and Theo since they'd all been assigned to the same hexagonal table at school.

"You *like* him," Sofia said. "I can tell by the way you stare at him."

Theo sat directly across from Odessa. Where else was she supposed to look?

"Yeah," Odessa said. "He's funny." She also thought he was smart, but she knew this wouldn't matter much to Sofia. In the world of fourth grade, funny mattered. Smart did not.

"But do you *like* him like him?"

Today Odessa had admitted that she thought he was cute, especially since he'd stopped cutting his hair, and that yes, she guessed that meant she *liked* him liked him.

This is just what Oliver mumbled to her: "*You like-like Theo Summers.*"

She'd always suspected that Oliver eavesdropped on her phone calls, and now she had the proof. So she shoved him.

Hard enough to knock him off his pigeon-toed feet.
And he fell.

They were in the kitchen, clearing the dinner dishes like Mom made them do every night before dessert. Tonight it happened to be butter-brickle ice cream, Odessa's favorite.

Mom was by the sink, exactly where she'd been

standing three days earlier when she'd thrown up her hands and said, "I. Give. Up."

One of the reasons Odessa loved words was that sometimes the very same words could have a totally different meaning. So tonight when her mother shouted, "I. Give. Up," she didn't mean *You can have what you want.* This time she meant *You are in huge trouble.*

"I'm tired of the fighting!" she hollered. "To your room, Odessa. Now. TIME OUT."

Odessa could have explained what had led her to shove Oliver, but she was too angry. Too tired of being blamed for his toadiness. So she stormed out of the room yelling, "My pleasure!"

8

"And don't come down until I say so," her mother called after her.

Odessa stomped through the house and raced up the narrow attic steps, slamming the door behind her.

She flopped down onto her bed. *I'm almost ten years old,* she thought, even though her birthday was still half a year away.

What ten-year-old gets a time-out?

Odessa jumped up and began to pace the creaky floorboards. *Oliver is shy with other people; why can't he be shy with me? Why is he always nosing around in my business?*

She wanted to smash something. When she felt this way she'd usually reach for the oversized sock monkey Sofia had given her on her sixth birthday and bite him on the belly.

He didn't seem to mind.

They had an understanding.

But the sock monkey was downstairs in the room that was now Oliver's, because her move to the attic wasn't finished. For example, she still had no desk. No mirror. She didn't have the posters she'd torn from the pages of the tween magazines Mom didn't like her to read.

Odessa noticed just then that despite having none of the essential things, she *did* have a hand-painted pottery cupcake sitting on top of her empty bookshelf.

A cupcake that belonged to Oliver.

Mom must have brought it up by mistake. Odessa's

hand-painted pottery was shaped like an ice-cream cone. They'd made these pieces at I Did It Pottery, on a recent Saturday afternoon with Uncle Milo.

Odessa reached for the cupcake, threw it to the floor with all of her strength, and watched, with wonder, as it smashed into tiny shards.

That felt good.

But what felt even better was the sensation of those shards crunching beneath the soles of her orange Converse high-tops.

So she stomped.

And she stomped harder.

She jumped up and down on that broken cupcake, smashing the shards to dust, until finally the creaky floorboards gave way beneath her, and she fell.

Have you ever fallen?

Down some stairs? Off the jungle gym? Out of your bed in the middle of the night?

Well then, you know what was happening to Odessa: that upside-down, over-under, inside-out feeling.

She landed with a thud.

Right in the middle of her bedroom floor.

It wasn't her old bedroom floor directly below the attic. This was the *attic floor*. The very floorboards through which she'd just fallen.

Odessa gripped her stomach. Then she scratched her head. This made no sense at all.

Mom's order rang in her ears: *Don't come down until I say so.* The type of order her mother called "nonnegotiable."

Even so, Odessa took the stairs quietly. When violating a nonnegotiable order, it's best not to stomp your way down from your room.

She found Mom and Oliver sitting at the dinner table, enjoying their dessert without her, which hardly seemed fair, considering that butter-brickle ice cream was *her* favorite, and nobody else's.

"Hi, honey," Mom said, grinning.

"Hello . . . ," Odessa said carefully.

Maybe all was forgotten. Maybe she should just take her seat and not offer any explanation for why she'd come down from her room without permission.

So she sat. Right in front of a piece of carrot cake.

Carrot cake was *not* her favorite.

And it was the same dessert they'd had the night before.

Odessa didn't want to push things, but she couldn't help herself. Sometimes things, like little brothers, needed to be pushed.

She asked politely, "What about the butter-brickle ice cream?"

"We don't have any," Mom said. "But I'll get some for tomorrow night, how 'bout that?"

Again, Odessa tried out her politest voice. "Yes we do, Mother. We bought it today. Remember? It's in the freezer."

Duh. Where else do you keep ice cream?

Odessa got up and went to the kitchen. She opened the freezer to find an empty space where the butter-brickle ice cream had been.

"WHO ATE ALL THE ICE CREAM?" she shouted.

Back in the dining room Mom and Oliver stared at her funny.

"Tonight we're having carrot cake," Mom said slowly. "And tomorrow, if you can find another way of asking, I'll be happy to buy some butter-brickle ice cream. Now take a seat."

Odessa sat. "But we had this last night," she said glumly.

"No we didn't." Oliver had frosting on his lip. "We had pineapple slices."

Odessa knew that if she opened her mouth to tell Oliver that, *actually*, they had pineapple slices the night *before* last, it would come out in a way that might get her sent to the attic again. So instead she pushed her carrot cake around her plate with her fork.

"Are you feeling okay?" Mom asked.

No, Odessa wanted to say. *There's no more butter-brickle*

ice cream, AND I don't understand why you're not still mad at me.

"My tummy hurts," she said.

Mom reached over and put a hand on Odessa's forehead. "Maybe you should go lie down." She tucked a strand of hair behind Odessa's ear.

As Odessa pushed back her chair and took one last look around the table, she noticed something else.

Something that gave her the same upside-down, over-under, inside-out feeling.

Mom and Oliver were wearing what they'd been wearing the night before, when they'd all eaten carrot cake, not pineapple slices, for dessert.

Odessa looked down at herself. Amazingly, she too wore yesterday's clothes, though she had no memory of changing.

She wasn't feeling well.

Not well at all.

Up in her attic Odessa threw yesterday's clothes in the hamper and put on her favorite pajamas. She crawled underneath the quilt of teddy bears and reached over to turn out her light. The last thing she saw before she closed her eyes and drifted off to sleep was this: Oliver's pottery cupcake.

Sitting on top of her empty bookshelf.

In one perfectly intact, un-stomped-upon piece.

23 Hours

Early the next morning, when Odessa's alarm clock began to tweet (she preferred the sound of birds to buzzing, beeping, and the *William Tell Overture*), she rubbed her eyes.

What a strange dream she'd been having.

Falling through floorboards. Broken pottery. Carrot cake that should have been ice cream.

Uncanny, she thought.

She got out of bed and dressed quickly. When she came down to the kitchen, Oliver was halfway through his glass of chocolate milk, and he stuck his tongue out at her from beneath a chocolate-milk mustache.

Mom slid a plate of scrambled eggs on rye toast in front of her and said, "Eat up. The clock is ticking."

This wouldn't have been odd if her mother said this

14

every day, the way her teacher Mr. Rausche always started each morning by saying, "Best feet forward."

But her mother had never said anything about the clock ticking, unless you counted *yesterday* morning, when she said this as she slid a plate of scrambled eggs on rye toast in front of Odessa right after Oliver stuck out his tongue from beneath a chocolate-milk mustache.

"I'm sorry to rush you, love," her mother said, "but I have a meeting. Chop-chop."

And yes, that was exactly what her mother had said the day before as Odessa reached for her fork. She said she had a "meeting," which Odessa knew meant she had a "job interview."

Mom hadn't worked in an office since Odessa was born, and Odessa preferred it that way, so she didn't much like it yesterday when she knew Mom was going off on a job interview, and she didn't like it any more today.

Odessa had already been here.

Here in this moment.

Today was yesterday. All over again.

Odessa felt dizzy. Clammy. The smell of the eggs made her want to throw up, and she might have, if it weren't for her absolute mortal fear of vomit.

She swallowed. Hard.

Eat up. The clock is ticking.

Sure, but why was it ticking backward?

At that moment, Odessa had two choices.

One: she could stand up and run around in circles, screaming and tearing at her hair.

Or two: she could shrug this off. Shake the dizziness right out of her head. Wipe the clamminess off of her palms.

She could choose to believe that she'd only dreamed this day. That she hadn't really lived it. That her dream from the night before was even more uncanny than she'd thought, because it had predicted what this next day would bring.

Odessa decided to go with option number two.

She kissed her mother good-bye out of sight of the school bus, and she climbed on board. She watched as Claire Deloitte placed her backpack on the empty seat next to her so that Odessa would have to sit someplace else. Thomas Macon folded a paper airplane and tossed it over his shoulder toward the back row, just like she knew he would, but this time Odessa ducked so that it missed hitting her between the eyes, as it had yesterday.

(Or in the dream she'd had that she was mistaking for yesterday.)

She went through the day like this. It was sort of like sleepwalking. She felt discombobulated.

She ate spaghetti and meatballs in the cafeteria again, she listened to Ms. Gomez conjugate the verb *to remember* (*recordar*), and she watched the same film about earthworms that was no more enlightening upon a second viewing.

She came home and ate a snack and went to her room and the phone rang and it was Sofia and they talked about homework and then Sofia asked if Odessa *like*-liked Theo Summers and Odessa admitted that she thought he was cute, especially since he'd stopped cutting his hair.

And of course Oliver said something about Theo Summers under his breath, proving that he'd eavesdropped on her conversation, and even though what she wanted to do more than anything in the entire world was to reach over and shove him hard enough to knock him off his pigeon-toed feet, she didn't.

She held her arms at her sides.

She went back to the table, sat down, and caught her breath, and a minute later her mother placed a bowl of butter-brickle ice cream in front of her.

She ate it.

It was her favorite, after all.

Odessa cleared her bowl and excused herself. She went upstairs to the attic, but not before grabbing a hammer from the tool drawer and slipping it under her shirt.

She got down right next to her floorboards. She pushed

them and listened as they creaked. She tried to pry one up, but couldn't. She tried another. And another.

The floor was solidly nailed down.

She put the hammer on her shelf, next to Oliver's pottery cupcake. She walked back and forth across the floorboards. She slid across them, as if she was skating on the pond near Uncle Milo's. She reached for the cupcake. She held it up over her head, but then she put it back on the shelf. She didn't have the *I need to bite my monkey on the belly* feeling. She was perplexed, not angry.

Odessa poked at the boards with her toe. She put both feet together and jumped.

Nothing.

She jumped again. And again. She closed her eyes, held her breath, and jumped as hard as she could.

And then . . . she fell.

Over-under, inside-out, upside-down.

She opened her eyes to find herself lying in bed.

Maybe I've hit my head, she thought. *And I've been in the hospital, and now I've been sent home, and everyone thinks I'm going to die, but here I am, finally, waking from my coma.*

That was the only explanation she could come up with, because she did not remember going to bed, and anyway, people in comas probably have strange dreams.

She crept downstairs in her pajamas to find her mother in the kitchen, washing dishes.

"Odessa, honey. I thought you weren't feeling well. What are you doing out of bed?"

She leaned into Mom's outstretched arms. She closed her eyes against her mother's chest and let her mother take in a few whiffs of her scalp. Typically, she didn't let her mom get away with this sort of behavior. She was in fourth grade. She wasn't a baby. Kids her age weren't supposed to allow their mothers to smell their heads.

But tonight it felt good.

Because maybe Odessa had just woken up from a coma.

"Mom?" she asked, without opening her eyes or disentangling herself.

"What, honey?"

"How long have I been asleep?"

"It can't have been more than an hour. You really should go back to bed."

Odessa could barely get out the next sentence. It caught someplace in the middle of her throat.

"What did we have for dessert tonight?"

Her mother chuckled.

"Is this about the ice cream again?" She leaned back and took Odessa's face in her hands. "I really didn't know how much you hate carrot cake. I promise that tomorrow I'll pick up some ice cream. Just for you. Deal?"

Odessa nodded, but only because she was unable to speak.

"Now, honey, I think you should go back to bed."

Odessa took the stairs slowly. Going back to bed meant sleeping only to wake up again on the same day *for the third time in a row.* She locked the attic door behind her.

20

She grabbed her journal and sat on the floor, because she still had no desk. She took out a pencil.

Despite being a group M speller, Odessa was excellent at math.

She did some quick calculations, and as she did she felt a clicking in her brain. Just like when a difficult math problem suddenly made perfect sense. She was too smart to believe there were actual cogs and wheels turning inside her head, but sometimes that was how it felt.

What caused this clicking was Odessa's memory of coming to her room the night before, between dinner and dessert. She'd come to use the upstairs bathroom, the one she liked best, and while in there she'd thought about something she wanted to write in her journal, so she darted up to the attic, sat down on the floor, and wrote the following:

If I stop caring that Claire won't talk to me anymore, she'll start talking to me again. Just like the way Oliver gives me back what I want right after I don't want it anymore.

Odessa flipped back a page in her journal and found the entry. She flipped to a fresh page and began to scribble furiously.

The first fall through the attic floorboards had taken her back exactly one day.

Twenty-four hours.

She landed on the floor of the attic because that was exactly where she'd been twenty-four hours earlier, writing about Claire in her journal.

She did some more calculations.

The second fall took place on the same day as the first. Butter-brickle ice cream day. Although she had taken it later, after dessert, because she held her arms at her sides and did not shove Oliver. And this time, her math told her, she'd landed twenty-three hours earlier.

Flabbergasting, she thought, tossing her journal and its scribbled equations across the room.

Was this it?

Was this her life?

Would she always have to relive this day?

Was she doomed to an existence of unappetizing cake made from a vegetable?

No! She wouldn't let that happen.

All she had to do was not jump. Easy enough. The clock would tick forward so long as Odessa walked lightly on her attic floor. Better yet, she could avoid the middle of her room at all costs.

Yes.

Avoid the middle.

That was exactly what Odessa Green-Light did for the next month.

22 Hours

Odessa had almost forgotten about those strange days of falling through the floor. She must have been running a fever. A high one, the kind that makes you hallucinate. Anyway, it was silly. Impossible. It didn't deserve her attention. Not another thought. She'd even thrown away her journal after picking out a new one with a hummingbird on the cover from the stationery store.

Odessa was moving forward.

Mr. Rausche had promised she could make the switch to group *N* after five consecutive perfect scores on her weekly word-study quizzes. So far Odessa had taken four, and she'd spelled each and every word correctly.

Odessa had her attic and she had privacy from Oliver, and she was starting to like the new house. The afternoon

school bus route took her by her old house, and she'd see someone else's shoes on the front porch, or someone else's bike out on the lawn, or deflating balloons tied to the mailbox, and though in the first days these discoveries made her feel like she'd swallowed a brick, lately she'd just think: *Look, someone must have had a birthday.*

Jennifer, the woman Dad was remarrying, had moved into his apartment. Jennifer was different from Mom. She wasn't tall and bony with soft parts Odessa knew how to find. Jennifer was soft all over, in a nice way, and she had brown curly hair and smelled good and her lips were always shimmery and her eyelids sparkled. Odessa had met her lots of times, and she was always really friendly, and once she even let Odessa wear some of her gloss when her lips were chapped, but Jennifer was like the shoes on the porch or the bike on the lawn—she belonged to someone else's family.

Odessa preferred her time at Mom's house. She liked the Green House more than the Light House. Especially since she'd moved to the attic.

She'd begged for a rug, and even though Mom wasn't usually quick to buy her what she wanted, she'd gone out and gotten her a purple cheetah print, which brightened up the room while also hiding the floorboards.

It was a win-win.

Odessa returned Oliver's pottery cupcake and collected her ice cream cone. She took her clock and another

one from the living room that nobody seemed to miss. This way, she could be doubly sure of the time.

Mom had gone on half a dozen job interviews. She'd wear a blazer with her jeans and tie her long hair up in a bun. Sometimes she'd even put on makeup. But so far, nothing seemed to work out. What luck!

Odessa and Sofia were moving up in Dreamonica, an online game world in which they'd built identical mansions and between them owned a dozen puppies. They were best friends in Dreamonica, like they were in real life, and their characters looked exactly the same, the opposite of real life. Mom allowed Odessa twenty minutes a day online, an improvement from the fifteen minutes she'd been allowed in third grade.

Odessa and Theo Summers had been moved to adjoining seats in the hexagon and assigned to each other as math buddies. Math was easy. It made sense. It was the opposite of silly or strange or inexplicable. Odessa was good at it, and what a lucky thing that she could be good at something with Theo Summers by her side.

So all was going pretty well, until another fateful Tuesday.

Tuesday meant the next day was a Wednesday, word-study day. It was to be the fifth quiz on which Odessa would get a perfect score.

But she forgot to study.

This time she couldn't blame Oliver. Or a field mouse.

Or the fact that Dad was remarrying. The only person to blame was herself.

This sort of thing happens, but it didn't happen often to Odessa. So when she arrived at school on Wednesday morning and Mr. Rausche said, "Best feet forward," Odessa felt a sudden chill. Sofia stared across the hexagon at her.

What's wrong?

Sofia knew how to read Odessa's face. They were best friends. They could communicate without using words.

I forgot to study!

Sofia cringed. She knew how important this quiz was to Odessa. *Oh no!*

Maybe she could have scored perfectly anyway, but she

was upset, and her fate was sealed with the pesky word *thorough*, into which Odessa inserted a *w*.

It wasn't a failure, exactly, but that's how it felt.

And anyway, *scrupulous* was a much better word than *thorough*.

She sulked for the rest of the day. Sofia reminded her that in Dreamonica it didn't matter if you knew how to spell *thorough*, you could still live in a mansion, but that didn't help much.

On the bus ride home, Odessa almost sat on Claire's backpack, just to see what she'd do about it. She almost tapped her on the head and said, "Hey? What gives? We were friends last year, not best friends, but friends. Now you won't even talk to me." But of course she didn't. She chose a seat alone and stared out the window. When the bus passed her old house, she cursed the new owners for not cutting the roses before they died on the vine.

Odessa couldn't even be cheered up by butter-brickle ice cream.

She stared at the dish in front of her as Oliver inhaled his while babbling on about recess handball.

She took a taste.

It reminded her of something.

Not of the ice cream parlor where she discovered that butter brickle was her favorite, where Dad first allowed her a cone in place of a cup. Unlike Mom, he didn't care if ice cream wound up on her dress.

No, this taste reminded her of something else.

Of those strange days when she fell through the floorboards and sat down not once, but twice to a piece of carrot cake. Those days when she figured she must have been struck by a terrible fever, because nothing about them made any sense.

Those days when she must have been hallucinating.

But . . . what if she hadn't been?

What if she really did fall through the floor? What if she really *could* go back? If she'd gone back twenty-four and then twenty-three hours, the next time she'd go back twenty-two. She could live this day again and study for the test and get her fifth consecutive perfect score, so that she could move up to group N.

What if?

That night, when Odessa went to bed under Oliver's old baby quilt, she had a dreamless sleep, the kind from which you wake up full of energy. Just what you need when you set your alarm for four a.m.

Tweet. Tweet. Tweet.

How she loved the sound of birds.

She didn't love waking up early, but she needed time to go over those words, to remember that there is no *w* in *thorough*. And she wanted to make certain there weren't any other words on her list that sounded as though they should contain letters they did not.

She wanted to be *scrupulous*.

She turned off the alarm. The ink-black sky gave her

nothing to see by. She stumbled to her desk, the one her mother had finally moved up to the attic, with Uncle Milo's help. She flipped on her lamp and looked at her calendar with the cats on it.

She removed Wednesday's picture of two Siamese kittens wrestling in a flower bed to reveal a fat Calico reaching for a ball of string. He was Thursday's cat, and it was Thursday. More specifically, it was Thursday at a little past four in the morning, one day after Odessa had failed to get a fifth consecutive perfect score on her word-study quiz.

She threw Wednesday's kittens in the trash and stepped into the center of her purple cheetah-print rug. She'd been walking around it for a month now, avoiding the floor underneath. It felt soft and inviting between her toes.

She tapped her foot lightly.

She got down onto her hands and knees and pushed at the boards beneath the rug, listening to them creak. She stroked the cheetah print with her fingers.

Odessa loved this rug, and wouldn't it be a terrible thing if she jumped through the floorboards and lost it? If the rug became stuck someplace between today and yesterday? Trapped in the *betwixt*?

Her attic would look so dull without it.

But worse, what if *she* got caught in the *betwixt*? What if *she* never made it back to yesterday? How would it feel to never see her family again? Mom? Dad? Uncle Milo?

Odessa was a reader, and she'd read books about kids

opening doors or climbing through wardrobes into other worlds, and though she loved these books, she didn't think she'd like to live in any world other than her own. She wanted to live with her own family, even if that family lived in separate places, and even if that family included Oliver.

She rolled up the rug and stashed it out of the way. Then she walked back into the center of the attic, quickly, before her fears could get the better of her, and she closed her eyes, held her breath, and jumped.

The next thing Odessa knew, she was lying in her bed.

She opened one eye and looked at her alarm clock.

6:07

She opened the other and looked with both eyes at the clock she'd taken from the living room.

6:07

From her dormer window she spied the first light of day—orange and pink and blue blended together like a watercolor painting.

She'd made it! It worked!

It was almost one full hour before she usually woke up. Far too early to start the day—unless it was a Wednesday, with a word-study quiz to prepare for.

Odessa climbed out of bed and kept to the edges of her room, avoiding the center of the floor. She raced over to her desk and stared at the picture of a long-haired white cat asleep on top of a washing machine.

Tuesday's cat.

This made no sense at all. How could it be Tuesday? It was supposed to be Wednesday.

Word-study day.

But then Odessa understood. It was 6:07, after all, so it took a moment to remember that she always removed yesterday's calendar page first thing when she woke up.

It was time to remove Tuesday's cat, because it was Wednesday morning.

She ripped the long-haired white cat from the pad, and there they were: two Siamese kittens wrestling in a flower bed.

It was twenty-two hours earlier.

Wednesday morning at seven minutes past six.

Odessa sat down at her desk with her word list and quizzed herself.

Over and over and over again, until it was time for breakfast.

Downstairs, Mom gave her cinnamon toast again (luckily, Odessa loved cinnamon toast), and she climbed

aboard the bus and watched Claire block the seat next to her with her backpack. She arrived at school, where Mr. Rausche said, "Best feet forward." Sofia didn't have to read her face. She wasn't panicked. She took her quiz and aced it.

There is no *w* in *thorough.*

That afternoon she was sent home with a new packet of words to study.

She was now a proud member of group N.

Odessa Green-Light was no longer smack-dab in the middle.

21 Hours . . . 20 Hours . . .
19 Hours . . . 18 Hours . . .
17 Hours . . .

Imagine everything you'd do over if given the chance.

That thing you said at lunch that made everybody laugh because it was stupid?

Forgotten.

The humiliating *thwack* of the dodgeball against your thigh and the red mark it left behind?

Erased.

The misunderstanding that sent you to the "take a break" chair, when you weren't really talking during social studies, you were only asking Jeffrey Mandel to return your pencil?

Over.

These are the sorts of things that sent Odessa back to the center of her attic floor, the rug rolled up and stashed

near the bookcase. She would shut her eyes tight, hold her breath, and jump.

She jumped to undo something about her day that had gone a way she didn't like.

What power.

How easy.

Still, there were choices to make.

What needed undoing?

And was undoing it worth living the whole day over again? Worth using up another jump back in time?

What about the things she would have to endure for a second time just to change the one thing she wanted to undo?

Take the farting incident.

Odessa knew that a loud fart could be a good thing *if you happened to be a boy.*

If you happened to be a girl, farting was a whole different story. It was something to be avoided at all costs. Something to live in mortal fear of. But living in mortal fear of something doesn't mean it won't happen to you.

Like vomiting. Odessa feared vomiting, but sometimes she'd get the stomach flu. Usually right after Oliver got it, because in addition to being a toad, Oliver was a walking germ-fest. Odessa feared shots. But she got them. She was afraid of thunder, but that didn't keep storms from coming.

Odessa feared farting.

In front of other people.

Especially farting in front of somebody who looked cute since he'd stopped cutting his hair. Somebody she *like*-liked.

But still, it happened in front of Theo Summers.

During math.

Multiplication tables, to be precise.

Theo looked at her and she looked away, but she could feel how hot her face was. She didn't need a mirror to know she'd turned scarlet. Lobster-colored. This happened when she got embarrassed, and it was why her mother sometimes called her Odessa Red-Light. Like getting stuck with the hyphenated *Green-Light* wasn't annoying enough—even her own mother teased her about it. Her own mother, who along with her father had *de*-hyphenated the whole family.

Odessa waited for Theo to make some joke to Bryce Bratton. But he didn't. And because of this, because he quickly looked down at the math problems on the hexagonal table between them, Odessa's *like*-like blossomed into full-blown love.

But Theo knew.

He had heard.

And he'd never forget.

This left Odessa with no choice but to go home and jump through the floor.

Still, there were parts of this day she didn't want to relive.

On the day of the farting incident, Odessa had a checkup after school at which she received not one, but three shots. And that night there was a terrible thunderstorm. The window-shaking kind. The kind that made her rethink wanting to sleep in a room alone.

But neither shots nor thunderstorms seemed very big at all when stacked up next to the horror of Theo Summers hearing her fart.

So that night, as the thunder rattled her bones and the lightning lit the darkening sky outside her window, Odessa rolled up her cheetah-print rug.

They'd just finished dessert. Chocolate banana pudding wasn't her favorite, but it was a close second. When she considered living through the shots and the thunder again, she thought: *At least there'll be pudding!*

Odessa tapped her toe on the exposed floorboards.

The thunder crackled outside. Terrifying. A sound like the whole world splitting in two. It reminded Odessa of the time she and Oliver dropped a watermelon out their bedroom window onto the back patio just to see what would happen.

What happened was that Mom got really mad.

Hurry! Jump. Get away from the thunder. Wake up again, start the day fresh, and avoid that terrible Odessa Red-Light moment.

But going back seventeen hours was different from leaving something behind.

The shots and the thunderstorm were still in front of her because . . . tomorrow wasn't really tomorrow.

Once she jumped, tomorrow would become today all over again.

16 Hours

Things might have continued this way, with Odessa correcting all of her awkward, embarrassing, unfortunate moments. The pesky happenstances that are a part of any fourth grader's life.

Things might have continued like this but for one simple fact: Odessa Green-Light was a curious girl.

The type who sought to understand why certain things were so. It was this part of her that hated spelling and its nonsensical rules.

So Odessa went in search of answers.

She wished more than anything that Claire was still speaking to her. They were friends last year when they were both in Room 22. They weren't best friends, but Claire was fun, and curious. She was logical and clear-headed too. Back in third grade they'd read a whole series

of mysteries about a boy named Benedict, and Claire had always solved the mystery *before* Benedict did. She didn't have to cheat and skip to the end to see how it all turned out, like Odessa.

But now Claire put her backpack on the seat next to her on the bus, the seat that used to be Odessa's, and they weren't in the same class this year. Odessa was in Room 28 with Sofia, which was nice, but not necessary, because Sofia was her best friend no matter what classroom they were in.

If Claire had still been speaking to her she might have been able to think three steps ahead like she had with the Benedict books and help Odessa find some answers about the attic floor. But no. Odessa was going to have to figure this out on her own.

Like she often did when things perplexed her, she opened up her hummingbird journal. She wrote down the things she understood, underlining them for emphasis.

Time is running out.

Each time she jumped she lost one hour, one chance.

There are only twenty-four chances.

Twenty-four opportunities to redo something, and now, with only sixteen opportunities left, she started to wonder: Had she frittered away the first eight?

I've been stupid.

She had no regrets about the farting incident, but the "take a break" chair? The red mark of the dodgeball and its *thwack*?

What a waste.

She began to understand the need to hoard her remaining opportunities.

Sixteen left. Sixteen!

She made a final note in her journal:

Don't be impulsive. Make it matter. THINK!

*

Weeks went by.

The air grew colder. The leaves went from green to red to brown before abandoning the trees altogether. The sky outside Odessa's dormer window turned black before dinnertime.

Dad and Jennifer were planning a spring wedding. Odessa's every other weekend with them was spent tasting cake and looking at flowers and trying on dresses. Odessa finally picked out a lavender one with spaghetti straps, which meant Oliver would have to wear a lavender tie, and she was looking forward to seeing that. He never wore anything but T-shirts and cutoff sweatpants.

Jennifer brought home samples of music for the reception. She'd play it full blast in the house and practice her dance moves. Dad would smile and shake his head. Jennifer knew how to make Dad laugh, which was good because sometimes Dad could be too serious. Sometimes Odessa would even dance with her.

All the wedding preparation reminded Odessa of when she and Sofia used to play princesses. Neither of them really wanted to be princesses—who could stand itchy clothes and perfect posture all the time?—but it was still loads of fun to pretend.

The only thing Odessa looked forward to with winter's arrival was the freezing of the pond near Uncle Milo's, where he took her ice-skating on Saturday afternoons. He took Oliver too, because Odessa never seemed to get to do anything, or go anyplace, without Oliver the Toad.

On a particularly gloomy Saturday, Uncle Milo, Odessa, and Oliver went to check out the pond, skates in the trunk, hot cocoa in the thermos, but it hadn't frozen over completely yet. Big shards of ice floated haphazardly, like pieces of a puzzle that would never fit together.

Oliver thought he spied a rabbit and went bounding off after it, maybe thinking he could coax it into his hands like that field mouse, and Odessa took the rare opportunity afforded by this moment alone with Uncle Milo to ask him some questions.

Uncle Milo was her mother's younger brother. Once he'd told Odessa a story about how when they were kids Mom had convinced him to do a trust fall backward so she could catch him. He closed his eyes, crossed his arms, and fell backward, but then she stepped out of the way and he cracked his head open on the kitchen floor. Odessa thought this was pretty funny in the way things are funny when they're the opposite of what you expect. She couldn't picture her mother letting her brother fall on his head, because Mom was the one who always told Odessa how she needed to show Oliver more *kindness*.

And she certainly couldn't picture Milo as a toad.

Uncle Milo was her favorite.

"Uncle Milo?" she asked. "Has anything ever happened to you that you don't really understand? I mean, like, something that makes *no sense?*"

"Of course, O." He smiled. Odessa loved his smile. And she loved when he called her O, except sometimes he called Oliver O too, and that she didn't like one little bit. "All the time. Most things in life don't make any real sense. That's what keeps us on our toes."

Odessa thought of Milo as someone with all the answers, but there were things even he couldn't figure out, which was surprising. And a little bit comforting too.

"Cool," Odessa said, though she was far from satisfied.

He squinted at her. "Are you okay?"

"I'm great."

"I know things haven't been easy. . . ."

"I said I'm great."

"I know you did. And I said I know things haven't been easy."

Odessa bit the inside of her cheek. She thought about that lavender dress hanging in plastic in the closet at Dad's. About Claire's backpack on the bus seat. About Mom's job interviews. About the word *like* and its different, confusing meanings.

"Uncle Milo, I . . ."

Just then Oliver came racing back, waving something in his hand. It was too small to be a rabbit. *It better not be another field mouse*, Odessa thought.

As he grew closer, he shoved the object into his pocket. When he reached them, he bent over to catch his breath, hands on knees, cheeks bright red with cold. Odessa resisted the temptation to call him Oliver Red-Light.

"You are never gonna"—*gasp*—"guess what I"—*gasp*—"just found."

Oliver was rarely right about things, but he was right about this.

Odessa would never have guessed.

Not if she'd had one hundred guesses.

He stuck his hand back into his pocket and took something out slowly, grabbing it by both ends and pulling it tight. He held it up proudly.

A one-hundred-dollar bill.

"Would you look at that. . . ." Milo slapped Oliver on the back. "It's your lucky day, O. You are one lucky little man."

Immediately, Odessa thought of her piggy bank and its twenty-seven dollars and eighty-three cents. She'd felt good about her savings. She'd saved six dollars and twenty-two cents more than Oliver.

She couldn't bear to do the math. She didn't want to know by exactly how many dollars and cents Oliver's savings now outnumbered hers.

Plus, there were so many things she wanted to buy. So much she could do with one hundred dollars. There were things a fourth grader needed that a second grader did not.

It wasn't fair.

"Where did you find it?" Odessa asked.

Oliver lifted his thumb over his shoulder and pointed behind him. He was still trying to catch his breath.

"Over there."

"Over *where?*" she asked. "Over where . . . *precisely?*"

Odessa had never stolen anything in her life. Sofia stole lip glosses from her older sister, and Odessa had told her it was wrong, but Sofia had just laughed and dug her pinkie deeper into the one that smelled like mango.

Now, as Odessa's plan began to take shape, she worried that she was about to do something kind of . . . wrong.

But how could it be stealing if she wasn't planning to take something *away from* Oliver? What if she was planning to get to that one-hundred-dollar bill *before* he did? Before he even knew there was a one-hundred-dollar bill to find?

"Over by that big boulder," Oliver said. "The one underneath that Christmas-y tree."

Uncle Milo laughed. He put both hands on Odessa's shoulders and squeezed. "You're not going to find another hundred-dollar bill, no matter how hard you look. It doesn't happen like that. Luck was on your brother's side today. Maybe tomorrow it'll be on yours."

Uncle Milo didn't know everything. He'd even said so himself. He didn't know that Odessa didn't need any luck.

She looked at her watch. All she needed was for Uncle Milo to take her home. Back to the magical attic that belonged only to her.

15 Hours

Money can't solve all your problems. This is something Odessa had heard adults say for most of her life. They also said that money doesn't grow on trees, but they were wrong about that, because Odessa now had one hundred dollars from beneath a tree in the woods. Uncle Milo had given her a high five when she'd found it, and Oliver had stared at her in disbelief and with a familiar envy. She felt a little guilty about going back and getting to the money before Oliver, but only a little. She was rich. That helped with her guilt, though it didn't help her figure out what was happening in the attic, because . . . money can't solve all your problems.

She continued her investigation by taking out mysteries from the library. Not the babyish Benedict ones any

third grader could solve. She went looking for *real* mysteries. There were so many of them, so many books with spines of every width and color. Maybe reading some might help her solve her own.

Sofia was not pleased.

They'd both started the series about the girl who moves to a new town and has to make new friends at her new school, but then there's this mean girl who will stop at nothing to destroy the new girl, and Odessa and Sofia were on book five when Odessa returned it unfinished at library time and checked out four mysteries.

That was one of the cool things about being in the fourth grade. You could check out four books at once. Second graders like Oliver could only check out two, but it hardly mattered, because Oliver wasn't much of a reader.

"Those look boring," Sofia said. "We don't read mysteries. Or books about fairies. And we don't like graphic novels."

Sofia had added this last category, Odessa knew, because that was the kind of book Claire read on the bus in the mornings.

"Yeah, I know. But I guess I'm just in the mood for something new."

Sofia sighed and rolled her eyes. She started to say something about how Odessa wasn't allowed to drop their series for a new one, but then Mr. Bogdasarian, the librarian, rang the bell that meant they were all to line up quickly and quietly. He timed them, and although Odessa always raced to her spot in line tight-lipped, she wasn't sure why she did. There never seemed to be any sort of prize for speediness.

When Sofia sighed and rolled her eyes, Odessa thought again, for the millionth time, about confiding in Sofia about the attic. About the loophole she'd found in time.

But something always stopped her.

Maybe it was that she knew how it would sound coming out of her mouth. *Impossible. Absurd.* And Sofia had a way of looking at Odessa when she didn't believe or understand or agree with what Odessa was saying—a sharp look Odessa could feel in the softest part of her center. She didn't like that feeling at all.

Or maybe it was that Odessa didn't believe Sofia could

help her solve her mystery. Help her understand the *why*.

It wasn't as if Sofia wasn't smart.

Sofia was in the level N word-study group too, which might have had something to do with how desperately Odessa had wanted to move up from the middle.

Sofia's math buddy, however, was Chester Spaulding, and everyone knew Chester wasn't as good at math as Theo Summers.

Anyway, Sofia didn't have much of an imagination, or Claire's detective skills, and she definitely didn't know about Odessa's house and its history.

For that Odessa turned to Mrs. Grisham, their landlady, who lived next door in a house that looked almost the same except it was pink. Odessa used to love pink, but she'd outgrown it, and now she wondered if when she got really old, she might love pink again.

Odessa hadn't seen much of Mrs. Grisham since they'd moved in, and she felt uneasy about just walking up to her front door and ringing her bell. Old people made her nervous. She didn't have any grandparents and she'd never had an older teacher, so she hadn't spent any time around old people.

Odessa picked up the newspaper that was sitting on Mrs. Grisham's front porch and tucked it under her arm. It took a very long time for Mrs. Grisham to answer the doorbell.

Odessa stood there, rehearsing what she'd say when

Mrs. Grisham finally made it to the door, but all she managed to blurt out was "Here's your paper."

Mrs. Grisham looked at Odessa the way Oliver looked at the various creatures he'd find in the backyard.

"It was sitting on your porch," Odessa added. "I didn't want anyone to take it."

"Has there been a rash of newspaper thefts in the neighborhood I don't know about?" Mrs. Grisham asked.

"Um, no. I just . . . I'm Odessa," she added, because she wasn't sure what else to say.

"I know who you are. You live in my house."

"Yes, I do."

"You didn't look too happy about living there."

"It's fine now," Odessa said. "I live in the attic."

Mrs. Grisham looked her up and down and then turned and went back inside. She didn't slam the door exactly, but she did close it rather abruptly.

The next afternoon Odessa noticed the paper on the porch again, and again she delivered it to Mrs. Grisham.

This time their exchange lasted longer.

Things continued this way. Most afternoons Odessa would pick up the paper from the porch and ring Mrs. Grisham's bell.

"Why are you always talking to that old lady?" Oliver asked. "She's weird."

"You're weird," Odessa snapped back. She gave him a shove in the direction of their house, as if she were urging

him home rather than just enjoying the pure pleasure she got from shoving him.

Odessa had never noticed Mrs. Grisham's paper on her porch before, but one thing was certain: since that first day she'd delivered it, Mrs. Grisham never seemed to go out and get the paper herself.

During their afternoons Odessa tried out all of her theories about the house.

She asked if magicians had built it.

"No," Mrs. Grisham answered.

Odessa asked if it had been struck by lightning.

"Nope," Mrs. Grisham said.

Odessa asked if, to the best of her knowledge, ghosts had ever been known to haunt her house.

"Not to the best of my knowledge," Mrs. Grisham sighed. She seemed to be growing tired of Odessa's line of questioning. "Look, don't worry about the house and just enjoy living there. Sometimes houses, like people, are peculiar. And sometimes they come along at just the right time. Now stop asking me so many questions. Do you want a cookie?"

Of course Odessa wanted a cookie.

So Mrs. Grisham started feeding Odessa homemade treats on her visits, and they sat in her front parlor, where she kept her enormous collection of owl figurines, and Odessa stopped asking questions. Instead she mostly talked about school, sometimes exaggerating details to make her stories more interesting.

And then, one afternoon, when Odessa rang the bell with the paper tucked under her arm, Mrs. Grisham took even longer to get to the door than she had on that first afternoon. She opened it only halfway. She wore a long floral thing with buttons that must have been a bathrobe.

A housecoat? A dressing gown?

Odessa wasn't sure what it was called, but she knew that even old women didn't go out in public in something that looked like that.

Mrs. Grisham managed a weak smile as she took hold of her paper.

"Thank you, dear."

It was the first time she'd ever called Odessa anything.

Mrs. Grisham started to close the door, without stepping outside for one of their chats and without offering any treats. Odessa grabbed the handle.

"Um, are you okay?"

"Yes. I'm fine. Just a little . . . oh, shall we say . . . *blue*."

Odessa loved the word *blue*. It said so much more than *sad* or *unhappy*. It was a word you could see. A word that painted a picture.

Odessa wasn't used to grown-ups telling her how they felt, unless they were feeling *fed up* or *out of patience*.

"Why are you blue?" she asked.

"Well, it's my birthday."

Her birthday? Birthdays were the happiest days of the year. Birthdays were the opposite of blue.

"So why aren't you . . . *jovial?*"

"Jovial?"

"You know, happy."

Mrs. Grisham smiled, and that made Odessa feel a little jovial herself.

"Oh, I suppose because when you get older, birthdays aren't all clowns and carousels and cotton candy."

Odessa thought Mrs. Grisham was closer to describing a carnival than a birthday, but still, she appreciated all those hard-c words strung together one after the other.

"Didn't you get any good presents?" Odessa asked.

Mrs. Grisham turned the newspaper over in her hands. "You brought me this," she said. "That's something."

"It's not much of a present. I mean a *real* birthday gift, with paper and ribbons and everything."

"I've never been much for presents," she said. "Mr.

54

Grisham used to give me a bunch of orange dahlias every year on my birthday. That was the best."

"Dolleeyas?"

"Yes, dahlias. My favorite flowers."

Odessa was about to ask what happened to Mr. Grisham and his dolleeyas, but then she stopped herself. She used *logic*, like Benedict. Mrs. Grisham was *blue*. She didn't have any dolleeyas. Therefore, there was no more Mr. Grisham.

"I have to go." Odessa turned and started to run.

"Thanks for the paper," Mrs. Grisham called.

"Happy birthday!" Odessa shouted over her shoulder as she raced home. She lived right next door, but still, she ran as fast as she could.

She found her mother in the kitchen, grating cheese.

"What's for dessert tonight?" Odessa asked, breathless.

"Please don't run in the house."

"Dessert," Odessa barked. "What is it?"

Her mother stared at her. "Melon," she said, drawing out the word.

"Water?"

"Are you thirsty, honey? What's going on?"

"No, I mean is it *water*melon?"

Her mother shook her head. "Cantaloupe."

Cantaloupe was *definitely* not worth sticking around for.

Odessa grabbed a fistful of grated cheese and shoved it in her mouth, dropping bright orange shreds of it on the kitchen floor.

"Odessa!"

Odessa knew grabbing cheese by the fistful would make her mother *fed up*, but she also knew it didn't much matter. She was already gone, running upstairs to the attic.

When she woke again, after the jump, it was 1:27 a.m. She pulled her comforter up to her chin, and she smiled because she had five more hours of sleep ahead of her.

Odessa loved sleep.

In the morning she ate her breakfast, and before she went out the door to catch the bus she handed her mother a note.

Odessa knew that sometimes she had better luck getting her mother to pay attention when she wrote down what it was she wanted to say. It hadn't worked with her move to the attic, but it had worked with other things.

She also knew it helped to use the word *please* as many times as possible.

Dear Mom,

Please can you buy a bunch of orange dolleeyas? And please put them outside Mrs. Grisham's front door. And please ring the doorbell so she knows to come to the door. But please don't stay around so she knows you left them.

Sincerely,

Your daughter, Odessa

P.S. Please!

When Odessa left for school that day, a day she had lived most of already, she felt the opposite of blue.

It was Mrs. Grisham's birthday, and she would find orange flowers on her doorstep. Her favorite. She'd have no idea who left them there, because she'd have no idea that she'd told Odessa how much she loved them. Maybe this would frighten her. Maybe she'd think it was the ghost of her husband. Or maybe she'd just gather them up in her arms and take a big whiff of them and shrug, knowing that there are some things in this world that don't make sense.

When Odessa delivered the newspaper that afternoon, it took Mrs. Grisham no time at all to come to the door. She opened it wide and grinned broadly. She didn't wear a long floral thing with buttons that must have been a bathrobe.

She wore a pretty red dress and shiny shoes.

14 Hours

Sofia was right. The mysteries *were* boring. And they didn't do anything to help Odessa understand what was happening in the attic.

Mrs. Grisham had told her to stop worrying, and Mrs. Grisham was an old person, so Odessa figured she must give good advice, because why else would you bother getting old?

That was just what Odessa was trying to do: she was trying to stop worrying and just enjoy the attic's strange powers.

She returned the boring, useless mysteries to the library and went back to the series about the new girl at school. There was no mystery as to how things would turn out for her—things always turned out just fine for this type

of character, and given the twists and turns in her own life lately, Odessa liked this sort of predictability.

She also checked out a graphic novel, thinking that maybe if she held it in her hand as she boarded the morning bus, Claire would offer Odessa the seat next to her.

Odessa had given up pretending she didn't care that Claire had stopped speaking to her. That wasn't working. And anyway, she *did* care.

She and Claire hadn't known each other forever like Odessa and Sofia, but they'd become friends last year in third grade and Odessa didn't understand what had happened since. At first she thought it was just that they didn't have the same teacher anymore, but then the backpack started showing up on Odessa's bus seat.

Claire didn't seem to have had any real friends before Odessa came along. She was skinny and knobby-kneed, and too eager to agree with whatever was said. It's hard to pinpoint why some kids are targets for the cruelty of others, but there was no denying that Claire Deloitte was a big, fat bull's-eye.

"Claire, did you see that movie about the aardvark and the pelican that opened this weekend? Everyone's talking about it," one of the girls might say at recess.

"Yeah," Claire would answer. "It was funny."

"Ha! Ha! Ha! There is no movie about an aardvark and a pelican!"

Or:

"Claire, don't you love that song 'Dream Detectives'?"

This song Claire had to know was real; it played anytime a radio switched on.

"Yeah. It's awesome."

"Oh my God! That song is sooooo stupid. It's, like, the stupidest song *ever.*"

Or this:

"Claire, when's your birthday?"

"It's on Oct—"

"Who cares!"

Maybe it was just because Odessa didn't pull any of these cruel jokes on Claire that Claire had attached herself to Odessa by the third week of third grade.

When it was Odessa's turn to stay in at recess to wipe down the desks, Claire would stay and help. If Odessa chose quiet reading time over working on the geography puzzle, Claire would read alongside her. Once Odessa opted to skip out on the birthday cake brought in by Sienna. Carrot cake. Yuck. Claire declined her piece too.

At first Odessa wondered about Claire.

Why didn't she stand up for herself? Why was she such a follower? But she stopped wondering, because she liked to be with Claire. Claire was smart. And she was funny. And despite the fact that she preferred books with cartoons, she too was a lover of words.

Now Claire spent most of her time at school with Maya, and that made Odessa feel *jovial* for Claire, because she didn't want her to be friendless.

60

So Odessa got on the morning bus with the graphic novel in her hands. She'd stayed up too late reading it cover to cover, and she was surprised by how much she'd enjoyed it.

She displayed the front of it as she approached Claire, who rested her arm on the dreaded backpack. Odessa took the seat in front of her.

As the doors closed with a *whoosh* and the bus lurched forward, Odessa turned around. She held the book out. "Have you read this?"

Claire glanced at the cover and then down at her lap. She nodded.

"Did you like it?"

Claire didn't respond. She probably thought Odessa was trying to catch her in a trap—asking for an opinion only so she could mock it.

"Well I read it last night and I thought it was awesome," Odessa said. "I totally didn't get why anyone bothered with graphic novels, like I thought they were going to be Calvin and Hobbes or Garfield or something, you know, baby stuff, but this book was really, really good."

Claire shrugged.

The bus stopped to pick up Mick McGinnis, and when it started up again, Odessa fell forward in her seat and dropped the book. As the bus climbed up the hill, the book slid back into Claire's row.

Claire picked it up, and for a moment Odessa thought she might shove it into her own bag or maybe toss it over

her shoulder or out the window, but she held it out to Odessa.

"If you liked this one," Claire said, "you should try *The Windchaser.*"

Odessa took her book back, feeling encouraged. Bold. "Would you mind putting your backpack on the floor so I can sit next to you?"

"No switching seats once the bus is moving," Claire shot back.

She pointed to the rules posted at the front of the bus. Right above *No Chewing Gum* and below *No Shouting* it said *Pick Your Seat and Stay There.*

Claire knew Odessa followed rules. It was something they had in common. But Odessa was obviously desperate. Desperate enough to switch seats on a moving bus.

"C'mon," Odessa whispered.

Claire shook her head no. She reached for her backpack and started digging around. Odessa knew this meant: *Don't talk to me.*

Odessa could feel opportunity slipping through her fingers.

"Listen, Claire," she blurted out. "I don't know why we aren't friends this year, but maybe if you just told me what I did, then I could apologize."

Claire looked at her. "What would be the point? You'd just say 'I'm sorry,' but you wouldn't really mean it. Apologies don't mean anything when you make someone apologize." She shrugged. "That's what my mom says."

Odessa's mother said this too. Their mothers must have read the same book about raising children. Mom never made her apologize to Oliver. Instead she'd make her ask, "What can I do to make you feel better?"

She tried this out on Claire.

Claire just sighed.

"I guess you could make me feel better by knowing what you did in the first place. But since that isn't going to happen, I'll just tell you, and then you can give me a fake apology and go back to hanging out with your real friends and leave me alone."

Odessa's stomach did a flip. Something like the upside-down, over-under feeling she got when falling. Odessa's stomach flipped because it was one step ahead of her brain.

She suddenly knew what Claire was going to say.

This was about that afternoon last summer when she and Sofia ran into Claire at the mall.

She asked what they were doing, and Odessa said they were going to see a movie, and Claire asked which one, and Sofia drew her finger across her throat behind Claire's back, letting Odessa know: *Do NOT invite Claire.*

Odessa's mom walked over and said hi to Claire and asked what she was up to. Odessa said that Claire was busy and couldn't come to the movie with them, even though Claire had said nothing of the sort.

Claire walked away fast, almost running, saying she

had to go meet her babysitter at the food court, and there was something about the way she almost-ran that made Odessa sad for Claire, but then she and Sofia went to see the movie, and it was really funny because this humongous dog talked with this New York accent and Odessa managed to block out the whole thing until just now, sitting on the morning bus.

Or did she really block it out?

If Odessa had really forgotten about that day, then why did she remember it so clearly right now?

Claire began to tell Odessa about that afternoon at the mall. How happy she was to see Odessa, because they hadn't seen each other since school got out.

Odessa was listening to Claire but at the same time she was cursing her attic floorboards. Why did it have to be a matter of hours? Why couldn't she go back months? If she could return to that day last summer, she'd have ignored Sofia's silent warning and asked Claire if she wanted to come to the movie, which she was hearing now from Claire would have been impossible anyway, because Claire had to be at her sister's play.

But of course that wasn't the point.

"I'm really sorry," Odessa said. "And you aren't making me say anything. I'm saying I'm sorry myself."

Claire sighed. "I wish that were true."

Odessa turned and faced forward. Her eyes stung with tears. She'd tried to be a good friend to Claire, and she'd

tried to be a good best friend to Sofia. But she'd done everything wrong.

She shoved the graphic novel into her backpack. How stupid to think that a book could fix things. The book was not the answer. The answer had been right there in front of her all along.

Odessa couldn't go back to the summer. But she could go back to this morning. She could leave the book at home and she could get on the bus with a letter in her hand.

It was easier to get people to pay attention when you wrote down what it was you wanted to say.

Odessa would do what she should have done months ago. She'd write a letter of apology, and she'd write it before Claire ever brought it up.

Odessa wrote the best letter she'd ever written. It took her three whole drafts.

Claire took it and shoved it in her bag without looking at Odessa.

But that afternoon, when Odessa got on the bus, Claire's backpack was on the floor, the seat next to her empty.

Odessa sat with Claire and rode the bus home.

13 Hours . . . 12 Hours . . .

Odessa had to admit that there were benefits to moving from a house you loved so your father could remarry someone who was not your mother, and the main benefit was that you got to have two Christmases.

At Mom's, Uncle Milo cooked breakfast while Odessa drew with her new artist's pencils and Oliver played with his new hamster.

Oliver had always wanted a hamster. He'd begged, cajoled, and bamboozled, but her parents had said no, because parents know that hamsters smell foul.

But now that the decision was Mom's alone, Odessa knew she'd given Oliver what he wanted more than anything, just like she'd given Odessa the attic she'd wanted more than anything, because there were other things

Mom couldn't give them, like a Christmas in their old house with their father.

And also, Oliver was lonely.

Odessa had wanted her own room, but Oliver had not. He pestered Odessa and mimicked her and eaves-dropped on her, but he hadn't wanted her to move out. He didn't want to sleep alone. Getting the hamster meant he wouldn't have to.

Milo suggested Oliver name him Mud, so that when people asked, Oliver could say, "His name is Mud." They all thought this was funny, even if Odessa wasn't sure why.

They went to Dad's apartment Christmas night. Dad and Jennifer had set up a tree twice as big as the one at Mom's and covered in fake snow. Odessa used to beg for a tree with fake snow, but her dad said they were "cheesy." Now Dad had one, and Odessa didn't know if he'd gotten it for her, or if Jennifer liked the trees with fake snow too.

There were other things Odessa and Jennifer both liked. They both liked radio 101.3, which played songs Mom called *insipid*. They liked sparkling lemonade, which

Dad kept stocked in the fridge. They liked to do crosswords, and sometimes they'd work together on one from a book Jennifer had bought of not-too-easy/not-too-hard puzzles.

That night there was a fire in the fireplace where the bulging stockings hung.

Uh-oh.

Normally, melted chocolate is one of the world's greatest inventions, but on Christmas night at Dad's the chocolate he'd put in their stockings melted all over the other things in there, like the animal erasers and the headbands and the tween magazines Mom didn't like Odessa to read.

They all laughed about it, and anyway, there were more presents under the tree with the fake snow.

Oliver got a new Star Wars Lego set, and Odessa received a new dictionary.

"Jennifer picked this out for you," Dad said, giving her a look. Odessa knew the look meant: *Give Jennifer a hug.*

Odessa looked away. "Thanks, Jennifer." She wasn't in a mood to hug Jennifer. Then she added, "I love it," because this might make Dad happy, and also, it was true.

Odessa opened the dictionary and inhaled its new-book smell. It was a grown-up dictionary with tiny print and no glossy photos. As she flipped through the pages, she saw that they were filled with purple marks.

"I hope you don't mind that I went through it," Jennifer

said. "I highlighted some of the unusual words I thought you might want to learn. It should help with the crosswords and Scrabble too."

Odessa had to admit, even though she didn't want to hug her, and even though she didn't want it to be true, that Jennifer had given her the best of all her Christmas gifts.

*

By the end of vacation Odessa was ready for school to start. She was tired of staying indoors. Tired of Oliver. Tired, even, of playing Dreamonica, in which she and Sofia now had more puppies and bigger mansions with swimming pools and waterslides and their characters were big TV stars. She was ready to leave the online world for the real world, but mostly, she was ready for recess.

Theo had been teaching her how to shoot baskets, and she wasn't half bad, but then Bryce Bratton had started saying they were in *loooooove*, so her lessons had come to an abrupt stop right before vacation.

Maybe over the break Theo would have blocked out Bryce, the way she'd blocked out that day at the mall with Claire, and they could start shooting baskets again. That was what she hoped when she went back to school that first day.

Odessa the Optimist.

But then Theo showed up with a new buzz cut and everything went downhill.

Odessa still thought he looked cute, because love means not caring if someone's hair is shaggy or bristly. Love means caring about what's on the inside and not on the top of someone's head.

So she was fine with the change.

She was *not* fine with what Sofia did.

During morning math Sofia sidled up to their side of the hexagon and said, "Oh my God, Theo, I can't believe you shaved off all your hair. Odessa liked it shaggy."

Ouch.

When Odessa had told Sofia she thought Theo Summers was cute since he'd stopped cutting his hair, she'd trusted Sofia not to tell anybody. Especially not Theo! That's what it means to have a best friend, whether in the real world or in Dreamonica. Your secrets are supposed to be safe.

What Sofia had done was no different from asking Odessa to trust her, and then stepping out of the way and letting her fall and split her head open on the kitchen floor.

After school Odessa went straight to her room and cried the tears she'd been holding in since morning math. She liked to imagine a place inside her, a place like that water tower not too far from the pond where she went skating, a big tank that could store all her bad feelings until she was somewhere safe enough to unlock that place and let everything out.

When she was done sobbing on her bed, she was still

angry and wasn't sure what to do about it. Sometimes shoving helped. Or throwing things. Also stomping.

What a terrible mistake.

And it was only the first of two terrible mistakes.

What she had was precious, she knew this, only thirteen opportunities left, and she knew to take great care with precious things. But she was just so angry, so *fed up*, that she'd gone and stomped on her attic floor without thinking about the consequences.

Mistake number one.

The next thing she knew it was thirteen hours earlier, and she was going to have to relive a day she wanted to forget.

It wasn't something she could undo, because it hadn't been her doing in the first place. And even if she could avoid it by knocking the hexagon over as Sofia approached or creating some other diversion, it wasn't going to take away the fact that Sofia had said it, that she had stood by and let Odessa fall back and split her head open on the floor.

Odessa decided, as she tossed and turned in her bed in the wee hours of a morning she'd already lived through, to be mature about it. To confront her troubles. To take Mom's advice and talk about her feelings rather than going around stomping and shoving. She would catch Sofia at school, before the first bell, and ask her nicely not to say anything about Theo's hair.

That was what she did.

Sofia wrinkled her nose. "Why would I say anything about Theo's hair?"

"Just don't. Okay?"

They were standing on the steps to school and right at that moment a bus pulled up. Theo climbed off with his new buzz cut, and Sofia's jaw dropped.

"How did you know?" she asked.

Mistake number two.

"Odessa! Have you guys been talking on the phone? Have you been emailing? Did you see him over vacation? Is something going on with you guys and you aren't telling me about it? Are you like *boyfriend-girlfriend* now? Geez! I thought we told each other everything."

She turned and ran up the stairs. Odessa watched her go while Theo, with his new buzz cut, walked right past her without saying a word.

Odessa thought about walking away from school, from math, from recess, from Sofia.

She might have if she'd had anyplace to walk to, but home was too far and she wasn't allowed to cross many of the streets on the way.

The first bell began to ring.

She'd never been late to class. She hadn't been late yesterday, because she hadn't talked to Sofia out on the steps. She didn't bother running. Late was late.

The fourth-grade rooms were on the second floor, but

the second-grade rooms were on the first, right by the stairwell, and as she approached Oliver's room she was surprised to find him sitting out in the hall, his face in Red-Light mode.

"Oliver?"

The hall was for the bad kids, the ones the teachers couldn't handle. Oliver was pesky, he was annoying, he was shy, but he wasn't *bad*.

"Go away," he said. "Please. Go away."

She recognized his *I'm about to cry* look, and because Odessa knew she'd do anything to avoid crying at school, she left him sitting there.

74

Without her asking questions, maybe Oliver could fill up his inner storage tank and hold it together until he got home and could be alone in his room.

Odessa tried to remember how he seemed after school on the yesterday that was now today. She couldn't remember. She couldn't, she realized, because she never bothered with how Oliver was feeling, especially yesterday, when she was so fed up. She'd sat next to Claire on the bus like she did every day now. She didn't notice where Oliver sat, because she never paid any attention to Oliver. But this afternoon she sat next to him. Luckily, Claire didn't seem to mind.

"What are you doing?" he asked.

"Sitting with you."

"Why?"

"Can't I sit with my brother if I want?"

"You never sit with me."

"I am today."

He turned and stared out the window.

"Why were you out in the hall?" Odessa asked.

He shrugged.

"Did you get in trouble?" Stupid question. Kids don't sit out in the hall just to breathe the fresh air.

"It wasn't my fault."

In Odessa's experience, most things were Oliver's fault, but this wasn't the time to say so.

"Whose fault was it?"

"Blake Canter is always picking on me, but I'm the one who gets in trouble."

Poor Oliver.

It was one thing to be the kid who got picked on. It was another thing entirely to be the boy who got picked on by a *girl* half his size.

"What happened?"

Oliver bit the nail on his thumb. That was what he did when he was upset or scared. He'd been doing it since he'd given up sucking it, at the mortifying age of seven.

"She took my hamster. Stole it from my backpack. She was waving it around and showing everyone and calling me a freak, and when I tried grabbing him back from her, Ms. Farnsworth told me since I can't keep my hands to myself I should go sit in the hallway."

"You took Mud to school?"

"Of course not. I took Barry."

Barry was the stuffed hamster Oliver had been sleeping with since forever.

"Why did you even take Barry to school?"

Oliver shrugged. "I don't have any friends."

She wanted to tell him that he wasn't helping matters by taking a worn-out stuffed hamster he refused to let Mom put in the laundry to school, that what he needed to do was be less shy and quiet, but she knew the damage was done. Once you're known as the boy who needs his stuffed hamster, it's a reputation that tends to stick.

Odessa leaned back in the bus seat and sighed. This day had been only a little bit better than this day had been before, and yet she knew she had no choice but to go back and live it all over again.

She thought about the randomness of things. Today had been a big mistake. It was her mistake number one. And yet . . . if she hadn't mistakenly fallen through the floorboards and had that fight with Sofia on the steps, she wouldn't have been late and she wouldn't have ever known that Oliver was having a day that was probably even worse than hers.

*

On the third take of this not-so-great day, Odessa snuck into Oliver's room while he was in the bathroom brushing his teeth, took Barry, and hid him at the bottom of Oliver's hamper.

On the bus she sat with Claire. Oliver was chewing his thumbnail. Odessa wanted to tell him that today would be a better day than it would have been had he found Barry, but she didn't. She didn't tell him for the same reason she waited for Theo to get off the bus before she asked Sofia, nicely, not to mention his hair.

If Odessa had learned anything from her adventures in the attic, it was to never make the same mistake twice.

11 Hours

It was another morning, with another one of her mother's "meetings," which meant that her mother was rushing Odessa to finish her breakfast (*Chop-chop!*) and to make some sense of the mass of tangles that was her hair (*Are small animals nesting in there?*) and to pick out something more appropriate to wear (*It's February, honey, not July*).

Odessa ate quickly, and she worked her hair with a brush, but she had no intention of changing her clothes. Girls in the fourth grade wore layered tank tops.

Her mother was opening and then slamming shut every drawer in the kitchen.

"*Somebody needs her cof-feeeee,*" Odessa singsonged under her breath to Oliver, who muffled his giggle with his hand.

"Not today," her mother muttered to herself. "Of all days, dear God, not today."

"What's wrong, Mom?"

"I just can't . . ." She picked up her purse and dumped the entire contents onto the kitchen floor. "Where on earth are the keys to the van?"

Mom always lost the keys to the van. Dad used to tease her that she should wear them around her neck like a "Latchkie kid." Odessa had never heard of the Latchkies or any of their children. Then Dad explained that a Latchkie kid is actually a *latchkey kid*, which is a kid who comes home from school to an empty house and has to let herself inside, fix her own snack, and get her homework done all by herself.

Odessa didn't offer to help. She wasn't much good at finding lost things, and even if she had been, the bus would be here soon, and even if the bus wasn't coming soon, she wasn't sure how she felt about Mom going back to work.

It sounded sort of dreamy when Dad first explained it, but that was back when Odessa couldn't imagine a life without Dad at work and Mom at home. That was before he moved to his apartment and Mom moved to the new house. And now that Mom was going on job interviews, Odessa imagined coming home to an empty house and fixing herself a snack, and she didn't find it dreamy at all.

She didn't want to be a latchkey kid. The girls in fourth grade didn't wear keys around their necks.

Odessa went off to school, leaving Mom sifting through gum wrappers and receipts on the kitchen floor.

Her day was uneventful.

She came home and brought Mrs. Grisham her paper, which she hadn't done in a while. Mrs. Grisham had baked ginger cookies, and Odessa wondered how many days she'd baked cookies without anybody stopping by to share them, so she ate four, but this didn't make her feel any better.

She went home and opened the front door. (She didn't need a key; it was unlocked.) She called, "Hi, Mom."

No response.

"Mom!" she yelled up the stairs.

Nothing.

She wandered through the kitchen, panic rising, and into the living room.

Mom sat on the sofa. The TV was on.

Some lady in a white billowy pantsuit was giving all the people in the studio audience some kind of prize, and then other ladies were jumping up and down and hugging each other, and while this should have been sort of exciting, or at least interesting, Odessa couldn't concentrate on what was happening because . . . her mother was watching TV!

In the middle of the afternoon!

Rule number one in the Green House: *No TV in the daytime.*

Okay, so maybe rule number one was *No hitting or*

pushing. No TV in the daytime was definitely rule number two.

"Mom?"

Oliver was sitting next to her. He didn't care about ladies giving away prizes to other ladies, but he would have been happy to watch anything, because he loved TV.

"Hi, honey," her mother said, eyes on the screen. "Good day at school?"

"Um, yes. Good day at home?"

"Sure."

"Did you find the keys?"

"No."

"So you missed your meeting?"

"Yep."

"Mom?" Odessa reached for the remote control. "Can I turn off the TV?"

Odessa was a keep-the-TV-on type, but she clicked the power button. She sat down next to Mom.

"I'm sorry you missed your meeting."

"Oh well, I suppose it wasn't meant to be."

"What do you mean?"

Mom stretched out her legs and pulled the throw blanket up to her chin.

"I mean if the job was the right job for me, then I would have made it to the interview. I wouldn't have misplaced the keys. The Universe would have seen to it that it all worked out."

"So it's the Universe's fault?"

The Universe. Why hadn't Odessa ever thought to blame her mistakes on the Universe?

Mom laughed. She nudged Odessa with her toe.

"Maybe you should give the Universe a time-out," Odessa said. "Send the Universe to its room."

Oliver jumped up and threw his arms out wide. "You should kick the Universe in the privates!"

"Inappropriate," Mom said, trying not to laugh. Then her smile disappeared. She pulled her feet back and curled them underneath her.

"You don't need a job," Odessa said.

"Yes, honey, I do. That's just the way it is now that I'm on my own."

Odessa wanted to tell Mom that she wasn't on her own. That she had Odessa and her toad of a son and Uncle Milo. But Odessa was quiet; she felt a sting in her eyes and didn't want to cry.

Mom looked at her. Mom knew how to see the sting even when the tears hadn't come yet. She was tricky that way.

"Oh, sweetie." She reached out and brushed Odessa's cheek. "Finding work is a good thing. I *want* to go to work as much as I *need* to. I'm ready to get back into designing. I miss it. I want to do something that puts me back out into the world."

"What was the job?" Odessa asked.

Her mother sighed. "Oh, just the kind where you get paid to do what you love."

Odessa loved making pottery. She loved the color magenta, lollipops that were too big to ever finish, and the feeling of fresh-out-of-the-laundry pajamas. She loved the smell of newly mowed grass. Butter-brickle ice cream. Theo Summers.

Odessa tried to imagine someone paying her for loving all those things.

"Sounds like a pretty good job," Oliver said.

Mom tousled his hair. "Stupid Universe," she said, even though *stupid* was a word Odessa and Oliver were not allowed to use.

"Stinky Universe," Oliver said timidly. Mom smiled.

"Contemptible Universe!" Odessa cried.

Mom put one arm around each of them.

Odessa had made up her mind, but there was no hurry to go to her attic and back to this morning to fix things. It was nice to just sit here like this.

"You know what?" Mom said. "The Universe wants us to have some ice cream."

Odessa and Oliver jumped up and raced into the kitchen. Oliver went for the spoons, Odessa for the bowls.

"Mint-chip or butter brickle?" Mom called as she headed for the freezer.

What a silly question. Always butter brickle.

"Well, would you look at that," Mom said as she stood

with the freezer door open, the cold rush of air blowing her hair off her face.

"What?" Odessa and Oliver asked in unison.

"The Universe has a very strange sense of humor," Mom said as she pulled out her frozen car keys.

10 Hours

Usually when Dad came to pick up Oliver and Odessa for their Wednesday-night dinners, he'd pull into the driveway and honk. Sometimes Jennifer was with him. Odessa liked the just-Dad nights, but ever since Christmas and the dictionary with the purple underlined words, she didn't mind so much when Jennifer came along.

On the Wednesday after Odessa had gone back to find Mom's keys in the freezer so Mom could make the job interview, Dad came to the front door and rang the bell.

Odessa opened it. "Why didn't you honk?"

"Is that a way to greet your dad?" He spread his arms out wide and she stepped into them. He pulled her close.

"That's better," he whispered into her ear. He smelled like his minty tummy tablets. Odessa missed that smell.

"OLIVER," she shouted up the stairs. "LET'S GO!"

"Wait a minute!" Dad said. "Let's go inside and talk a little."

Odessa didn't like any sort of conversation that adults announced you were having before you had it. First there was the "talk" about how Mom and Dad decided it would be better to live apart, and then the "talk" about how they were going to sell the house, and of course the "talk" about Dad getting remarried.

"Can't we just go to dinner?"

Mom walked up and Dad put his arm out. It was sort of like a handshake, but a little bit like a hug.

"Come on into the kitchen," Mom said.

Odessa followed them.

"How're things?" Dad asked Mom.

"Oh, you know, pretty good," Mom answered.

There they were, walking and talking like two old friends meeting each other on the street.

Her parents could be so weird.

Oliver came downstairs and took a look at the three of them around the kitchen table. Odessa could tell he was just as confused and uncomfortable as she was.

"So your dad and I want to talk to you about some changes," Mom said.

"I know there have been so many lately," Dad added, "and I'm sorry for that, I truly am, but sometimes change is good, and change can be exciting, and in this case you

should be proud of your mother for getting a really great job."

And proud of *me*! Odessa wanted to yell. *I'm the one who found her keys.*

"You got a job?" Oliver asked, shocked, like it had never occurred to him that one of her "meetings" might lead to that.

"Yes, honey, I did. At JK Design Studio. I'm going back to interior designing. I'll be doing some landscaping work too."

"That's great, Mom." Odessa tried her best to sound excited.

"Yes, it's great, but it means we have to make some new arrangements. I'll be out of the house more than I'd like."

I'd like you to be out of the house not at all.

Odessa didn't say this out loud. She sat there fingering her necklace with the peace sign, imagining how a key might feel hanging from her neck on a shiny new chain.

"I've talked to Mrs. Grisham next door," Mom continued. "She's agreed to watch you on the days you don't have after-school activities."

"The landlady?" Oliver asked.

"Do you know another Mrs. Grisham who lives next door?" Odessa snapped. Oliver's face fell.

"She used to be a teacher, so she can be of some help with your homework."

If Mom couldn't be home, at least it would be Mrs. Grisham and not some stranger greeting her after school. Mrs. Grisham was her friend, even if she was old.

"And you can always call me at work if you need anything at all," Dad added.

Odessa looked at her father. What she wanted to say was: *Why are you even here?* But she knew it might come out sounding mean, so she searched for better words.

"Why are you even here?" she asked, because sometimes only certain words work.

Dad cleared his throat and exchanged a look with Mom. "Because in spite of all the changes, we're still a family."

If we're still a family, why are you remarrying Jennifer?

Odessa didn't say this out loud.

Instead she grabbed her coat and went to dinner with Dad and Oliver, just the three of them, and afterward Dad pulled into the driveway and honked. Mom came to the front door.

They waved at each other and smiled as Oliver and Odessa walked into the house.

Odessa thought about that smile upstairs in her room. The way her parents almost hugged. How proud Dad seemed of Mom for getting that job at JK Design Studio.

She sat down and opened her new dictionary. When the world confounded her, words brought her peace. She read some of the words Jennifer had underlined in purple.

She liked the ones that meant something other than what you'd think.

Gumshoe: a detective. NOT a person who has gum on his shoes.

And she liked the ones with meanings that matched the way they sounded.

Enigma: something that is not easily explained or understood.

*

Mrs. Grisham started watching them the following Monday. Odessa and Oliver arrived home to the smell of some-

thing delicious that turned out to be made of something not delicious at all. Zucchini bread.

Odessa knew few things with the sort of certainty that she knew zucchini does not belong in an after-school snack.

Oliver took one look at it and went straight to his room.

Odessa and Mrs. Grisham sat in the living room and talked, and it felt like those afternoons at Mrs. Grisham's house, except that they weren't surrounded by owl figurines, but by photographs of a family that didn't include Dad.

Later that week, the snack was pumpkin muffins. An improvement for sure, but still missing the mark.

Odessa ate a muffin and polished off a glass of cold milk. Mrs. Grisham asked about her day, and she said it was fine. It was easier than telling her she saw Sadie Howell talking to Theo Summers at recess and that this wasn't good at all because everyone knew that Sadie, with her pale blue eyes, was the prettiest girl in the whole fourth grade.

Mrs. Grisham was a friend, but Odessa didn't need to tell her *everything*.

On her way upstairs to call Sofia, which she still did despite the "Odessa liked it shaggy" comment, she paused outside Oliver's door. She could hear him talking quietly on the phone. Didn't he know that she used the phone every day after snack?

She put her ear to his door. Even though she hated when he eavesdropped, she had to listen.

Who was he speaking to?

He'd said he had no friends, but this couldn't be true. Everyone has some kind of a friend, even shy kids like Oliver.

"It's okay," he was saying. "You're going to be okay. I know you feel bad, but I'm here. I'll help."

Odessa creaked open the door.

"Oliver?"

He sat on the floor with his back to her, holding something in his lap.

"It's Mud," Oliver said. "He's really sick."

Odessa sat down next him and watched as he stroked his hamster. His best friend.

"His heart is beating really fast and his breathing sounds weird."

"Maybe you need to take him to the vet. Let's go tell Mrs. Grisham."

"No," Oliver blurted out. "No way."

Odessa looked at him.

"Remember Truman?" he asked.

Truman was their old cat. Mom had him since before she'd met Dad. They'd taken him to the vet one day because he wasn't eating his kitty food, and he never came home again. Oliver was barely old enough to remember Truman, but he'd since been terrified of vets. And people doctors too.

"But maybe the vet can help him." Odessa touched Mud gently.

Oliver shook his head no as a tear made its way down his cheek. Usually Oliver's tears irritated Odessa. He knew how to cry at just the right time, in just the right way, so that he always looked like an innocent victim.

Poor Oliver, she thought.

Usually when someone said, *"Poor Oliver,"* it was immediately followed by *"You're older, Odessa. You should know better."*

But today she really felt those words: *Poor Oliver.* The realness of that tear made Odessa want to help him.

"Wait here." Odessa went into Mom's medicine cabinet and took out the grape-flavored chewable Motrin. Mom gave it to her in the middle of the night when she woke up with the feeling like her knees were on fire, or sometimes her ankles, and occasionally her feet. The doctor called these "growing pains," but Odessa was never any taller in the morning.

She also took chewable grape Motrin when she had a fever or her teeth hurt and that time she'd stepped on a bee when she'd gone outside in bare feet right after Mom had said, "Put some shoes on, you could step on a bee!"

Odessa knew Mom's medicine cabinet was off-limits. She knew never to take any medicine all by herself, without adult supervision—that was why medicine came in bottles most adults had trouble opening. But chewable grape Motrin came in a box, and anyway, giving it to a hamster was different from taking it herself.

Odessa held the purple pill in her hand. She braced for the feeling of Mud's nose and whiskers on her palm, but he had no interest in her offering.

"Maybe we should crush it up and put it in his food," Odessa suggested.

Oliver shook his head. "He's not eating."

When Truman needed medicine Mom would pry his mouth open, shove the pill down his throat, and hold his jaws closed until he swallowed it.

She looked at the pill and at Mud's mouth. The pill was almost half the size of his little face. She couldn't see how this could possibly work.

"Maybe put it into his water," Oliver said.

Odessa nodded. Sometimes, not often, but sometimes, he did have brilliant ideas.

Oliver crushed the pill into the top of Mud's water

bottle and gave it a good shake, then put it back on the side of the cage. He placed Mud in a patch of sawdust just under the small metal spout.

He sniffed it.

His whiskers twitched.

He sniffed it again.

Then Mud stuck out his tongue—so little and pink—and started to drink. Odessa couldn't believe how small his tongue was. And his teeth! No bigger than grains of rice. She had to admit, he was sort of cute as he stood on his hind legs and held on to the drinking spout with his tiny little paws.

Oliver breathed a sigh of relief as a third of the purplish water slowly drained from the bottle.

He looked at his sister. "Thanks," he said.

Odessa smiled.

She went up to her attic, her chest swelling with pride. It felt good to help someone, even if that someone was a rodent who belonged to a toad.

She called Sofia, but Sofia's mom said she was doing homework and that they could talk about Dreamonica later. Odessa didn't say: *I need to talk about Sadie and why she's all over Theo, not my fake mansion with the water-slide!*

She sat at her desk and pulled out her folder. Perplexors: math problems disguised as word problems. They made her brain hurt. She put those back and took out her

word-study sheet. The quiz, as always, was on Wednesday. Tomorrow. She looked over her list.

> **neighbor**
> **brought**
> **tongue**
> **height**
> **weird**
> **believe**

And her favorite: **misspell.**

It was nice to know that Mr. Rausche had a sense of humor.

Odessa stretched her legs and caught the cord of her desk lamp with her sneaker, pulling the plug clear out of its socket and plunging her room into almost-blackness. That was one thing about living in the attic that Odessa did not love—her small window didn't let in much light.

She grabbed her pen that was also a flashlight and crawled underneath her desk. Her father had given her this penlight. It said Clark Funds on it. She'd always wondered why Dad had given her Mr. Funds's pen, but now she was glad he did, because she'd have had a hard time finding the socket without it.

Just as she went to put the plug in, Odessa spied a little door. Well, maybe it wasn't a door, because it had no handle, but it was a small square-framed space, just big enough for somebody to crawl through.

She shined the light of Mr. Funds's pen on it.

How peculiar, Odessa thought.

She reached over to give the door a shove, and just as she did, she heard a bloodcurdling scream come from beneath her.

"Noooooooooooooooooooooooooooooo!"

Odessa scrambled out from under her desk and down her attic steps and threw open Oliver's door to find him lying in his bed, curled around Mud's lifeless small body.

"He's not breathing!" Oliver wailed.

Mrs. Grisham raced in. She took the hamster from Oliver and looked him over carefully. She put him up to her ear as if he were a telephone.

"Oh dear," she said.

Oliver began to sob uncontrollably.

What came tumbling into Odessa's mind just at that moment was a purple word from her new dictionary.

Slipshod.

It referred to something done in a sloppy way with poor attention to detail, and though Odessa understood it to apply mostly to the way things are built or constructed, she couldn't help but feel, at that moment, that *slipshod* might also describe her whole *feed-the-sick-hamster-some-chewable-grape-Motrin* plan.

Would it have been such a bad idea to read the label?

"It's her fault," Oliver cried. "It's all her fault."

Mrs. Grisham looked at Odessa.

"W-w-well," Odessa stammered, "I . . ."

Then she ran from the room.

*

Ten hours earlier found Odessa standing on the sidewalk waiting for the bus to school. Oliver was saying something to her, but Odessa wasn't listening. She probably didn't listen the first time he'd said it either, but she wasn't listening this time around because she was waiting for Mom's car to turn the corner.

She was going to save Mud, even though Oliver had been so quick to tattle on her. It didn't seem fair to punish a poor hamster for her brother's being a toad.

To think she'd felt guilty about that one-hundred-dollar bill! Oliver didn't deserve good luck. It was no wonder the kid had no friends. Who tattles on someone for doing what she thought was the right thing? For trying to be a decent sister?

He babbled on and Odessa put her hands over her ears. No reason to be nice to him.

Just then Mom's car came into view.

It was a new ritual since she'd started work. Odessa and Oliver walked to the bus stop, where they'd meet Ben Greenstein and his mother, who waited with the three of them until the bus arrived. Mom would leave the house right after the kids and honk and wave as she drove past on her way to work.

Odessa flailed her arms wildly. "Stop!" she yelled.

Mom pulled over.

Odessa ran to the passenger door and opened it.

She spoke without stopping to breathe. "You have to take Mud to the vet—it's really important—he's really, really sick—and Oliver is too scared after what happened to Truman to tell you—but if Mud doesn't see a doctor he's gonna die."

Odessa slammed the door, ran to the bus, and climbed on.

She sat next to Claire and smiled. It was nice having her as a bus friend. She shut her eyes and took a silent vow never to enter her mother's medicine cabinet again. Never

would she bear the responsibility of taking another's life, even if that life belonged to a smelly hamster with rice-sized teeth.

She didn't talk to Oliver once all day.

Walking home from the bus stop that afternoon, Odessa thought about how she could get Oliver to repay her. He owed her big-time. The problem was, he didn't know he owed her. He didn't know she'd gone back and helped him. No matter. She'd figure out a way to make him pay.

When they walked through the front door, Odessa did not smell pumpkin muffins. And she did not find Mrs. Grisham waiting for them in the kitchen.

Mom sat at the table with a serious look on her face. A face that said: *We need to talk.*

"It's Mud." Mom held out her arms to Oliver. "He isn't going to make it. I took him to the vet, but there's nothing they can do to save him."

9 Hours

Odessa had started to see herself as someone with limitless capabilities. Kind of all-powerful.

Odessa Almighty.

No more.

As it turns out, going back in time can't fix everything. Mud's demise made that clear.

Now she was just *Odessa Who Can Go Back and Correct Mistakes, Sometimes*—a title that didn't have quite the same ring to it.

She told herself that she had never killed the hamster in the first place. Just believing, briefly, that she *had* caused Mud's death . . . it didn't fit with how she saw herself.

She was a giver, not a taker.

A fixer! Not a breaker.

And now that she knew Mud was going to die anyway, she felt . . . well, better.

Oliver, however, was not recovering speedily. He rarely smiled, and had no energy to be his pesky self.

Mom offered to get him a new hamster, but he refused.

"How about a guinea pig? They're hardy!"

"No thanks."

"I'd consider a ferret."

Oliver shook his head.

"You know, we could always go back to being a cat family."

He didn't even bother to respond.

"Hey," Odessa said. "Remember when your bike got stolen and then Dad went out and got you a new one and it was way better than the one you used to have?"

Oliver looked at her. For a minute she thought he might tell her to *shut up* or ask why she had to be such a *stupid butt-brain*, but he just walked off and closed himself in his room.

Odessa listened outside his door. Was he crying? Talking to his stuffed hamster, Barry? She heard nothing.

This silence was maybe the worst sound of all.

She thought of giving him the hundred-dollar bill. Maybe that would cheer him up. But she decided against it: money can't buy happiness. At least, that was what grown-ups said.

Oliver was particularly glum over the weekend. Be-

cause they shared a room in what was now Dad *and* Jennifer's apartment, it was hard not to notice the depths of his *blueness*.

She didn't know how to cheer him up, but that didn't stop her from trying. One attempt, a happy dance, ended with her twisting an ankle.

He wouldn't play Scrabble. Jennifer had picked up a deluxe version, the kind where the board spins to face the next player, and Odessa brought along her new grown-up dictionary with the purple underlined words, but Oliver shook his head. "No thanks."

Odessa set up a runway for a fashion show, and Jennifer let her borrow her heels. She wore her lavender dress

even though the wedding was months away, but Oliver refused to put on his suit with the matching tie.

Jennifer tried too. She suggested a Lego challenge: Who can build the tallest structure in three minutes? Oliver took a pass.

And then on Saturday morning, while they were watching TV, the only activity Oliver would engage in, his favorite commercial came on. It was for a car driven by hamsters in baggy pants and gold chains, hamsters that could break-dance. Every time Oliver saw this commercial he'd laugh until he cried, except for this Saturday morning when he started crying without any laughing first.

Odessa sat across the room, stunned. She wanted to go comfort him somehow, but she took too long, and before she knew it Jennifer hurried to the couch and put an arm around the sobbing Oliver.

That was when he shouted at her.

"Don't touch me!"

Shy, timid Oliver roared like a lion.

Dad came storming into the room. "What's going on in here?"

"Nothing," Jennifer said. She stood, hands deep in her pockets. "Oliver's just upset."

Dad looked from Oliver to Jennifer and back again, and then at Odessa, as if she could do anything other than keep her heart from pounding its way right out of her chest.

The first thing she wanted to do was run upstairs to her attic. To turn back the clock and reach Oliver first. That way, if he'd shouted, he'd have shouted at her. That's the way things were supposed to be. Brothers are supposed to shout at sisters. Not at the woman your dad is going to remarry.

But Odessa couldn't run upstairs, because she was at the Light House: Dad's. Her attic was at the Green House: Mom's.

"Oliver?" Dad looked at him.

The room felt like it was shrinking. It felt like someone had turned up the thermostat.

"It's okay, Glenn," Jennifer said.

More than anything, at that moment, Odessa wished her mom was there. She'd know what to say to make the room expand, and cool down, and feel normal again.

Odessa looked at the clock above the sofa. They weren't going home until tomorrow evening, and that would be too late. She couldn't fix a thing.

Jennifer walked out of the room. Dad sat by Oliver and all at once Odessa felt that water tank inside herself filling up, not with tears, but with rage.

If Dad hadn't left their old house, if he hadn't de-hyphenated the family, they wouldn't be in this apartment, and there wouldn't be an almost-stranger named Jennifer in the other room, and Oliver wouldn't be looking so miserable because he wouldn't have screamed, and

anyway he wouldn't have even been given a hamster who died, because when Dad and Mom lived together they said no to rodents.

Odessa went and took her brother by the hand. It had been so long since she'd held it. She could feel that it had grown bigger. She pulled him into their bedroom. They spent most of what was left of the weekend in there. Odessa wrote in her journal. Oliver played with his Legos.

When Dad dropped them off on Sunday evening he honked, Mom came to the door, and they smiled at each other. As Odessa walked up the steps, she thought again about their smiles and about all the things she couldn't fix.

Still 9 Hours

Odessa's tenth birthday was approaching, and she found herself wondering if this was what it meant to grow up. Did the world just get more and more mysterious? More *incomprehensible*? More *bewildering*?

There was the attic floor, of course, and then the door with no handle under her desk. There was how your best friend could step out of the way and let you split your head open, yet continue to be your best friend. There was the way two people could smile at each other, and then one could go and *re*marry somebody else.

She wished she could just live in Dreamonica, where she got to make every decision—how many puppies, how big a mansion, even what color hair and eyes she had.

And speaking of eyes, there was Sadie Howell, who had turned her attention to Theo Summers, big-time.

Odessa could not compete with those pale blue eyes; she couldn't even match their shade when she designed her online self.

Smile, blush, giggle. Smile, blush, giggle.

That was Sadie Howell. Hovering over Theo's desk. Sitting next to him at assemblies. Running up to him at recess.

Smile, blush, giggle.

Odessa couldn't believe this sort of thing worked. It made Sadie look kind of dumb, or—as Uncle Milo liked to say—one fry short of a Happy Meal.

But Theo seemed to fall for it. Without his shaggy hair to hide behind, Theo had no choice but to stare right back into Sadie's eyes.

All this time Odessa had thought the secret lay in math! If she could show Theo how good she was at solving equations, he'd see that she was worthy of his love.

It seemed so stupid now. Maybe Odessa's Happy Meal was the one missing the fry.

She needed a plan. Solutions to mysteries didn't fall from the sky. They didn't materialize out of thin air or show up in the bottom of a box of Honey Nut Cheerios. Library books didn't unravel mysteries, and you couldn't buy answers with a one-hundred-dollar bill. Asking the grown-ups in your life a whole bunch of questions wasn't any help either.

She needed to *do* something.

Odessa decided to start with the mystery that seemed the most solvable: the door with no handle in her attic. She needed to open that door. She needed Uncle Milo, because for one thing he was handy, and for another, if the door opened onto a secret world or an alternate universe, he was the person she'd want to take with her when she abandoned her old life for a new one.

But Milo hadn't come around in a while, and when Odessa asked Mom why, she smiled a goofy smile.

"He's been busy."

"Doing what?"

Uncle Milo was famous for doing nothing.

Mom grasped Odessa's hands and leaned in close, barely able to contain her excitement. "He's been spending time with a nice young woman named Meredith."

Meredith? *Meredith?*

Odessa immediately pictured this Meredith with pale blue eyes.

Smile. Blush. Giggle.

"He's bringing her to dinner," Mom said. "Saturday night."

Dinner was always better when Uncle Milo came over, but Uncle Milo always came alone.

Meredith? Odessa anticipated the evening with a combination of giddiness and dread.

She felt downright *griddy*.

What if Meredith didn't like children?

What if she was a sour-faced adult with no sense of humor? What if she smelled funny or had horse teeth?

Or what if she was nice and friendly and pretty like Jennifer, but still a stranger who didn't belong in the family?

Saturday morning was haircut day. It had been three months since the last visit to Snippity-Do-Dah, which only meant that Odessa's long, straight hair was a little longer and a little straighter. Oliver's short hair had grown shaggy, though not in a cute-shaggy way like Theo Summers's—more in an I-just-crawled-out-from-under-a-rock-shaggy way.

Odessa liked Snippity-Do-Dah because they gave out lollipops, and not the tiny kind you could crunch your way through in two seconds. Their lollipops lasted.

Odessa stared at herself in her mirror. She pulled long strands of hair over her face and then folded them up to just above her eyebrows, so she could see what she'd look like with bangs.

Cute.

She turned her head away and then whipped it back around to the mirror, trying to catch herself off guard. She wanted her knee-jerk reaction.

Still cute.

She picked up the phone to call Sofia. Sofia would have an opinion on bangs. She was full of opinions. She would have an opinion about bangs in general, and

about bangs on Odessa, but Odessa put the phone back down.

She didn't totally trust Sofia. And she was still a little mad at her. Sofia didn't know about the "Odessa liked it shaggy" comment, so she probably thought everything was fine between them.

But what about her reaction when she thought Odessa and Theo were hiding a secret boyfriend-girlfriend relationship? It was as if she couldn't believe Theo would ever like Odessa in that way!

Odessa had gone back and fixed all that, but still, she knew . . . even if Sofia didn't. That made it hard to trust her, though they were still best friends in real life and in Dreamonica.

It was complicated.

In the car on the way to Snippity-Do-Dah, Odessa said, "I'm getting bangs." It felt good to have made this decision without Sofia's approval.

"Oh, honey," Mom said. "Are you sure?"

"It's just bangs, Mom," Odessa shot back. Bangs were easy. Simple. Bangs were not at all complicated.

"Well, it's up to you, I suppose, but I just want to make sure you've given it some thought."

Sadie Howell had bangs. Odessa couldn't go to Snippity-Do-Dah and ask for pale blue eyes, but she could ask for bangs.

Big mistake.

When she got home Odessa rushed to her room to see what she could do about her new, not-so-fabulous look. She stared at the mirror that only an hour ago had told her bangs were a good idea. Cute, even.

Stupid mirror.

Odessa grabbed her green crushed-velvet headband. Her favorite. She wore it most days anyway, so maybe nobody would notice if she used it to hold those horrible bangs up off her forehead. But her hair just poked out and looked weird.

She had only nine falls through the floorboards left. Five fingers on one hand, four on the other. You don't need to be a math whiz to understand that nine is not a large number.

Odessa had a feeling there were important things to do with these opportunities. She wasn't sure what, exactly, but she knew she needed to make them count.

Should she use one to undo a haircut?

Probably not. After all, hair grows back.

But Odessa couldn't afford to look not-so-fabulous. There was Sadie Howell. And Meredith was coming for dinner.

Bangs mattered. Bangs were important.

*

Back at Snippity-Do-Dah, sitting in the bright yellow swivel chair, Odessa looked at herself in the mirror.

Bangs. How stupid!

"Just a little off the bottom," she said. "Thank you very much!"

8 Hours

Meredith did not have pale blue eyes or horse teeth, but she did have a good sense of humor. And she was a third-grade teacher, so she liked kids.

Odessa's third-grade teacher had been Ms. Albright. Ms. Albright was the last person in the world Odessa could imagine Uncle Milo bringing to dinner. She also couldn't imagine calling Ms. Albright by her first name, whatever that was.

She thought about the kids in Meredith's third-grade class. What did they call her? What would they think about Odessa calling her Meredith?

Odessa wore her favorite outfit—her peace T-shirt, gray skinny jeans, and pink Vans. She brushed her bangless hair until it shone.

As usual, Oliver didn't put any effort whatsoever into his appearance.

"You should change," Odessa said.

"Why?"

"Because you look like a toad in that shirt. And Meredith is coming over. And if you act like you look—that is to say, like a toad—she may decide she doesn't want to ever have children with Uncle Milo because maybe they'd get your toad genes." Geez. Oliver could be so annoying. And so clueless. "Toad," she said one more time before she slammed his door and walked away.

Odessa was glad she'd bothered with her outfit. Meredith had red hair and three piercings in each ear. She wore tall boots and a denim dress, and she looked much cooler than Ms. Albright ever did.

Meredith smiled at Milo a lot. And he smiled at her. Odessa was smiling too. It was a regular smile-fest. Except for Oliver.

Odessa felt something like guilt tug at her. Maybe she was responsible for Oliver's mood. But what could she do? He looked like a toad in that shirt. And it was her duty as his sister to tell him so.

By the time Mom brought out dessert—chocolate mousse—Odessa loved Meredith. She was deep in an *I want you to be my aunt* sort of love, and because she loved Meredith this way, she felt really bad about having to do what she was going to do next.

She needed Uncle Milo's help with the door with no handle, and she didn't know Meredith well enough yet to know what kind of company she'd be in an alternate universe, if that was where the door led. She needed to get Milo alone.

"Can you come up to my room?" Odessa asked.

"Sure, O," Milo said, and he grabbed Meredith by the hand. She had small fingers with perfectly manicured silver nails. "Let's go."

"Not her," Odessa said. "Just you."

Odessa knew how she sounded. But she couldn't think of any other way to ask, and since she couldn't come out and explain why she wanted only Milo, she was left with no choice but to come off as rude.

Uncouth.

Milo looked wounded. He turned to Meredith. She took her hand out of his and placed it on his shoulder.

"It's okay, baby." *Baby?* Meredith looked at Odessa and winked. "Sometimes a girl just needs a little alone time with her favorite uncle. I totally understand."

Odessa didn't know how to wink, so she didn't wink back.

Milo followed Odessa up the stairs while Meredith used her third-grade teacher skills to try to interest Oliver in a game of Uno.

"What's this all about?" Milo asked once they were safely in the attic. She searched his eyes for the twinkle they usually got when she and Milo were in the midst of conspiring.

No twinkle.

His eyes looked like Mom's did when Odessa left dishes in the sink, or her shoes at the bottom of the stairs.

"I need your help," she said. "I really, really need your help."

Milo softened. "Talk to me," he said.

Odessa reached for Clark Funds's penlight and shined it on the door with no handle.

Milo got down onto his knees.

"It's a crawl space," he said.

"What's that?"

It sounded fun. Like the indoor playground at the

118

mall Mom used to take her to when she was little, before Odessa realized that there was cool stuff you could buy at the mall.

"It's sort of like another attic. Sometimes it's used for storage."

Her attic had an attic?

"I need to get in there."

Milo narrowed his eyes. She saw just the slightest hint of a twinkle.

"I *need* to," she pleaded.

He reached over and gave it a shove. It wouldn't budge, but Odessa could have told him that.

"It's painted shut," he said. "We've just got to loosen up the edges."

He reached into the pocket of his jeans, pulled out a Swiss Army knife, and ran it along the perimeter of the small square entry. White chips of paint fell onto the floor.

Milo gave it another shove. The door shifted slightly but still wouldn't open. He worked his knife around the edges again, and this time he leaned against the door with his shoulder.

Finally, it gave way, and Milo tumbled forward, hitting his head on the wall with an alarming *whack.*

"Nothing to worry about," Milo said as he rubbed the spot just above his right eyebrow. "I don't really use my head much anyway."

Odessa hesitated. She'd visualized so many possibilities

for what lay beyond that door with no handle that she was suddenly afraid to look inside.

She wasn't afraid of finding *something*.

She was afraid of finding *nothing*.

She stared into the darkness.

"Well," Milo said. "My work is done here."

He stood up to leave. Odessa opened her mouth to ask him to wait, because what if an alternate world really did lie beyond that darkness? What if she was about to step into a new life? She'd need Milo by her side.

But she didn't say anything, because she knew what was inside that door. She knew it in her bones.

Nothing.

Milo started down the steps, but then he stopped. "You know," he said, scratching his head, "you really should try to be a little more patient with and nicer to your brother. I know it isn't always easy, but . . . he's your person in this world. And you're his. You'll need each other, all your lives."

He closed the door behind him.

Odessa sat still for a moment before grabbing Mr. Funds's light and switching it on. She didn't see the point of sitting around feeling guilty.

She held the penlight in front of her. It only lit up one small patch of darkness at a time. If Odessa were more courageous, she might have climbed inside the crawl space. Instead she sat at the edge of the opening, shin-

ing the light's small beam all around, illuminating wooden boards and cobwebs.

Just as she was about to give up and figure out how to close a door with no handle, the beam caught something.

She moved closer, holding the penlight out straight.

A small owl figurine.

Just like the ones that filled Mrs. Grisham's front parlor.

Odessa leaned in to grab it. She didn't disappear into an alternate world, but she did get her lungs full of dust. She took the owl out and wiped it off with the hem of her T-shirt. She held it and stared at its gold glass eyes.

Why was Mrs. Grisham's owl in her attic? What had she been doing up here? Did she know more than she was letting on?

Odessa placed the owl on her desk, right next to her cat-of-the-day calendar. She sat down in her swivel chair and looked at it.

Owls were supposed to be wise, weren't they? In cartoons they always had glasses and funny square graduation hats.

Please, she pleaded with the small figurine. *Help me. Solve my mysteries.*

And what she heard it say was: *Whoooo.*

Whoooo.

Whoooo do you have in this world?

She had to hand it to the owl. It was an excellent question. Who *did* she have in this world?

Dad was remarrying Jennifer. Mom had a new job. Sofia couldn't be trusted. Claire was just a bus friend. Mrs. Grisham was probably hiding something from her. Milo was falling in love with Meredith.

Oliver.

Odessa had Oliver.

Milo was right. He was her person in this world.

Odessa reached for her dictionary.

She needed the soothing power of words. She put her hand on top of it as if she were swearing on a Bible. She opened it and began to flip through the pages, slowly at first, then faster. She loved the sound of pages being flipped, the rush of air they gave off. She stopped, placing her finger randomly inside, and the word she was looking for found her. There it was, underlined in purple.

Compunction: regret; the state of feeling sorry for something.

Compunction. It was different from feeling *blue*.

She thought of Oliver and how she'd spoken to him tonight and how he'd lost the power to smile and how he

had no friends other than one dead hamster and one dirty stuffed one. How she'd stolen a hundred dollars from him, robbed him of his one triumphant moment.

Compunction overwhelmed her.

When Mom came knocking at her door saying "Come down right now, young lady, you're being rude," it was a relief. A big fist had reached inside Odessa's chest and was slowly squeezing her heart and lungs tighter and tighter. She stood up, but that squeezing feeling held firm inside her.

Without stopping to think, Odessa marched to the center of her room, rolled up her cheetah-print rug, and jumped.

*

After her third visit to Snippity-Do-Dah and her third lollipop she couldn't crunch through in two seconds, Odessa brushed her hair shiny and went down to Oliver's room.

"You should change," she said.

"Why?"

"Because that shirt is too small for you and Meredith is coming for dinner. And you want to make a good impression. It's the first step toward making a new friend."

Oliver smiled at her. "Will you help me pick something out?"

"Sure," she said, and she reached over and touched his freshly cut hair.

7 Hours

Suddenly it all made sense. The reason. The purpose. After all, people don't just go falling through floorboards backward in time *willy-nilly*.

Finally, Odessa had a mission.

Project Oliver.

She would use her power to help the most powerless person she could think of. She'd make up for not having always been the world's greatest sister.

Oliver didn't know what to make of Odessa's sudden attention. He eyed her with suspicion, the way any younger brother might whose previously mean or indifferent older sister started saying things like:

"Time to lose the Power Rangers lunchbox. How about getting a Bakugan one?"

Or:

"Maybe you should take tae kwon do."

And:

"Why don't you see if that kid Jack can come over sometime? But don't call it a *playdate,* that's too babyish."

She tried not to be bossy; she knew from experience that it wouldn't help Oliver see things her way.

Everyone needs friends, especially shy kids, so Odessa decided she'd become Oliver's first friend. If he had one, others were sure to follow.

She started sitting next to him on the bus. Claire didn't seem to mind. She would turn around in her seat to talk to them, and Odessa figured it couldn't hurt Oliver's reputation to be seen with two fourth-grade girls, even if one was his sister.

A few mornings she walked Oliver to his classroom so she could give Blake Canter a look that said: *Don't mess with my little brother, even if you are littler than he is.*

After that, she wasn't sure what to do. How do you help a toad become a prince when there's no way you're ever going to kiss him?

*

Odessa showed Mrs. Grisham the owl she'd found in the crawl space. Mrs. Grisham looked up from the honey spice cake she was slicing. It was a Wednesday, a *dinner out with*

Dad day. Even if Odessa *did* want to spoil her appetite, she wasn't sure she'd do it with a honey spice cake.

"Oh, I remember that one. I haven't seen it in ages."

"That's because I found it in my attic. In the crawl space."

"Huh. I wonder how it got in there." Mrs. Grisham turned it over in her hand, and then held it out to Odessa. "Here, it's yours. Finders keepers and all that."

Odessa took it back. She'd already tried asking Mrs. Grisham all about the house and the attic, and she hadn't gotten anywhere, but she decided to try again.

"Did you ever spend time in the attic?"

"Of course. It's my house, after all."

"Did anything strange ever happen?"

"Strange things happen all the time. Now eat your cake."

Odessa took a few bites, just to be polite. Then she went upstairs and looked out her small window onto Mrs. Grisham's house next door. It looked the same, except pink. She knew from being inside that the rooms were similar, but darker and more filled up with stuff. And now she saw—it should have been obvious—that Mrs. Grisham's house also had an attic.

What if that attic had magic powers too? What if the answer to Odessa's biggest mystery lay up a narrow flight of stairs in the house next door?

Odessa waited until Saturday.

Saturday afternoon was the one time Odessa knew for sure that Mrs. Grisham left the house. She went to the farmers' market in town, where she'd buy fresh vegetables that she'd try to hide in Odessa's and Oliver's afternoon snacks. She'd buy herself a bunch of dahlias too.

When she left, Odessa walked around the outside of her house, trying all the windows and the back door. Everything was locked. Odessa had never burgled anybody's house, though she did so love the verb *burgle*.

Stupid! Of course Mrs. Grisham locked her door and all her windows. Nobody wants burglars. Especially not old ladies who live alone.

Odessa would have broken a window if she hadn't been afraid of cutting herself. She'd have kicked down the door if she had known tae kwon do.

She went back to her own house and up her attic stairs.

*

When she opened her eyes again it was 7:15 that morning. She scrambled for her bathrobe and slippers. Mom and Oliver were still asleep, so she tiptoed out of the house.

She'd never rung Mrs. Grisham's bell so early. What if old people slept late? What if she turned off her hearing aids and didn't hear the doorbell? What if she answered without any teeth?

All these questions raced through Odessa's mind as she stood on the porch, but they turned out to be all for nothing because Mrs. Grisham answered quickly, dressed and with a full set of teeth.

"What brings you here at this hour?" she asked.

"I can't find my green velvet headband. Maybe I left it over here?"

Mrs. Grisham let her in.

Odessa made a show of looking around the room, all the while waiting for Mrs. Grisham's attention to somehow get diverted.

"And you need this headband at a little past seven in the morning?" Mrs. Grisham arched an eyebrow.

"Hair emergency!"

Odessa looked underneath the sofa.

Mrs. Grisham stared.

Odessa lifted up and then replaced a pile of books on the coffee table.

Mrs. Grisham cocked her head.

Then a miracle occurred. Miracles, like answers to mysteries, don't usually fall from the sky or materialize out of thin air.

But this one did.

A teakettle whistled someplace in the back of the house.

"I'll be right back." Mrs. Grisham turned to follow the sound.

Odessa ran to the front window and undid the lock.

6 Hours

At first, breaking into Mrs. Grisham's house was exciting.

Odessa the Gumshoe.

After watching her neighbor leave for the farmers' market, Odessa went to the front porch, heart pounding. The window she'd left unlatched that morning slid right open and she crawled inside.

In the attic Odessa found boxes, musty furniture, and old-lady stuff. She shined Clark Funds's penlight all around. Nothing interesting. She cleared a space on the floorboards and jumped, over and over, as hard as she could, waiting for that over-under, inside-out, upside-down feeling.

Nothing.

When she crept back down the attic steps and out that

front parlor window, what she'd done suddenly seemed wrong. Inexcusable. It felt way worse than taking the one-hundred-dollar bill. She ran home and hid in her room and vowed she'd never burgle anyone ever again.

*

The next Monday she could hardly look Mrs. Grisham in the eye.

She'd come home on the bus alone, because Oliver had gone to Jack's house. He'd listened to her! And now he was going to play with a friend! Project Oliver was right on track.

"I have homework," Odessa said as she passed through the kitchen. She didn't even pick up one of the oatmeal cookies still cooling on the rack.

"Wait," Mrs. Grisham said. "You might need this."

She reached into her apron pocket and pulled out Clark Funds's penlight.

"You seem to have left it upstairs," Mrs. Grisham said. "In my attic."

This was a huge Odessa Red-Light moment. Maybe the worst ever.

"I . . . I . . . I . . ."

What to say? She wanted to run. Flee up to her attic and jump through the floorboards. Erase this moment. Wipe it off the map.

But she couldn't.

There was nothing she could do to prevent Mrs. Grisham from finding her penlight and figuring out that she'd violated her trust by *burgling* her house. It was too late. Too much time had passed. She didn't have enough hours left to go back that far.

"I'm sorry," Odessa said. "Really sorry. I just . . . I was just . . . I was just trying to figure something out."

"Did you?" Mrs. Grisham asked.

"Did I what?" Odessa asked.

"Figure it out?"

"No."

"And does it matter?" Mrs. Grisham asked.

Odessa thought about this. Did it matter? Did the *why* of it all *really* matter? She had to admit, now that she thought hard about it, that despite her desire to understand why and how things worked, it didn't. What mattered was the *what*. *What* she did with her power.

"I guess it doesn't," Odessa said.

"Okay then." Mrs. Grisham pointed to the cooling rack. "Cookie?"

Odessa took two.

*

Odessa developed a Grand Master Oliver Plan.

A GMOP.

It came to her while she was sitting in the principal's office. She'd never been to the principal's office, but despite all the things she'd learned this year—three-digit multiplication, world capitals, how to apply deodorant—she still hadn't figured out how to control her impulse to shove.

It was a Thursday.

PE day.

This meant that the fourth graders ate lunch earlier than usual, overlapping with the second grade in the cafeteria.

Odessa watched Oliver walk in. Before Project Oliver she would have pretended she didn't know him, but today she waved to him from across the room.

Odessa could see that his shoelaces were untied. He hadn't mastered the art of tying his own laces. How a boy could be as skilled as Oliver at building with Legos and yet so *ham-handed*, Odessa could not understand.

She stood on her chair so he could see her and she mouthed the words: *Your shoelaces.*

He looked at her with befuddlement.

This time she whisper-yelled: *"Your shoelaces!"*

In addition to not being able to tie his shoes properly, Oliver apparently could not read lips.

Odessa cupped her hands to her mouth and shouted: *"YOUR SHOELACES!"*

He heard her.

So did Blake Canter.

Rather than stopping in his tracks and bending down to tie his shoes—rather than listening to his sister—Oliver took a step forward with his tray in his hands, and when he did, Blake Canter took her little hot-pink sneaker and stood on his dangling shoelace.

Oliver's fall was *epic.*

The clatter of the dishes. The crashing of the silverware. The tray sliding ten feet across the cafeteria floor. It was a *cacophony*—but the laughter was the loudest sound of all.

It echoed off the cafeteria walls.

Oliver lay on the floor. Odessa could see that he wasn't hurt, so she ran right by him and up to tiny Blake and gave her a shove, hard enough to knock her off her hot-pink feet.

The evil little she-troll burst into tears.

And now Odessa sat face to face with Ms. Banville, the principal.

While Ms. Banville remarked on how *surprised* she was, how *puzzled* to see Odessa in her office, when Odessa had always been such a *model* student and blah, blah, blah—Odessa wasn't listening.

She was doing math in her head.

If she went straight to the attic after school she'd have time to go back and catch Oliver before lunch and tie his laces for him.

She saw no point explaining Blake Canter's trolliness.

Why bother, when Odessa would erase this visit to Ms. Banville's office, Oliver's epic wipeout, and the echoing laughter in the cafeteria?

She'd wipe it all off the map.

Odessa took stock of Ms. Banville's office. Her big swively chair, the photographs of curly-headed children, the diploma on the wall, and the big banner above her window that said FEBRUARY IS PRESIDENTS' MONTH.

This meant many things. It meant that they ate cake for George Washington's and Abraham Lincoln's birthdays. It meant a week off when some people did boring things like visit relatives, while others did awesome things like go to the Harry Potter theme park.

And it meant that someone at school got to be President for a Day.

It worked like this: they had an all-school assembly at which Ms. Banville would read a riddle, and whoever solved it first got to skip the next day of classes and sit in the principal's office acting like the principal, or the president, which meant making announcements over the loudspeaker and signing attendance slips, and—most important—it meant you were cool for one day, and usually that coolness lasted for a long time.

As Ms. Banville rattled off Odessa's various punishments—a written apology to Blake Canter, an essay on how words, not fists, are the way out of conflict, and no recess for two weeks—Odessa studied that sign.

FEBRUARY IS PRESIDENTS' MONTH.

Her GMOP started to take shape.

She would help Oliver win President for a Day! She would hand him a moment of triumph. Make up for the one she'd taken away.

Odessa had some planning to do, but for now, she needed only to go home and back six hours so that she could start this day over and tie her little brother's shoelaces in triple knots.

5 Hours

When the time came to select the President for a Day, Odessa was so excited to begin her Grand Master Oliver Plan, so proud of herself for coming up with it, that she failed to account for the problem of the shrinking of time. Since there were only five hours left, and since the assembly took place first thing in the morning, Odessa couldn't wait until she got home from school to jump through the floorboards. That wouldn't leave her enough time to give Oliver the answer to Ms. Banville's riddle.

None of this was on Odessa's mind that morning. She ate her cinnamon toast and rode with Claire to school, all the while picturing herself the hero. The one who saved her brother, who put his needs above her own. After all, Odessa wanted to win President for a Day herself. Who

wouldn't? All that attention! Even better than pale blue eyes.

She was filled to the brim—to the very top of that tank inside her—with pride. She was such a good person.

Odessa the Selfless.

She arrived at school and filed into the gym along with everyone else.

She took her seat and listened as Ms. Banville said: "I'm going to read this year's riddle. Please don't shout out the answer. Raise your hand and wait to be called on." Then she leaned in close to the microphone.

Slowly, and with a fair amount of drama, she read from a slip of paper:

> *You can find me in darkness but never in light.*
> *I am present in daytime but absent at night.*
> *In the deepest of shadows, I hide in plain sight.*
> *What am I?*

A few hands shot up and then some came down just as quickly. Odessa leaned back into the bleachers. She didn't even try to solve the riddle. She didn't need to.

Ms. Banville called on a fifth grader.

"I don't know . . . maybe dreams?" she said.

"Good guess, Rochelle," Ms. Banville said. "But no, that is incorrect."

She wandered over to a kindergartner who had both

his hands in the air and was waving them so wildly they'd snagged the curls of the girl sitting next to him.

"Yes, Jeremy?"

She held the microphone to his mouth.

"Elmo?" he said.

The whole school laughed, but not the way they laughed in the lunchroom at Oliver. Or the way some girls used to laugh at Claire. They laughed because little Jeremy was adorable with his crazy hands and out-of-the-blue answer.

When do kids go from adorable to just plain weird in the eyes of everyone around them?

There were a few more guesses—*an owl, a bat, an invisible friend*. One third grader said "Big Bird" and then sulked when he didn't get a laugh.

Ms. Banville read the riddle aloud again. She scanned the bleachers.

"Theo?"

Odessa turned around and saw Theo, her Theo, with his hand in the air.

Both Theo and Odessa were good at perplexors. "If Bob eats apples but not bananas and Bertha likes pears but not oranges" and those sorts of problems. But this one was different.

Theo dropped his hand into his lap and tugged at his T-shirt. "Um, the letter *D*?" he said.

Sofia grabbed Odessa's knee and gave her a *The boy*

you love is about to win! squeeze. It was the perfect moment between two best friends. Nobody knew. Nobody saw. Nobody embarrassed anybody.

Ms. Banville gave a sly smile and motioned for Theo to come down from the bleachers. He stood next to her.

"How do you mean?" she asked.

"Well, there's a *d* in *darkness* but not in *light*, and there's one in *daytime* but not in *night*, and then, like, there's one in the middle of the word *shadows*. So . . ." He shrugged.

Odessa had known Theo was smart, but she hadn't known he was *brilliant*.

"Congratulations," said Ms. Banville, putting a hand on his shoulder. "Tomorrow you will be President for a Day."

Applause filled the gym, and nobody clapped harder than Odessa. She was so swept up in his victory, in his breathtaking intellect, in her sudden vision of Theo as the

President, arm in arm with Odessa, his First Lady, that she almost forgot what she had to do.

Get home. Back to the attic. She looked up at the clock. *Oh no!* She couldn't wait until after school.

Sofia looked at her. She sent a silent message: *Are you okay?*

Odessa nodded.

She thought of running home. Of all the streets she was forbidden to cross. Even if she had the courage, the house would be locked. Though she was happy she wasn't a Latchkey Kid, right now it was very inconvenient that she didn't have a key around her neck.

She needed a Plan B.

Vomit.

Her most feared thing in the world.

The fourth grade was lining up to go back to their classrooms. Sofia linked her arm through Odessa's. A cluster formed around Theo with lots of back-slapping and high-fives and all those things boys did when what they really wanted to do was hug somebody.

Theo looked happy, in his bashful way. He wasn't a bragger. He had *humility*.

Odessa felt a pang of regret. Of compunction.

Theo had won the contest fair and square. No luck, only his brilliance, which was the very core of why she loved him, long hair or short. And now she was going to snatch this victory right out of his hands.

He would never know, of course, but she hoped any-

way that he'd find it in his heart to forgive her for what she was about to do.

She broke away from Sofia, ran to the front of the line, and grabbed Mr. Rausche's sleeve.

"Uuuuggghhh." She clutched her middle. "I feel like I'm going to throw up." Even saying the words made her healthy stomach turn.

Mr. Rausche looked her over, making a face. "Odessa Light-Green . . ."

Come on, Mr. Rausche, is this the time for a cheapo name joke?

She made an overly dramatic groaning noise.

"Hurry," he said. "To the nurse's office. Go."

The nurse kept her distance from Odessa as she speedily dialed her mother's cell phone.

Voice mail.

"Have a seat," she said to Odessa. "We have to wait to hear back from your mommy."

Mommy. How embarrassing. Did this nurse realize she was in the fourth grade?

"I can't wait," Odessa said. "I have to go home NOW."

"I've left a message. I'm sure she'll call back when she gets it."

"But," Odessa said, "I'm running out of time."

The nurse looked puzzled. How could Odessa make this woman understand? She had to get home so that she could jump back and give Oliver the answer.

Then . . . it came to her. Sometimes there's another

143

solution right under your nose, but you fail to see it because you're too focused on the obvious.

"If you can't reach my mother," Odessa said, "can you call my father?"

The nurse nodded wisely, as if this were an unusually intelligent idea. She checked Odessa's file, and dialed.

Odessa knew Dad would answer. He always had his BlackBerry within arm's reach.

The nurse hung up. "He's on his way."

Odessa's heart soared. It wasn't that she'd be able to beat the clock, it was that Dad, with all his markets and stocks and trading and his new apartment and his new almost-wife, still could make time for her. His sick kid.

Or his fake-sick kid.

When she climbed into his car, he handed her a bottle of ginger ale and one of her favorite magazines. He put on 101.3, the station she and Jennifer both loved. Odessa was in a hurry, but still, she wished the drive would last forever. She tilted her seat back a little. Dad took her hand.

Just then the next wrinkle in her plan occurred to her.

"Dad," she said. "You need to take me home."

"Where do you think I'm taking you? I'm taking you home, so you can rest up and feel better."

Odessa swallowed. "No, Dad, I mean home. To Mom's house."

Dad pulled the car over to the side of the road. He reached into his glove compartment and took out a roll of his minty tummy tablets.

"My apartment is your home too." He turned to face her. "I know you don't spend as much time there as you do at your mother's, but that's because of our schedules and my work, and we're just trying to make things easier for you and Oliver. That doesn't mean that you shouldn't feel like you are at home with Jennifer and me."

Why'd he have to look like he'd just lost his favorite hamster? And why'd he have to say Jennifer's name?

Odessa stared straight ahead, out the windshield of the car that wasn't moving. Even though it was her favorite station, a song she didn't like played on the radio.

"I know, Dad. It's just that I really need to go to Mom's house. The Green House. I need to go to my room. My own room. My attic room. Please. I know you don't understand, but I really need to go there. Can you take me there?"

"Your mother is at work. I don't have a key."

"Mrs. Grisham has a key. We can borrow hers."

"Wait here," Dad said. He climbed out of the car with his BlackBerry and paced up and down the sidewalk with it pressed to his ear.

"Fine," he said as he started the car engine. "I talked to your mother. I'll wait there with you until she gets home."

Odessa's feet felt heavy as she climbed the stairs to the attic. She told Dad she was just going upstairs to change into pajamas.

It was so nice to have him there. He was in his regular seat on their couch, waiting to start a movie on pay-per-

view, one of the stupid comedies they loved watching to-gether. It felt almost normal to see him there. She could imagine all four of them together, in this new house.

She didn't miss her old house. She just missed her dad.

She looked at her clocks.

12:47

The assembly started at nine. She had some time to spare. Just enough for a movie she'd seen a billion times before.

She ran downstairs.

"What happened to your pajamas?" Dad asked.

She threw her arms around him. "Thanks, Dad," she said.

"For what?"

"For picking me up. For the ginger ale and the magazine. For leaving work early. For taking me here. For watching a movie with me."

"You don't have to thank me, sweetie. I'm your dad."

"I know, but I just feel thankful so I wanted to tell you, because if I don't I may not get the chance again and I don't want to live with *compunction*."

Dad squinted at her, then reached over and put his hand on her forehead. "Did the nurse take your temperature?"

She grabbed the blanket and put it over the both of them. She rested her head on his shoulder and they watched their movie and Odessa dozed off for a minute, and when her eyes snapped open again she thought, quickly, of two things.

One, that it wasn't strange, not strange at all, to have Dad in Mom's house. And two, that she'd better hurry upstairs or else her whole GMOP would fail.

"I've gotta go," she said, jumping up and running to the attic with the sort of energy not typically possessed by a sick child. "I'll be back," she called.

She wished that she didn't have to leave. That they could sit together until Mom got home. Mom would walk in and see Odessa and Dad on the couch, and maybe they'd smile at each other. Maybe they'd have dinner together. Maybe he could stick around until bedtime.

But she had to go back for Oliver—and there she was, filing into the gym with her class at 8:58 a.m.

The second grade had already arrived and taken their seats on the bleachers. Odessa broke from the line and ran over to her brother. She grabbed him by the collar and leaned close in to his face.

"The letter *D*," she whispered.

He tilted away from her, as if he were protecting himself from an incoming slap to the cheek. "Huh?"

"Just listen to me for once, Oliver. It's the letter *D*, okay? The letter *D*. That's the answer. I know you're shy, but you have to raise your hand and say 'The letter *D*.' That's all you have to do. I'll give you a hundred dollars if you just say 'the letter *D*.'"

She turned and ran back to join her class, taking the same seat, one row in front of Theo.

Ms. Banville started in with her instructions about not shouting out the answer, and Odessa watched Oliver. She knew that look. Pure panic spread across his face.

She glared at him. *The letter* D, she mouthed silently.

He shook his head slowly: *No*.

His shoulders slumped and he looked down at his feet, refusing to meet her gaze across the bleachers even though she sent him the strongest telepathic message she could: *Don't wimp out. Do it. Raise your hand. Don't be a toad. I wasn't planning on giving you the money, but I will, I really will, if you just do it!*

Finally, after answers of dreams and owls and bats, Ms. Banville called on Theo.

"Um, the letter *D*?" he said.

Oliver finally turned his eyes back to Odessa and shrugged.

Sorry, he mouthed.

You should be sorry, she thought. *After everything I went through for you—you blew it! I tried to help you, but you, Oliver Green-Light, are a helpless toad.*

Sofia squeezed her knee again—*The boy you love is about to win!*—and again Odessa enjoyed basking in Theo's brilliance, but she was mad at Oliver. Really mad.

Once a toad, always a toad.

On the bus home she sat next to him for what she'd decided would be the very last time.

Before she could say anything he blurted out, "I don't know how you knew the answer, but however you found out, it isn't fair. I don't want to be a cheater. And anyway," he said, his eyes welling up with tears, "I don't want to be President for a Day. Maybe you do, but I don't."

"What! You don't? What do you want, then, Oliver? Really. What do you want?" She was almost shouting at him now.

"I just want to be normal. I just want my old life back," he said, sniffling. "I just miss my old life."

A hole ripped in the water tower inside her and she could feel her anger draining from her body.

Of course. There it was.

Oliver missed his old life.

Odessa missed her old life too.

She reached into her backpack and took out her sweatshirt. She handed it to her brother so he could wipe his tears.

"Don't worry, O," she said. "I'll get you your old life back. I promise. I can fix this." Then, if only to convince herself, she added: "I have the power."

4 Hours

With Dad's wedding only a few weeks away, Odessa didn't have a lot of time to get her old life back.

But then she thought about how quickly things could change. One day Dad lived with them, the next he didn't. Mom said, "We're putting the house up for sale," and suddenly it belonged to someone else. Mrs. Grisham showed them around the new house, and the next week they were moving in.

Change can happen quickly, and Odessa just needed to be quick about it.

To *re* something means *to do it again.*

Dad needed to *re*marry Mom, not some woman named Jennifer. Just because Jennifer was nice to Odessa and had sparkly eyelids and shimmery lips didn't mean she needed

to marry Dad. Odessa didn't want to hurt Jennifer, she really didn't.

Maybe when all this is over, Odessa thought, *I'll find someone nice for Jennifer to marry.*

But first things first. It was time to re-hyphenate her family.

She started with her lavender dress. It was so beautiful, so twirly and delicate. She hated to see it get ruined, but she had to do what she had to do.

It was a Saturday morning and she asked to try it on again. "It's just that I love it so much," she said.

Jennifer was in the kitchen making crepes, her specialty. They were delicious, covered in powdered sugar and chocolate. As Oliver carried his to the table, Odessa twirled right into him, slipping her hand under his plate and flattening it to her chest.

"Oliver!" she shouted.

He stared at her openmouthed.

She shot him a look: *I've got this. This is all part of my plan.* But he didn't understand. Oliver couldn't read lips, and he wasn't so great at reading looks either.

"*I-didn't-do-it-it's-all-your-fault-you-knocked-into-me!*" he screamed.

Jennifer grabbed a kitchen towel, but it was no use. The chocolate was everywhere. The lavender dress turned a not-very-attractive maroon.

Dad stood there with his hands on his hips.

"I'm soooooo sorry." Odessa tried to sound remorseful. "I didn't want to ruin your wedding."

"It's okay," Dad said. "We'll just have to get you a new dress."

"But it won't be this one. And I'm supposed to wear this one."

"It's just a dress, Odessa." Dad reached over and steadied his hand on the still-shaking Oliver. "And I guess this means Oliver doesn't have to wear his lavender tie."

That was Odessa's next plan, to draw on Oliver's tie in permanent marker. Now that wouldn't work either.

Okay. Think big.

It took her the rest of the weekend to work up the courage, and then, finally, on Sunday afternoon, shortly before Dad was to drive her and Oliver back to Mom's, Odessa started looking for the scissors.

If this had been the Green House she'd have known where the scissors were, and she wouldn't have had to ask Jennifer. If she hadn't had to do that, she might have gotten away with her plan. But she did have to ask. And so Jennifer must have wondered where Odessa had wandered off to with those scissors.

Oliver and Dad and Jennifer were doing a puzzle, a big one of underwater sea creatures. It looked as if it could take days to do, which was why Odessa figured she had some time to spare.

She pretended she was going to the room she shared

with Oliver, but when she saw no one was looking, she snuck into Dad and Jennifer's bedroom and closed the door. She found Jennifer's wedding dress hanging in the closet in a white zippered bag.

Odessa planned to quickly snip the straps with the scissors, but when she took the dress out and laid it on the floor she decided that maybe the straps weren't enough. What if Jennifer just pinned them?

She'd have to cut a hole in the middle. It wouldn't be easy: there was some sort of hard, underwire thing, and also, the fabric was so beautiful, so delicate, sewn with little tiny beads. She ran it through her fingers, feeling regret, *compunction*. But she'd made her brother a promise. Promises were precious too.

She grabbed hold of the scissors. She picked up the dress and searched for its middle.

Just then she heard Jennifer's voice.

"What is going on in here?" She was calm but mad. Yes, mad for sure. Jennifer was always so nice, so friendly: it was the first time Odessa had seen her mad. She looked like she'd maybe stopped breathing, but then she managed to shout out: "Glenn!"

Odessa could lie. Say she had no intention of ruining the dress, but there she sat with the scissors in one hand and the dress in the other. How could you not put two and two together?

Dad came running and froze in the doorway.

Odessa thought right then of a poem she'd loved when she was little about this kid who doesn't understand money and ends up giving away a dollar in exchange for five pennies. His dad's face turns red, and the kid thinks it's because his dad is proud, but of course he's not proud, he's angry. And when Odessa saw her father's red face she wondered if maybe he was the opposite of that dad in the poem—though he looked angry, maybe he was really proud.

Couldn't he see that she was trying to save her family? That it didn't matter about the dress, that what mattered was trying to do the right thing?

"Jennifer," he said. "Can you give me a minute alone with my daughter?" He reached out and pulled her into a hug. He was a head taller than Jennifer, and he kissed her curly hair. He let her slip slowly from his grasp and she left the room.

He turned to face Odessa and crossed his arms. She closed her eyes so she wouldn't have to see his reddening face. *Please, please, please be proud.*

He wasn't.

"Your dress yesterday," he said. "That wasn't an accident."

Like he'd been doing at the table, he was putting together the pieces of a puzzle. "And now this, Odessa. I hardly know what to say."

"Dad," she whispered.

"Quiet," he snapped. "I'm talking."

Dad never snapped. Odessa started to cry.

"This behavior is inexcusable. It's mean and hurtful.

You need to use your words, Odessa. I don't know how many times we have to tell you that. You need to talk when you're angry, not push or hit or act out like this." He gestured to the dress and the scissors on the floor.

"It's just . . . ," she said, choking back tears. "It's just . . ."

Dad came and sat next to her. His face had returned to normal Dad color. That was when Odessa found her words.

"It's just that you're supposed to love Mom."

"Oh, sweetie," he said, taking her chin in his hand and turning her to face him. "I do love Mom. I'll always love Mom."

"Then why are you remarrying Jennifer?"

"Because," he sighed. "Things change."

He said more, about two people growing apart, realizing you're different from who you once were, and blah, blah, blah.

Odessa was not listening.

She'd heard what she needed to hear. *I'll always love Mom.* When they talked about the divorce with Odessa and Oliver, her parents said things like *We still care about each other* and *We'll always be in each other's lives,* but this was the first time Odessa had heard him use the word *love.*

Words count. There are so many to choose from, and Dad had chosen *love.*

That was all that mattered.

And yes, things change. Odessa knew this better than anybody, because she had the power to change things.

Things change.

Before he drove her home, back to her attic, Odessa apologized to Dad. It was harder to know what to say to Jennifer.

She couldn't look her in the eye.

"It's not about you," Odessa said. "You're nice. You're always nice to me. You let me wear your lip gloss. And you gave me that dictionary with all the purple words. And your dress is so pretty."

Jennifer put a hand on Odessa's shoulder and squeezed. Odessa understood that squeeze: *It's okay.*

Still she added, "What can I do to make you feel better?" She wasn't just repeating what Mom had forced her to say when she upset Oliver. She really did want to make Jennifer feel better. She didn't want to hurt her.

Jennifer smiled. "You've already made me feel better."

Odessa wasn't sure she believed Jennifer, but it didn't matter. Soon enough that dress would be back hanging in the closet. The scissors would be back in the drawer. No one would stare at her with shock, or go red-faced with anger.

Unfortunately, it was too late to do anything about her lavender dress. She'd ruined it Saturday morning and she couldn't go back that far. She did so love that dress. But that was okay. She wasn't going to need it.

There would be no wedding between Dad and Jennifer. Odessa was going to change that too.

3 Hours

It was time for Odessa to admit that her GMOP needed an accomplice. Her GMOP was now a GMOOP—a Grand Master Oliver/Odessa Plan.

Plan to Go Back and Fix What Really Matters.

Plan to Re-Hyphenate the Family.

Plan to Get Our Old Life Back.

A plan this big required a coconspirator.

Though Uncle Milo was always her first choice when it came to a partner in crime, he was an adult, and he was Mom's brother. Odessa crossed him off her list.

It was time to fix things with Sofia.

Time to tell her everything.

Sofia was coming for a sleepover. They still talked on the phone all the time and played *Dreamonica* online, but it had been months since they'd had a sleepover. Time had

almost erased Odessa's anger about the Theo haircut incident. It was funny how time could do that—change things without your even knowing.

Or it could have been that Odessa didn't care as much about what Sofia did or didn't say about Theo, because a miraculous thing had happened on Monday.

Theo asked her about math camp.

He asked *her*. Not Sadie Howell.

He told *her* his mom was signing him up, and he wondered if Odessa might want to sign up too, because, he said, applications were due at the end of the week.

Theo Summers. He asked if she wanted to go to math camp.

Math camp.

What a magnificent pair of words.

Mom had already signed her up for Camp Kattannoo, the same place she and Oliver went every summer—she had a collection of tie-dyed T-shirts and a drawerful of lanyards to show for it. Though she planned on getting her *old* life back, that didn't mean she couldn't go to a *new* summer camp.

Their conversation went like this:

THEO: Hey, what are you doing this summer?
ODESSA: (too embarrassed to say the word *Kattannoo* out loud) Going to camp. It's pretty cool. We design clothes and do weaving.

THEO: Oh. Sounds cool.

ODESSA: (Did she really just say "do weaving"?) It's okay, I guess.

THEO: Well, my mom signed me up for math camp. Applications are due by Friday.

ODESSA: Math camp?

THEO: Yeah. I thought maybe you might, you know, wanna go too.

ODESSA: Me?

THEO: (scratching his buzzed head) Yeah, you. You know, since you're like my math buddy, I thought you might want to go.

ODESSA: (cheeks in full Red-Light mode) Okay. I'll talk to my mom.

When she got home that afternoon, she wondered if the conversation had really happened. It seemed too good to be true. She'd always been told she had an "active imagination." Maybe it had run wild. Willy-nilly. Maybe she'd lost her marbles.

She wished she could go back and relive it, but she couldn't, because although it had happened at the end of the school day and she had the time, she only had three opportunities left to fix the Things That Really Mattered. It would be selfish to use an opportunity just to hear Theo say those words again, and she was no longer Odessa the Selfish.

So instead she inscribed the conversation into her journal, and while she did, she was able to decode the true meaning behind Theo's words:

Theo: Hey, what are you doing this summer?
(What he meant: I like you so much more than Sadie Howell.)
Theo: Oh. Sounds cool.
(What he meant: You are brilliant, just like me.)
Theo: Well, my mom signed me up for math camp. Applications are due by Friday.
(What he meant: I prefer girls with brown eyes.)
Theo: Yeah. I thought maybe you might, you know, wanna go too.
(What he meant: I can't face the summer without you.)
Theo: (scratching his buzzed head) Yeah, you. You know, since you're like my math buddy, I thought you might want to go.
(What he meant: I know we're only in fourth grade, but we'll be in fifth grade soon, so I think we should get married.)

Maybe it was this, the fact that Theo wanted to marry her, that made Sofia's comment those months back about his hair seem insignificant.

So she'd forgiven Sofia.

Odessa the Absolver.

Mom had ordered pizzas. There was talk of make-your-own-sundaes. It was shaping up to be a great sleepover.

Up in the attic, Odessa asked Sofia to swear herself to secrecy.

"Cross your fingers."

Sofia did.

"Now cross your toes."

Sofia removed her slippers. Four crossings were enough to gain Odessa's trust.

Odessa knew that most stories began at the beginning, so she started with the night she smashed Oliver's I Did It pottery. She told Sofia how she'd come downstairs to a plate of carrot cake. She told her about all the embarrassing things that had happened at school that Sofia didn't know about because Odessa had wiped them off the map. She told her about breaking into Mrs. Grisham's house. And Oliver's fall in the cafeteria.

Sofia hardly moved, hardly breathed. Her eyes barely blinked.

Odessa didn't tell her about the hundred-dollar bill, because she still felt a little guilty about it, just a little, and she didn't tell her what had happened with Theo and his haircut, because she figured there was no point in bringing up Sofia's less-than-perfect behavior when they were right in the middle of patching things up.

"So," Odessa said. "I realized this all must be for some-

thing. It has to have a purpose, right? And I don't want to go back to change the small things. I want to use these last opportunities to change what really matters. I want to get my old life back."

"Are you for real?" Sofia asked.

Odessa nodded.

Sofia made a face. She looked to Odessa, then to the attic floor, and back to Odessa again.

"Show me how this works," she said.

"I just roll up the carpet, close my eyes, and jump."

"That's all?"

"Yep."

"Show me."

"I can't," Odessa said. "I think there's only three times left and I have to make them count."

"Well," Sofia said, twirling a strand of blond hair on her finger, "if you want my help you have to show me how this works."

Odessa tried explaining again to Sofia why she didn't want to waste the opportunity when there wasn't something she needed to undo, but Sofia said, "Show me." She crossed her arms. "Or I'll tell."

"You'll *what*?"

"I'll tell. I'll tell your mom, or my mom, or somebody, everybody, about how you think you can turn back time by stomping on the floor." Sofia chuckled.

It wasn't a friendly sort of laugh.

Odessa couldn't believe her ears. Her ears that were

turning bright red with anger. She and Sofia were best friends. They had identical mansions and a dozen puppies, and they talked on the phone every day, and Odessa had hurt Claire terribly just to please Sofia, and they could communicate sometimes without using words.

Odessa tried this now. She looked at Sofia. She tried saying with her look: *Do you even know what you're doing? How you sound? What it means for our friendship? I'm asking you to catch me and you're stepping out of the way and letting me fall and split my head open.*

Sofia stared back. "Show me."

Odessa began to roll up the rug.

She stashed it next to her bookcase, made her way to the middle of the floor, and glared at Sofia.

"Hold on," Sofia said, scrambling to her feet and over to where Odessa stood. "I want to go with you."

"Why?"

"Because you're my best friend."

In a flash, Odessa played out two scenarios. In the first one she grabbed Sofia by the hand and they jumped together, back three hours to find themselves in their own homes preparing for their sleepover. She'd pick up the phone and call Sofia and listen to her marvel about the magic of time travel, and maybe even apologize for doubting her. Then she'd come over and they'd stay up all night whispering and plotting and putting the final touches on her GMOOP.

In the second scenario she'd shove Sofia out of the way and go back the three hours on her own, back to preparing for a sleepover at which she would not reveal the secrets of the attic.

Odessa chose option number two.

Despite what Dad had said, and Mom had said, and even Ms. Banville had said about how words rather than fists (or scissors) are the way out of conflict, Odessa gave Sofia a huge shove. Strong enough to knock her off her toe-crossing feet.

And then Odessa jumped.

Alone.

2 Hours

Odessa tried using words. If words really were the way out of conflict, then words should have helped her. Words should have been able to get her old life back.

But words weren't enough. Words were failing her. They didn't help with Sofia and they wouldn't help with Mom and Dad.

She couldn't just come out and tell Mom that Dad still loved her. Mom wouldn't believe her. And Dad wouldn't remember saying it, because Odessa had gone back and never asked for scissors, and she'd never taken the dress from the closet and Dad had never stared at her red-faced and disappointed. But Odessa knew. That was what mattered. And now all she had to do was confirm what she suspected: that Mom still loved Dad too.

She called another family meeting.

She couldn't just call a meeting to ask if they still loved each other, so instead she talked about math camp. She loved repeating her conversation with Theo—how *he'd* asked *her*. She'd told Mrs. Grisham and she'd told Uncle Milo and Meredith and she'd already told Mom and Dad and she'd even told Oliver, but still, she so enjoyed reliving it.

Mom and Dad sat and stared.

"This is about math camp? Really?" They exchanged a look.

"You said we make all the big decisions together. As a family. Because we're still a family. Right?"

"Yes," Dad said. "We're still a family. But I'm not sure going to math camp qualifies as a big decision."

"It's big to me," Odessa offered lamely.

"Far be it from either of us to stand between our daughter and math. Of course you can go to math camp." Mom reached over and mussed Odessa's hair as if she were a child. Still, it was better than smelling her head. "Now hurry up and get out of here so you can have your dinner with your father and get home in time for bed."

It was a Wednesday. Dinner-with-Dad night.

"Why don't you come?" Odessa asked.

"Oh, no, honey." Mom didn't even look at Dad. "This isn't my night. This is Dad's night."

"Dad, you don't mind if she comes, do you?" Odessa

could feel Oliver's eyes on her. She could feel his wonder and awe.

Odessa the Brave.

"Um, well, no, I guess I don't mind."

What followed was an awkward exchange where Mom kept saying no, she couldn't, and Odessa kept saying of course she could, and Dad kept mumbling something about how it was okay by him, and then Odessa used the most powerful word she knew, the long, drawn-out *pleeeeeeeeeeeeeease?*

That was how they all wound up at Pizzicato for dinner together, the same place where Dad had told Odessa and Oliver that he was *remarrying* Jennifer, on the night before they moved into their new house with Mom.

But this night was the opposite of that night. This

night was *jovial*. They laughed and ate too much pizza and drank too much sparkling lemonade, and afterward as they walked back to Dad's car Odessa took each of her parents by the hand. If she hadn't been in the fourth grade and about to embark on a major relationship with a boy with buzzed hair, she might have jumped and let her parents swing her back and forth, back and forth, like she had when she was younger.

In the car Mom sat up front and Dad reached across her and took his minty tummy tablets from the glove compartment. Odessa inhaled their smell. Everything felt perfect. Once they reached home it would become clear that this was how it should always be, the four of them together.

But Dad dropped them off and drove away with a few short honks and a wave.

She'd have to do more.

*

The next weekend at Dad's, Odessa tried reminding him of all the ways Jennifer was not Mom. Jennifer was nice and pretty and she smelled good, but she belonged in someone else's family.

Mom belonged; Jennifer did not.

"Remember our family trip to Mexico?" Odessa put the emphasis on the word *family*.

"Of course," Dad said.

"That was the best."

And then:

"Remember that necklace you gave Mom for her birthday a few years ago?"

"Yes, I remember," Dad answered.

"That was one beautiful necklace." This time she put the emphasis on *beautiful*.

Odessa loved words. Even when you used the obvious ones, you could add so much meaning by just leaning on them a little.

But words had their limits. Dad reached over and gave Odessa's arm a squeeze. The squeeze was harder than the kind you give when you want to say I love you. This squeeze said: *Lay off the Mom stories in front of Jennifer.*

Nothing seemed to be working, but Odessa didn't lose faith. She knew what she had to do.

Stop the wedding.

She'd seen enough TV and movies to know that there was always a moment, an opportunity for someone in the audience to stand up and say: *I object!*

And this was what she'd have to do. She'd have to make Dad see, in that moment before he said vows he didn't really believe in, that he was remarrying the wrong person. She would stand up and she would grab her mother by the hand and she would shout: *I object!*

Or *I protest!*

Something like that.

The problem, however, was this: Mom wasn't invited

to the wedding, and Odessa's gesture was going to be a lot less grand without Mom there as a visual aid.

Odessa paced around her attic floor, squeezing the owl figurine in her fist. She talked to the boards as if they could listen.

Help me. You are here for a reason. I have this power for a reason. How can you help me stop this wedding? How can you help me realize my GMOOP?

Going back two hours couldn't change everything. It couldn't make Odessa live in her old house or make Mom and Dad still be married to each other or make Oliver less of a toad or make Odessa taller with pale blue eyes. It couldn't make Sofia trustworthy, or make Milo want to be with her more than with Meredith, or make Mrs. Grisham's husband still alive so she wouldn't be alone. And it couldn't make Mom appear at Dad's wedding so that Odessa could shout *I object!* and he'd see her and realize that he was making a big, fat mistake.

The attic could do none of that. She could only go back and fix something about her day that had gone in a way she didn't like.

And what she didn't like about the day that was rapidly approaching was that Dad was going to stand up and promise to love and cherish *Jennifer.*

She sat. And she thought. And she grabbed hold of her dictionary. And she thumbed through its fresh-smelling pages and all the purple words that couldn't help

her. Jennifer had given her this dictionary. Jennifer was nice and thoughtful; someone else would want to marry her someday. Odessa felt *compunction*—she wanted Jennifer to be happy, she didn't want to ruin her wedding, her moment of triumph, but . . . Dad belonged to Mom.

She picked up her journal and a pen, but she couldn't get beyond the blank page. She stared at the phone, but there was nobody to call.

So she went to see Mrs. Grisham. Sofia was her best friend. Claire was her bus friend. Mrs. Grisham was her old friend.

It had been a while since she'd knocked on her door. Because Mrs. Grisham watched them after school, Odessa didn't have occasion to go to Mrs. Grisham's house, but this Sunday, one week before the wedding, that was what she did.

They sat together in the familiar parlor with the owl figurines.

Odessa stared at her shoes.

Mrs. Grisham let her stare. She didn't ask her what was wrong or why she was there or even if she wanted a cookie. She let her sit there silently, with all the eyes of those owls on her, while she figured out what she wanted to say.

"I don't know how to fix things."

Mrs. Grisham waited.

"I thought I could go back and fix things," Odessa continued. "That I could make changes, the kind of changes that matter, and I made a promise to my brother, and I have this power, this special power, and I kind of feel like you gave it to me, like you trusted me with the attic, you told me that I'd love living there, and I do love living there, but . . . I'm failing." Odessa's words got caught in her throat. "I can't change the big things. The Things That Really Matter," she croaked.

A long silence followed, during which Odessa swallowed back the tears that threatened to fall. She was in fourth grade. She wasn't a baby. She didn't want to cry.

"You've probably made more changes than you realize," Mrs. Grisham said.

"But I need to do more. It's not enough."

"So do more."

"But my powers . . . the attic, the magic, this power to go back . . ."

"Nonsense," said Mrs. Grisham. "Power comes from you. Not from magic."

"But I . . ."

"Nonsense."

Odessa wasn't used to Mrs. Grisham speaking to her this way. Rudely. Curtly. Dismissively. Plenty of adults spoke to kids this way—sometimes Sofia spoke to her this way—but never Mrs. Grisham.

Odessa went home deflated. She lay down on her bed and stared at the ceiling. She turned onto her side and caught sight of the door with no handle.

The crawl space.

She screwed up her courage, made her way to the opening, and climbed inside. Cobwebs brushed her face and tangled in her hair. There wasn't room to stand and jump, so Odessa squeezed her eyes tight, hugged her knees to her chest, and wished as hard as she could: *Take me to an alternate world. Pleeeeeeeeease. I want to go someplace else. Somewhere different. I don't want to be here, where I can't change the things that matter.*

She sat like that, hunched over into herself, until the dust made her cough, her muscles ached, and she shook with cold.

Odessa felt the weight of her own failure all week long, and then, because time ticks forward, not backward, the morning of the wedding arrived.

Odessa woke in her attic to the ray of light shining in through her small dormer window. She walked over to her calendar with the cats on it and removed Saturday's cat to

reveal Sunday's cat: a fat tabby in a black tuxedo and top hat.

Dad wasn't fat, and he wasn't wearing a top hat to the wedding, but still, the coincidence made her laugh.

She took out her new dress, light yellow and not nearly as twirly as the lavender one, and she laid it out on her bed. Then she looked at that bed and wished she could just crawl back into it and sleep until Monday. She couldn't. She knew that. But she *could* buy herself two more hours of sleep.

So why not?

The power to go back in time wasn't going to stop this wedding, but it could put it off just a little longer. And the bed looked so inviting. All week long she'd been sad. She was so, so tired.

Odessa went to the center of her room. She rolled up her cheetah-print rug. She closed her eyes, held her breath, and jumped, not knowing that she'd be racing right back to this same spot in a few short hours, using up her final opportunity, needing that final hour, to go back and change her future.

1 Hour

Odessa put on her dress and spun around. Then she spun harder. She got a little bit of twirl out of the edges of the pale yellow fabric, but still: disappointing. She went downstairs and knocked on Oliver's door. Mom stood next to him at the mirror, helping him with his pale yellow tie.

Odessa watched Oliver checking out his reflection. He looked the opposite of toadlike. Handsome, even. And Odessa could see from the way he stared at himself that he could see this too.

Mom was still wearing her bathrobe, but it was white, and Odessa could imagine her standing next to Dad in a white dress with delicately sewn beads and a wire thingy in the middle that made it hard to cut through. Mom

could be the bride. Suddenly Mrs. Grisham's words came back to her.

Power comes from you, not from magic.

She couldn't give up. She had to get Mom to that wedding so that she could stand up and shout *I object!* and Dad could see he was making a big mistake.

"Mom, you need to get dressed."

"Why?" she asked. "I'm not going anywhere. Just to the movies with Milo and Meredith, but that's not until later."

"Just go put something nice on, will you?"

Mom looked at her and then at Oliver, and then she smiled, almost as if she understood.

"Well, you two do look dashing. I suppose I shouldn't just stand around here in my pajamas. I'll go get dressed and then we'll have a proper sit-down breakfast." She took in the sight of Odessa and Oliver in their matching outfits. "Me and my two gorgeous kids."

Odessa asked Oliver to set the table and he said he would, without sticking his tongue out or anything, and Odessa grabbed a piece of paper and a pencil and sat down to write a note.

Sometimes it was easier to get Mom to pay attention when she wrote down what she wanted to say.

Dear Mom,
   I need you to come to the wedding with me so that Dad can see that he is making a big

mistake and so that I can say I object! and then we can go back to living together as a re-hyphenated family. Please. It is my GMOOP.

Love,

Odessa

She folded the note and then she folded it again. Her pale yellow dress had no pockets, so Odessa stuck it under her plate. She wanted it nearby when she gathered the courage it would take to hand it to her mother.

When she came back downstairs, Mom looked beautiful. Mostly, Mom looked tired, or frustrated, or just Mom-like. But this morning she wore a pretty flowered shirt, jeans, and boots with heels, and though that was a far cry from a white gown with tiny beads, it would have to do.

They sat and ate and talked as if it were just another morning, just another day, though of course they all knew it wasn't. Odessa mostly pushed her food around on her plate. She knew something that her mother and brother didn't. That today would be the day they'd begin their old life again.

Odessa pictured that calendar cat, the one in the tuxedo, standing with his paw around the waist of a cat in a flowered shirt, jeans, and boots with heels.

She smiled.

"Someone's happy," Mom said.

"Mom." Odessa felt her power, the power Mrs. Grisham said came from her, not from magic, rising up from her chest to her face, making her go warm, and probably red-cheeked too. "Mom, there's something I have to—"

Just then the doorbell rang.

Mom stood up. "I have a surprise."

Odessa and Oliver followed her to the front door. There stood a man in a black suit and a black cap. Behind him in the driveway was a long black stretch limousine.

Odessa could hardly believe it.

She'd always dreamed of riding in a limousine. In the pages of the tween magazines Mom didn't like her to read, the young stars of the shows Mom didn't like her to watch rode around in them. She'd asked, begged, cajoled for a ride in one.

Once, before their family trip to Mexico, she'd asked if they could take one to the airport.

Mom had said, "Isn't the fact that we're taking you on an airplane to another country enough for you?"

So Uncle Milo had driven them in his beat-up wagon.

And then she'd asked again on her ninth birthday for a ride in a limousine to anywhere: around town, Pizzicato, the Dairy Whip for an ice-cream cone.

But Mom had said, "No, that's absurd, you're nine years old."

If there was one thing Odessa could count on, it was Mom saying no to the things she wanted most of all.

"Your father sent the limo for you." Mom gestured to the man with the hat in his hands. "He'll take you to the church. Dad will meet you there."

One part of Odessa wanted to forget the note clutched in her palm and run to the limousine, climb in, blast some music, turn on the colored lights, pour herself some water in a champagne glass, and inhale the fancy polished leather.

"Cool," Oliver said. "This is so cool."

"Wait," Odessa barked. Oliver froze. "Mom," she said. "You have to come with us."

Mom laughed. Her eyes quickly welled with tears. "I can't go with you, honey. This is your father's wedding. It's his moment."

"But you need to."

Mom's tears made their way to her cheeks now, and Odessa knew that those weren't happy tears. Happy tears catch at your eyes. These trailed down her face.

"Here," Odessa said, and she handed her mother the note. It was one of the moments when words wouldn't have come anyway, so she was glad she'd written them down.

Mom unfolded the note and read it. She made a sound and then covered her mouth with her hand. The tears were sobs now, and even though Odessa never would have thought watching her mother cry like that could make her *jovial*, that was exactly what happened.

Mom loved Dad too.

That was why she sobbed like that.

"Come on, Mom," she said, and took her by the hand. "Let's get in the limo."

Mom wrapped Odessa in her arms. She buried her face in her scalp and took a deep whiff. Odessa tried to break free, but her mother's grip was fierce.

"You're a great kid," Mom whispered. "And I love you. And I want you to go get in that car and go to your father's wedding and I want you to have a good time. Do that for me, okay?"

"Not without you," Odessa said. "Mom. Please."

Mom shook her head no.

"Pleeeeeeeeeeease?"

Right then Odessa felt Oliver's not-so-small-anymore hand in hers. He gave her a tug.

"Let's go," he said. "It's gonna be okay."

Odessa looked at Oliver. She looked at Mom. She looked at the man with his hat in his hands who had taken several steps back from where they stood.

I can fix this, she thought. *I have the power.*

"Can I have your business card?" she called to the man.

"Excuse me?"

Mom chuckled. "He's legit, Odessa. Just get in the car."

"Please, sir," she said, using her politest voice. "May I have your business card?"

The man stepped toward her and reached into his inside jacket pocket. He pulled out a card with gold lettering and held it out. Odessa took it.

World-Class Limousines:

Let us take you for a ride you will never forget.

And at the bottom: the telephone number.

"Thanks!" she called over her shoulder as she ran from the entryway. What she didn't count on was Mom running after her.

"Come back here!" Mom shouted. "You can't run away from this."

As Odessa raced up the stairs she studied those numbers. She knew she couldn't take the card with her, so she needed to memorize them.

Luckily, Odessa was good with numbers.

She got to her attic a few steps ahead of Mom. She didn't bother with the rug. She didn't have the time, and anyway, what did the rug matter? The rug was a small thing. If she'd learned anything, it was that the small things didn't matter.

*

Odessa sat at the breakfast table in her pale yellow dress that didn't twirl. She had a pen in her hand and a blank piece of paper in front of her. She took the paper and balled it up and threw it in the trash.

She grabbed the phone in the kitchen and dialed the numbers still fresh in her mind.

"World-Class Limousines," a voice chirped.

"Yes, good morning." Odessa used the most adult voice

she could muster. "I'm sorry to tell you that we have to cancel an order. The car coming to One Twenty-One Orchard Street. Please refrain from sending it." She paused, not sure what else to say. "That is all."

"Will do," the voice said, and hung up. Odessa hadn't expected that to be so easy.

Oliver cocked his head. His look said, *What was that all about?* but Odessa just pretended she couldn't read looks.

Right then Mom came downstairs in her pretty flower shirt, jeans, and boots with heels. Again, Odessa thought she looked beautiful.

They sat and ate breakfast and the doorbell didn't ring.

Mom looked at her watch.

The doorbell still didn't ring.

Odessa cleared the dishes, careful not to spill anything on her pale yellow dress. She wanted to look her best when she shouted *I object!*

186

Mom was pacing now. She picked up the phone and hung it up again. She went to the front door, stepped outside, looked up and down the street, and came back in again.

"Oh boy," she said.

"What is it, Mother?" *Odessa the Innocent.*

"There seems to be a problem with your ride to the wedding."

"Why don't you just take us?"

"Because I shouldn't be the one to have to drive you. It's his responsibility to make sure you get there on time today of all days." Mom picked up the phone and dialed, held it to her ear, and then hung it up. "Voice mail. Typical."

She picked up the phone again. This time she called Uncle Milo. Uncle Milo, famous for doing nothing, had something he had to do that morning that prevented him from driving his niece and nephew to their father's wedding.

How Odessa loved Uncle Milo.

"Mom," Odessa said. "We have to go. We can't miss the wedding. Please. Time is running out."

As Mom went to get her keys, Odessa darted back up to the attic. She stood and looked around the room she loved so much, and she wondered if she'd be saying goodbye to it soon. With Mom and Dad getting back together, maybe they'd buy their old house again, or maybe get a new one.

She stood on her cheetah-print rug, the rug that hadn't been lost in the betwixt.

"Thank you," she whispered to the floor. "For everything."

She ran back downstairs, and they all piled into the station wagon that was not a limousine and sped off to the wedding Odessa was going to stop.

The streets she knew so well rushed by outside her window. Inside, her heart felt full to bursting.

Her new life was about to begin.

Or maybe it was that her old life was about to begin again.

Time can be tricky that way.

The New New House

Odessa sat down on a cardboard box marked *Odessa's stuffed animals*. She wasn't sure she was going to unpack this box. She wanted her new room to be grown-up. A fifth grader's room. Maybe she'd have Uncle Milo carry the box down to the basement for storage, since the new house had no attic.

This house was theirs. A forever house, Mom called it.

"Forever?" Odessa asked. Forever was a very long time, and time couldn't always be trusted.

Mom put a hand on her head and smiled. "Forever for now."

They'd bought it from a couple whose kids had grown up and gone off to college. There were someone else's scribbles on the kitchen wall and scuff marks on the stairs

from someone else's shoes, but Odessa didn't mind. They could paint the walls and refinish the wood. This was their *forever for now* house.

Odessa and Oliver wouldn't have to switch schools, but they would ride a new bus. She worried about Claire and their bus friendship, but then Claire said, "Why don't you come over after school sometime? We can hang out at my house."

So that was just what Odessa planned to do.

The new bus wouldn't take them by their old house, or their old old house. It traveled a new route that went by Dad and Jennifer's apartment, where it would pick up Odessa and Oliver every Thursday morning now that they'd turned dinner-with-Dad night into sleepover-at-Dad-and-Jennifer's night.

Dad and Jennifer's wedding had turned out differently from how Odessa had planned—obviously—because here they were, married to each other, four months later.

They were married, not *remarried*.

When Odessa had arrived at the church that morning with only minutes to spare, Mom had pulled up to the entrance and kept the car running.

"Hurry up," she said. "You're late."

"You have to come," Odessa said. "Come inside with me."

"No, honey. You have to do this on your own. Not on your own," she corrected herself. "You have to do this with your brother. Your person in this world."

"Mom, please," Odessa pleaded. She wished she'd written that note. Wished she had a slip of paper that said what she needed to say, because it was hard to speak with the car running and the clock ticking.

"Please come inside so that I can shout *I object!* And Dad can see that to *re*marry means to do it again to the same person and then we can go back to our old lives and you won't have to go to work and Oliver will be happy and maybe we can move to a new house together but I still want my own room."

She held her mother's hand firmly, but she could feel Mom pulling away. Usually it happened the other way around—it was Odessa who tried to extract herself from a parental grip.

Mom took a deep breath and let it out again. Gathering up her courage, Odessa hoped, to walk inside the church.

"There are three things I want to say to you." Mom turned around in her seat completely, so that she faced Odessa and the struck-silent Oliver.

"One: I'm happy. I love my job and I love my kids and I'm starting to really like life the way it is. I love your father because he is the father of my children, but I do not want to be married to him anymore. I. Am. Happy."

She held up two fingers, the way the teachers at school did when they wanted to make sure the class was still paying attention.

"Two: It's okay for you to go in there and have a good

191

time. I don't want you to root against them out of some sort of loyalty to me. Everything will be better if everyone is happy. So let them have this day, and try to enjoy it too. Weddings are fun and you're dressed to kill. And whether you have a good time or not is entirely up to you."

"And three." She took her three fingers and reached out to stroke first Oliver's and then Odessa's cheek. "I am so proud of both of you. You are growing up so fast and so beautifully."

Odessa noticed Oliver's hand in hers. She couldn't have said who had taken whose hand first. He pulled her toward the car door.

Words.

There would be no pushing or shoving or stomping or shouting *I object!* Mom had used her words. And they'd made Odessa see things differently, which, after all, is the purpose of words.

Odessa and Oliver got out of the car and stood in front of the church. Mom smiled and waved, gave a quick honk, and drove off.

*

Now, as Odessa unpacked her light yellow dress and hung it in her new closet, she thought about that day four months ago when Dad stood at the altar with Jennifer. He looked so tall and handsome. Her eyelids sparkled and her lips shimmered even more than usual. They held each other's hands and looked into each other's eyes and it was as if no one else was even in the church. When the minister asked if anyone had any objections, Odessa knew she couldn't object to Dad and Jennifer, she'd just have to get used to Dad and Jennifer, and maybe that wouldn't be so hard.

Later she danced with Dad, and she danced with Jennifer, and even Oliver danced like those hamsters in the commercial he loved, and what she'd thought would be the worst day of her life turned out to be lots of fun, just like Mom said.

Odessa returned home that night after Dad and

Jennifer left for their honeymoon, and she went to her attic. She rolled up her rug, closed her eyes tight, and jumped, not because she wanted to undo anything about that day—the day was sort of wonderful—but because she wanted to see what would happen.

Was she really out of opportunities to make a change? To undo something about her day that had gone in a way she didn't particularly like?

She jumped and she jumped harder, pounding her feet against the floor until her mother finally came upstairs and asked, "What is this racket all about?"

"Nothing, Mom," Odessa said. "It's all over now."

*

Odessa took a look around her new room. There were more boxes to unpack than she remembered packing. She pulled out her certificate from math camp and hung it over her desk. She and Theo weren't in the same group, but they shot baskets together during free time and sometimes ate lunch together. The math was hard but not too hard, and she'd made friends with a girl who didn't go to their school, a summer friend, and Theo had started growing his hair shaggy again.

She could hear Oliver in his room next door. He was singing a song from Camp Kattannoo. He'd made friends there. Friends who were not furry and small and smelly. He

was doing okay without her and her GMOP or GMOOP. He was looking forward to the third grade.

She'd given him a housewarming gift. A huge pirate Lego set he'd had his eye on for months.

"Wow! This thing costs like a hundred dollars!"

Odessa knew exactly how much it cost.

She heard a knock on her door. She figured it was Oliver, because she'd reminded him all through the move about knocking and privacy and not listening in on her phone calls.

Or maybe it was Sofia, who'd said she wanted to stop by to check out Odessa's new room, and Odessa had said *Come on over* because she still loved Sofia. Sometimes Sofia wasn't the world's greatest best friend, but other times she was.

She opened the door.

It was Mrs. Grisham.

Even though it had only been a day since she'd seen her, and even though she'd never done it before, Odessa gave her a big hug.

"You left this behind," Mrs. Grisham said, reaching into her pocket and pulling out the small glass owl. "I found it in your attic."

"It's not my attic anymore."

"No, I suppose it's not." She stared into Odessa's eyes. "But it was for a time."

Mrs. Grisham stepped inside and took a look around

Odessa's new room. She walked to the center of it and stood. She tapped her foot on the floor.

Like Odessa hadn't already tried that!

There was nothing at all magical about this new room, and that was perfectly fine by Odessa.

"You're going to love it here," Mrs. Grisham said, just as she had that first time she showed Odessa the attic house, although now Odessa knew that her bark wasn't an order, it was just the voice of someone who has lived a long time and knows certain things.

"I think I will," Odessa said. "I think I'm going to love it here."

She took the owl from the old woman's hand and she put it on her desk.

Her desk. Her room.

Her home.

Forever, for now.

About the Author

DANA REINHARDT lives in San Francisco with her husband and their two daughters. She is the author of *A Brief Chapter in My Impossible Life*, *Harmless*, *How to Build a House*, *The Things a Brother Knows*, and *The Summer I Learned to Fly*. Visit her at danareinhardt.net.

THE GATHERING DARKNESS

SURVIVORS

RED MOON RISING

ERIN
HUNTER

HARPER

An Imprint of HarperCollinsPublishers

Special thanks to Gillian Philip

Red Moon Rising
Copyright © 2017 by Working Partners Limited
Series created by Working Partners Limited
Endpaper art © 2017 by Frank Riccio
All rights reserved. Printed in the United States of America.
No part of this book may be used or reproduced in any manner whatsoever without
written permission except in the case of brief quotations embodied in critical
articles and reviews. For information address HarperCollins Children's Books, a
division of HarperCollins Publishers, 195 Broadway, New York, NY 10007.
www.harpercollinschildrens.com

Library of Congress Control Number: 2017934809
ISBN 978-0-06-234345-1 (trade bdg.) — ISBN 978-0-06-234346-8 (lib. bdg.)

Typography based on a design by Hilary Zarycky
17 18 19 20 21 CG/LSCH 10 9 8 7 6 5 4 3 2
❖
First Edition

PACK LIST

WILD PACK (IN ORDER OF RANK)

ALPHA:

female swift-dog with short gray fur (also known as Sweet)

BETA:

gold-and-white thick-furred male (also known as Lucky)

HUNTERS:

SNAP—small female with tan-and-white fur

BRUNO—large thick-furred brown male Fight Dog with a hard face

MICKEY—sleek black-and-white male Farm Dog

STORM—brown-and-tan female Fierce Dog

PATROL DOGS:

MOON—black-and-white female Farm Dog

TWITCH—tan male chase-dog with black patches and three legs

DAISY—small white-furred female with a brown tail

BREEZE—small brown female with large ears and short fur

CHASE—small ginger-furred female

BEETLE—black-and-white shaggy-furred male

THORN—black shaggy-furred female

OMEGA:

small female with long white fur (also known as Sunshine)

PUPS:

FLUFF—shaggy brown female

TUMBLE—golden-furred male

NIBBLE—tan female

TINY—pale-eyed golden female

PROLOGUE

Darkness lay thick in the den, with only a faint smudge of moonlight shining through the entrance. Lick tried not to shiver as she blinked rapidly. Although the den-smells were warm and comforting, it couldn't be so very cold and lonely out there in the silver glow of the Moon-Dog . . . could it?

Beside her Grunt was still snoring, and Wiggle was making little squeaky noises, his lip quirking back as if he was dreaming of prey. How could her two litter-brothers sleep? The three of them had something to do—something that couldn't wait!

Lick nudged each of her brothers with her nose, shoving Wiggle harder when he grumbled and resisted.

"Wake up," she whispered. "Come *on.* We have to go!"

Grunt gave a tiny groan of protest, but as he woke properly he blinked hard and stumbled to his paws. Then he nipped

1

Wiggle on the ear to rouse him.

"Hurry up, Wiggle," he growled. "Lick's right. It's time!"

They were making an awful amount of noise, or so it seemed to Lick, but the adult dogs of their new Pack didn't stir. She could hear snores and sleepy murmurs, and the occasional scrape of claws from a dog on a dream-hunt, and she could just make out furred flanks, rising and falling in the darkness. *We'll make it out of here. We have to!*

There was a strange little ache in Lick's belly as she took a last look at Lucky, Martha, Mickey . . . at all the dogs who had cared for them, who had found them and taken them in after their Mother-Dog went to sleep and didn't wake up. This Pack had been kind to them, and Lick wished she could say a proper good-bye.

But if we wake them up, they'll stop us from leaving.

"Come on, Lick." Grunt's low voice was at her ear. "Don't change your mind now! This Pack thinks we're bad dogs. Well, we're real *Fierce* Dog pups, and we'll be fine without them!"

"I know," sighed Lick softly. "I know, it's just that—"

"They're only kind now because we're little." Grunt shook himself angrily and whispered, "They won't be kind when we're big Fierce Dogs and they're scared of us!"

"Of course. We'll never really belong in this Pack." Lick gave

her brother a quick nuzzle. "Let's go. But try to be quiet!"

Wiggle was trembling with fear as the pups crept cautiously up the earth slope to the mouth of the den, but Lick and Grunt goaded their smaller brother on with nudges and gentle nips. When they emerged into the faint moonlight, all three of them froze for a moment. The grass beneath Lick's paw pads was damp with dew, and the night air smelled sharp as her nostrils flared. She had to look strong for Wiggle, and that made Lick feel a little braver herself.

But it's a big world out here. . . .

Slowly, quietly, the pups edged forward, huddling together and staying as low as they could. Wet grass tickled Lick's belly and chin, and she wanted desperately to sneeze. *But I can't.*

Up ahead, a large shadow moved against the tree trunks, and Lick shrank back. Along with her brothers, she held her breath as she watched the Patrol Dog Moon slink along the camp's border, her ears pricked and nostrils scenting the air for trouble.

But Moon wasn't scouting for three small pups within the camp itself. Her shape vanished into the shadows, and Lick breathed a sigh of relief. Quickly the three Fierce Dogs scuttled to the tree line that marked the camp's border, their pawsteps sounding terribly loud to Lick's quivering ears.

If the den had felt dark, the woods beyond the camp somehow seemed even blacker. Small creatures rustled in the grass, making the pups jump, and when a night bird screeched overhead, Wiggle started in terror and almost stumbled. Grunt's head was lifted high, his jaw clenched stiffly, and although Lick reckoned his fearlessness was a bit of an act, she didn't want to look like a coward herself. Wiggle was pressed so tightly against her flank, she was sure she was the only thing keeping his trembling little body upright.

"Where's the rock?" asked Wiggle plaintively, when they'd padded in silence for what felt like forever.

"Not far." But Lick was beginning to doubt herself—and she had a feeling Grunt doubted her too, from the resentful glances he was shooting her. If they could just find that oddly shaped gray lump of stone, the one that looked like a crouching giantfur, she'd know exactly where they were, and they could follow the river upstream. . . . "We've passed Giantfur Rock loads of times with Martha. It can't be much farther to the river."

"If we're going the right way," grumbled Grunt.

"Maybe we passed it already?" suggested Wiggle nervously.

"I don't think so." Lick hesitated, one paw in the air.

Grunt glanced to the left and right, licking his small jaws. "I

think you've taken us the wrong way, Lick."

"*You're* the one who said we needed to go downwind of that big tree!" Lick snapped.

"And it was you who said we had to cross the little stream!"

Lick opened her jaws to quarrel some more, but she could hear Grunt's breath rasp as he glared at her. His forelegs shook, and she realized he was just as scared as she was.

"It doesn't matter whose fault it is," she whined miserably, her ears drooping. "We're lost and we're all by ourselves and I don't know what we're going to *do*!"

Wiggle gave a despairing whimper and lay down with his head on his paws. "We're lost!" he echoed.

"We'll be all right." Lick tried to comfort him, but she didn't sound convincing even to herself. *We can't be lost. This is silly!* She lifted her head determinedly and sniffed the air. "That way, I'm sure . . . maybe . . ."

The other two just stared, looking very reluctant to believe her.

"Come on!" Forcing her ears up, Lick chose a likely-looking direction and picked up a paw. But it felt heavy, and she realized her legs were aching. Miserably she set down her paw once more, and her ears drooped. "I don't know," she mumbled. "I don't know the way."

Silence fell around the three pups, and they stared at one another in lonely misery and terror. Even the trees' shadows seemed to draw tighter around them.

Then, in the stillness, there was a rattle and rustle of leaves.

Lick couldn't help giving a yelp of shock, and she spun around to face the pale shape that was pushing through the undergrowth toward them. Out of the scrub came a small black nose, quivering whiskers, and then, abruptly, a bright and friendly white-furred face.

"Daisy!" squeaked Lick. The sickening fear gave way to almost unbearable relief, and her small legs suddenly felt weak and shaky.

"Lick! Grunt, Wiggle—what are you doing out here in the middle of the night?" The little white dog gazed at the pups, her dark eyes full of concern. "You could have been hurt!"

Lick and Grunt traded guilty glances, while Wiggle sniffled unhappily, staring at his paws.

"We were running away," blurted Lick at last.

"You were?" Daisy's eyes widened in disbelief. "But why?"

"No dog wants us in this Pack." Grunt's face grew surly and resentful. "We're better off on our own."

"Oh, Sky-Dogs, of course that's not true—not either part!" Daisy sprang forward on her short legs and began to lick them

all frantically. "Of *course* we want you in the Pack, pups—and of course you're better off with us! Every dog needs a strong Pack, now that the Big Growl has changed the world!"

"But the Pack Dogs don't like us," muttered Grunt.

"Now, come on back to the camp with me." Ignoring his sullen words, Daisy licked Grunt's nose until he sneezed. "Lucky wants you in our Pack, and so does Mickey. And Martha, and me. And if any dog doesn't, they'll soon come around. Don't you worry, pups!"

Lick exchanged a look with Grunt. Wiggle was clearly desperate to go back with Daisy; his eyes were suddenly brighter and his pricked ears quivered with frantic hope. Grunt looked too tired to argue anymore. And if Lick was honest, she felt very relieved indeed that they'd been found.

"All right, Daisy." She couldn't stop a yawn from escaping, and her jaws widened with it till her eyes were squeezed tight. She shook herself and blinked rapidly. "We'll come. But it's such a long way back. . . ."

"Oh, little one." Daisy laughed fondly. "It's not half as far as you think. You've barely reached the edge of the first hunting ground."

Lick's ears drooped and her body sagged. *So much for our big*

7

escape. And no wonder we couldn't find Giantfur Rock. It's still far, far away.

All the same, she felt her heart lighten a little as she followed in Daisy's pawsteps. Exhausted as she was, she only wanted to curl up in that cozy den once again, and not even Grunt's rebellious muttering behind her could change her mind.

And I do want to belong to this Pack. Maybe Daisy's right. They'll get used to us, and they'll like us in the end.

I want my Mother-Dog, but she's gone to sleep forever.

So I want to belong. I want a Pack.

Lick glanced skyward with a terrible pang of yearning. *Why can't I belong?*

CHAPTER ONE

Drowsy and content, Storm lay stretched out in the Sun-Dog's light. The peace of the glade was broken only by the squeaks and yelps of the four pups who romped and played outside their den, as their parent-dogs, Alpha and Lucky, looked on. One eye open, one ear pricked, Storm watched them. There was a strange warm feeling in her chest. For some reason, she realized with surprise, just watching the pups' playtime made her happy.

The little dogs were so joyful and carefree, as if the terror of their near drowning in the Endless Lake had been completely forgotten. Storm was glad the experience hadn't affected them too badly, and she could understand why: Lucky, the Pack's Beta, had a way of making the tiniest of pups feel secure and cared-for . . .

. . . *even a pup who isn't his own.* Storm felt a twinge of gratitude as memories of her own turbulent puphood came back to her. She

and her brothers had had nowhere else to go, no dog to take care of them, but Lucky had stepped in to take the place of their parent-dogs. Despite Lucky's love and care, she thought with a pang of loss, her brothers hadn't made it in the end. . . .

But I did. I survived, and now I live for all three of us. And that's because of Lucky.

The atmosphere of peace in the camp felt reassuring. It was good to see her Packmates, young and old, looking so content. The whole camp felt bathed in happiness and goodwill. The Pack needed a break from the suspicion and fear that had haunted them for so long. This sun-high it seemed every dog had decided to push the problem to the back of their minds. Many of them believed that the traitor in their ranks—the bad dog who had done so many terrible things—had been Arrow, her fellow Fierce Dog, who had left the Pack with Bella. They thought that with Arrow gone, they must be safe.

It was so tempting to believe that . . . but Storm was *sure* that Arrow was innocent. And if that was true, then the bad dog who had laced the prey pile with clear-stone and framed the loyal Patrol Dog Moon for stealing prey had not been found. Whisper's murder had still not been solved.

Storm suppressed a shiver at the memory of Whisper's death.

The threat was still real—she knew it, even if she wished she didn't. The bad dog could right now be planning another attack. But even so, in this moment she couldn't help enjoying the new peaceful spirit among her Packmates.

I just wish I could believe it was over. . . .

Storm raised her head from the ground and caught sight of Snap. The hunt-dog was padding toward her, her jaws full of soft moss. Her ears were pricked, her tail wagging.

Snap set the moss gently down beside her. "Storm! I brought this for you—I thought you looked a little uncomfortable. Here, put it under your forepaws."

Storm blinked, grateful and surprised. She hadn't really noticed before, but her forepaws were resting awkwardly on hard stone. Half rising, she pawed the moss onto the flat boulder beside her and sank down again. Now her stretched-out paws felt as if they were floating on air. "Thank you, Snap, that was thoughtful."

And unexpectedly kind, she thought as she watched Snap nod and pad away. Mickey's mate could be short-tempered—and what was more, Snap had been one of the dogs who suspected that the traitor must be a Fierce Dog. With Arrow gone, those dogs' suspicions had fallen squarely on Storm herself. Now, though, Snap seemed to regard Storm as a hero. Every dog here knew that it was

she—the Fierce Dog—who had dived into the Endless Lake and pulled Tiny out, saving the little pup's life with a trick Martha had taught her long ago.

It's a really nice change, thought Storm. *I'm not sure I realized just how much their suspicion was upsetting me until they started trusting me again.*

Sighing contentedly, she let her eyes drift shut. Spots of light danced behind her eyelids, and she observed them dreamily till they dissolved into blackness. That was when the less pleasant thoughts began to drift in: *But I know we can't afford this sense of peace. After all that the traitor dog has done . . . spreading blood and panic in the camp, killing that fox cub to cause a war between dogs and foxes . . .*

She wished she could believe those terrible crimes had been committed by one of the dogs who had already left the Pack. It couldn't have been Bella or Arrow, of course—Storm knew they weren't capable of such evil, however much the other dogs distrusted them.

But what about the dogs of Terror's old Pack? What about Ruff, or Woody, or Rake? Or even Dart, who had been in the Wild Pack from the beginning but had left it to join up with those three deserters? They'd been gone by the time the rabbit blood was smeared all over the glade, true, but they could have sneaked back somehow to plant it. . . .

Another warm flank settled down against hers, and she opened her eyes to see that Mickey and Snap had joined her in her patch of sunlight. Instantly she felt reassured again. Storm felt small paws on her back and turned her head as Lucky and Alpha's pups began to clamber all over her, swatting her tail and nibbling at her ears. "Tiny!" she yelped at the smallest of them.

Tiny took no notice, chewing happily on one ear as the bigger, shaggier Tumble rolled off and began to attack Storm's hindpaw. The two other female pups, Nibble and Fluff, seemed to be fighting to the death along Storm's spine, and when she shook them off, they climbed straight back on and charged at each other again.

"I'd give in, if I were you." Mickey laughed beside her.

Storm rolled onto her side and batted idly at Tiny, who yelped in delight. Nibble and Fluff, forgetting their tussle, threw themselves at Storm's throat and chewed it with their small soft mouths, growling and giggling. Storm gave a dramatic groan of defeat and waved her paws in the air. Tumble jumped onto her shoulder and began to yap, tossing his small head in triumph.

"Pups, pups, I'm beaten!"

"Grrrrr!" Tiny had most of one of Storm's paws in her jaws.

"We've conkw . . . conqu-wered the Fierce Dog!" cried Tumble.

"Hooray!" barked Fluff and Nibble.

Storm lay helplessly beneath them, grunting out laughs. Deep in her belly she could feel that unaccustomed warmth and affection. *They're not even a little bit afraid of me anymore. Not since I rescued them from the Endless Lake. In fact, I think they really like me. . . .*

"Storm, Storm! Tell us a story!" Nibble was prancing up and down right in front of her nose.

"Yes, a story!" chorused Fluff and Tiny.

"Or we'll beat you again!" growled Tumble, right in Storm's ear, making her jump.

"Oh, I'd love to, pups. . . ." Storm half rose, shaking herself. *Especially since you've all finally learned to say "Storm" instead of "Torm"!* "But—hold on, Tumble, don't bite me!—I can't think of one . . . wait . . ."

"*I'll* tell you a story." Alpha's amused voice came from behind them. "So long as you leave Storm alone, pups. Let's give her some peace!" The beautiful swift-dog licked Storm's muzzle affectionately, and then settled down on the grass. The pups finally abandoned Storm and nestled eagerly against their Mother-Dog—all except Tiny, who stayed firmly between Storm's paws. Storm gave her a gentle lick on the top of her head.

Alpha winked solemnly at Storm, and Storm thumped her

tail gratefully. "I'll tell you another story of the Wind-Dogs if you like, pups."

"Oh, the Wind-Dogs!" Fluff barked excitedly, her shaggy dark-brown ears shooting up. All the pups loved Alpha's stories of her favorite Spirit Dogs. Alpha, like all swift-dogs, was closely connected to the Wind-Dogs. That gave the pups a special relationship with them, too.

"Well," began Alpha, crossing her forepaws and settling down to tell her tale. "You all know that with every turn of the four seasons, the Wind-Dogs chase the Golden Deer around the world. And that every year, when the Golden Deer is caught, Long Light dies, and Red Leaf begins as the Earth-Dog prepares for Ice Wind."

"Yes, yes, yes. We remember." Excitedly Tumble climbed over Nibble to hear better, and she shook him off.

"In the proper order of things, the Golden Deer rises again with Tree Flower and the start of the next Long Light. But once, many years ago, Long Light passed without the Wind-Dogs catching the Golden Deer."

Fluff gasped. "How did that happen?"

"No dog knows, pups. But because the Golden Deer ran free,

Red Leaf never came, and neither did Ice Wind. The Wind-Dogs chased the Deer anyway, pursuing it fiercely, desperately, but they were tired—*so* tired—and they were afraid that this time, it would never be caught. But if the Deer ran free forever, it would put the whole world out of balance!"

The four pups could only stare at their Mother-Dog, wide-eyed. Storm watched them with amusement.

"Finally the Wind-Dogs ran out of breath and it seemed as though the Deer would run forever. What was to become of the land without Red Leaf and Ice Wind? Without the cold seasons, plants and trees cannot rest and grow!

"But that, pups, was when the first Swift-Dog arose from her den. She was shocked to see the Golden Deer still running free. But she knew what to do." Alpha's face grew solemn. "She sprang to her paws and ran alongside the Wind-Dogs—she could catch up with them, because unlike them, she was fresh and rested. 'Look,' she said, 'how my body is light, and my legs so long and thin. I can run, and I'm not tired. Let me carry on the chase!'

"Well, the Wind-Dogs were so tired by now that they agreed to let the first Swift-Dog take her chance. And soon they saw that she was right: Her body was as light and agile as a bird in flight, and her long legs ate up the ground. The Golden Deer had

run far and fast, pups—but it too was tired now. Up a long hill it raced, with the brave Swift-Dog gaining on it. And when the two reached the summit, the Swift-Dog gave a mighty leap—*and brought down the Golden Deer!*"

The pups were beside themselves with excitement, yapping and squeaking. "Yay! The first Swift-Dog!"

"And so balance was restored to the world. The Wind-Dogs were pleased with the first Swift-Dog, proud of her bravery and determination. So they swore that from that moment on, any mortal dog who caught the Golden Deer—or one of its shadows— would be granted long life and good luck, for them and their pups and their Pack."

"Hooray!" barked Tumble, spinning around in delight. "One day I'll catch it!"

"No, *I* will!" yapped Fluff, shoving him with a paw.

"Me! Me!" squeaked Tiny, making all of them laugh.

Storm managed not to join in the laughter, however affection-ate. She gave the little pup a gentle nuzzle. *I wouldn't risk hurting her feelings.* "Why shouldn't you catch the Golden Deer, Tiny? You're very brave and determined."

Tiny gazed up at her with adoration. "Thank you, Storm!"

There were some dogs in the Pack who thought the Golden

Deer was nothing more than a story, a fable to tell pups. *But I know differently,* thought Storm, excitement and anticipation stirring in her belly. *I've seen it. Lucky almost caught it, not so long ago. He got within leaping distance of its shadow. . . .*

Storm watched the pups as they began to yawn and settle. *If life in the Pack stays quiet, I could go out hunting for it before the end of Long Light. Not just for Tumble, Nibble, Fluff, and Tiny; I could do it for the Pack, too . . . prove how grateful I am that they've accepted me. And it would show them, finally, that this is where I belong.*

Abruptly filled with energy, Storm jumped to her paws. "Alpha, is it all right if I go for a run now—on my own? That story made me want to stretch my legs!"

Alpha looked a little taken aback, but she nodded. "Of course, Storm. And I know what you mean. Talking about running makes me want to run, too!" She glanced at her pups and gave an amused sigh and a shake of her head. "Not right now, though . . ."

With a last nuzzle of Tiny's shoulder, Storm turned and bounded out of the camp. *I probably won't see the Golden Deer, but who knows? Perhaps it's still around. At least it's worth a try! If I can just catch the scent—*

But it wasn't the scent of deer that filled her nostrils as she raced through the underbrush. It was the smell of a familiar dog,

and she was almost on top of him before she skidded to a halt.

"Bruno!"

Storm's heart sank a little. Bruno had never quite accepted her as a member of the Pack, and he had a deep mistrust of all Fierce Dogs. Even during these last few days when the rest of the Pack had been so nice to Storm, Bruno had still been standoffish. She hadn't expected to run into the big dog, but he was on patrol, of course. The Pack's numbers had dwindled so badly, even hunt-dogs were having to take their turn on patrol duty. Storm stiffened and tucked her ears back, waiting for a snide comment.

"Storm." Bruno too looked somewhat surprised, but his brown eyes softened as he watched her. "You're out patrolling too?"

"Just a run," she muttered. "I'd better get going—"

"Storm, wait." Bruno took a pace toward her. "Just a moment. I need to say something. I'm—I'm sorry . . . for how I've behaved."

Storm felt her jaw hang loose. She could only stare at Bruno in distrust.

"I mean it," he went on. "I've been unfair to you, and I apologize. I don't think you're the bad dog, I really don't."

Storm sat back and scratched her ear with a hindpaw, playing for time. *Am I hearing this right?* "But you don't like Fierce Dogs—"

"I still think Arrow must have killed Whisper," Bruno

mumbled. "Well, it was either him or one of the foxes. But I watched you save Tiny from the Endless Lake, and I knew that I'd been wrong about you. You're a good dog, Storm. I'm sorry I didn't believe you. And I'm sorry for all the trouble I've caused you."

Storm stared at his mournful, penitent face. How many times had she seen it twisted with meanness and suspicion? However carefully she examined it now, she just couldn't make out if there was something harder behind his remorseful eyes. *How can I trust him?*

She stood up again on all four paws. "But you're still blaming Arrow. You still think all Fierce Dogs are bad. We didn't *ask* to be born Fierce Dogs."

"Arrow's different." His eyes were beseeching. "I *do* still suspect him. We don't know him, not really, we never did. And now he's left the Pack, and taken Bella with him. But it's not about him being a Fierce Dog, Storm. I won't ever judge you for that again. I know now it was stupid."

Storm licked her chops. Bruno did look genuinely upset. Could she really keep arguing with that miserable expression? "If that's true, Bruno, then . . . I guess I can accept your apology."

"It is true, I promise. Listen, Storm, I have to go catch up

with my patrol." The big dog's ears were pricked eagerly, but all of a sudden he crouched, his paws stretched out, his head lowered close to the ground. "But please believe me when I say I regret all of it."

He wouldn't fake that submission, would he? He's always said exactly what he thought. Storm pinned her ears back, shocked but reluctantly pleased. *I would never have expected Bruno to care about my feelings. But hard as it is to believe, I think he's for real.* Tentatively she began to wag her tail.

"All right. . . . All right, Bruno. And thanks. I . . . appreciate you saying this."

"Good." Bruno darted forward to touch her nose with his. "Thanks, Storm. That means a lot to me."

As she watched his retreating haunches, Storm sat back again, flummoxed but filled with growing happiness. *I can hardly believe it. Bruno meant that, I'm sure of it. He doesn't hate me anymore. The whole Pack accepts me.*

Things really are getting better. This is where I belong.

CHAPTER TWO

The grave was such a peaceful place. Shaded by trees, surrounded by the scents of the forest, dappled in sunlight. Storm stood by it, gazing down at the place where the Pack had brought Whisper to return to the Earth-Dog. The ground no longer looked freshly turned; mosses and grass and tiny purple flowers grew on its surface. Whisper was becoming part of the land again, part of the forest, just as the Earth-Dog promised all dogs.

It felt right. Storm bowed her head, then turned to leave.

And jumped, her heart thrashing. Whisper himself stood before her: not part of the earth after all, but himself again, his eyes bright but fearful, his ears pinned back.

"Don't forget me, Storm, all right?"

Her throat felt dry, but Storm shook her head. She rasped, "Of course I won't forget you, Whisper! But we need to move on . . . the whole Pack needs to look to the future."

Sadness filled the gray dog's eyes, and he shook his head. "Oh, Storm."

Storm's belly felt cold, and she shuddered. She couldn't take her eyes off Whisper's.

"You can't move forward yet, Storm. Please." He gestured with his head. "First you have to look behind you."

She didn't want to turn and look, but she had no choice. Fur prickling, she turned, slowly.

Two graves.

Two graves.

Whisper's grave was just as it had been, settling into the life of the forest, the undergrowth beginning to creep across his resting place.

But beside his, a second grave was freshly dug, the turned earth dark and moist.

"Who?" Storm barked, her voice choked and harsh. "Whose is it, Whisper?"

She heard only silence. When she glanced back, Whisper had vanished. Frantically Storm began to dig, clawing at the earth, kicking it clear with her hind legs. She dug and dug, desperate. The soil was loose, and easy to pull up, and she was soon deep down in the grave, deeper than they'd ever buried Whisper. Still she clawed and kicked, and still there was no body, no dog.

Where is the corpse? How far down must I dig? Storm jerked up her head and howled aloud into the shadowy forest.

"Whose grave is this? Whose?!"

* * *

She started awake in her own den, shaking violently. Terrified, she peered at her paws. She was relieved to see there was no mud on her claws—she had not been digging in her sleep.

But it felt as if she had. She could imagine the dirt's grittiness caught between her paw pads; she could even taste it in her mouth. And as much as she spat and shook herself, she couldn't get rid of it.

It was early; the Sun-Dog had not yet shown his shining hide through the trees, though the promise of his glow had paled the edge of the sky. Storm shuddered, trying not to whine. *I didn't wake any other dog, thrashing around. Oh, thank the Sky-Dogs. How could I ever have explained this horrible dream?*

The taste of dream-mud, and the sensation of dirt in her claws, stayed with her all morning; she could not forget the sight of that fresh grave next to Whisper's. *I never found a body. But Whisper was trying to tell me something, I know it.*

Will another dog die? Who will it be?

Me?

She still hadn't managed to shake off the fear by the time she joined Beetle and Thorn for their early patrol. The two dogs greeted her with friendly enthusiasm, but Storm herself struggled

to look cheerful. She was irrationally certain that her fur was filthy with grave dirt.

"What's wrong, Storm?" Beetle furrowed his brow.

She shook herself for the umpteenth time, though there was nothing to dislodge. *It was a dream, for the Sky-Dogs' sake.* "Nothing. Let's go."

The two litter-siblings exchanged doubtful glances, but Storm gave them no time to ask more questions. She led them on their familiar route, heading in a wide circle toward the longpaw town. There had been more activity in the deserted settlement lately, and Alpha wanted every dog to keep a close eye on the goings-on.

The three dogs slowed their pace as a shattered line of low buildings came into view. With a nod to Thorn and Beetle, Storm lowered her shoulders and crept through the long grass, her ears quivering with alertness. A sharp scent came to her nostrils: tangy and piney, like a freshly broken branch.

Alpha's right. The longpaws are back. And they've been busy.

There were fences now, their wood white-pale, smelling freshly cut by sharp longpaw weapons. The ground had been flattened out in long, dark strips. Beside the strips of flattened soil, great square holes had been excavated, and more fresh-cut wooden posts had been driven into their edges. Slumbering nearby were

the vast yellow loudcages the longpaws used to dig and flatten and smash.

"Don't wake the loudcages," whispered Beetle, his tail stiff and quivering.

"I don't think we will," murmured Storm. "They've obviously been hard at work."

Thorn's eyes were narrowed, and her hackles were raised. Both the litter-siblings looked nervous and hostile; they hated longpaws, and no wonder—their Father-Dog, Fiery, had been captured and killed by particularly vicious ones. Again Storm recalled that terrible evening when Lucky and Alpha's pups had splashed recklessly into the Endless Lake and almost drowned. Thorn was one of the dogs who had gone to save the pups, but just when it had mattered most, she couldn't bring herself to set a paw on the beach—because there had been longpaws there. Her fear had defeated her, brave as she was.

"Are you two all right?" Storm growled, glancing at both dogs with concern.

"We're fine." Thorn's voice sounded choked, but there was a determined light in her eyes. "Let's keep going."

"Stay close together, then," Storm said. "We'll be safe if we protect each other."

Even more cautiously than before, they slunk through the grass toward the town. Storm could sense the fear and anger emanating from Thorn and Beetle; their fur was rank with it, but they pressed on bravely. Tall, shadowy figures moved in the half-destroyed buildings, and the three dogs could hear the barks of longpaws communicating with one another.

"I can't stand the thought of longpaws so close to our camp," whispered Thorn. "After what they did to our Father-Dog."

Beetle shuddered. "Longpaws are bad, Storm."

"These might be different longpaws," suggested Storm uncertainly. "The better kind, like the one on the beach that Mickey rescued from the giant wave. These ones don't have the shiny black face masks that hide their eyes, or the yellow fur."

I'm trying to convince Beetle and Thorn, but I'm not even convincing myself. They're probably right. And this can't be good for the Pack. Even that nice longpaw on the beach tried to make Mickey go with him in the loudbird. . . .

Worse, the deep pits and the ravaged earth of the settlement reminded her of the grave from her dream. Storm's fur prickled and her hackles quivered. *It's all wrong. Something terrible is coming: The dream told me so, and all this longpaw activity only makes it more certain.*

But I can't put my paw on what it will be. . . .

* * *

"To me, Pack, and listen for a moment."

Alpha was sitting up, watching the Pack patiently as the lowest-ranking dogs finished eating their share of the prey pile. The Moon-Dog, only her half-turned haunches visible, was still low on the horizon; but higher in the sky, there were dark clouds, and occasional drops of rain fell on the gathered Pack. Normally they would all hurry to their dens now, but Alpha looked serious and intent, and her dark eyes glowed with determination. Every dog sat up and paid attention. Sunshine, the Omega, swallowed her last bite of mouse, licked her paws clean, and pricked her feathery ears.

Alpha nodded in satisfaction. "Now. We need to discuss the longpaws Storm, Beetle, and Thorn saw on their patrol today. There are many more of the longpaws than before, and they and their giant loudcages are making great changes to the land. Will they come closer to the camp? And if they do—how will we respond?"

In the thoughtful silence that followed her statement, two dogs jumped to their paws, growling. Beetle and Thorn, Storm realized with surprise.

"We attack them, of course!" Thorn's bark resounded strongly through the glade.

"We drive them away," agreed her litter-brother, his eyes hard. "Before they can do even more damage to our Pack!"

"It's *our* territory," added Thorn. "Not theirs! They abandoned it."

Storm stared at the two litter-siblings, uneasy. She knew there was more to this than the desire to protect their territory. The change in Thorn since this afternoon was striking, and unsettling; clearly she'd regained some of her courage, but what Thorn and Beetle wanted was no less than revenge for Fiery—and that, Storm knew, could never end well. Not against longpaws with loudcages and deadly loudsticks.

"So what do you say, Alpha?" barked Beetle. "Will we defend our territory?"

Alpha stood up on her flat rock and looked sternly at the two of them.

"No," she said, quietly but clearly. "We will not fight longpaws. That has never worked for any dog. You two may be too young to have learned this, but I know it well—and so does Beta, who was in the Trap House with me." She glanced at her mate, Lucky.

Beetle looked surprised and angry at Alpha's calm refusal, but Thorn pricked one ear forward, as if suddenly less sure. "What's a Trap House?"

Storm shifted her attention from Thorn to Alpha. She wanted to know that, too.

"I'll explain, and then you might be less inclined to tangle with longpaws." Alpha lay down again, her paws in front of her. "Longpaws are not content to let free dogs be free, even when we *don't* bother them. They capture free dogs and hold them prisoner in steel cages. These places are cold, and cramped, with barely room for a dog to stand—there's no chance to roll, or run, or jump." She sighed, a sad, faraway look on her narrow face. "And sometimes they take dogs out of those cages, yes—but those dogs disappear, and they are never seen again."

Storm felt a great shudder run through her hide. Beetle still looked angry, but Thorn's rage seemed tinged with fear once more.

"All right," said Thorn after a moment, bowing her head. "We accept your decision, Alpha."

"Of course you do," Alpha answered gently. "I'm sorry, Thorn and Beetle, but this is the only way."

"Looks like we don't have a choice," grumbled Beetle, but he lay down and ducked his ears submissively.

"There's a chance the longpaws might leave us alone." Mickey the Farm Dog stepped forward, the voice of reason as always. "If we don't trouble them, they might not trouble us."

"That's not what happened to Fiery!" snapped Moon, rising to her paws. Then her body sagged, and she sighed. "Longpaws will always hunt us down—just like they hunted down my mate. I'm not angry now, like Thorn and Beetle are. I'm just sad. And I don't want what happened to Fiery to happen to any other dog." She twitched her tail and looked keenly at Alpha. "Will we have to move camp again?"

"I'm not sure." Alpha looked down at the rock beneath her paws. "If the longpaws want this territory, though, we may have no choice."

Storm gasped. Would it really come to that? She'd been so preoccupied with the threat of the traitor within the Pack, she hadn't thought that such danger could come from outside.

Several of the dogs gave angry, protesting growls.

"This is our home!" yelped Snap.

"We've fought so hard, and worked so hard," added Daisy miserably. "This is our home now."

"And it's perfect," whined Sunshine. "The glade, the pool, the cliffs where we can watch for trouble . . ."

"Where would we go?" asked Breeze. "The other dogs who have left the Pack have surely claimed all the best territory nearby. We'd have to travel very far before we could settle again." She

glanced at the four small pups, her face full of worry.

"I don't know." Moon sighed, scraping the earth with a claw. "I'd travel any distance to keep my pups safe—and I'm sure Alpha and Lucky think the same. The pups would manage, if we all helped them."

"My brothers and I traveled with Lucky and Mickey, when we left the Dog-Garden," Storm said quietly, half-afraid to remind the Pack of her Fierce Dog home but determined to reassure Breeze. "We were about the same age then. They have a whole Pack, and their Mother-Dog and Father-Dog. They'll be all right."

"I agree," put in Mickey gently, giving Breeze a lick. "Longpaws may not all be bad, but the pups will be safer if we stay away from them."

Third Dog Twitch nodded. "It's a big decision to make, Alpha. Perhaps we shouldn't be too rash, but we should all think hard about our future."

Lucky, who had been quiet till now, gave a growl. Gently he licked Tumble's small head. "It's the pups who are the future of our Pack, and I don't ever want to see them in longpaw cages."

Alpha gave a sharp, quiet bark. "Very well. The discussion is over for now. There's much for every dog to think about. Talk

about it among yourselves. We will come together again soon and decide what to do. I know it's a hard bone to chew, my Pack."

In ones and twos, the dogs drifted away toward their dens. Only a little rain had fallen, but cold drops still spattered on their fur as the clouds blustered above them, and Storm found herself tired, and eager for her dry, peaceful den. She set off in its direction, nodding to Chase and Daisy, who were on patrol duty for the night. But just as she was about to enter the welcoming warmth of her den, two shapes caught her eye at the edge of the forest.

Storm hesitated. It was Beetle and Thorn, and they were deep in a quiet, intense conversation. *It must have been tough for them tonight,* she thought, *being told hard truths about the longpaws.* It had to be difficult for the two young dogs to choke down Alpha's ruling: to accept that they could never have revenge for their Father-Dog.

But the litter-siblings were as close as two dogs could be, and Storm knew they were resilient. She would not interfere; everything would be fine. Thorn might be terribly afraid of longpaws, but Beetle was the best dog to reassure his sister, despite his own fears. The two of them had always helped each other since their Father-Dog's death.

They're hurting, and angry, and afraid, Storm realized, *but they've got*

each other. And I'd probably say the wrong thing anyway. I'm not very good at comforting.

She turned away, shaking off her unease, and padded into her den to sleep.

CHAPTER THREE

The Sun-Dog's rays were growing warmer by the day, and dazzling spots of light dappled the little freshwater pool. Storm lounged sleepily by Lucky and his pups. Even Tumble, Fluff, Nibble, and Tiny had run out of energy and had flopped in a pile beside their Father-Dog.

It reminded Storm of when the pups were very small, which didn't seem all that long ago. How had the time passed so quickly? Only recently, curling up and snoozing was all they had ever done; they had barely been able to lift their heads or open their eyes. Now, their parent-dogs spent most of their time and energy trying to round them up, and the four pups were constantly chattering and squealing and bouncing and play-fighting. Lucky looked relieved to see them sitting still for a while.

Even as Storm watched them, though, Tumble stirred,

wriggled away from his litter-siblings, and trotted toward the pond. The others were quick to follow, and Lucky gave a small, half-suppressed groan.

Storm laughed softly. "They don't stay still for long, do they?"

"They certainly don't." But there was adoration in Lucky's eyes as he gazed after his pups.

Tumble hesitated, a tail's-length from the pond's edge, and the others followed his example, hanging back warily. It was long moments before the shaggy golden male pup summoned up the courage to dip his forepaws into the pond. He tilted his head uncertainly and retrieved one of his paws. Beside him, Nibble dipped in the very tip of a forepaw. Tiny shrank back, ears low, tail tucked between her legs.

Fluff stepped past Tumble, a determined look on her face. She managed to step into the water with all four paws, and that encouraged the others. Tumble and Nibble took deep, shaky breaths and joined her at the pond's edge; Nibble sniffed at the sun-dappled surface and sneezed.

"It's all right," she said confidently, and took a pace forward.

The bank must have sloped down sharply at just that point. The little tan pup stumbled and fell into the water with a splash,

and her three litter-siblings instantly erupted in panicked barks and yelps.

Tiny gave a miserable, terrified howl. "Help, Lucky, help!"

Springing up, Lucky was at the water's edge in an instant, and leaned down and seized Nibble's scruff. Storm too was on her paws, ready to help, but it was obvious that Nibble was fine now. Lucky set the sodden pup down on the bank, and Nibble shook herself violently. She was trembling.

"Nibble," he scolded her gently, "the water there isn't that deep. You wouldn't have been in trouble if you hadn't panicked. And that goes for you three, too." He nodded sternly at Tumble, Fluff, and Tiny. "You must learn to keep calm."

"I'm not going in, even if it isn't deep," yelped Tiny. "Water can eat you."

"Yes, look how the Endless Lake grabbed Tiny!" yapped Fluff.

"The Endless Lake grabbed Tiny because the Lake-Dog is wide awake and lively, and he likes to pull at a dog when you least expect it. And the Endless Lake is so huge, a pup can disappear in it," explained Lucky patiently. "This pond is sleepy and calm. Truly, pups."

"Well, I'm still not going in it again," said Nibble stubbornly.

She shook more water out of her fur and shuddered.

"All right, pups," sighed Lucky. "I'll take you back to the den."

The pups' ears all pricked up with relief, and Tiny turned and aimed a high-pitched growl back at the surface of the pond, as if it were an enemy she had beaten in a fight.

This is wrong, Storm thought, alarmed at Tiny's anger and at Lucky's resignation. *She shouldn't growl at the River-Dog like that! What if they make an enemy of her for life?*

"Wait, Lucky!" Storm padded to his side. "This is crazy. We can't let the pups be scared of water forever."

"That's true," mused Lucky, "but they're still very young, Storm. Maybe we should give them more time."

The pups nodded their enthusiastic agreement.

"Come on, Lucky." Storm straightened her spine and faced her Beta. "This is important. What if we have to cross a stream to reach a new camp? What if they have to escape a giantfur across water?"

"Yes," said Lucky slowly, "you're right. But what are you suggesting, Storm?"

"Martha taught me and Wiggle and Grunt to swim at the same age your pups are now," said Storm firmly. There was a small twinge in her belly as she remembered the huge, gentle water-dog

who had been her foster Mother-Dog. "Martha wouldn't want these pups to be afraid of water! I can teach them to have courage, to not fear the water, exactly as Martha taught me. The pups can grow up to be friends with the River-Dog."

"No, Lucky!" exclaimed Nibble. "Don't let Storm put us back in the water!"

Tiny shrank back behind her braver sister. Tumble put on a fierce face, drawing back his lip in a snarl.

Lucky lifted his head, facing Storm. Then he gave her a tiny nod. He turned to his pups.

"Storm's right," he told them sternly. He bent his head to lick Nibble's long snout. "Do you know what we've all learned, pups, all the dogs who survived the Big Growl?"

They shook their heads, wary and nervous.

"The Big Growl taught us that every dog fears something," he said gently. "I was once afraid of Trap Houses, and Fight Dogs, and losing my independence. But I also learned it's important to face your fears—to look them in the eye and challenge them. And facing my fears is how I survived and found the Pack."

"Sweet isn't afraid of anything," objected Fluff loyally.

"No, my pup. No dog is fearless. Not Storm, not Bruno, not even Snap or Mickey. How can any dog show courage if they're

never afraid of anything? Your Mother-Dog is scared of many things, but she knows she has to be brave and *face* those things. And so must you—especially if you want to be Alphas of your own Packs one day!"

Tumble's ears pricked up at that. "I want to be Alpha one day. . . ."

"Me too!" Fluff knocked her shoulder into his.

"Perhaps you'll all be Alphas." Lucky laughed. "So, should we start practicing now?"

Storm wagged her tail and gave Lucky a nod of gratitude. *Lucky has always respected my opinions; even when we've had our differences.* His approval gave her a warm feeling of belonging all over again.

Hesitantly the pups followed as the two adult dogs led them past the pond and toward the river. Storm felt so proud of the pups as they bounced along behind her, over the field and past the edge of the woods, through the high grass where they sometimes hunted rabbits. It was the farthest they had ever been from the camp. Although the river was much smaller than the Endless Lake, they all slowed down and sniffed nervously at the soft ground under their paws as Lucky came to a halt on the sandy riverbank.

"Now, pups." Lucky turned to nuzzle the trembling little dogs. "Remember: Storm and I won't let anything happen to you, so don't fear the water. We'll be with you the whole time."

It was Tiny who crept forward ahead of the others, ducking her head and wagging her stumpy tail.

"I know that, Lucky." Her voice was small, but brave, as she tilted her little head to gaze at Storm. "Will you teach us now?"

"Tumble, that's wonderful!" exclaimed Storm, paddling at the golden pup's flank to shield him from the full strength of the current. "That's right, keep your nose clear of the water, but don't panic if a wave splashes up. Good!"

"Catch me!" yelped Nibble as her Father-Dog caught her gently in his jaws and tugged her closer to shore.

"Good job, Nibble. But don't get too overconfident!" Lucky licked her nose.

"I'm swimming!" yelped Fluff, splashing out into the deeper water.

"Hey!" Storm swam to her and herded her back toward the shallower water. "That's good, Fluff—but listen to your father! You mustn't take the River-Dog's good mood for granted."

Finding her paws in the shallows, Fluff nodded and shook her fur vigorously. "All right, Storm. But the River-Dog won't hurt us, I know it!"

Tiny sidled up to her litter-sister. Shyly she said, "You're really good at swimming, Fluff."

"You will be too, Tiny!" said Fluff reassuringly. "Don't be scared of River-Dog. She's just very big and strong, and we need to trust her."

"And *respect* her," Lucky added, laughing as he paddled to shore. "Now, stay in the shallows for a while, pups. I'm tired!"

They yapped their agreement, and, braver now, waded close to the bank. Storm watched them with amusement as Lucky came to her side, and they flopped down together on the crescent of gritty sand.

"That was a good idea, Storm," said Lucky. "You were right. And look at them now! You're a good teacher. You'll be a terrific Mother-Dog yourself someday."

"Humph." Storm wriggled a little uncomfortably. She wasn't at all sure she wanted noisy, disobedient pups of her own, however sweet. She changed the subject swiftly. "The water looks good, don't you think? Clean and clear."

"I was just thinking that," mused Lucky. "The River-Dog

doesn't look sick at all anymore. Maybe the effects of the Big Growl are fading. The Spirit Dogs are setting things right, as they always do."

Storm nodded doubtfully. "I suppose, even if they're wounded, the Spirit Dogs will always put things right in the end?"

"Yes. They always come back." Lucky laid his head on his paws and gazed sadly at his frolicking pups. He gave a deep sigh. "I'll be sorry if we have to leave this place."

"I know. It's just about perfect."

"And it's not only the place." His ears drooped. "I wish I could meet Bella's pups when they're born. At least while we're here, Bella knows where we are, and I can believe she'll come back to see me someday. If we leave, I may never meet the pups at all. I wish I'd fought harder to stop her and Arrow from leaving the Pack, Storm. If I'd known about her pups, maybe I would have."

"I wish they hadn't left, too," said Storm quietly. "Arrow was— well, he wasn't a brother to me, like Bella is your sister. But he was the only Fierce Dog I really knew, the only one I ever got to talk to. It would have been fun to see Fierce pups grow up—but this time, raised by kind parent-dogs. I'd have liked that." She sighed. "And it would have been so good for the Pack, too—to realize that it's a dog's parents and friends and Pack who make them what

they are, not their Fierce Dog blood."

Lucky gave her a gentle, consoling nudge and laid his head upon her neck.

A breeze ruffled the surface of the shallows where the pups were playing. The water splashed Tiny's nose, making her jump and yap in surprise. Fluff was teaching her litter-siblings a jumping game over the tiny waves, and showing them how much fun it was to flop on their bellies in the shallows. Beside Storm, Lucky gave a gruff chuckle and lifted his head.

"We both miss Bella and Arrow," he murmured, "but it's hard to be sad here and now, Storm. Look at them: We've taught them how to trust the River-Dog again."

As Storm watched him watching the pups, she felt a warmth that had nothing to do with the Sun-Dog's rays. Lucky was right. Their Pack was still in danger, but they had faced danger before. Lucky and his pups were still in trouble, but she was determined to make sure they had a future.

CHAPTER FOUR

"*I want you to take charge* of the first hunt today, Storm." Alpha's tail swished as she walked up to the den entrance. "The prey pile has been running low, so we'll need you to bring back plenty of food."

Storm scrambled to her feet, blinking in the Sun-Dog's light. "Of course, Alpha! I've been looking forward to a hunt."

"I'll send some of our strongest hunters with you." Alpha touched her nose to Storm's. "You're more than capable of leading them. Moon and Chase will go with you to scout, and, let's see . . ." The swift-dog looked around the glade, and her eyes fell on Bruno, who lay in the sun, talking with Breeze. The brown Fight Dog looked happy as he spoke, and Breeze was nodding, her eyes soft. But they were instantly alert at Alpha's bark.

"Breeze, Bruno! I'm sending out a hunting patrol."

Both dogs got eagerly to their paws and bounded across to

Storm and Alpha; Chase and Moon were already on their way over from their own dens.

"Storm will lead the patrol," announced Alpha as the hunt-dogs gathered around.

No dog spoke. Despite how kind her Packmates had been lately, Storm felt a flicker of anxiety as she met their eyes. They were all watching her with keen anticipation. There wasn't a trace of resentment in any dog's gaze, and Bruno looked positively enthusiastic about following her lead. Once again a wave of quiet happiness rippled through her. *Things have changed so much lately.*

She couldn't repress a happy bark. "All right. Let's go! We've got work to do!"

Storm led her patrol out of the glade and through the forest, enjoying the softness of moss and grass beneath her paw pads, and the cool breeze that brought with it a tantalizing promise of prey. Tree Flower was drawing to an end, warming into Long Light, and the forest was alive with the rustle of prey. Storm licked her jaws in anticipation.

"Let's split up into smaller groups," she told the others. "There's so much prey, that will maximize our chances. Bruno and Chase, why don't you head to the hunting meadow below the cliffs?"

"Sounds good to me," growled Bruno, and the two dogs veered off.

"He didn't even argue," marveled Moon as she watched Bruno and Chase disappear into the long grass. The three female dogs padded on through trees bright with new green and yellow foliage, their paws silent on fallen blossoms. "Well done, Storm!"

"It seems like Bruno's not suspicious of you anymore," said Breeze. She looked cheerful as she sniffed the wind. "I'm really glad—there's a much happier atmosphere in the camp now!"

"I'm glad too," said Storm softly. "It does make life a lot more peaceful."

"And that's good for the pups," agreed Breeze. "Oh, what a beautiful day for a hunt!"

Storm gave a soft growl of agreement. There couldn't be a more pleasant way to spend the hours of the Sun-Dog's journey: padding quietly through the forest, noses twitching and ears pricked in concentration. For a while there was a companionable silence between the three Packmates as they focused on their search.

"Oh!" exclaimed Breeze. "Did I scent a rabbit just now?"

"I did, too." Storm halted and sniffed the wind. The rabbit scent was mingled with something meatier.

Deer!

"Moon, you go after those. Breeze, you can help Moon drive the rabbits, but keep scouting between the groups, too—you never know what else might pop up. Meanwhile, I'll check out that deer scent. If I catch sight of anything, I'll call you back—it might take a few of us to bring one down, but it would be more than worth it."

Moon gave her an approving growl and a nod, and set off after the rabbits, with Breeze in tow. Every dog was listening to Storm's orders, and she felt her heart beat with a fierce pride.

I think Alpha knew how well this would go; she must have known about Bruno's apology, too. What a wise leader she is—and kind, too. She knows I needed this.

There was a little nibble of guilt in her belly, though. Storm was aware she had more than one reason for choosing the deer scent for herself. *If I can get a sign, just an inkling that the Golden Deer is nearby . . .*

She shook herself. *Stop dreaming, Storm, and start hunting!*

A warm, rich odor clung to a tussock of grass at her shoulder. Storm hesitated, snuffling at it, filling her nostrils. Not the Golden Deer, with its particular, unique spiciness; but the scent definitely spoke of deer, and made her mouth water. Casting around for the strongest trail, Storm found a promising direction and followed it, muzzle close to the ground.

It led her across the meadow, the trail strong and easy to follow until it dispersed among a cluster of cottonwood trees. Storm walked between their smooth silver trunks, keeping her head low and her paws quiet. Above her the new leaves fluttered, casting strange dappled shadows, but the paleness of the foliage made it simple to spot the group of dark, moving shapes where the trees were thickest.

There was a clump of goat's beard growing between the trees, its tall plumes of feathery flowers making good cover. Storm slunk in among the plants and lay low, watching the deer. Their odor was very strong now, and she was downwind and perfectly placed. Could she even take one of them down alone? *Just one . . .*

Or perhaps she should be patient and follow the original plan. She could track the herd, then go back for the others—who must have caught some small prey by now—and then they might have a chance to catch two deer. *Two deer would feed the Pack for days,* she thought hungrily.

The peace in the little copse was deep and blissful, broken only by the rustling of breeze-blown leaves and the contented munching of browsing deer. So it chilled Storm's spine when a searing howl echoed across the grass.

The deer bolted instantly, their hooves a light thunder on the

soft grass. Breathless and afraid, Storm leaped to her paws. The howling was too high-pitched and wild for her to identify the voice, but it was undoubtedly a dog, in pain and terrified. That dog needed help. There was no question of not responding.

Bounding out of the goat's-beard bush, she veered through the tree trunks and raced across the grassy meadow. Her thoughts tumbled over one another even as she sprinted, desperate to reach the distressed dog. *We should never have split up. We still have an enemy, and that bad dog is still among us!*

Oh, Sky-Dogs, I hope I'm not too late—

She plunged into another thickly wooded patch of forest, nearly tumbling over in her speed. The howling was closer now. *It's Moon!*

The deer-scent in her nostrils had been overwhelmed by the reek of rabbit, so she knew she was on the right track. But that scent in turn was abruptly swamped by the pungent, pervasive odor of wild garlic. It seemed to fill Storm's whole skull, making her eyes water and her nose sting. Her sense of smell was useless now—she could only strain her ears forward and crane them to the side, hunting for clues, trying to home in on the source of the howling.

She was so busy listening, focused on the terrible cries, that she almost careered into the steep hollow that opened before her paws. Scrabbling to a halt just in time, she stood on the edge, surrounded by a thick tangle of tough grass and more pungent wild garlic. Panting, Storm stretched out her neck and peered down the slope. It was almost vertical, a hidden trap for any unwary dog.

"Moon!" she barked. She could make out Moon's black-and-white fur through the undergrowth; the Farm Dog was sprawled at the foot of the sharp drop. *"Moon!"*

The pale shape moved, struggling to rise. Heart in her throat, Storm watched as Moon got gingerly to her paws, head hanging down. At least she had stopped howling, but there was still shock and pain in her blue eyes.

Moon tilted her head up, meeting Storm's frightened stare.

"Moon, are you badly hurt? What happened?"

The Farm Dog lifted a paw, wincing in agony. Next to her, Storm could make out a dead rabbit, its head and flank patched with blood. All around Moon were scattered rocks, some larger than a dog's head. They were smeared with fresh earth.

Those rocks have only just fallen!

"Moon, are you all right?" she barked again, torn with anxiety.

Moon gave a low growl, one that swelled with anger till it was almost a howl again.

"No, Storm, I'm *not* all right." Moon's white muzzle curled back to show angry fangs. "I've just been attacked!"

CHAPTER FIVE

"Hold on, Moon. We'll get you out of there." Storm crouched at the edge of the drop, pricking her ears forward and peering over. It was a horribly long drop—Moon hadn't been badly hurt, but that must have been by pure luck. If she'd fallen another way, the fast-running hunt-dog might have broken her neck.

Was she pushed? Is there an enemy nearby? Storm gave a few rapid, loud barks of summons, then turned back to her friend. "What happened, Moon?"

"It was a stupid accident," growled Moon, pawing awkwardly at the dead rabbit. "I was so focused on tracking this rabbit, but I couldn't rely on my nose because of the stench of that wild garlic up there. I had to keep my *eyes* on the wretched creature. So I never saw the land fall away."

"It could happen to any dog," Storm told her, relieved. "I can't

smell a thing, either. You were lucky you weren't knocked out, and that you could howl. I came as soon as I could."

"Oh, you weren't the first," snarled Moon.

Storm flinched back, startled. *No, I got here ahead of the others— wait! Moon said she was attacked.* "What do you mean?"

"I tried to climb out of here at first, but it was hopeless. Too steep, and the slope is crumbly. I knew I'd have to howl for help, so I did—and some dog came, all right. Some dog came, saw me down here, and dislodged these rocks to topple them onto me!"

Storm felt her heart thunder against her ribs. *What? Is the traitor here, now?*

She glanced around and spotted a crumbling overhang a little to their right. It wouldn't be hard to loosen stones from there and send them tumbling down on a dog lying below, as helpless as a wounded deer.

Storm's stomach plummeted, but she also felt a throb of excitement. Moon was all right, and perhaps she had seen the traitor!

"Who, Moon?" she asked breathlessly. "Who did this?"

"I don't know!" Moon gave a strangled howl of frustration. "I couldn't see from here. The dog was nothing but a shadow. But that . . . that *creature* shoved the rocks down deliberately—that much I *do* know!"

Storm tried to beat down her disappointment. The priority here was to get Moon out of her predicament. "You're lucky you weren't killed. Can you walk?"

Moon staggered to her paws and gingerly tested her weight. "Nothing's broken, I don't think. Just bruised."

"You'll be fine," Storm reassured her. *It could have been much worse.* "Where *are* the others?"

Pawsteps and harsh panting echoed abruptly at her ear, and Storm jumped back in shock. When she turned, Bruno, Breeze, and Chase were at her side, out of breath from running, their eyes full of panic. *Of course I didn't smell them coming,* she realized, annoyed at herself. *It's that Earth-Dog-cursed garlic.*

"What happened?" barked Bruno.

"It's fine," Storm reassured him, gesturing to the precipice with her nose. "Moon fell, but she's not badly hurt."

"No thanks to that traitor dog!" barked Moon angrily from below them. "I thought our territory had been cleared, but the bad dog has struck again! I could have been *killed.*"

Chase gave a sharp yelp of horror, while Bruno looked shocked into silence, and Breeze growled in appalled dismay. "How did it happen?"

"Moon fell by accident—but then a dog pushed those rocks

over on top of her." Storm stood back to let her three Packmates peer over the edge. "We can't worry about that right now, though. We have to get her out."

"How can we pull her up from all the way down there?" Bruno's eyes were wide and afraid.

"We don't have to." Storm scratched experimentally at the steep ground. "Look, the earth is crumbling. I'm sure it can be loosened. We'll dig until the slope's shallow enough for Moon to climb."

"Good thinking," yapped Chase, and she set to work. The others joined her, scraping and digging, kicking the loose earth away with their hindpaws.

It was tougher than Storm had expected. All four dogs were soon panting hard, and their progress was slow. Below them, Moon scraped weakly at the foot of the drop, doing her best to help. Storm's paw pads ached; she could feel stinging scratches on them from the dry, stony ground, and she could hear Bruno's harsh, exhausted breathing at her ear, but at last the slope was excavated enough.

"Try now, Moon," barked Storm. "Breeze, Chase—give her a helping paw."

Moon took a determined breath. Scrambling and scrabbling,

she hauled herself up, slipping now and again despite the dogs supporting her flanks. At last, Chase and Breeze got her to the rim of the hollow, and Moon flung herself over it with a last desperate gasp.

The white-and-black dog stood trembling for a moment, her flanks heaving, as the other four dogs licked her face and shoulders. "Well done, Moon," murmured Breeze, nuzzling her.

"Well done, all of *you*," Moon said. "I just wish I'd been able to *see that dog!*"

Storm turned and studied the land around them. The overhang didn't look particularly unstable, and there was no better time than the present to investigate. She began to climb up toward its jutting tip.

"Hurry, Storm," Moon growled, an edge of panicked anger in her voice. "I want to find any clues that might tell us who pushed those rocks down."

"Storm will find anything there is to find." Breeze looked anxiously toward Storm, who nodded. "But, Moon, your legs are unsteady. Lean on my shoulder and we'll start back to camp."

Moon's breathing was still harsh and rapid, but Breeze's words seemed to calm her. She nodded. "All right, Storm. Go ahead and investigate. But I want to hear about anything you

find." She propped her shoulder against Breeze's, and together the two female dogs began their slow trek back in the direction of the camp.

Storm watched them go, then turned and continued toward the overhang, her heart beating hard. She placed her paws carefully as she climbed up the bare rock. It was solid, and no dislodged stones rattled down beneath her treads. She scented the air and the rock, but once again, all smells were smothered by another odor—one that didn't belong there.

Storm edged out more confidently onto the jutting rock's flat top and gaped at the shocking mess that had been left on the overhang's surface. The hollow, raw gaps where the loosened stones had been: Those she was expecting. More surprising were the ragged plant stalks that had been torn up by the roots and strewn around.

Wild garlic.

The uprooted plants hadn't grown here, on the bare rock. The traitor had dug them up, brought them up here, and scattered and trampled them all across the jutting overhang, and the reason was obvious: Storm could detect no trace of the bad dog's scent. She growled angrily at the coldhearted deception.

One thing's for sure: This was a trap. A planned, deliberate, cruel attack. The culprit thought it through.

Whoever had covered the camp in rabbit blood, whoever had hidden savage shards of clear-stone in the prey—the same warped, calculating mind had devised this trap. Her anger turning to fear, Storm shuddered.

Below, Chase and Bruno were staring up at her, blinking against the sunlight. Storm shook herself and trotted back down to join them.

"Come on," she said in a low voice. "We'll catch up with Breeze and Moon. There's nothing to be discovered up there."

"What about the hunt?" whined Chase.

"It's more important to get back and tell Alpha about this." Storm set off toward the glade. "The forest will wait for us, and so will the prey. But the traitor could strike again at any moment."

Is Alpha ever going to stop that furious pacing? wondered Storm. Agitated, the swift-dog strode one way and then the other, over and over again, her thin tail lashing. "This is terrible news, Storm," she said at last. "I thought perhaps our troubles were finished. I thought it too soon."

Storm didn't respond.

I hoped so too. But I never really believed it. I only wish that knowing something like this would happen meant I could have stopped it! The injustice of it made her want to howl. What good was it being aware of the danger they were in if she couldn't do anything about it?

At last, Alpha came to a halt and gave a sharp bark. "Beta! Third Dog! To me."

Twitch and Lucky had been hovering nearby, aware that something was very wrong, and they bounded quickly across to their leader. Their eyes darkened and their tails stilled as they listened to Alpha retell Storm's story. By the end, when Alpha fell silent, they were exchanging glances full of fear and fury.

"This can't go on," said Twitch softly.

Lucky nodded in agreement. "Alpha, I think we need to hear everything that today's hunters can tell us. Let's find out what the others in the party have to say—they might have noticed something strange, even if they didn't realize it at the time."

"A good idea, Beta." Alpha turned her slender head and barked, "Chase! Bruno! Breeze! To me, now."

Storm felt a small wrench of unease in her gut. She didn't want all the hunters to fall under suspicion. This had been her hunt, her responsibility; the thought of more trouble and resentment

stirring in the Pack as a result of her patrol was horrible. *Oh, I hope Alpha doesn't start throwing accusations. . . .*

But her anxiety turned quickly to resentment. As Alpha finished asking her questions and pricked an ear, Chase took a pace forward.

"The trouble is, none of us saw anything, Alpha." She lowered her head respectfully. "Maybe if Storm hadn't split us up and sent us in different directions—"

"Hey!" protested Storm. "We agreed on that tactic!"

Chase gave her a sidelong look, not quite meeting her eyes. "Well, you *were* the one who sent Moon after the rabbits. . . ."

Storm stiffened, feeling a growl rise in her throat. "I don't like what you're implying, Chase."

"Wait." Breeze stepped between them. "Storm didn't know the hollow was there. None of us did! And you know, maybe it was actually an accident—"

Moon gave a furious snarl, and Breeze shrank back. "Are you calling me a liar, Breeze? I'm sick and tired of not being believed! It's like being accused of prey-stealing all over again—which I *still* didn't do, by the way!"

"Stop, stop." Twitch limped forward on his three legs to touch his nose gently to Moon's, then to Breeze's. "No dog is being

accused of anything, Moon." He nuzzled Storm, including her in his conciliatory words. "We're just trying to work out exactly what happened, and when. Now isn't the time for us to turn against each other. It's more vital than ever for the Pack to stay friends—to stay loyal to one another. It seems to me that this infighting is exactly what the traitor dog is trying to provoke."

Alpha nodded. "Wise words as usual, Twitch. Storm, Moon: He's right. There are no accusations here, believe me."

Tipping her head back, she let out a short, summoning howl and waited as the Pack hurried to gather around her. She gave each dog a long, steady gaze as they waited expectantly.

She cleared her slender throat. "Pack, I have something to say; and please don't think I suspect any particular one of you of being responsible for the terrible things that have happened lately. That's important."

As their tails twitched and they gave hesitant nods, Alpha raised her head. "We thought our troubles were over and that the traitor had left our territory. But today Moon was attacked when she was outside of camp on a hunt. A dog she didn't see pushed rocks on her from above, hurting her." There were whimpers of dismay from the gathered Pack, and Alpha growled them into silence and continued. "Since we don't know who did this, we

can't punish any dog. But we can try to keep ourselves safe. When any of us are outside the camp, we must stay in pairs. That will be the rule from now on. It's only sensible for every dog to have another who can vouch for them. Not to keep an eye and a nose on them—I want to emphasize that—but simply to be relied on as a witness. I wish this wasn't necessary." Alpha shook her head sadly. "But as much as we all hoped it were otherwise, it seems our Pack's troubles aren't over. Not yet. But with caution and sense, we can prevent another dog from being harmed. Be careful, my Pack, and be safe. That's all."

Every dog padded away, looking reassured and somewhat mollified. *Every dog,* realized Storm with a sinking heart, *except for Moon.* There was fiery resentment in the hunter's eyes as she slunk toward her den, and Storm hurried to catch up and walk at her side.

They walked together in silence till they reached the entrance to Moon's den, then sat down. Hesitantly Breeze and Chase joined them, glancing at Storm for her approval. Storm nodded silently, though she could feel the hair on her hide rise with the force of anger emanating from Moon.

"You're not happy, Moon." Storm licked her chops, feeling like a fool as soon as the words were out. *Of course she's not happy! Her face*

is as dark as the Sky-Dogs before a thunderstorm.

Moon growled under her breath. "I respect Alpha, of course I do. I wouldn't ever speak ill of her, but . . . Storm, what is she actually going to *do* about the traitor? We're all supposed to watch each other—what use is that? It just makes every dog suspicious, and the bad dog isn't stupid enough to make a move while it's being watched!"

"It's a difficult situation for Alpha," began Breeze lamely. "I know she tries. . . ."

"She's our Alpha! She's there to do difficult things, make hard decisions!" Moon lay down, head on her paws, glowering at the forest. "The traitor targeted me, Storm. Those rocks were pushed down *after* I howled for help. The bad dog knew who I was, which means they *wanted* to hurt me!"

Storm swiveled an ear toward Moon and widened her eyes. "What, Moon? Say that again. They heard you howl, identified you, and *then* they loosened the rocks?"

"Loosened them, and shoved them down on me," snapped Moon.

"So the bad dog knew it was you, specifically. You weren't visible from atop the overhang—I had to lean out over the edge just to get a glimpse—so they must have recognized your voice."

"That's what I'm saying." Moon's lip curled. "Between this, and framing me for prey-stealing—whoever the traitor is, they've got it in for me, Storm."

"Moon, I know it must have been terrifying," said Chase soothingly, "but the truth is, the whole Pack is being targeted. Maybe it's just bad luck that you've had the worst experiences. No, don't snarl at me like that! I'm just trying to make you feel better. It could honestly be a case of being in the wrong place at the wrong time."

Moon subsided with a sigh, though the snarl still lingered on her lips. "Maybe," she grunted.

Giving her a lick, Storm got to her paws and padded off, absorbed in thought. *Maybe Chase is right,* she thought. *But it does seem like a nasty coincidence. Maybe, in Moon's case, it's more than simple bad luck. . . .*

Her paws splashed in something cold and wet, and she gave a yelp of surprise. Preoccupied with the Pack's dilemma, she hadn't realized she'd paced as far as the pond. Storm blinked, then gazed down at the play of sunlight on the gentle ripples. As the water grew still again, her own reflection gazed back at her, troubled.

The dogs who had suffered at the paws of the traitor: Did they have anything in common? Storm wondered. Was there

something particular about them that attracted the bad dog's malice?

If she couldn't work out the traitor's motive, how could she possibly work out who it was?

And far more important, she thought with anguish: *How can I even begin to figure out how to stop them?*

How can I find the bad dog—before something even more tragic happens to the Pack?

CHAPTER SIX

Storm scrambled to her paws, filled with resolution. *For once, I'm not a suspect. Alpha and Beta both trust me now—perhaps they'll start listening to me. I bet Alpha hasn't thought about who the bad dog is targeting. I have to bring it to her; maybe she'll have noticed something else I've missed.*

The Sun-Dog was loping down toward the tops of the trees that surrounded the camp, his light slanted and golden the way it was whenever evening drew near. Storm paused to stretch, enjoying the late warmth. *It's always good when the Sun-Dog begins to linger longer, when Ice Wind is finally long gone. It's not all bad omens these days; we just have to get through this awful time with the Pack intact. We can't lose any more dogs.*

Storm let herself yawn widely, blinked, and caught sight of Twitch.

Her ears pricked up, and she trotted over to him. She liked

their gentle, three-legged Third Dog; and didn't every dog trust him? "Twitch, can I talk to you?"

He glanced over at her, his tail wagging in welcome. "What can I do for you, Storm?"

"I'm going to talk to Alpha. Will you come with me?" After all, Twitch was one of the other dogs most affected by the traitor's attacks.

He nodded solemnly, his eyes warm. "Of course I will!"

Together they approached Alpha and Lucky's den; Storm felt somehow stronger with Twitch at her side. He was such a level-headed, kind dog, and she felt a sudden fierce need to protect him from the traitor. She had to protect *every* dog; this was her Pack, and a Pack Dog was what she was, right down to her claw-tips. *I won't let the bad dog win.*

Alpha and Lucky were relaxing at the mouth of their den, but Storm could see the alert twitch of their ears, the narrow keenness of their eyes. They looked protective and anxious as the pups romped and played, and Storm missed their simple, fond joy in the pups' antics—a carefree pleasure that she'd seen only the day before.

Curse that bad dog, Storm thought angrily.

Alpha and Lucky listened patiently as Storm talked about her

certainty that there must be some logic behind which dogs the traitor targeted. *They're taking me more seriously because Twitch is here,* she thought, and was glad she had asked him to come along.

When she had said her piece, Alpha licked her chops thoughtfully and gave her Beta a swift glance. Lucky nodded, almost imperceptibly.

"Storm, we share your worries," said Alpha, frowning. "Somehow this situation is more frightening because we have no clues; we don't know where to begin. But you seem to have given this a lot of thought, so tell me: Do you have *any* theories about the culprit?"

"I ... I'm not sure," sighed Storm, sitting back on her haunches. "I'm sorry, Alpha. I can't think which of us would do these things. But I have thought about who it *can't* be."

"Go on," Twitch encouraged her.

Storm took a deep breath. "Well, I think we need to look at which dogs the bad dog is targeting. There might be some reason for it we can't see yet. For instance, Moon has been attacked, so it isn't her—and there's no way Thorn and Beetle would put their own Mother-Dog in such danger." *Or frame her for a theft she didn't carry out,* she thought inwardly, but it didn't seem right to mention that aloud when it was Alpha who had punished Moon for it.

Today's incident with the rocks was proof enough.

"I agree," said Alpha, her expression inscrutable. "Are there any more?"

Storm nodded to the Third Dog. "Not Twitch, obviously; he was badly hurt when the prey was sabotaged. He wouldn't do that to himself. Not either of you two," she added in an embarrassed mumble, half glancing at Alpha and Lucky. "You wouldn't hurt your own Pack."

Alpha gave a soft laugh. "Don't be ashamed to include us, Storm. You're right, of course, we wouldn't hurt our own Pack—but we have to consider every dog's motives, just to be certain. Go on."

"Breeze is out of the question; she was with your pups when the rabbit blood was scattered over the camp. And . . . there's me. I haven't any proof, but *I* know it isn't me." Storm raised her head with nervous defiance.

Alpha nodded thoughtfully, looking very serious. "It narrows it down a little, doesn't it?"

"I suppose so," growled Storm. "But beyond that—I just don't know. I can't imagine any of the rest of our Packmates behaving this way. What possible reason would they have? I just wish we knew *why* all of this is happening. It seems like there must be some

logic behind which dogs have been targeted."

"But what could the connection be?" Lucky asked thoughtfully. "The dogs who have been hurt . . . besides Moon and Twitch, there was Whisper. . . ."

Twitch shuddered at the mention of the murdered dog, his eyes sad. "Bella was the worst affected when the prey pile was poisoned," he remembered.

And then there's me.

Storm's stomach gave a sickening lurch. If specific dogs were being targeted, then she was one of them. Always, when something bad happened to the Pack, Storm had come under suspicion. Every single crime that had been committed was one it looked like Storm could have been responsible for; she'd always been alone, so she never had proof of where she had been and what she was doing.

And why would I? I don't know when the attacks are going to happen; if I knew that, I'd be the bad dog myself. If I had a witness, I'd be in the clear.

She hesitated, unwilling to share this realization. You could *see* a dog being poisoned, or pelted with rocks—being turned into a suspect was just as hurtful, but it was invisible. What if the others didn't agree?

Before she could speak again, Alpha was shaking her head

doubtfully. "I agree that there must be some connection, but I don't know what it could be. Whisper, Bella, Moon, Twitch . . . all these dogs came from different Packs, originally. They're hunters and Patrol Dogs and scouts. Except for being part of this Pack, I don't see what they have in common."

Storm felt her shoulders droop sadly. "Neither do I," she said. "I wish I did."

"Don't worry. And don't ever feel like you can't come to me with your thoughts, Storm," Alpha told her gently but firmly. "We have to be able to talk about this, to discuss it, or we'll never move any further forward. I think you're right: We have to do our best to work out who else it *can't* be. It's the only way we'll ever discover who it really *is*."

Storm sagged with relief. *Alpha and Lucky are taking me seriously. That has to be good.* She shivered. *I can't bear the thought of finding out one of my Packmates did this—but we must find the bad dog.*

Lucky was staring straight ahead, his yellow tail thumping in a slow rhythm. "It's hard to take in," he murmured. "Rake, Ruff, Woody, and Dart are long gone, just like Bella and Arrow. I doubt very much they'd come back to our territory just to do this, to hurt us. And the dogs who are still here . . . it's not that I don't take you seriously, Storm," he added hurriedly, "but it's a lot for

any dog to contemplate. Little Sunshine, a killer? Or Daisy?" He licked his chops. "Bruno? He might be surly sometimes, but he has never been anything but loyal to the Pack. The same goes for Snap. Mickey—no, I just don't believe he's capable of it. Chase? I don't know her as well as I know the others, but I've been Pack-mates with her long enough—and I know she's a good dog, a good *Pack Dog*. I know it in my bones."

"That's the trouble," sighed Alpha. "We only have our bones to go on, and that hasn't helped us so far."

Storm's head dipped. Well, what had she expected? That Alpha or Beta would have instant, easy answers? Maybe deep down, she actually *had* thought that.

No. Be sensible, Storm, she scolded herself, *and take this problem one bite at a time.* She'd decided to talk to her Alpha, and she'd done it, and that had been the right thing to do. Now, at least, she knew she wasn't the only dog gnawing over the mystery.

But she knew she couldn't leave it like this; she couldn't just drop all the responsibility at Alpha's den mouth like an unwanted chunk of rabbit. As Storm padded away from the leaders' den, she felt her muscles tense with determination.

I can't just wait around, wondering if Alpha's come to any conclusions. What if another dog gets hurt in the meantime? I need to take action, protect

the Pack—even if that means nothing more than talking things over with my Packmates.

The dogs who had been targeted were the ones least likely to be guilty—so she should talk with them. There was a chance they'd seen something—something that was significant, but they didn't realize it at the time. And it might be hard for dogs to think about the attacks—and the chance there might be more—but discussing it openly might actually make them just a little safer. They'd be on the alert—and that felt like the most useful thing Storm could do for them right now.

A dark-brown shape was heading for the camp border at the edge of the glade, about to vanish among the tree trunks. Storm gave a soft bark.

"Breeze! Wait."

The brown dog turned to give Storm a quizzical look over her shoulder. "What is it, Storm? I'm supposed to meet Daisy to patrol."

"I'll be quick." Storm swallowed. "It's just—I need to talk to you. About the bad dog."

Breeze's brow furrowed. "The bad dog? Why would you want to talk to *me* about that?"

"I'm sure the traitor will strike again, Breeze. It's awful to

think about, but I believe we have to. It's the only way to ensure that we might be ready for another attack." Storm licked her jaws. "I've been trying to work out which dogs *didn't* do these things. Right now, that's easier than trying to imagine which dog is actually capable of them."

"What's your best guess at the moment, Storm?" Breeze asked. She sat back on her haunches, tilting her head curiously.

"I think we can eliminate the dogs who have been targeted . . . Twitch, Moon, Bella, and . . . well, clearly Whisper is out of the question." Storm felt a stab of grief at the mention of poor Whisper, and she shivered. "And I know you were with the pups when the camp was polluted with that blood. But the trouble is, it could be *any* other dog."

Breeze shuddered. "Sky-Dogs," she whispered softly. "I can't bear to think about it."

"But we have to," Storm pointed out. "And I know you observe the camp a lot, while you're taking care of the pups, and—well, I suppose I'm asking if you've seen anything?"

"Like what?" Breeze twitched her ears forward, looking puzzled.

"That's the trouble, I don't *know*," exclaimed Storm in frustration. "Just something unusual: maybe a dog who seemed to be in

the wrong place . . . something that seemed normal at the time, but looking back it was . . . just not quite right. Out of character."

"Oh. I do see what you're nibbling at." Breeze's eyes narrowed in concentration. "Truly, Storm? I can't think of anything. There hasn't been anything . . . well, *strange* that I've noticed around camp lately. No dogs behaving oddly or differently, nothing like that."

"Oh," sighed Storm. "Well, it was worth asking."

"Of course it was," Breeze told her. "And I'll be even more watchful now, I promise. We all have to stay alert. If anything strange happens, I'll tell you at once."

Storm nodded, suddenly feeling unbearably tired. "Thanks, Breeze."

"It's nothing. Now, why don't you go to your den?" Breeze nuzzled Storm's neck fondly and gave her ear a lick. "You've had a tough day. Maybe things will look clearer in the morning, after a good night's sleep."

"You're probably right." Storm touched noses with the gentle-eyed dog. "Good night. And thanks."

Breeze padded off into the trees, and Storm trudged to her den. Her legs suddenly ached with weariness, and she sank gratefully onto her bedding. She expected to drop off instantly, but sleep evaded her like a dodging, darting squirrel.

Her mind clawed at the mystery of the bad dog, and her eyes kept flicking open. However much she tossed and turned, and dragged her bedding into new positions, she just could not drift into blissful unconsciousness.

What if it isn't only one dog? she asked herself, even as she squeezed her eyes shut and willed sleep to come. *Maybe there's more than one traitor.*

Could it really be one—or more—of my dearest friends?

Opening her eyes again, Storm stared miserably at the exposed roots that poked through her den wall. Daisy was such a sweet-natured dog, brave and kind. And she was *small* . . . not that size always mattered, if a dog could catch an enemy unawares.

Mickey was a big dog, but his mild nature made him an even less likely culprit than Daisy. Snap or Bruno? Snap was quick and cunning, and Bruno was certainly fierce and burly enough to take down most dogs. But despite her differences with both of them, Storm couldn't believe it of either Snap or Bruno.

The least likely bad dog of all was Sunshine. She was little—but like Daisy, that didn't have to matter. *She still has teeth.* Storm's mind recoiled from the idea. Sunshine had always seemed so happy to be Omega; she was more content than any dog in the Pack, as if she'd found true meaning in her life.

But what if she wasn't happy with it anymore? Could the little dog be simmering with resentment beneath it all? Had she secretly rebelled at her status, at having to make do with the last and smallest prey every night?

It was no use; sleep wouldn't come. Staggering to her paws, Storm slunk from her den and walked in a daze around the camp's border. The night was clear and starlit, the sky still dark blue rather than black, the air fresh with the scents of oncoming Long Light. But as she paced, she realized the stars were vanishing one by one, beginning at the horizon; light rain began to speckle her coat. Storm craned her head to peer at the sky. Clouds had obliterated the stars, and the raindrops were cold despite the change of season. She gave a long sigh and trudged on, sniffing dutifully at the border as she walked.

The rain was falling harder now; her fur clung to her skin, heavy with wetness. The clouds seemed to be thickening rather than clearing, and something in the atmosphere made the hairs on her spine lift. Glancing up again at the sky, she saw Lightning Dog race in an instant from the clouds to the earth. In his wake came the thundering rumble of the Sky-Dogs; they always seemed to chase Lightning when he sprinted, just for fun.

Her eyelids felt impossibly heavy. *I might sleep now.* Storm padded

back to her den, tail drooping and dripping; she didn't even have the energy to shake herself. Curling up on her soft mossy bedding—*Sunshine brought this for me; how could she be bad?*—Storm was at last overwhelmed by a long, dark, and dreamless sleep.

Storm had no idea how long she'd slept. She was jerked into wakefulness by a terrible, wailing howl that made her clench her teeth.

The Sun-Dog is up and running—it's morning. She shook herself, stumbling a little as a fog of drowsiness clung to her.

The high howl came again, splitting the air—a horrible sound of grief and desperation. Now Storm was fully awake. Tightening her jaws, she sprang out of her den and raced toward the source of the dreadful noise.

She wasn't alone; alongside her ran Snap, Breeze, and Mickey. Moon hurtled from her den and joined them.

"What's happening?" cried Sunshine, frozen in terror as they passed her. "What's wrong?"

"Who knows?" barked Snap.

"It's coming from High Watch!" gasped Mickey.

Chase bolted out from the trees and ran with them. Sunshine took off in pursuit, small legs a blur beneath her shaggy white coat, but she was soon left behind. Alpha sprang from her den,

and when the pups tried to follow, Lucky summoned them back with a bark that was not to be argued with. He shielded the little dogs with his body as he stared after his running Pack.

Storm's heart thundered as she saw Alpha first catch the leading dogs, then streak ahead. She was so fast! Alpha raced up the winding path to High Watch. The track underpaw was slippery with mud after the heavy rain, and all the dogs stumbled and slithered as they followed, leaving deep claw marks in the loose, wet earth.

The line of Packmates was much more strung out by the time Alpha leaped up the last rocky ledge to the cliff top and vanished over it. Storm was only a few paces behind her, though, and with one bound she was on the plateau and sprinting after her leader. The pounding steps of her Packmates echoed behind her, one by one, as they too reached the summit.

Not again, Storm kept thinking. *Please not again. Let it be an accident. Let it just be that the High Watch dog has gotten caught in thorns—who's on High Watch, anyway?*

Cold terror swept through her lungs and belly as she remembered. *Daisy!*

Alpha skidded to a halt on the damp grass ahead of her, and Storm almost collided with the swift-dog. Mickey, Snap, Breeze,

and Chase were at their side in an instant, but Storm didn't turn to look at them: She felt a rush of pure relief. In front of Alpha stood Daisy, alive and well—but quivering with shock and terror. Her little head was raised to the Sky-Dogs, her jaws open wide as she howled and howled in despair.

"Daisy! *Daisy!*" commanded Alpha. "Daisy, *what is it?*"

Her sharp words finally penetrated the little dog's head. Daisy turned, eyes filled with stunned misery, and stared at her Packmates.

"Bruno . . ." From a howl, her voice had fallen to a high, tortured rasp. "It's *Bruno*. There."

Alpha stiffened, and stared past Daisy. "What?" Her voice made Storm's blood run ice-cold.

"He's dead." Daisy's voice faded, choked with horror and grief. "Bruno . . . my friend Bruno . . . He's *dead*."

CHAPTER SEVEN

"No!" Mickey's agonized howl shattered the awful silence.

Storm was frozen where she stood. She felt as if she were viewing the scene from outside—floating—watching herself and the rest of her grief-stricken, disbelieving Pack. Daisy nodded feebly at a large slab of rock near the cliff edge; Alpha's paws shook as she walked toward it. There was a dark smear of blood across the pale stone, but Bruno was mostly hidden; Storm could see only a single lifeless paw.

Snap was nuzzling her mate, Mickey, trying frantically to console him. Chase and Breeze stood flank-to-flank, dumbfounded. Moon gave a high, whimpering howl of distress; as soon as Thorn and Beetle appeared, they ran to her, licking comfortingly at her raised throat. Between the bigger dogs, a small dirty-white shape pushed through, last to arrive, panting from the exertion.

Sunshine crept closer to Daisy, her dark eyes stunned, her whole body shaking. "Is it true? Did I hear that right, Daisy? *Bruno?*"

Daisy could only nod once, miserably. Even her wiry fur seemed to droop.

Mickey shook himself violently, his jaws clenched. He took a couple of steps forward and placed his paws on either side of the two little dogs, sheltering them. Dropping his head, he began to lick their ears gently.

Those three and Bruno, they were all part of the Leashed Pack after the Big Growl, Storm realized with a wrench in her belly. *They learned to survive together, without their longpaws. They were all so close. Perhaps that shared history makes their bond even stronger than the ones between regular Pack Dogs. Does it make their grief far deeper, too?*

Storm's heart ached for them; she could not imagine how they were feeling. She hadn't known Bruno for as long as they had, but she too felt hollow with grief and shock. She and the big dog had only just started to get along like true Packmates. As Alpha stalked stiffly behind the rock slab and stared down, Storm started hesitantly toward her, Chase and Breeze at her tail.

"No," snapped Alpha, clearly and sharply. "All of you, stay back."

As they halted, she sniffed at the ground and at the covered corpse. After a long time, she raised her head and sighed deeply. She turned to her Packmates.

"Only a large, vicious animal could have killed Bruno," she said, her voice rough and raspy. "But that rain last night—it's washed away any traces. There are no paw prints. There's no scent."

"Large and vicious," growled Snap, leaving Mickey's side to take a couple of paces forward. "You mean a giantfur, maybe? A giant sharpclaw? Or . . . could it have been a dog?"

Alpha was silent for long moments, licking her chops. She glanced back at what lay behind the rock, and when she turned back to the Pack, she didn't quite meet any dog's eyes.

"Yes," she admitted at last. She sounded as if she could hardly get the words out; as if her jaws were full of poisoned prey. "Yes, it could have been a dog. I think . . . I'm almost certain . . . Yes. It was a dog."

Gasps and muffled whimpers erupted from the Pack. A low, agonized growl sounded from Mickey's throat.

Alpha drew herself up stiffly. "All of you, return to the camp. Except for you, Mickey," she added as he began to protest. "And Storm and Breeze, and Moon. You four can help me move Bruno. We can't leave him up here. We'll bury him next to Whisper."

A cold chill went through Storm's rib cage at the sound of the gray dog's name. *Whisper.*

Whisper tried to warn me!

He knew this was going to happen. My dream was clear. Perhaps I could have stopped this. . . . Perhaps I was supposed to stop this. . . .

But how could she have foreseen it? Guilt flashed through her. Bruno had been one of the Packmates she still suspected of possibly being the bad dog; could there be a worse, more tragic proof of his innocence? And who would want to hurt Bruno? He could be grumpy and abrasive, but his size and strength belied a surprising gentleness.

I didn't see it coming. But I should have. Whisper warned me. He warned me.

Mickey nudged Daisy and Sunshine with his nose and shepherded them away, muttering pointless reassurance; Daisy was still shaking as she set off back down the cliff path. The rest of the Pack followed, their tails hanging low, and Mickey stood and watched them go. His chest was heaving, Storm noticed.

Mickey's pain was awful to see. Turning tactfully away, Storm paced over to the slab of rock. For a moment she hesitated, and then she stepped around behind it.

Sky-Dogs! Storm sucked in a shocked breath.

No wonder Alpha had sent the rest of the Pack away. No dog should see this, if they didn't have to—and especially not little Sunshine. *I wish Daisy hadn't found him. She shouldn't have seen this either. . . .*

Bruno did look almost as if a giantfur had attacked him, but Storm knew why Alpha had instantly suspected a dog. The injuries were just too vicious, too *deliberate* to be the work of some raging animal.

The big dog's throat had been torn out. That was bad enough—a horrible echo of what had happened to Whisper—but far worse, his entire lower jaw had been ripped away. Blood was splashed on the rock and on the grass around him; he lay in a dark congealing lake of it. His eyes were open, glazed in death, and his expression was more one of shock than terror.

Storm took an instinctive step back. She could hardly bear to look at the evidence of poor Bruno's violent killing, but there was something even worse about the state of his body. Her stomach twisted sharply.

His jaw . . . torn right away from his skull.

Storm felt sick, her belly and fur tingling with a feeling of familiarity—but she could not put her paw on why it was so familiar. . . .

"Let's get to work," Alpha said, softly but clearly. As if a trance had broken, the other four dogs shook themselves and prepared to drag Bruno as carefully as possible down the steep and winding cliff path.

It was a long, difficult, painful task; Bruno's body was heavy and the thudding sound it made as they maneuvered him down the steeper shelves was awful. Behind them, a thin, dark smear of half-dried blood marked their path. Once they were down among the trees, the ground was at least flat, but the big dog was an awkward burden to drag through the pine trunks and the thorny scrub.

The four Packmates and their Alpha had to take frequent breaks, but at last, exhausted and panting hard, they released Bruno in the dappled light of the forest clearing. His big frame flopped to the ground, lifeless, and rolled slightly down a shallow slope.

Inwardly Storm shuddered. There was Whisper's grave, overgrown with grass and moss, dotted with tiny purple flowers. It was settling back into the paws of the Earth-Dog, just as it had been in her dream.

And now we'll dig that fresh grave. The one Whisper told me we'd dig.

They set to work, tearing and clawing at the soft earth, kicking

the loosened mud aside till they had created a hollow deep enough to keep Bruno safe from surface scavengers. *Deep enough to deter foxes,* Alpha had said when they'd buried Whisper; but Whisper had been a smaller dog. It was a much bigger job to bury Bruno, but at last the hole was deep enough, and together they dragged Bruno to its edge. With a shove from Mickey and Storm, he rolled and thudded into dark, moist, exposed earth.

My paws. They're shaking. It was just exhaustion, Storm told herself, but she knew that wasn't true. It was shock and grief—and fear. *My dream. This is just like my dream.*

I didn't know I'd feel so strongly about losing Bruno. I didn't get along with him well—not till the end—and he made trouble for me. But he wasn't a bad dog. He certainly wasn't the *bad dog.*

Misery choked her. *Bruno and I had only just learned how to get along, Earth-Dog. And now he's dead, and you've taken him.*

Moon gazed down into the grave, her drooping ears pricking up suddenly with sad curiosity. "Bruno's jaw," she murmured, her eyes distant. "He looks—it looks just like what happened to Terror. Remember, Storm?"

"That doesn't mean anything." Breeze's voice held an edge as she sidled closer and pressed her flank to Storm's. "Just because it's what Storm did to that mad dog Terror—there's no way she'd

do such a thing to Bruno. He was our Packmate!"

Storm felt her stomach shrink within her, and she couldn't help cringing. Breeze always meant well, but there were times Storm wished she'd keep her jaws shut. Moon was staring at Breeze, her eyes startled.

"I didn't mean that at all," Moon stammered. "You know that, Storm, don't you? It was just a . . . an observation. A big, strong dog—as big and strong *as* you—did this. That's all."

Storm nodded quickly. "I know. Of course."

But the air was suddenly crisp with unease, and Storm felt heat run through the skin beneath her fur. Moon looked guilty, Breeze exasperated, and Alpha and Mickey simply uneasy.

"We should get back to the camp soon," said Mickey, just as the silence was growing unbearable. The Farm Dog's voice still sounded hoarse and rough, and again Storm felt a sharp twist of sympathy for him. No dog liked to bury an old friend. "Come on. We have to cover him."

"Of course." Breeze nuzzled him gently. "Then he'll truly be with the Earth-Dog, Mickey."

It didn't take nearly so long to kick and scrape the soil back over Bruno's corpse. When he was hidden from sight and the earth was piled back, it made Storm feel sick with despair. *He's*

gone. We won't ever see him again—except, maybe, in dreams.

The sad and silent group plodded back to the glade, each dog lost in thought. Alpha picked up her pace as they reached the camp border, and she trotted in ahead of the others, barking a summons to the whole Pack.

"Pack! To me!" She stood patiently while the dogs gathered around her. Storm couldn't help noticing that no dog's tail wagged; every Packmate stood straight, their heads high and their faces somber. "I've been giving this a lot of thought, and I have come to a decision. Since it seems obvious to me now that poor Bruno was killed by a large dog, watches will be taken only by smaller Packmates until we have dealt with this."

"But . . ." Sunshine, shivering, crept forward, her shoulders low and humble. "Alpha, us small dogs won't be any match for the bad dog, if it attacks. . . ."

Alpha closed her eyes and gave a heavy sigh. "I know, Omega. But all of us bigger dogs will be watching one another. That means the traitor won't have a chance to bother you. I hope." She licked the little dog's nose. "You're the only dogs I can afford to trust with this, Sunshine. I know you won't let me down."

Storm could only listen, her mouth dry, a hollow sensation in her stomach. *I'm the biggest dog here. And the strongest. Now that Woody has*

left and Bruno is dead—even I think I'm the most likely suspect.

Even as the horrible thought struck her, from the corner of her eye Storm saw Snap lift her head. The smaller dog gave a whine to draw Alpha's attention.

"I hate to say this, but I'm going to. I *must*." Snap shot a glance at Storm, and Storm almost recoiled at the hostility in her eyes. Snap's hard brown stare was fixed on her, but Storm got the clear impression that Snap was talking to every dog *but* her. "The only dogs big enough to kill Bruno would be Storm and—*maybe*—Mickey or Lucky." Snap licked her jaws and narrowed her eyes. "But Mickey couldn't have done it. He was with me. And Lucky was Bruno's Packmate, for a long time. They all survived the Growl together. They were friends, we all know that."

"What are you saying, Snap?" Alpha's tone was calm and steady.

It's obvious what she's saying. Storm felt the weight of horrible inevitability pressing down on her shoulders.

Snap sat back on her haunches, looking grim. "Every dog knows that Storm hated Bruno."

The heat of rage was a physical force in Storm's chest, swamping her misery. She struggled to hold the fury back, but it was too strong. It escaped her in a violent, angry bark.

"That isn't true! I never hated Bruno! *He* hated *me*. But we made up! I wouldn't hurt him. I was *glad* that we had become friends, after everything that had happened. . . . Bruno even apologized to me!"

Chase shut one eye and swished her tail doubtfully. "That doesn't sound much like Bruno to me."

He's right. Desperately Storm turned to Lucky—but to her dismay, even the Pack Beta looked unsure. *Lucky! You were like a Father-Dog to me! How can you believe this?*

She felt as if an enormous boulder were crushing her to the ground. *I can't prove it—no one saw us talk. There's no way I can prove that Bruno said he was sorry!*

"It's true!" To Storm's surprise, it was Daisy who trotted to the center of the circle. The little dog's eyes still looked hollow and grief-stricken, but there was a determined set to her jaw.

"Bruno told me!" announced Daisy, fixing Alpha with her most resolute gaze. "We talked about it only the other day. He said he was worried, and he felt guilty—that he'd maybe been unfair to Storm."

Alpha looked startled. "Did he tell you he'd apologized to her?"

"No . . ." Daisy admitted. "He didn't say *that*. But he *was* sorry.

He told me so. And if Storm says he did, then I believe her." She turned and gazed steadily at Storm, who felt her heart turn over with gratitude.

"I agree," Sunshine piped up, wagging her ragged plume of a tail. "Storm would never hurt Bruno, anyway. I *know* she wouldn't. She's a kind, good dog!"

Alpha nodded, got to her paws, and looked around the Pack silently, as if coming to a decision. Storm waited with her heart beating high in her throat.

Alpha and Beta know me. They must know I wouldn't do this. But could she be certain? However much they cared for Storm, they hadn't done a great job of standing up for her recently.

"Storm is a member of our Pack," Alpha said at last. "A *loyal* Packmate who has stood by us in many dangers—who has fought off enemies, and *saved my pups*. I will not have the members of this Pack turning on one another; that's exactly what the traitor wants." Storm's ears pricked up with relief as Alpha's eyes grew brilliant and ferocious. "No dog is to accuse any other from now on, unless they have some proof. Wild accusations and arguments do not help the Pack, or any dog in it! Is that understood?"

Snap's head and tail drooped, and she gave a resentful growl, but she lowered her shoulders and gave a single nod. "Yes, Alpha."

She shuffled back to a dazed Mickey's side.

Warmth returned to Storm's belly and limbs. *Alpha trusts me,* she thought, *and so does Omega. And so do many dogs in the ranks between them. I don't have anything to fear from my own Pack.* The relief made her dizzy.

Chase grunted and growled. "Alpha . . . there is another dog who could have killed Bruno."

Alpha swung around sharply. "I said no wild accusations!"

"I'm not making one." Chase took a pace forward, and raised her head to stare at Alpha.

"Hush, Chase!" Breeze nudged her anxiously. "Don't say—"

"I am going to say it," she snapped at Breeze, and returned her gaze to Alpha's. "I think—it might have been the Fear-Dog."

There was a moment's shocked silence. Then Mickey gave a dark growl of derision. "There's no such thing as the Fear-Dog!"

"Exactly, Mickey." Snap barked a laugh of agreement. "And even if there was, Spirit Dogs don't go around tearing out throats. They don't bother themselves with flesh-and-blood dogs like us!"

Storm listened in silence as others in the Pack began to ridicule Chase's claim. She should have felt reassured by Mickey's scorn, by Snap's dismissal of the whole mad idea of murderous Spirit Dogs. . . .

But she wasn't nearly so sure.

My dreams. I've dreamed of the Fear-Dog; that has to mean something. Even Lucky trusts the power of dreams—after all, they showed him the Storm of Dogs long before it happened. She shuddered.

The Fear-Dog was an invention of the mad Terror—or so they'd thought. Every dog in the Pack knew the great, black, snarling Spirit Dog had just been a story that Terror had made up, to strike fear and obedience into his own cowering Pack.

But what if he's real?

When the dogs of Terror's former Pack had joined the Wild Pack, they'd brought the stories and the belief and the legend with them, the way they'd brought their own scents, their own ears and tails and paws: that was how deeply they'd believed in Terror and his fake Spirit Dog.

But what if a spirit can become *real?* wondered Storm, her gut icy-cold. *Can it be created out of stories? If enough dogs believe, does a Spirit Dog come into being?*

What if it wasn't just the stories they brought with them?

What if they brought the Fear-Dog himself?

CHAPTER EIGHT

Storm paced the camp's border, over and over again, every muscle and nerve drawn tight. Beyond the trees, the Sun-Dog was creeping below the horizon, gilding the pine trunks with his golden glow, and Storm couldn't help feeling that even he—even that great Spirit Dog—was slinking away to avoid her. Perhaps the Sun-Dog had a problem with Fierce Dogs, too? *Maybe,* thought Storm, *even the Sun-Dog is made a little nervous by the presence of such a big, ferocious—* Fierce—*dog. Perhaps he, too, rejects dogs like me. . . .*

Storm was beginning to grow very tired of all this. None of the Pack dogs would meet her eyes, however hard she glared at them. If she turned her head and caught one of them watching her, she saw only fear and suspicion in their swiftly averted faces.

Did it mean nothing when all of you began to trust me? Have you forgotten how I saved the pups? Have you forgotten I'm your loyal Packmate?

Daisy stood up for me. Sunshine did, too. And Alpha trusts me absolutely!
So why can't all of you?

She turned her stare on Snap, but the hunt-dog looked sharply away, glowering at the ground. Mickey rose to his paws, looking embarrassed, but when he took a pace toward Storm, Snap muttered something that she couldn't hear. Mickey swallowed, gave Storm a hesitant, sympathetic glance, but sat back down.

Even you, Mickey? Even you?

She didn't know which feeling was stronger: the anger or the hurt. Their suspicion stung her like a swarm of bees in her belly.

It was not so long ago that they couldn't be nice enough to me. Snap brought me soft moss to lie on. And now . . . Storm growled, deep in her throat, and paced faster, breaking into a trot.

It would be best if she could tire herself out before it was time to sleep, but her brain was buzzing with resentment and fury. She couldn't imagine ever sleeping again. On she paced, walking and running around the clearing, until the Sun-Dog had vanished altogether and the Moon-Dog had risen in the gray-blue sky. *She* at least wasn't turning her face away from Storm; she shone full and round and bright on the glade, lighting every pair of suspicious eyes with her silver glow.

One by one, the Pack members were padding to the center

of the camp, gathering in their circle for the Great Howl. Storm hung back, reluctant to share space with any of them, her anger still hot in her throat.

But as they settled, sitting or lying down, giving one another friendly licks and flicking their ears as they greeted one another, Storm began to relax.

It's time for the Great Howl. The whole point is to bind us together, as a Pack. It's what the Moon-Dog wants. And it's what we need right now.

Her stiff legs trembled as she stalked forward to join the Pack. *Maybe this Howl will make everything the way it was again. Maybe this will fix things.*

Maybe this is my last chance . . . my last chance to prove I belong in this Pack.

And if I can't show them, if I can't make them believe it . . . what then? What will I do? Misery and confusion sank into Storm's bones.

She sat down, her tail curled tight against her, picking a spot where her flanks wouldn't touch any other dog. No dog moved closer to her; maybe they could feel the rage that lifted the fur of her hide. *Maybe they're afraid of me.*

Maybe they're right to be.

Storm tilted back her head to stare morosely at the Moon-Dog. Then she narrowed her eyes. There was something odd

about the great silver Spirit Dog now. Her glow had dulled, and Storm wasn't the only one who had noticed it.

Around her, dogs were shifting, fidgeting, muttering. Ears were tucked tightly back, claws scraped nervously at the earth. *Is it a cloud?* wondered Storm.

But as the Moon-Dog rose higher, the cloud didn't pass. The pale disc reddened, as if it was stained with blood. Stars were blinking into life, glimmering in the darkening sky, and Storm realized suddenly: *There are no clouds.*

What's happening?

A whimper from Sunshine broke the silence. "The Moon-Dog is angry!"

Storm glanced at her, shocked. Maybe the little dog was right. When Storm turned back to the sky, the Moon-Dog's hide was not silver at all: She looked like a giant, sinister red eye, staring at the Pack with a dull, blank rage. It reminded Storm of something . . . something awful. Abruptly she realized: It looked just like the mad dog Terror's crazed glare.

A ripple of icy fear ran beneath Storm's fur, mixed with a horrible shame. *Have I caused this? Has the Pack? The things that have happened lately—have we done this to the Moon-Dog? Is she really this angry with us?*

A quivering voice broke the silence. "The Fear-Dog," whined

Breeze, crouching low to the ground. "It's the Fear-Dog."

Chase gave a low, terrified howl. "The Fear-Dog has cast his shadow over the Moon-Dog! Is he *eating* her?"

Chase and Breeze both believed firmly in the Fear-Dog, Storm remembered: They had both been members of Terror's Pack. But the others were cowering now too—even Mickey had pressed himself to the earth, trembling.

"Is it a sign?" whined Beetle. "Is something bad going to happen?"

"Quiet, now!" Alpha took a step into the circle. "There's nothing to be afraid of, my Pack. There's no such thing as the Fear-Dog!"

"Yes," whined Chase. "There is. Look at him."

"No!" barked Alpha. "That's no Fear-Dog, It's just . . ." Her voice trailed off, her ears tucked back, and her tail trembled anxiously. "It's the weather. That's all. Just the weather. Rain's coming."

But that's no cloud. Storm stared at the rust-red Moon-Dog. *There are no clouds tonight. . . .*

"I've never seen this happen before," said Moon, her eyes wide. "There's never been a cloud like that. Not ever!"

"Is it hurting the Moon-Dog?" whimpered Omega in distress.

"If that *is* the Fear-Dog, he's harming her!"

"Pack! Stop worrying." Lucky sprang forward past Alpha. "This is not the Fear-Dog!"

"I agree with Lucky," declared Twitch, stepping forward to stand beside the Pack's Beta. "This is something we haven't seen before, but it's natural. It's only a mood of the Moon-Dog." He drew a breath. "But since she's in a bad mood, maybe it's best that we don't Howl tonight."

"That's true," said Lucky. "It's clear the Moon-Dog is not herself. Alpha, do you agree?"

"Yes." Alpha nodded firmly. "Let's leave our Howl till the Moon-Dog is more kindly inclined toward all dogs. But listen to Beta and Third Dog, Packmates. There is no such thing as the Fear-Dog."

She sounds determined, thought Storm, eyeing Alpha. *She sounds convincing. But there's fear in her eyes, too. Alpha's as confused and unsure and distressed as the rest of us. . . .*

Storm swallowed hard, suddenly more afraid than ever.

"I don't know what's happening," Alpha went on, a hint of a tremor in her stern voice. "But it has nothing to do with Terror's wild stories. Go to your dens. We will leave the Moon-Dog to rest and recover; she will be our beloved Spirit Dog again soon."

One by one, the dogs rose to their paws and slunk off toward their dens, watched by that great round red eye. Around them everything seemed so still and quiet, thought Storm, as if the forest itself were afraid of the Moon-Dog tonight.

She gazed up at the great Spirit Dog in awed trepidation, feeling the dark night press in on her hide, and a violent shudder ran through her bones.

Rain. It fell in a torrent from the sky, relentless. The black downpour was so heavy it was hard to breathe, and water streamed into her eyes and nostrils.

Water? Storm wasn't sure. Was it blood, then, or only the stench of it? It seemed that blood filled her mouth and her head; it streamed into her eyes, it drenched her fur. That meant it was a dream, she was sure. Only in dreams did the sky rain blood.

And yet it felt real, all real. Blood in her eyes or not, Storm could see enough. She could see too much.

All around her, dogs were battling to the death. Fighting, biting, scratching, and snarling. Dogs collided in a mass of violent confusion, slithering in the mud. High above, the Sky-Dogs were joining in the fight; thunder crashed and rolled, and Lightning streaked across the sky in white flashes, over and over again.

Despite the chaos and the noise and the driving rain, nothing could blunt Storm's sense of smell. The stink of blood was thick on the sodden air; she tasted

its rusty tang in her mouth.

Lucky and Terror were locked in combat, rolling over and over on the slippery ground, the golden dog's jaws tearing at Terror's ear. There were so many other dogs Storm knew—of course there were. She remembered this battle against Terror's Pack too well. It was real. The place and the struggle were real; the blood was real.

But why was she back here? Why was it happening again?

Bella and Martha and Moon were in the heart of the chaos, fighting with savage desperation. She could see Twitch, snarling and biting at dogs of his own former Pack; of course, this was when he had finally turned against Terror's brutal rule. But others had stayed loyal to the mad tyrant: dogs Storm now knew as friends were attacking her Pack. There were Splash, Chase, and Breeze, fighting in a frenzy. Off to her flank she saw Ruff and Rake, Whisper and Woody, their teeth snapping wildly at her Packmates.

The smell of the blood and the rage of the storm thrilled through her bones. Through the blinding rain she saw Terror throw off Lucky and charge straight toward her. She wasn't afraid. She leaped gladly to meet him, her jaws open in a snarl of fury.

I want this fight!

She crashed into Terror head-on, their jaws locking in a deadly struggle. His mad yellow-red eye glared into hers, but she wasn't scared of this brute; she bit and tore, feeling her fangs sink into his flesh.

And suddenly, horribly, her hold broke. Terror fell away, flailing and uttering a gurgling, agonized howl. His dismembered jaw was still caught between her teeth; she spat it out, tasting blood on her tongue. Her mouth was full of that dark, thick fluid.

But of course it was. She'd tasted it from the start. This was always going to happen. It was always meant to happen.

On the ground, in the sticky, sucking mud, the maimed Terror writhed and squirmed in agony, his face disfigured almost beyond recognition, his life spilling out of him. Storm felt no pity. She gazed down at the dying dog, his lifeblood filling her mouth and nostrils, seeping through every fiber of her body. Triumph surged through her, making her bones thrum with a fierce and lethal joy.

She became aware of eyes fixed on her, and she jerked her head up to look around. Dogs were staring at her, their faces full of horror and shock. And fear. Terror's Pack and her own friends: They had all gone unnaturally still, the battle forgotten, to gape at her victory. They were afraid of her; she could see it in their wide white eyes.

And between them . . . other dogs skulked. Shadow dogs, with featureless faces.

Watching her. Watching, and seeing, and knowing what she was. . . .

Storm woke with an abrupt, awful jolt. Her paws were no longer half sunk in mud; she stood on dry, dusty earth that was littered

with twigs and leaves. The rushing sound of water still filled her ears, but it wasn't raining; the noise was the river, flowing only a rabbit-chase away. She stared at it in shock, watching the dance of moonlight on its surface.

I did it again. I walked in my sleep.

A sickening rush of disappointment flooded through her. *I thought it was over. I haven't sleepwalked in so long. I hoped it would never happen again.*

The dream was still vivid in her head. She could still see the horrified faces of those dogs, Terror's Pack and her own. The worst of it was, it was no dream, but a memory. It had happened; she had done that awful thing, and her feeling of triumph and delight in Terror's death had been real.

I ripped off his jaw. I remember how it tasted. It didn't disgust me: I loved that moment. It tasted . . . good. Like victory.

I remember I was glad.

And Bruno had died like that. Bruno's life had ended in just the same way as Terror's: his jaw torn savagely from his head.

The terrible things that have happened lately . . . Are they because of Terror? Has it all been about that insane dog?

The red Moon-Dog that rose tonight had reminded her so vividly of his crazed eyes. And Bruno's death had echoed Terror's.

Perhaps the Fear-Dog was not only real but haunting their Pack, seeking revenge for his disciple-dog?

Alpha doesn't believe in the Fear-Dog. She says he isn't real.

But Chase believes. Breeze believes. They thought the Fear-Dog spoke through Terror.

Terror thought that, too.

Storm's head spun, and she stumbled, feeling faint. *How can I fight a Spirit Dog? That is a battle no mortal dog can win.* Despair and fear made her dizzy, and she wanted to howl in misery.

Along her trembling hide, a breeze whispered. Leaves rustled in the branches above her, and the gentle tumbling sound of the river was suddenly clearer. A night bird cried somewhere in the trees, and a beetle scuttled in the grass beneath her paws. It was as if Earth-Dog were trying to wake her up, making the world around her solid and true, a place she could know with her nose and eyes and ears and paws.

No. No, there's no Spirit Dog behind these attacks. That traitor dog is as real as I am.

There was no questioning the facts: Bruno had suffered the same fate as Terror, and that had to mean something. But it did *not* mean that the Pack was being hunted by a ghost. Terror was dead and gone to the Earth-Dog. As for the Fear-Dog: He didn't

even exist. Storm knew that in her head and in her heart.

She clenched her jaws and narrowed her eyes. *Think, Storm! Think with your brain, not your frightened belly.*

Bruno hadn't been there on that horrific night. He hadn't been part of that battle. But his death had to point to . . . something. Could the bad dog be one who was there the night of Terror's death?

Many of those dogs had already been targeted by the traitor. Even Whisper, though in that battle he'd fought loyally for Terror.

It wasn't Lucky; she knew that as surely as she knew anything. Lucky would not, *could not* do that to another dog; what was more, he was the Pack's Beta. He had led the Leashed Dogs out of the Empty City to safety, and a new life. And he would never invite fear into the Pack to threaten his own pups. If there was one dog Storm could be sure of, it was Lucky.

Breeze loved the pups, too, and devoted her life to protecting them; Twitch and Moon had both been targets of the bad dog's deadly malice. *Chase?*

Storm pictured the small dog in her mind. She was little, but quick, and ferocious. Chase could stand up for herself; there wasn't much that frightened her, except the imaginary Fear-Dog.

And the bad dog hadn't brought chaos or violence or misery to Chase.

Closing her eyes, Storm tried to go back into her dream. She could recall so vividly the sensations that had flooded her body: fury and infinite strength and a fearless certainty. Nothing had mattered in those moments but putting an end to Terror. She could have torn the jaw off a giantfur, never mind a big, burly, mad dog.

Nothing could have stopped me. Nothing.

Chase was little, but size mattered nothing next to rage. Perhaps Storm wasn't the only dog who had felt that power: the fire in the blood that burned everything it touched.

Could Chase be the bad dog? I know Lucky trusts her, but Lucky trusts every dog.

That's his weakness. . . .

CHAPTER NINE

Dawn was breaking as Storm slipped back into camp, the early rays of the Sun-Dog burnishing the pine trunks and turning the low mist silvery-gold. It was easy enough to sneak past the Patrol Dogs, now that their numbers were stretched so thin. *That should worry me,* thought Storm. *But there's so much more to worry about. And I don't think the biggest danger lies outside the camp.*

How strange *it is,* she realized as she stepped across the boundary and felt the weight of fear settle once more on her shoulders. *The borders of the camp are what protect us . . . or rather, they are* supposed *to. Instead, it feels like they're trapping us. We're penned together inside our own territory, like dogs in a Trap House, and danger is right in here with us.*

Still, Storm felt a huge sense of relief as she crept back into her den. She did not want any dog to know she had been wandering alone in the night—not even the ones who were aware of

her unnerving problem, like Daisy, Twitch, and Lucky. *Some of my Packmates mistrust me enough already. I can't give them any more reasons to suspect me.*

She felt guilty and ashamed, but she played the part of a dog who had slept the night through in her den, emerging a little while later to stretch and yawn and claw the dewy grass. As it was, she was attracting a few suspicious glances and sidelong stares. Storm ignored them all—she supposed she couldn't blame them for being afraid, even though she *could* blame them for casting their fears onto her.

Her own attention was focused on Chase. The little dog was well aware of her gaze, Storm realized: She kept turning to meet Storm's stare, her own eyes nervous. Her tail twitched and she shook herself uncomfortably as Storm watched her go about her morning duties. *Chase is keeping as much distance as she can between us,* Storm noticed.

I should try not to alert her. But still she couldn't tear her attention away from the small scout dog.

"Storm!" Alpha was padding toward her across the clearing, her ears pricked.

Storm jumped up, glad to have a distraction. "Yes, Alpha?"

"I'm going to send you out hunting with Chase and Thorn, but I want you to combine that with patrolling." The swift-dog swept her tail thoughtfully back and forth. "Because we're so short of Packmates, we are going to have to start doubling up on duties. Just keep an eye on the borders as you hunt."

"Absolutely, Alpha." Storm nodded.

"Wait, Alpha!" Moon was bounding over. "Did I hear you mention Thorn?"

"Yes." Alpha flicked her ears back, surprised. "What's wrong, Moon?"

"I don't think Thorn should be going out just now." Moon's gaze slid toward Storm, and though she quickly looked back toward Alpha, Storm felt a sting of hurt in her chest.

"What, Moon?" she growled. *Is she really afraid that if Thorn goes out in my company, I'll end up hurting her? I thought Moon was on my side—I saved her from that pit! I'd expect this from Snap, but not from Moon. . . .*

Alpha stepped between them before the black-and-white Farm Dog could reply. "There's no reason why Thorn shouldn't go out just now," she told Moon crisply. "Storm, go find her." Alpha paused, then said, "I've chosen Storm to lead this hunt. She is a powerful and *trustworthy* young dog. Do you disagree with my

judgment, Moon?" There was a warning in Alpha's eyes.

Moon's ears went back and she shook her head. "Of course not, Alpha. Storm . . . I'm sorry."

Storm nodded, trying not to let her relief show on her face.

"You can tell Beetle at the same time that I want him on High Watch," Alpha added. "Breeze is going there, too. I want dogs to take High Watch in pairs from now on; it's safer."

Chase, ears swiveling toward Alpha, padded up. "You want me on patrol?" she asked. "Did I hear you right, Alpha?"

"A combined hunt and patrol," Alpha corrected her. "We have to use all dogs' talents more flexibly from now on. Go on, Storm. Go and find Thorn."

Moon looked sulky, but she remained silent as Storm and Chase padded off. Storm could feel her haunches prickling with the Farm Dog's glare, but she didn't turn to look back. *I mustn't lose my temper—even though I have good reason to. That would be disastrous right now.*

She slanted a look at Chase, pacing silently at her side. The scout dog was keeping quite a distance from her—a little farther than Storm would be able to lunge, she couldn't help noticing. Tension crackled between them; Storm could feel it in the rising hairs of her hide. She was too angry, though, to break the silence

herself. The resentment simmered hot in her throat and chest. *Sending me and Chase out together—this is the worst pairing imaginable right now! Can't Alpha feel it?*

Not a word was spoken between the two dogs as they padded through the trees, so Storm heard Beetle and Thorn before she saw them. Twigs cracked, a body thumped against another body, and there was a protesting yelp.

"Beetle, you have to come at me lower!"

"We're supposed to be practicing for a fight," came his growl. "Block me properly if you don't want to be hurt! I can't help it if your jaw got in the way."

"That's not the point, you idiot. There's no point attacking a tall creature high up! Then they can get at your belly!"

"Not if I'm fast enough." Paws pounded through leaves and there was another thud, and the rustle of forest litter as a dog rolled. "Thorn! That's cheating; stop dodging!"

"*It* would dodge."

"No, it wouldn't, it might have a stick or something. Face me head-on—*I'm* the one who needs to be ready to dodge if it tries to hit me!"

"Fine! Just remember I'm not the enemy. Attack lower down, I tell you. Don't go for my throat first—knock my legs away!"

Storm broke into a bound and pushed through a tangle of shrubs into a small clearing. "Hey, you two. What are you doing?" She tilted her head and frowned as they both turned toward her.

"Practicing our fighting," said Beetle sullenly. His tail was low, and he shot his litter-sister a glance that was half-angry, half-guilty. Thorn nodded, almost imperceptibly, and sat back on her haunches.

"We need to be ready for something like a giantfur," Thorn told Storm defiantly. "Especially if the Pack's moving on somewhere else. We could bump into anything."

Storm narrowed her eyes and looked from Thorn to Beetle. His tail was twitching nervously at the tip, a giveaway sign that he was hiding something. "Giantfurs don't use sticks. And the best tactic for a dog to use on a giantfur is to *run*."

"Well . . . it's like Thorn said," mumbled Beetle, glowering at the ground. "We need to be ready for *anything*."

Chase had followed Storm through the bushes and was looking suspiciously at the two young dogs. "That doesn't sound like any fighting I've ever heard of. You'd be better off practicing moves that'll be useful against a bigger dog. That's what you're more likely to meet, and there are all sorts of tricks you can use. Practice *those*—anything else is a waste of time and energy."

Storm blinked and forced herself not to look at her hunt companion. *Have you been trying out those tricks against a bigger dog lately, Chase?* She gave Thorn and Beetle a low growl. "Anyway, whatever you're doing, it's time to stop. Alpha wants you to come on a hunt with us, Thorn. We'll be patrolling the borders as we go. Beetle, you're to join Breeze up on High Watch."

"Fine." Thorn shook bits of leaf and twig and soil from her fur and trotted forward. "That sounds like a good idea." She hesitated. "Storm, listen . . . can you not mention to any other dog what we were doing? You too, Chase."

Storm flicked an ear forward. "Why not?"

Thorn glanced at Beetle, a look of slight embarrassment on her face. "We want to get it right. It's hopeless trying to practice when lots of dogs are giving you different advice."

Beetle growled in agreement, shooting a meaningful glance at Chase.

"All right," said Storm doubtfully. It seemed a strange request, but Beetle and Thorn were proud and prickly. *I guess they'd hate to make fools of themselves, especially after Chase and I have both told them they're doing it all wrong. Besides, the tension in the camp is still so high, it's probably not a good idea to get any other dog thinking about fighting.* "We won't let on that you're trying out new moves. Not till you're ready."

"Thanks." Thorn wagged her tail and trotted happily to Storm's side. "I'm ready to go. Which direction?"

Storm felt grateful to her. Thorn didn't flinch or avert her eyes or keep her distance; she even licked Storm's muzzle in a friendly gesture.

"Out toward the meadow first, I think, Thorn. We need to more or less circle the camp. Beetle, you'd better head up to High Watch. Breeze must be there already."

"I'm on my way." Beetle turned with a flick of his tail and loped from the clearing.

Thorn stayed companionably close to Storm's flank as the dogs headed toward the meadow, while Chase scampered ahead to scout for prey. With the small dog out of earshot, Storm could forget about her, and she found herself glad, after all, about Alpha's choice of her other hunting partner. Thorn seemed to know instinctively when Storm needed her to head off and circle a likely spot, and she was on constant alert, her nose sniffing the air and the undergrowth, her ears pricked high. Best of all, Thorn was easy company. She didn't fidget and jump all the time, as if expecting Storm to turn and tear out her throat.

I'd almost forgotten how relaxing that is.

Storm was reminded, though, every time Chase doubled back

to make a report. The little dog's head would appear through the bushes, and she'd give Storm a hard and wary glance before telling her where the rabbits were concentrated, or where she'd scented out a likely nest of voles.

She's making me nervous, Storm realized. *Is she watching me like that because she's frightened of me? Or is it for some other reason?*

She might be working out how to catch me unawares....

"There's a big warren up ahead," Chase told them on her third report. "The rabbits are enjoying the sunshine; they don't look alarmed. If we approach from downwind, we can get close enough to catch at least two."

Storm suppressed a shudder. *They're enjoying the sunshine. They don't look alarmed. We can get close enough....*

Is that how you creep up on everything, Chase?

She shook herself. *Don't be ridiculous, Storm—that's how every dog hunts. Don't start feeling sorry for a bunch of rabbits just because she's making you nervous.* "That's good, Chase. Thanks. Thorn, why don't you take the northern flank?"

Thorn tilted her head to one side. "I thought Alpha wanted us not to hunt alone?"

Storm gave a nod. "We're still hunting together. I'll stay low in the grass and go at them head-on from here, and you should be

able to intercept them when they run."

"Great, Storm," said Thorn enthusiastically. She spun around and bounded toward the edge of the meadow.

It worked just as Storm had hoped. By the time the rabbits had fled in a panic toward Thorn's ambush, and Storm and Chase had made havoc among the stragglers, they had caught three rabbits between them: two sizable bucks and a smaller doe. Storm stood panting over the corpses, pleased with the result.

"Good work, Thorn. And you, Chase. Right, we'd better not rest on our paws. Let's keep looking." She gave a sharp, low bark as the small dog turned away. "Chase, wait!"

Chase glanced back, one ear pricked, a distinct nervousness in her eyes. The whites showed at their edges. "What?"

She looks like she thinks I'm going to bite her head off. Storm bit back her resentment. "Don't go too far, that's all. Stay in barking distance, and don't go farther than we can smell you. Thorn's right; Alpha doesn't want any of us to go off alone."

"Fine." With a nod, Chase bounded ahead again. Storm flicked an ear toward the undergrowth; yes, she could still hear the rustle of the smaller dog as she moved through the scrub. If there was trouble, she and Thorn could be with Chase in moments.

Thorn trotted at Storm's side once more, calmer now that

she'd used up some energy. "Storm, can I ask you something?" Even for a dog tired from a hunt, Thorn sounded subdued.

Storm twitched her other ear toward her. "Of course. What is it?"

Thorn seemed lost in thought for a few paces, as though arranging her words before she spoke. Pausing, she snuffled at a tree stump, then walked on.

"It's about the day my Father-Dog died. Our Father-Dog."

Storm's heart sank. *I'm not good at this kind of conversation....*

"I've been thinking about it a lot lately," Thorn went on. "Beetle and I—well, we were so young back then. Moon didn't tell us many of the details of what happened to him. I suppose she wanted to spare us."

"I suppose she did," Storm mumbled. Desperately she sniffed the air, almost hoping she'd have to break off this discussion to run to Chase's aid. But the small dog's scent was still clear, and there was no tang of fear or panic in it. *She's fine. And that's good. But quick, Chase, find some prey before I have to answer any awful questions about Fiery....*

Thorn was still talking. "Moon won't talk about that day, but you were *there*, Storm. You sneaked out of camp and followed the search party. You were younger than us, even, but you saw what

happened. You had to deal with that knowledge then. So I think we can now."

Storm's heart plummeted even further. "Are you sure?"

Thorn nodded. "I want to know the truth about that day, Storm. Beetle does too. Will you tell us what happened? We want to know how our Father-Dog lost his life."

Storm's pawsteps slowed. This might be awkward and difficult for her, but Thorn had a point. "I think that's fair," she said at last, quietly.

But I'm not sure I want to remember. The details were awful. I'd forgotten how young I was. A shiver ran beneath her fur, for more than one reason. *I wasn't even* Storm *then; I was still* Lick.

But Thorn's right. She and Beetle have a right to know about that day.

She looked into Thorn's eyes—wide, and full of desperate hope—and she knew that she was going to have to walk back into this terrible memory.

"I don't remember all the details," she said at last, truthfully. "But I guess I remember enough. I'll tell you what I can."

"Thank you, Storm," said Thorn. She gave her a sideways glance, her eyes nervous but hopeful.

"It was so unexpected," Storm began. "I remember Fiery got caught in some kind of tangle of ropes. There was nothing he

could do—and nothing we could do to help him. Fiery *made* us leave him." In a thornbush beside the two dogs, dew had caught on a spider's web, sparkling and pretty; but the fragile threads trembled from the hopeless struggles of a fly. The spider was already moving deliberately toward its catch. "It was like that," Storm said softly, nodding toward the web. "No dog could help."

Thorn shivered and swallowed. "I remember you coming back to the Food House and telling us. And I remember how our old Alpha said there was nothing we could do, that we had to leave him. Moon was furious."

"I know," Storm sighed. "Remember how determined she was? If no other dog would go after Fiery, she was going to go alone."

"She faced down the old Alpha," said Thorn quietly. "That big, scary half wolf. And Lucky too, and some of the others. I was so proud, and Beetle and I wanted to go with them, but Moon wouldn't let us."

"Lucky wouldn't let me go, either," said Storm with an amused growl. "That's why I had to sneak after them."

"I wish we had, too," muttered Thorn.

"I know," said Storm hesitantly. "But, Thorn? I think it's for the best that you didn't. You can remember your Father-Dog the way you knew him—as a strong and fine and brave dog. He'd only

just challenged that Alpha for the Pack leadership, remember."

"Yes." Thorn was quiet for long moments. At last she said, "And when you found him?"

Storm gave a long sigh, closing her eyes briefly. "He was so changed. What the longpaws had done to him . . . I still hate them for it."

"So do I," murmured Thorn. "So do I. But please go on, Storm. Tell me everything."

Storm grunted awkwardly. *This is the most difficult part. I don't know if I can bring myself to say a lot of it.*

"The longpaws had him in a Trap House," she began, and she heard the growl in her own voice. "Well—not a Trap House like the one Alpha talked about earlier. It was more like an enormous loudcage, but the back of it was full of wire traps. And it's just like Alpha described; they were so *small*. No room to run or jump." Storm shuddered. "And your Father-Dog—he wasn't the only one. They had all kinds of animals in there. Foxes, coyotes, birds. There was a sharpclaw, I remember. Even a deer, crammed into such a tiny space. I never thought I'd feel so sorry for prey animals—or for a *coyote*."

Thorn's voice was very small. "What did they do to them?"

"I don't really know, but . . . they gave them bad water, I know

that much. It was the longpaws who made your Father-Dog sick. Even after being trapped and stuck behind that wire, he would have stayed strong. But the longpaws poisoned him." Storm's muzzle curled back in a helpless snarl. "They poisoned all those creatures."

"I know," said Thorn. "I've never understood why they'd do that. If they wanted my Father-Dog dead, why didn't they just ki . . . kill him?"

"I never understood why they didn't do that, either." Just the memory of it was bringing all of Storm's fury back. "All of us— Lucky, Bella, Martha, and Twitch, and your Mother-Dog—we got all the traps open. We couldn't leave any creature in that place; it was horrible. A lot of them ran free, but some were too sick to get away. Your Father-Dog was one." Storm swallowed hard. "We managed to get him out of that place, but he was hurt badly."

Thorn was silent, padding beside her.

Storm licked her jaws. "There was a Fierce Dog there. One of the Pack from the Dog-Garden, I think. He was called Axe." She stopped herself suddenly.

Should I even have mentioned Axe? she wondered uneasily. *Do I really want to remind Thorn about our Fierce enemies from the Dog-Garden?*

But Thorn wants the whole truth . . . and it's part of the story. Storm

sighed. "Axe was a true follower of Blade, the Fierce Dog Alpha, and I don't think I've ever seen a dog so angry. He hated those longpaws, hated what they'd done to him, and he wanted revenge. We tried to stop him, but he was in such a rage. . . ."

"What happened to him?" Thorn asked breathlessly. "Did he get his revenge?"

"He tried." Storm hunched her shoulders, hating the way she could still see Axe's enraged face in her mind's eye. "He ran straight to their house, a house on wheels, and he challenged them to come out and face him. Well, they did. They came out with a loudstick, and they killed him with it."

Thorn gulped. "They hit him?"

"No, a loudstick's different. The longpaws don't even have to touch you with it. They point it, and it makes a tremendous noise, and a dog drops dead." Storm shook herself. "Don't *ever* go near a longpaw with a loudstick, Thorn. They're deadly."

"But the rest of you, you escaped. . . ."

"We did. We got Fiery away, I guess because the longpaws were busy with Axe. But Fiery was so weak from the poisoned water. When Terror and his crew attacked us on the journey home, he couldn't defend himself. They . . . they killed him, Thorn. He tried to fight, because he was still such a brave, good

dog—but Terror's Pack killed him."

"And you killed Terror." Thorn lifted her head, a look of fierce gladness in her eyes. "You protected the Pack, and you avenged my Father-Dog. Terror deserved to die, Storm, and I'm happy you killed him."

Storm said nothing.

Thorn lowered her head again, seeming deep in dark thoughts. Bitterly she growled, "But Terror would never have been able to put a claw on my Father-Dog if the longpaws hadn't done what they did. *They're* the ones who are really to blame."

"Yes," agreed Storm. "But there's no way for any dog to fight the longpaws, Thorn. Axe tried it, and look what happened to him. It was best to just run, and leave them far behind. And to know we should never, ever go near them again."

Thorn padded on for a while in silence. Storm did not feel it was wise to interrupt.

"There must be a way," Thorn muttered at last.

Storm swiveled an ear at her. "What?"

"Nothing."

It wasn't nothing, Storm thought, a chill of trepidation running through her bones. *What did she mean by that?*

But Thorn would not say anything more, and Storm was just

125

glad the young dog was content with what she'd been able to tell her. Storm hated reliving the past, especially the horrible parts of it, like Fiery's death. Some of the others in the Pack were gentle and empathetic, able to handle such conversations—but Storm wasn't one of them.

Who would have thought just *talking* could be so hard? If only Martha had still been here to explain the horrible events of that day to Beetle and Thorn. *She would've handled it so well,* thought Storm. *Much better than I did.*

It's done now, she decided. *I've told Thorn what I can, and I've warned her about the dangers of the longpaws. Maybe she'll be able find some peace. Just please, Thorn, tell Beetle yourself. Don't ask me to go over it again for him. . . .*

She was just glad down to the tip of her tail that it was all over.

Anxiety was still nibbling at a corner of Storm's mind as the three dogs padded back into camp after sun-high. She shook it off. There were more important things to think about than that awful discussion—real, solid things, like their excellent haul of prey. They'd found another rabbit, out on its own; Thorn had managed to trap a squirrel before it raced up a tree; and Chase had sniffed out a nest—not of voles but of equally delicious rats. *Alpha will be pleased with us,* thought Storm. *And we're all home and safe. Chase couldn't*

go far from us, but she still found that nest and dug it up. We've done a good job, we kept an eye out for one another, and we're in one piece.

What was more, they had all remembered to check the borders for strange scents as they hunted, and they'd found nothing untoward. As she and Thorn and Chase passed the boundary into camp, their heads were high, their muscles relaxed, their tails waving loosely. It felt good to be home. One by one they dropped their jawfuls of small bodies on the prey pile, and Storm felt warm with the knowledge of a job well done.

Beetle was already back in camp, his and Breeze's turn at High Watch over for the day. Thorn barked a greeting and bounded over to her litter-brother, and Storm watched them nuzzle and lick each other happily. It was a lovely sight in the late afternoon, but it gave Storm a pang. *I wish at least one of my litter-brothers had lived. I'd have had some dog to talk to, to confide in, to make plans with. . . .*

Sure enough, as she watched, Thorn and Beetle fell into a deep, quiet conversation, their heads close together. Storm sighed, shaking off the twinge of jealousy. Chase had dashed off to be with another group of dogs as soon as the prey was delivered; the scout dog clearly couldn't wait to be out of Storm's company.

"Storm!" Alpha was trotting toward her, her tongue lolling from her slender jaws. "Lucky and I just took a look at the prey

go far from us, but she still found that nest and dug it up. We've done a good job, we kept an eye out for one another, and we're in one piece.

What was more, they had all remembered to check the borders for strange scents as they hunted, and they'd found nothing untoward. As she and Thorn and Chase passed the boundary into camp, their heads were high, their muscles relaxed, their tails waving loosely. It felt good to be home. One by one they dropped their jawfuls of small bodies on the prey pile, and Storm felt warm with the knowledge of a job well done.

Beetle was already back in camp, his and Breeze's turn at High Watch over for the day. Thorn barked a greeting and bounded over to her litter-brother, and Storm watched them nuzzle and lick each other happily. It was a lovely sight in the late afternoon, but it gave Storm a pang. *I wish at least one of my litter-brothers had lived. I'd have had some dog to talk to, to confide in, to make plans with. . . .*

Sure enough, as she watched, Thorn and Beetle fell into a deep, quiet conversation, their heads close together. Storm sighed, shaking off the twinge of jealousy. Chase had dashed off to be with another group of dogs as soon as the prey was delivered; the scout dog clearly couldn't wait to be out of Storm's company.

"Storm!" Alpha was trotting toward her, her tongue lolling from her slender jaws. "Lucky and I just took a look at the prey

127

pile. What a good catch—well done!"

"The hunt went well." Storm felt a glow of happiness at the praise from her leader. It was quite hard to make Alpha happy these days, with all the stress she was under as both Pack leader and Mother-Dog, and Storm felt as if she'd completed another successful task.

"And you didn't run into any unforeseen problems or dangers?"

Storm shook her head. "Chase didn't scout too far from us, and we all kept each other safe. We each knew where the others were, all the time; the new system worked well, Alpha." She hesitated. *Perhaps now is a good time . . . while the worry is still fresh in my head.* "Alpha, may I speak with you?"

"Always, Storm. I told you that." Alpha licked her muzzle fondly.

Flank-to-flank, the two dogs paced toward Alpha's den, where Lucky, as always, was watching the pups. While they were still out of his earshot—and safely distant from any other dogs—Alpha stopped and turned to Storm.

"I've tried my best, Storm. I've done what I can to stop the other dogs from gossiping about you. I hope—"

"No, Alpha—no, it's not that!" Sitting back on her haunches,

"No, but—"

"Believe me, it's normal that Thorn still talks about Fiery. It's normal that she wants to know as much about him as possible—including his death. It's all part of coming to terms with losing him."

Alpha's dark eyes were gazing intently into hers, sympathetic but a little condescending. Storm could see clearly that the swift-dog did not really grasp what she was being told; she didn't know what it was about the things Thorn had said that had so unnerved Storm.

But I don't know how to explain it. I can barely put it into words in my own head, let alone describe it to Alpha. It was just . . . Thorn's face. Her eyes. Her voice . . .

Briefly Storm shut her eyes, defeated. "All right, Alpha. I understand."

"Good. I'm glad you felt able to come to me, Storm, but on this—I really don't think it's the problem you think it is." Alpha flicked out her tongue and gave Storm's nose a quick lick. "Do you feel better?"

"Yes, Alpha," she lied. "Thank you."

She watched Alpha get to her paws and pad lightly back toward her den. The Sun-Dog was nearly at the end of his run, and dogs

were stirring all around the glade, clearly beginning to turn their thoughts toward the prey pile.

I still miss Fiery.

The thought surprised her, and gave her a pang of sadness. The big dog had had such a strong sense of justice and fairness; he might have looked ferocious and brutal, but he had been the gentlest and wisest of dogs. *He was one of the dogs who showed me that a Fierce exterior isn't all there is to me. I learned that just by watching him. And he never acted as if my being a Fierce Dog was anything to fear. If he was still here, would I feel more at home in the Pack?*

Fiery had just challenged the half wolf when he died. That malicious half wolf who so hated Storm and ruled the Pack with cruelty—so many dogs were afraid of going fang-to-fang with him, but not Fiery. Storm's own words to Thorn came back to her. *Your Father-Dog was so strong and fine and brave.*

What would their Pack be like now if Fiery had lived and taken leadership of the Pack? *Would the Pack have broken up the way it did? Or would Fiery have found a way to keep us together?* For a moment she allowed herself to imagine the luxury of a Pack united, a strong Pack, a leader who had identified and dealt with the traitor before that dog could even begin to sabotage their lives. . . .

Storm shook herself. *No. That's disloyal to Alpha. The bad dog is so*

cunning and deceitful, any leader might have had the same trouble.

Still, she wondered: Had it all begun when Fiery lost his life? His death had led to Terror's. And Terror's death, she felt increasingly sure, had led directly to all their problems now.

Bruno was killed the same way Terror was. I can't get that out of my mind. It can't be a coincidence.

Storm blinked, her eyes suddenly focusing. Chase was staring straight at her, with an expression of baleful suspicion. Quickly Storm looked away, her gut twisting with alarm.

The Moon-Dog was rising over the treetops, though the sky was not yet dark. *And she is white,* realized Storm. The angry red glow of the previous night had vanished. *Has the Moon-Dog forgiven us?*

Or maybe—just maybe—she's telling me that I'm on the right track. . . .

Maybe I'm close to solving the mystery.

CHAPTER TEN

The Moon-Dog was still in the sky when a cold nose shoved Storm, waking her. Disoriented, blinking hard, Storm could make out her pale glow at the mouth of her den. *What? It's still dark. Well, only just . . .*

That wet nose nudged her again, and a voice said, "Storm! Wake up!"

"Lucky?" She staggered to her feet, still bleary from a vague, clinging dream. "What's wrong? What is it?" Shaking her head to clear it, she tensed her muscles and drew back her lip. *If there's trouble, we'll deal with it—*

"Nothing's wrong." Lucky didn't look scared; his tongue was lolling happily.

As her eyes adjusted, Storm could make out figures behind Lucky, all with their ears and tails as high as his. Mickey and Snap

stood there—and Chase, she realized with a twinge of apprehension. *This is big for a hunting party these days.*

"We got up to take over the night patrol," said Mickey, gesturing to his mate, "and—well, can you smell it?"

A breath of morning wind stirred the bedding at her paws; Storm flared her nostrils to search it for clues. *Sky-Dogs!* She started. The scent had a sweet-and-spicy edge that was very distinctive.

"The Golden Deer!"

"Yes!" Lucky could barely suppress his excitement. "Will you come with us, Storm? You're one of our best hunters, and I don't want to take any chances."

A thrill of anticipation and pride rushed through Storm's blood. "Of course. Let's go!"

As the other dogs turned to lope away from her den, Storm followed at a run, full of unexpected energy. They picked up speed as soon as they crossed the camp boundary, as if no dog could wait to find the trail.

Two shadows loomed from the trees ahead of them: Thorn and Beetle, returning from their night patrol. They looked surprised, but the hunting party barely paused to greet them, bounding on through the undergrowth. Storm let the joy of running sweep

through her, stretching her legs and leaping obstacles with grace-ful ease. As the Sun-Dog's first rays broke through the tree trunks, her nose tingled with the scents of waking prey.

A gray flash caught the corner of her eye, and she veered side-ways in pursuit of a startled squirrel. It fled before her, shooting up a smooth pine trunk just as her teeth snapped on thin air, but she couldn't even be disappointed. She felt happier than she had in days as she doubled back to join the group.

The others looked as if they were enjoying themselves as much as she was. Their tails were high, their tongues lolling, and they barked to one another as they ran, but no dog chatted with Storm.

Lucky was too preoccupied with sniffing the air and peering at the horizon between the trees. *He's been obsessed with catching the Golden Deer for so long,* thought Storm. *Oh, Sky-Dogs, let this hunt be a successful one! If we can catch the Golden Deer, good fortune will come to the Pack. And maybe that good fortune will be followed by more. . . . Maybe the bad dog will be forced out of hiding, and dealt with.*

The Pack could really be happy again. . . .

Snap and Mickey were wrapped up in an intense conversation as they trotted after Lucky, their heads close together and their eyes affectionate. Storm had no intention of interrupting such a private moment. Chase didn't speak to Storm, either, but that was

no surprise. The scout dog kept eyeing her—whether with nervousness or malice, Storm couldn't tell—and when Storm caught her gaze, she turned quickly away and ran on even faster.

For an instant Storm stiffened, the glow taken off her happiness; then she forced herself to relax. *Chase acts so anxious around me—if she's really the traitor, and she's onto me, I'll need to act fast. But I'm not sure. I'm going to have to talk to her.*

And that means she'll have to talk to me. . . .

Lucky was slowing down now, and Mickey and Snap were holding back too, all of them sniffing around uncertainly for the Golden Deer's scent. But instead of staying with the hunters, Chase had put on a burst of speed, darting ahead through the bushes to perform her usual scouting duties.

She's not supposed to go so far off on her own . . . Storm thought, and overtook Lucky to follow Chase. The small dog's paws pounded even faster, her legs a blur as she raced to avoid Storm.

What is she doing? Exasperated, Storm speeded up. She bounded after Chase, losing sight of her briefly as she rounded a copse of bushy trees. Storm raced after her, spotting her again, just ahead.

Abruptly Chase skidded to a halt and spun around, sending a flurry of leaves into the air. Her whole body bristled with tension.

"What do you want, Storm?" Chase's glare flicked past

"No, but—"

"Believe me, it's normal that Thorn still talks about Fiery. It's normal that she wants to know as much about him as possible—including his death. It's all part of coming to terms with losing him."

Alpha's dark eyes were gazing intently into hers, sympathetic but a little condescending. Storm could see clearly that the swift-dog did not really grasp what she was being told; she didn't know what it was about the things Thorn had said that had so unnerved Storm.

But I don't know how to explain it. I can barely put it into words in my own head, let alone describe it to Alpha. It was just . . . Thorn's face. Her eyes. Her voice . . .

Briefly Storm shut her eyes, defeated. "All right, Alpha. I understand."

"Good. I'm glad you felt able to come to me, Storm, but on this—I really don't think it's the problem you think it is." Alpha flicked out her tongue and gave Storm's nose a quick lick. "Do you feel better?"

"Yes, Alpha," she lied. "Thank you."

She watched Alpha get to her paws and pad lightly back toward her den. The Sun-Dog was nearly at the end of his run, and dogs

other dogs, Storm thought, but she wouldn't

len behind—and then fixed again on her,

a halt too, blinking in surprise. *She's really*

eathe deeply, Storm took a step back. She

ok threatening, Storm. That won't help any dog.

uld hear Lucky's trotting paws on the

ed to relax a little now that their patrol

t she growled, "Why are you following

t." Storm managed to put light humor

ver her shoulder and saw Lucky, still

out, trying to find the scent again.

"You know that's not what I mean."

hase, I . . . I don't know you very well.

ight. We're, ah . . . we're Packmates,

know each other a bit better. Don't

r chops. "I don't smell the Golden

might have lost the scent. Maybe

n we could . . . talk."

Oh, Sky-Dogs, that sounded lame. She gazed brightly at Chase, meeting only an apprehensive stare.

"There's nothing to know," snapped Chase at last. She was edging sideways, toward Mickey and Snap, who had entered the broad glade by now.

Storm followed her. "Of course there is," she told her cheerfully. "Where did you live when you were a pup? That sort of thing. Like . . . well, Lucky found me when I was a pup, and he brought me back to this Pack because my Mother-Dog had died. What about you? How did you come to be in Terror's Pack?"

Chase's lip curled up, displaying her white teeth. For a moment, Storm thought she'd blown it. *She won't give me an answer now. Storm, why do you have to be so clumsy when you talk to other dogs?*

Just as she was about to apologize and turn away, Chase snapped, "My Pack left me."

"Oh!" Storm blinked at her. "Oh no. That must have been a bad time for you. Why did they do that?"

"It was the right thing to do," Chase growled. "I was young and sick; what good was I to a Pack?"

Storm thought of Wiggle, her litter-brother. He had been small and sickly, but Lucky would never have abandoned him. . . . "How did you survive?"

t the swift-dog, warmth spreading through
Alpha had been standing up for her, even
other dogs she was good. She went on, cer-
tell Alpha her worries. "It's not me I want
."

ked one ear and frowned. "What about

about Fiery's death. Out on the hunt
o learn exactly what happened."
er head thoughtfully. "That must have
and I'm sorry you had to deal with it.
I'm only surprised she took this long
ave been able to deal with it earlier."
lay down on the ground, sighing and
a, she seemed almost too interested.
worried she's planning something."
looking a little surprised. Then she
down with her nose nearly touching
want you to worry about this when
ms. I suspect you're overthinking
ember your Mother-Dog or your

"Oh, I'd have starved if it hadn't been for Terror." Chase hunched her shoulders. "He found me, took me in. He gave me a home and Packmates. Terror was a crazy dog," she said, looking defiantly into Storm's eyes, "but he wasn't *all* bad."

Nonplussed, Storm stared after Chase as the little scout dog turned and ran off.

Terror wasn't all bad. . . .

An image of Twitch came to her mind. Their Third Dog had once been a member of the half wolf's Pack; but when he lost all strength in one of his forelegs, the old Alpha threw him out of the Pack, to live or die as chance took him.

But Terror brought him in. Twitch had to chew off his crippled leg while he was in exile, so he only had three to run on—but still Terror made him part of his browbeaten Pack. Terror had bullied and hurt all his Packmates, but they'd stayed, out of fear. Or maybe they'd had nowhere else to go.

Were all of Terror's dogs broken? Storm wondered. *They weren't all starving or crippled like Chase and Twitch, but maybe some of them were broken on the inside.*

Maybe, she mused, they had other reasons for staying.

What would it be like, being a dog like that? Broken and lost, with no Pack to call home?

And how would a dog like that feel when a powerful Alpha rescued them and brought them into his Pack?

I always thought Terror's Pack hated and feared him. Storm swallowed hard. *Maybe I was wrong.*

How might it make such a dog feel, to see her Alpha killed the way Terror was? Maybe Chase resents me because she's angry and grieving. This astonishing new idea rooted Storm to the spot, confused.

She was so preoccupied that she barely heard Lucky's frantic bark. When he repeated it, his voice filled with excitement, she shook herself and turned to stare at him.

"Come on! This way!"

Lucky sprang across the clearing, through a belt of trees, and out into a meadow dotted with cottonwood trees. Caught unawares, Storm had to race to catch up.

Mickey, Snap, and Chase were at Lucky's heels. Storm leaped over a fallen branch and sprinted after them, her confusion forgotten for the moment. *He's scented it! The Golden Deer!*

The small hunting pack plunged into the wood on the far side of the meadow, none of them taking any heed of the racket their paws made on the dry litter left over from last Red Leaf. Storm could smell an elusive, drifting scent, but it was already fading. A good way ahead, there was the crack and rustle of undergrowth as

a big animal raced away, fleeter than any dog.

No, this is hopeless, Storm realized with a pang of disappointment. *It's too fast, and it had too big a head start.*

Lucky slid to a halt, panting, but his eyes were shining as Mickey and Snap and Storm trotted to his side.

"That's the closest we've gotten to it yet!" he exclaimed.

Storm watched him fondly. He was almost hopping on the spot in his delight. It was hard to feel too let down when Lucky was so happy just to have come this close.

Mickey shook his head. "You know, I'm not sure that was the Golden Deer," he said. "It might have been just a normal one. I don't think the Golden Deer would make so much noise. It flies like a shadow, doesn't it?"

"It's still a shame we missed it," pointed out Snap, panting. "The Pack could have used a perfectly ordinary deer, too."

Storm flared her nostrils, breathing in deeply, searching the breeze. There wasn't a hint of that spicy, sweet odor; it was hard to tell if the creature they'd chased was the Golden Deer or not.

Still, I'd like to think it was.

Chase caught up to them, her shorter legs trembling as she halted. "No luck, then?"

"No, but we're *definitely* getting closer," said Lucky with

satisfaction. "We'll catch that Golden Deer one of these days. It's an omen that we'll get through our troubles." He turned to them with a grin, his tongue hanging from his jaws.

Storm hoped with all her heart that he was right. She wished she could be as optimistic about her strange talk with Chase as Lucky was about not catching the Deer.

Things are more uncertain than ever. If the Wind-Dogs really want to give us a sign, I wish they'd hurry up.

CHAPTER ELEVEN

They had run a long way in their pursuit of the Golden Deer's enticing scent, and the journey back was not nearly so thrilling. Storm's paws dragged on the grass, and her hide prickled with warmth. The Sun-Dog was high overhead by now; she wondered what Alpha would say about their long, unauthorized absence.

Mickey, Snap, and Chase were clearly thinking the same; their tails and ears drooped as they plodded on. Lucky, though, was still in an upbeat mood. It was starting to grate on Storm's nerves.

"Next time we'll catch the Golden Deer. We're getting closer every time, and now we know some of its tricks!" Lucky's tail swished enthusiastically. "If we can just catch it, our fortunes will turn. The Wind-Dogs will reward us by making the new pups wonderful hunters. And if the pups grow up happy and strong, the whole Pack will surely thrive once more!" He bounced along

143

the path ahead, making Storm want to bite his perky hindquarters. Did he *really* feel as happy as he seemed, or was it all a show, to keep his Pack's spirits up? If it was the latter, it wasn't working on Storm. . . .

"Hush, Lucky," said Mickey suddenly, halting.

I'm glad some dog said it, thought Storm, rolling her eyes. But clearly Mickey had another reason for silencing his leader. He crept forward past Lucky, placing his paws very quietly.

"We've reached the longpaw settlement," he murmured, glancing back at the others.

Sure enough, the clearing ahead was a churned-up longpaw mess. The longpaws must have decided the ruined building a little way away was beyond repair, so they had started to dig and build on this open patch of land beside it. The ruin backed onto the forest; the dogs had indeed reached the edge of the town.

Slumbering yellow loudcages rested on the turned black earth, their great grooved paw marks scarring what had once been grass. Some of them growled and rumbled softly, and Storm could hear longpaws barking to one another. Her ears twitched wildly at the echoes of clattering and clanging.

At least Lucky had stopped chattering and started paying attention. He stood very still, his ears pricked and his nose

sniffing the air. His head swiveled suddenly, and he nodded at a big metal box on the far edge of the clearing.

"Look at that," he murmured. "No—*smell* that!"

Storm sniffed. Sure enough, a scent was drifting powerfully from the box, strong and rich and slightly tinged with rotten things. As the dogs watched from the shadows, a longpaw sauntered up to the box, lifted its top, and tossed something into its gaping mouth.

"Are they feeding it?" Confused, Snap tilted her head to the side.

"Not the box." Lucky grinned mischievously. "Us."

"Huh? But what *is* it?" asked Chase, wide-eyed.

Mickey stood stiffly, watching the longpaw. "It's a spoil-box," he told them. "When a longpaw has something he doesn't want, he puts it in a spoil-box. There's nothing here for us. We should move on." He backed away.

Lucky, though, was quivering with excitement, his tail lashing. "Mickey, you know as well as I do . . ." He licked his jaws. "One of the things they put in spoil-boxes is *food!*"

Storm gaped at him. "Lucky, you're not suggesting we steal longpaw food?"

"Well, *they're* not eating it." Lucky sat back on his haunches.

"Every dog here is hungry, right? We've run a long way and caught nothing."

"But . . . *longpaw* food? Why would any dog want that?" She shuddered.

"I agree," growled Snap.

"Use your nose! Can't you tell how good it is?" Lucky licked at the air itself, drool escaping from his jaws. "We need energy for the return journey, Packmates. And there's food here for the taking."

Eyeing him sidelong, Storm raised her muzzle to sense the odor again. She had to admit that despite the hint of something rotten, it *did* smell good. . . . It was strange, but rich and intriguing.

"But *can* we eat longpaw food?" asked Chase doubtfully.

"Sky-Dogs, yes!" exclaimed Lucky. "It's delicious!"

"I don't know," muttered Storm. "What will Alpha say? What if the longpaws come after us?"

"Alpha won't mind one bit," Lucky reassured her. "As for the longpaws—like Mickey told you, if it's in the spoil-box, that means they don't want it. Besides," he added determinedly, "it'll be good practice for all of us. A dog has to be wily and quick to sneak past longpaws."

"I'm still not sure . . ." murmured Mickey.

"Mickey, *you* know how good it tastes. And besides, we'll still have to go out on a proper hunt when we get back. If we eat a little something now, we'll be better prepared for that, because we'll be stronger. There's no point staggering home hungry, if we're just going to be too weak to catch anything for the Pack." Despite his stern words, Lucky's eyes glinted with anticipation.

"Well, it's true that longpaws are lazy," admitted Mickey. "If they're not in loudcages, they don't chase you far, even if they do see you on their territory. It's just . . ." He half closed his eyes, as if thinking hard. "Well, Lucky, don't you think it's a bit of a Leashed Dog habit, eating longpaw food? I thought we were past that."

Lucky shook his head. "No, Mickey. The longpaws won't be *feeding* us—we're *taking* what we want. From under their noses! It's what I did all the time, when I was a Lone Dog in the city. And no dog ever called *me* a Leashed Dog!"

A small fire of excitement was kindling in Storm's belly, against her better instincts. Lucky made it sound fun. And she *was* rather hungry. And the Pack's Beta seemed to want to cheer them all up. . . .

"I think . . . I think I want to do it," she said slowly.

"Wonderful, Storm! I knew you would." Lucky licked her nose. "Come on, the rest of you—don't lose your nerve. Think of

the Pack—and just smell that grease!"

"Fine." Mickey sighed, but his tail too was beginning to twitch with anticipation. "All right, Lucky, you've talked me into it."

"Then I'm in, too," said Snap, with an indulgent sigh.

"And me," added Chase. "I admit, it does smell good."

Lucky's obvious delight made Storm glad she'd agreed to the crazy escapade. He was fizzing with new energy as he led them at a trot around the edge of the churned mud. All of the dogs—except Lucky—cast anxious glances in the direction of the longpaws, but they seemed entirely preoccupied with their loudcages and their tools. There were no loudsticks in sight, to Storm's great relief. As they approached the spoil-box, though, Lucky grew warier, creeping low to the ground and keeping one eye on the longpaws.

The smells from the box were overpowering now, and almost irresistible. Storm felt saliva gathering at the corner of her mouth, and she saw the others licking their lips and jaws.

"Right," said Lucky. "You and I are the biggest, Storm. Let's get into that spoil-box!"

Stretching up on his hind legs, he grabbed the top edge of the box with his forepaws. Storm followed his example, nosing at the lid, and when it came loose at one corner, she seized it in her teeth. It tasted of bitter metal, but she didn't care—the scents coming

from inside were just too good.

"That's it, Storm." Lucky worked a paw under the top, prizing it away farther. At last he could shove his whole head in, and suddenly he was scrabbling and kicking, hauling himself up till he was balanced on the edge of the box. Just before he toppled in, he gave a thrust of his shoulders. The lid bounced up and teetered. Taking his lead, Storm took a giant leap, landing on the rim and slamming her forepaws on the lid. It flapped back and fell fully open.

Awkwardly she tumbled down into the spoil-box beside Lucky. He grinned at her. His fur was crusted with crumbs and grease and bits of food, and as she struggled upright she realized, aghast, that her once-shiny coat was the same. Then she caught the scent of the discarded food again, and she no longer cared about the state of her fur.

Both the dogs propped themselves up, placing their paws on the inner rim of the spoil-box and peering down at their companions below.

"We're in!" announced Lucky with a rumble of laughter. "Where are the longpaws?"

Snap wagged her tail. "They're still making so much noise, they haven't heard you."

"Even though you were also making a *lot* of noise," added Mickey with a grin.

"Right. Let's get to work!" Lucky dived back into the spoil-box.

Storm thrust her muzzle deep into the pile of discarded rubbish. "Mmmm!"

"I know!" yelped Lucky. "Look at this stuff!" He grabbed something to show her: a half-chewed meaty bone that was covered in some kind of brown crust.

"Is that *dirty*?" Storm pinned her ears back, but Lucky laughed.

"It's meat—*chicken* is the longpaw word. The brown stuff is something they put all over it, for some reason—well, I know the reason. It tastes *good!*" He threw her the scrap. "Don't eat the bones, they splinter!"

Storm ripped the meat and crust from the bone, chewing. "Oh, it does taste good! Is there more?"

"Plenty." Lucky dug with his paws, tugging out thin boxes with his teeth. He stretched up and dropped them onto the ground outside the spoil-box, where the others were waiting. In a few moments, Storm could hear the rip of paper and the chomping sounds of happy dogs.

Delirious with excitement, she scrabbled in the pile at her paws. A good smell wafted from a bag; she tore it open. Inside

were two pieces of soft white stuff with cold spicy meat inside.

"Sandwiches, they call those!" Lucky told her. "And only half eaten!"

Storm was astonished at how good it all tasted. *Why in the name of Earth-Dog would the longpaws throw this stuff away?* She was glad they had, though. Together she and Lucky excavated the pile, eating some of the food themselves, tossing the rest of it out to the others. She couldn't see Mickey, Snap, or Chase, but she could hear their excited yelps, their noisy chewing, and the occasional thump of their paws on the side of the spoil-box as they reached up to beg for more treats.

If this is how Leashed Dogs get to eat, I can almost see the attraction! Storm gulped down a thin piece of salty meat.

"They must be hardworking longpaws." Lucky laughed. "They eat a lot."

"They leave a lot, too," added Storm, licking a wrapper clean of grease. "May the Sky-Dogs look kindly on them!"

Lucky chuckled, raking through paper and boxes and coming up with treasure: a chunk of something that reeked as if it had lain at the bottom of the spoil-box since Ice Wind, but Lucky insisted that was how it was *supposed* to smell. "It's called cheese," he said. "It's delicious."

"I think I'm full," he gasped after he had chomped down half of it. He tossed the rest over the edge to their Packmates with his jaws.

Storm had her snout in a stiff box that held remnants of still-warm, very spicy meat. "There's rice in this," she mumbled through the box. "Like we had in the Food House that time!"

"I don't know if I'll be able to climb back out," groaned Lucky. His belly did look more than comfortably rounded, thought Storm with amusement.

Twisting, she grabbed the edge of the spoil-box with her fore-paws and craned out to look at the others. Mickey was sprawled on his flank, looking content, and Snap had flopped across his legs. Chase was contentedly licking her paws clean of grease.

"I think every dog's full," she told Lucky. "Chase, where are the longpaws?"

The scout dog blinked and twisted her head. Then she gave a yelp of alarm. "There's one coming!"

"Let's get out of here." Lucky hauled himself up onto the edge of the spoil-box and jumped down, and Storm followed him. Both gave grunts of shock as their paws hit the ground heavily. *Oh,* thought Storm, *I've eaten too much.*

Mickey and Snap had sprung to their paws, barking in

warning, and Chase had already begun to run. As Storm and Lucky regained their footing, the four bolted after the little scout dog, as fast as their full bellies would let them.

Storm heard the pounding steps of longpaws behind them; she glanced over her shoulder as she ran. They were yelling, but they were already slowing down. *Just like Mickey said—they're too lazy for a hunt.* One of the longpaws flung an empty box that fell far short of the fleeing dogs, but Storm realized that they were all barking with laughter.

Thanks for the prey, longpaws! she thought mischievously as she raced after her Packmates into the trees.

They couldn't run for long, but they didn't have to. Lucky slowed to a placid trot as soon as the longpaws were out of sight, and the others fell in behind him. Storm licked her jaws. *Oh, I can still taste that crusty bird. . . .*

"I admit it, Lucky," growled Mickey happily. "That was one of your best ideas ever."

"*All* my ideas are the best ever," said Lucky grandly, drawing more amused barks from the others.

Storm picked up her paws happily, a new bounce in her stride. It felt good to have an adventure, she realized—one that wasn't

fraught with danger and misery. Her Packmates looked cheerful too, joking and teasing Storm and Lucky about the state of their coats. Once or twice all the dogs paused for a moment so that Mickey, Snap, and Chase could lick the two thieves' greasy fur.

Well, Mickey and Snap had fun licking Storm's fur, nibbling at scraps of food. Chase, she noticed, still didn't come near her. The small dog saved all her joking for Lucky and the others.

Does she know I suspect her? If she is the traitor, does she think I'm onto her? I have to watch her closely from now on.

It was painful to feel so close to an answer, to justice for Bruno and Whisper, and yet still so far away. But perhaps there was another dog she could talk to, if Chase kept avoiding her, one who knew Chase and knew what it was like in Terror's Pack. If Chase was the bad dog, her Packmate Breeze *must* have some inkling of it.

Still, Storm tried to let herself relax and enjoy the attention of the other dogs while she could. She had not felt this lighthearted in a very long time. *It feels good,* she thought. *It feels almost better than "sandwiches" taste!*

By the time they'd gotten closer to the camp, the heavy stuffed feeling had subsided, and they were all ready to go back on the hunt. And with the prey plentiful and their energy fully restored, the five hunters were able to catch several gophers and rabbits for the Pack.

Alpha gave Lucky a rather stern look when the hunters finally padded back into the camp, but between the prey they'd brought back with them, and the fun of the spoil-box story, she didn't stay annoyed for long. The whole Pack hung attentively on their tale of adventure at the prey pile that evening, and the pups especially demanded that the details be told over and over again. Sunshine was thrilled to hear a story that involved nothing more dangerous than some stolen food.

"I wish I'd been there," she confided in Storm as the dogs began to rise and pad to their dens. "It sounded fun!"

"I wish you had, too," Storm told the little Omega fondly, licking her bedraggled ears.

"I want to come next time!" barked Tumble, romping around Storm's paws with his sisters.

Storm laughed. "You're not big enough to climb into the spoil-box!"

"I will be, one day," he said indignantly. "I'm going to be *enormous!*"

"Me too!" yapped Tiny, not to be left out.

"Pups, pups! Leave poor Storm alone!" Breeze trotted up and nuzzled them affectionately. Alpha and Lucky were deep in a serious conversation, Storm noticed; Breeze must have been asked to

look after the pups once the Pack had eaten.

"Breeze," Storm greeted her. "I'd like to talk to you, but I guess it's not a good moment?"

"No, it's fine," said Breeze, her eyes bright. "The pups can play a little farther away. Go on, pups, but stay where I can see you!"

"I'll look after them," offered Sunshine. "I'd love to play for a while."

"Oh, Sunshine, thank you," said Breeze warmly.

"Yay!" yelped Nibble. "Yes, Sunshine, come and play!"

With happy yips they tumbled over her, and the little dog led them away to another part of the clearing, chuckling as Fluff and Nibble pounced on her fluffy tail.

The two bigger dogs watched them for a moment, tails thumping the ground in amusement. Then Breeze turned to gaze at Storm.

"What is it, Storm? What did you want to talk about?"

Storm sat back on her haunches and took a deep breath. "I wanted to ask about Terror's Pack. What it was like. You know, life under his leadership . . . was it very hard?"

Breeze lay down, looking thoughtful. "It was certainly difficult. You know how . . . well, the rages he flew into. We had to pad carefully around him."

Storm nodded. "Yes. I can imagine. But do you think any dog misses him? Mourns him, even?"

"Oh, Storm. I don't know. I suppose it's . . . hard to mourn a dog like that. We all lived in fear." Breeze tapped her tail against the ground. "Why are you asking about Terror's Pack now?"

Storm hesitated for a moment. *Can I trust her?*

I have to trust some dog! And Breeze is sweet, and intelligent, and she loves the pups. And she knows Chase, maybe better than any dog. . . .

Tightening her jaw, she made her decision. "It's Chase in particular. She worries me, Breeze."

Breeze tilted her head, studying Storm's face. "Go on."

"I've noticed something." Storm took a heavy breath. "All the dogs who have been targeted, all the victims of the traitor—they were all there the night Terror was killed."

"Are you sure?" Breeze frowned. "Moon, yes. And Twitch . . . but Whisper was a member of Terror's Pack. And Bruno wasn't there."

"That's true," admitted Storm. "But Whisper was there, even though he was on the wrong—I mean, the other side," she corrected herself tactfully. "And Bruno was killed in exactly the way I killed"—she choked slightly on the words—"the way I killed Terror."

"I'm not sure that proves anything," said Breeze doubtfully. "It could be a coincidence."

"Breeze," blurted Storm. "Do you think Chase could be the culprit? The traitor?"

Breeze stared at her for a moment, silent, but her expression was deeply thoughtful. "Storm," she said at last, "Bruno must have been killed by a much bigger dog. Alpha said as much."

"Well, that bothered me," Storm admitted, staring at the ground. "But—oh, I don't know. Bruno was lying there so peace-fully—apart from his injury, I mean. Maybe the bad dog caught him when he was asleep? Or maybe his jaw wasn't torn off till he was dead."

"It's possible, I suppose, but . . ."

"You see, I think Chase might have been trying to tell the Pack something," exclaimed Storm. "Sending us a message—showing us why Bruno had to die, why the Pack should be destroyed."

Breeze shook her head slowly. At last she sat up and scratched her ear. Then she reached forward and touched her nose to Storm's.

"No. No, I just can't believe that, Storm. Chase would never do such things. I've known her for a long time and she's a good, loyal dog. A *Pack* Dog."

Storm gazed into Breeze's eyes, worried and suddenly embarrassed. *Have I said the wrong thing? Have I been a fool to accuse Chase?*

"That . . . that does make me feel a bit better, Breeze. If you really think so . . ."

"I do." Breeze nuzzled her gently. "But you've given me a lot to think about, Storm. I won't tell anyone about our conversation, and I'll think hard about this. We have to solve the mystery before anything else happens to the Pack."

"Thank you, Breeze." Storm dipped her head in gratitude and watched the gentle brown dog as she trotted back to the pups.

I'm just glad Breeze didn't bite my nose off for accusing her former Packmate. I'm still not as sure about Chase as she is, but she does have good judgment. And she won't betray my confidence, I'm certain of it.

What made her most grateful of all, though, was that Breeze had taken her seriously. *She was willing to listen. She didn't immediately assume that I must be the one who's responsible. That means a lot.*

Storm padded back to her own den and settled on her bedding. A sense of calm filled her. *I've done what I can for now. And it felt good to talk about it.*

For the first time in a long time, she felt as if she might get a good, peaceful sleep.

CHAPTER TWELVE

When Storm was woken again the next morning, it wasn't by Lucky's gentle prodding her or an excited gathering of hunters. Outside her den there was a flurry of frenzied barks and howling cries. She jerked up, instantly wide awake.

I didn't have nightmares, or walk in my sleep. But these days *any* noise in camp was something to worry about.

She could make out only a few words clearly, but they were enough. *Bad dog. Savage. Breeze.* She shook herself violently and bounded out of her den.

Almost the whole Pack seemed to be assembled, crowding around a figure on the camp boundary. *Not another killing!* Storm's blood froze. She didn't stop running, though. She shouldered through her gabbling, frantic Packmates to the front of the crowd.

Please, not another killing . . .

Breeze was standing there, but she was barely identifiable. Her head and tail hung low, and she was shaking uncontrollably. Her brown hide was covered in bleeding scratches, but the blood was streaky, because she was sodden and dripping and smeared with mud, and there were strands of waterweed caught in her fur. Storm barely recognized her gentle eyes: They were wide and terrified, the whites starkly visible all around them.

"Breeze!" she barked in shock, and sprang forward to press her head to the smaller dog's neck. Breeze flinched as if she was in pain, but she held her ground. Then she sagged against Storm's body for support. Behind her somewhere, Sunshine was whimpering in terror.

"What happened here?" Alpha pushed between Mickey and Chase, looking horrified. "Breeze, what happened to you?"

"I . . . don't know . . . I'm not sure." Breeze couldn't stop trembling. "I woke up being dragged through the woods." She coughed painfully, and a trickle of water ran from her jaws. Her chest heaved.

"By a dog?" demanded Alpha urgently.

"I don't know—yes, yes, I think it was a dog. A big one. I fought, Alpha, I did . . . I tried to howl, but—"

"Hush, Breeze," said Storm urgently. "Save your strength."

"She has to tell us what happened, Storm," said Alpha, a little more gently. "Do you have any idea who it was, Breeze? Did you know this dog?"

"I don't know. I'm sorry, I'm sorry. I couldn't pick out a clear scent over the stink of mud and river-water. And there was also so much of that wild garlic and—so many smells. . . ." She panted, gasping for breath—as much from terror as from exhaustion, Storm guessed. "It pulled me a long way. It was so strong, I couldn't fight it—and then it . . . it flung me in the river. Oh, Storm, the water was so fast and deep. *I thought I was going to drown.*"

"It's all right, Breeze. You're safe." Storm licked at her neck and back, trying to warm her up.

"The River-Dog must have let you go," said Mickey, his eyes wide. "Maybe Martha was looking after you."

"Yes," said Sunshine. "Martha must have helped." She began to whine, mournfully, and Daisy nuzzled her.

"Maybe it *was* Martha," panted Breeze weakly. "Something must have helped me. I managed to swim to shore and drag myself out, but I could feel the River-Dog trying to pull me down." Her shaking grew more violent again, and there was a sob in her voice. "That bad dog was big, Alpha, and it tried to kill me. I know it wanted me dead!"

No dog could say anything. The whole Pack stared at Breeze in pity and horror. Storm could feel the thrill of fear skittering from dog to dog, tingling on every hide.

Twigs cracked as Moon and Snap trotted into camp. The two Patrol Dogs halted and blinked at the gathering of Packmates.

"What happened?" asked Snap as she and Moon exchanged bewildered glances.

"There's been another attack," Alpha told them grimly as they padded over. "You two were on patrol: Did you see anything? Hear or smell something unusual?"

"Nothing," said Moon, gazing at Breeze in dismay. "We didn't smell any intruder. I'm sorry, Alpha."

Alpha curled back her lip, showing her teeth. "Don't feel bad. This traitor is cunning; they masked their scent again. Even Breeze herself couldn't identify her attacker."

"I'm sorry too," said Breeze miserably. Her flanks were still heaving, but she seemed slightly calmer. "If only I hadn't been in such a panic, if I'd focused harder. . . ."

Storm stared at her. *What must that have been like? To be dragged across the ground in darkness by a huge dog—to be so terrified and in pain that you couldn't even recognize your attacker?* Breeze must have been traumatized, Storm realized, and her heart clenched with pity.

"No dog would have been able to think clearly during such a vicious attack," Alpha reassured the gentle brown dog.

"If only I had a *clue*," whined Breeze in frustration, her voice shaking. "I'm furious with myself. I'm so sorry, Alpha. All I know is that it was big. Not Storm, though—it couldn't have been—it was another big dog."

Storm, still propping up Breeze with her flank, tried not to sigh. It was heartening that Breeze still believed in her so strongly that she wanted to get in front of any accusations—Storm was the biggest dog in the pack, now that poor Bruno was gone. But all Breeze had done by insisting how much she trusted Storm was draw every dog's attention. Storm saw a mixture of curiosity and mistrust in her Packmates' gazes.

Sunshine gave a choked howl and backed closer to Lucky. Storm twisted one ear toward her in surprise. *Surely she's not scared of me?*

"No dog's accusing any other dog, least of all Storm." Lucky spoke firmly, giving Sunshine a reassuring nuzzle. "The most important thing right now is for us to go out there and try to find some clues while the trail is fresh—if the bad dog has been careless enough to leave any traces. We have to find this traitor before they strike again."

"We've said that before," growled Snap softly, lashing her tail in frustration. "We've searched and searched, and *still* the bad dog attacks us."

."So now it's more urgent than ever," snapped Alpha. "Lucky's right. We'll go out in teams of three; that seems safest. I will assign each group a patch of territory, and I want you all to search thoroughly. Check every tree stump, every hollow. Look under rocks if you have to; we can't afford to miss anything that might tell us this dog's name."

It didn't take Alpha long to organize the dogs into groups of three; clearly, thought Storm, she wanted to get out there and hunt for clues before the trail could be swept away by rain or wind, or the simple passing of time. Storm herself was teamed with Daisy and Mickey. As soon as Alpha called the names, she felt a rush of relief. There could not be two dogs she trusted more. And at least she hadn't been paired up with Chase again.

This means I won't be able to keep an eye on her. Though . . . I don't think Chase could have dragged Breeze like that. She's too small—this may prove that the bad dog is a large one, or at least a very powerful one. Storm licked her jaws. *But I don't think I could have stood another day working with Chase, anyway. Not when I can smell her suspicion of me.*

The three Packmates set out as quickly as they could, making

their way through the forest and across the meadow toward the river. Alpha had told them to check every paw-space of ground between the river and the cave they suspected was a giantfur den, which they always gave a sensibly wide berth—not even a bad traitor dog would risk venturing too close to that.

They moved as quietly as possible, placing their paws with caution on the rustling leaves and grass. Storm's fur prickled with nerves. Fear that she might miss a speck or a hair kept her senses jangling with alertness. *This could be our big chance, after all. There's been no rain since Breeze was attacked. If we can find just a single claw mark* . . .

Even Daisy was quiet and intent, her usual lively chatter silenced. It wasn't until they had paused at the edge of the meadow that she spoke.

"I know it wasn't you, Storm. You would never hurt Breeze."

Storm halted, surprised by the tone of Daisy's voice. There was a hint of desperation in the way she spoke. And the little dog hadn't said, *It's ridiculous!* Or, *Impossible!* Or, *It's out of the question!*

Just: *You would never hurt Breeze.*

And it had sounded almost like she wanted to also ask, *Would you?*

Storm paused, her jaw clenched tight as she waited for the terrible question, but to her relief, Mickey interrupted. "Remember

to keep your ears open as well as your nostrils. I don't think we should talk, or distract each other in any way. This is too important."

Storm nodded. *He's right.* She and Daisy once more fell silent, lowering their snouts to breathe in every possible scent as they made their slow and careful way toward the river.

The stench, when it hit her, was sudden and overpowering. And all too familiar—

"Fox!" she snarled.

The others had scented it too: Their heads snapped up at the same moment Storm's did. A reddish-gray tail was just disappearing into the riverside underbrush. Storm bolted after it, plunging into the bushes, her whole head filled with the fox's musky odor.

The fox was quick and nimble, darting between rocks and squirming under thornbushes that Storm couldn't hope to penetrate; but she could hear Daisy scrambling through the brush, coming after their quarry at a wide angle. She was aware, too, of Mickey's running paws on the edge of the meadow, skirting the bushes but keeping pace with the sly creature. *All I have to do is keep harrying it,* she thought grimly. *However fast it can wriggle through brush, Mickey's going to overtake it once we're on the flat land.*

Sure enough, as she raced up a low slope through a tangle

of branches, she saw Mickey's shape up ahead; he was facing her and the fox, his shoulders low and hackles high. His bared teeth glinted in the light. From the side, she saw Daisy tearing through the scrubby undergrowth, dodging obstacles with agile grace despite her stubby legs.

The fox scrabbled to a halt when it saw Mickey, and Daisy was blocking its escape toward the meadow. With a squeal of fear, it spun and hurtled back the way it had come.

Storm was ready for it. She braced herself on her forepaws, lunging forward and snarling. The fox, out of options, tried to skid to a stop and tumbled head over heels. Sprawling in front of her, it rolled swiftly onto its belly and cowered.

"Dogs not hurt fox," it rasped, its tongue hanging out of its jaws. Its eyes were angry and scared.

"That depends on you," growled Storm.

Abruptly the fox's eyes popped wide, and recognition sparked in them. "Ah! Ah! Good dogs, yes, you dogs not hurt poor fox."

"What?" A sickening claw of dread tugged at Storm's gut. *Wait a moment—this fox looks familiar—*

"You good dog. Well. You not-so-bad dog. You let poor fox go now. Yes, yes. Let fox go."

Daisy and Mickey were behind the creature now, blocking its

escape, and they were both staring at it—Mickey with guilt in his eyes. The fox glanced over her shoulder.

"You not-so-bad dog too." She sat up on her haunches, looking more confident. Ignoring Daisy, she stared straight at Mickey. "You smart dog like this one. Yes, two of youse. You let Fox Mist go now."

Storm shot Daisy a nervous glance. The little dog was watching the fox, appalled. Hesitantly Daisy stepped closer, sniffing; then she flinched back in revulsion at the strength of the odor. She walked a full circle around the creature, studying her from ears to paw-tips.

Daisy's dark eyes turned to Storm, then to Mickey.

"Isn't this the fox we captured before?" she demanded. "This is the one Alpha told us to punish."

"Um, it could be . . ." began Storm.

"I'm . . . not sure I would recognize . . ." Mickey licked his chops.

"Yes, yes!" interrupted the fox. Storm saw Mickey wince. "That Fox Mist! Now you let go again."

"What?" Anger flared in Daisy's eyes. "You two were supposed to mark her. She looks pretty unscarred to *me!*"

Fox Mist was creeping delicately toward the gap between

Storm and Daisy. Storm slapped a paw on the ground to stop her. "Just stop right there," she growled.

The fox flinched and sat down again, curling her tail around her rump and placing her head on her forepaws as if she wanted to look as small as possible. Storm couldn't stomach the idea of hurting her, though. Her sly little escape attempt had at least given Storm a chance to avoid Daisy's angry question.

Storm lowered her head to glare straight at the fox's nervous face. "You've obviously been slinking around our territory all night. Did you see anything?"

"What anything?" The fox seemed to decide on a change of tactics, tilting her head winsomely. "What means nice dog, good dog?"

"Stop that stupid flattery." Storm growled low in her throat. "Anything odd. Strange dogs prowling. Unusual behavior. You're not a fool—you know the kind of thing I mean."

"I see not anything." The fox hunched her shoulders in a gesture of helpless apology. "Nothing funny, no dogs I don't know. Only dogs from nice dog's Pack, they sniff the ground, they look everywhere, foxes go hide."

"That would be Moon and Snap on patrol," growled Mickey. "That's no help."

The little fox shrugged again, her eyes open and innocent. "All dogs is looking the same to me anyway." Suddenly she brightened. "No, I see something!"

"What?" Storm tensed. "What did you see?"

"I see dead dog." The fox frowned solemnly. "Dog all dead, dog all bitten and dead. Just like poor fox cub in forest." For an instant, her expression hardened and grew viciously hostile; then she seemed to master herself, and the submissive tone was back. "Up on cliff. Poor, poor dog."

"That was days ago." Storm's belly clenched in disappointment.

"Yes, yes. Two fox-moons, three fox-moons, maybe. Big, big dead dog. I see big dog get dead."

Storm started. "Wait. You *saw* Bruno being killed?" Her heartbeat raced, thrumming in her throat and chest. *This is it! She saw the murderer!*

Mickey's and Daisy's jaws had fallen wide, and they exchanged shocked glances. Daisy jumped to her paws; her eyes slanted, a little guiltily, toward Storm, before fixing excitedly on the fox. "Was it a dog you'd seen before? A dog you *knew?*"

The fox lifted a paw to lick it, looking smugly pleased at their reaction. "I not know dog."

171

Daisy's little body sagged with what looked, to Storm, suspiciously like relief. "Another big dog, then?"

Storm stared. *What do you mean, 'another big dog'?* Sadness threatened to choke her. *Oh, Daisy, you honestly thought the fox was going to name me, didn't you?*

"'Big' dog?" The fox set her paw back down. "How I know?" she scoffed. "I tell you, all dogs is looking same! Fox little!"

"But you must have *some* idea!" cried Daisy. "Look at me, look at Mickey here, look at Storm. You must have been able to tell what sort of size the killer was!"

The fox narrowed her eyes, tilting her head to one side and studying all three dogs. "Humph," she said at last. "This dog that kill dogs *and not just fox cubs*—it not so big. No, not so very, very big. Maybe not bigger than *you*."

She was looking straight at Daisy.

Mickey looked as stunned as Storm felt. Daisy was just blinking, speechless.

"How can . . . ? That's not possible!" yelped the little dog.

"It's not," barked Mickey. "A dog Bruno's size, taken out by a dog your size? It's *not* possible. It's ridiculous!"

Except that I thought not so long ago that it was perfectly possible, remembered Storm, *if Bruno's jaw had been gnawed off* after *he was killed.* But

still . . . it did not seem likely. *A dog of Daisy's size would have exhausted itself biting off Bruno's jaw. . . .*

The three dogs were so taken aback, they were too slow to react as the fox shot suddenly past Storm. A streak of gray, she vanished into the bushes with an impudent flick of her tail.

"Let her go," growled Mickey angrily. "She's clearly told us all she knows."

"Sure," said Daisy, her voice brimming with fury. "Let her go—just like *you* two did before!"

Storm licked her jaws, distressed. "Look, at least now we know something—"

"*How* can either of you believe a word a fox says?" demanded Daisy. "You can't trust a fox! And you can't make *friends* with them!" The little dog's hackles bristled; her legs were stiff and her tail quivered as she glared at Storm and Mickey. "How could you have let her go? You said you'd punished that fox! You *lied!* You lied to our Alpha!"

"Daisy," pleaded Mickey, "you have to understand. We're not *friends* with that creature, we just—it seemed wrong to scar her. It would have been . . ."

"Unnecessary," put in Storm.

"Yes, and *brutal*," Mickey added. "She was pregnant with cubs!

We thought it would be wrong."

"What does it matter what you thought?" Daisy looked less furious now, and more stunned with disbelief. "That wasn't your decision to make—you had no right to judge! You went against Alpha's orders, both of you!"

"We . . . we just couldn't go through with it," began Mickey, but Daisy gave an angry yelp, cutting him off.

"And *then* you came back to camp and you *lied!*" Her dark eyes blazed. "You lied in our faces. You lied to the whole Pack."

Storm couldn't say a word. She was too shocked by the sight of Daisy in a rage—*a justifiable rage,* she realized miserably. The little dog's face was full of horror, and revulsion, and worst of all, savage disappointment.

"You lied to us all," Daisy spat, turning her tail on both of them. "How can any dog trust either of you now?"

CHAPTER THIRTEEN

"I cannot believe this. I can't. But I have to."

Alpha's voice was like a longpaw whip, cutting Storm to the bone. She had no idea what her leader's expression was like; she couldn't look at the swift-dog's face. Storm just stared at the ground beneath her nose, wishing she could sink into it and hide between the Earth-Dog's paws for a while: maybe a whole turn of the Moon-Dog. It should be easy enough: Like Mickey beside her, she was already pressed low to the ground, submissive and ashamed.

Alpha's terrifying, enraged voice rose to a howl. "The pair of you betrayed the Pack!"

"We're so sorry, Alpha," whined Mickey.

"You!" Alpha snarled at him. "I would never have believed this of *you*, Mickey!"

Against all her better instincts, Storm's hackles began to rise. *What does Alpha mean by that? Is she saying that she would expect it from me?*

Remorseful as she was, it burned Storm's pride that she had to cower here in front of Alpha with the whole Pack watching. *I don't care what they think. It would have been wrong to wound that fox for no reason. It was a stupid order!*

I know we shouldn't have lied to the Pack. But I'm not sorry I took mercy on that fox. I'm not!

Resentment burned in her belly, a small ember of pure rage and hate. Didn't they all call her dangerous? Didn't they think *she* was the brute around here?

Yet their beautiful swift-dog Alpha was the one who'd given that stupid, brutal command—*and she stands there implying that she wouldn't have expected better of me!*

And humiliating me like this, in front of the Pack that already distrusts me . . .

Aware that her bitter fury must be showing in her eyes, Storm forced it down like a tough bite of prey. *I have to submit. It's Pack rules.*

Just bear it, Storm.

Still unable to look at Alpha's face, she flicked a quick glance at the rest of the Pack. None of them looked sorry for her, or even for Mickey. Every dog avoided her eyes, but she could see that

their expressions were sullen and angry.

"Disobeying an order's bad enough," barked Chase, "but lying to the Pack?"

"It's not acceptable. I don't care if they thought they knew better than Alpha." That was Daisy, still clearly seething with shock.

"No dog knows better than their Alpha," came Sunshine's small voice. "That's Pack law."

Sunshine? The little Omega's disapproval hurt Storm worse than any other dog's contempt.

"You will both eat last tonight." Alpha's tail lashed the air. "And not just tonight. That will only be part of your punishment; you both need to learn a harsh lesson."

"Alpha." Storm lifted her head defiantly. "If the fox had been terrified of us, it wouldn't have talked to us. At least we know now that Bruno's killer was a smaller dog."

"Hah!" barked Moon with contempt. *One of her pups was killed by a fox,* remembered Storm. "You believe a single word a fox says? Are you really that foolish, Storm?"

Lucky was gazing at Storm with pained disapproval. "That fox wanted to get away from you—it would have said *anything*, Storm. Foxes cannot be trusted. Not ever."

"But, Lucky—"

"And what's more," he growled loudly over her protests. He glared at her. "What's more, foxes are cunning. It would take one look at you and know what you wanted to hear: that the killer was a small dog, smaller than *you*."

Storm felt as if he'd kicked her in the ribs with his hindpaws. "Lucky, that's not true, you know it's not. There were three of us there and—"

"That's enough!" He silenced her with a cold bark. "Be quiet, Storm. You've said *more* than enough. Don't talk to me again until you're ready to be a true Pack Dog."

She couldn't speak. She stared at him, the hurt burning through her like a forest fire. She could only plead with her eyes— *Lucky! You know me better than this. . . . Or, are you the same as the others? Have even you always been suspicious of me, deep down?*

Lucky stared at her for a few long moments, then turned away in disgust.

The mood among the Pack was dark as they gathered around the prey pile later that evening. Storm found it hard to care that she and Mickey would be the last ones to eat; misery and anger had killed her appetite anyway.

There was none of the chat and banter and joking that usually accompanied the assembly of the Pack. Subdued, arriving in ones and twos, every dog lay down, heads on their paws, and watched the prey pile silently. Alpha sat in her usual place, her face stony. Lucky, beside her, was solemn and thoughtful; even the four pups were quiet.

What Mickey and I did seems to have been the last bone that choked the dog. I'm sure in normal times, Alpha wouldn't be this angry and unforgiving.

It was as if Alpha's and Beta's approval and trust had been a strong beam of sunlight warming her flank, and now the Sun Dog had hidden behind a black cloud, and she felt even colder than before he'd turned his face on her.

One by one, Alpha called up the dogs, her voice short and sharp. Any low conversations that accompanied the Pack's meal were stilted, and soon over. No dog seemed especially hungry. Storm thought with longing of how she and Lucky had raided the longpaws' spoil-box with Mickey, Chase, and Snap. They'd had so much fun, and they'd joked and boasted with the Pack about their escapade. Every dog had liked them, and every dog had appreciated the prey they'd brought back.

How can things have changed so quickly?

At last Omega had eaten her fill, and Alpha barked, "Mickey."

As the Farm Dog sloped forward, his tail low, Storm thought, *Even Mickey gets to eat before me. It's obvious who Alpha blames most.*

When it was her own turn, Storm grabbed a rabbit leg and returned sullenly to her own place, gnawing at it with little interest. She was still eating when Alpha growled, "Pack, I want to hear your reports. What did the patrols find today?"

"Not much," said Moon wearily. "We saw some blood, on the path and on bushes. It was Breeze's." She nodded at the brown dog, who still looked weary and nervous. "There were tracks in the path, like something had been dragged along—but we couldn't make out any other scent."

"It was the same with our area," added Snap. "We saw the trail, but caught no scent. This dog is cunning."

"We didn't see anything," said Thorn apologetically. "But then, we weren't where Breeze said she was dragged. We tried to find any spots the bad dog might have crossed as it approached the camp, but there was nothing. Not a single paw mark."

"Whatever dog we're up against, it's horribly clever," said Sunshine in a small voice.

"Yes," agreed Alpha. "You haven't remembered anything else, Breeze? Anything that could help us?"

"I'm sorry." Breeze's head and tail drooped. Her scratches had

stopped bleeding, but they still looked nasty. "It was so confusing. And terrifying. And so dark."

"It's all right," said Alpha, though she growled the words through gritted teeth. "It's not your fault." As she said that, she turned her head to gaze directly at Storm and Mickey.

As if it's our fault! Storm felt hot rage in her throat.

"Storm. Mickey." Their leader's voice was curt. "You will take High Watch tonight."

"Yes, Alpha." Mickey crouched submissively, his tail tucked between his legs. That was probably more sensible, Storm thought, than glaring in defiance. But she couldn't help it.

"Not just for tonight," Alpha went on. "You will both stay up there for three full journeys of the Moon-Dog and the Sun-Dog. You can take turns sleeping, to relieve each other during no-sun."

Storm got to her paws, shaking at the injustice, but she couldn't speak—even if Alpha would have allowed her to. Instead, the swift-dog went on, "Your time on High Watch would be longer, by the way, if the Pack didn't need you to hunt. And when you return? You will both still be held in disgrace. You will be considered bad dogs until you prove yourselves worthy of the name Pack Dog once more."

The rest of the Pack remained motionless, staring at Storm

and Mickey, but Snap bounded to her paws. "Alpha!"

Alpha didn't even look at her. "Yes, Snap?"

Storm saw the way that Snap's tail was quivering and knew what the small dog was going to say. *I don't even have the energy to growl at her now. . . .*

"That's where Bruno was murdered! You can't send Mickey up there for three days—not with *Storm!*"

"Quiet," said Lucky tersely, standing up. "That's enough, Snap. This is Alpha's decision. Mickey will be fine."

"You don't know that—!"

"Beta said *enough!*" Alpha turned at last to Snap, glowering. "If Mickey and Storm trust each other enough to conspire against the Pack, and defy my orders, then they can certainly trust each other on High Watch."

There was no sound for a moment. Snap stepped back, still looking unhappy.

"Now," said Alpha. "Both of you. Get yourselves to High Watch, and out of my sight."

CHAPTER FOURTEEN

Distantly, from across the river and the meadow, the noise and clatter of the longpaw town was winding down. Some lights flickered off; others began to shine like tiny Moon-Dogs as the gray dusk deepened. Longpaws barked farewells. Loudcages growled, rumbled away, and faded.

It was funny how far sounds traveled, thought Storm, gazing down toward the broken settlement. *The place is just as far away as it was before, but the noise is so much clearer from up here. The Wind-Dogs must carry it.*

Behind her, Mickey paced up and down the path the Pack had beaten on the cliff top. He looked so tired, Storm realized, but he was trying to keep himself alert. He kept turning, almost against his will, to look at the rock where Bruno's body had been found.

With weary paws, his head sagging, he plodded over to where

Storm sat looking landward. "Have you seen anything new?"

"No," she sighed. "It's just the same as last night."

"I'm starting to wish that something *would* happen," yawned Mickey. "It would be less tiring if we had something to do."

And we'd be of much more use to the Pack, thought Storm resentfully. *I don't think I can stand another day and night of this. Another idiotic decision from Alpha, though I'd better not say so to Mickey.* "I don't want to be assigned to High Watch again till next Tree Flower," she grumbled. "I'm sick of this."

Mickey made a sound that might actually have been agreement; Storm wondered if he was as annoyed at Alpha as she was. "Well, it'll be over soon."

"Yes, though not soon en— Wait, what's that sound?" Storm got to her paws and pricked her ears, staring down at the longpaw town. "Look. It's Beetle and Thorn! What are they doing?"

Mickey came to her side and peered down. The dusk was deepening, but the weak glow that lit up the digging-and-building area picked out the movement at the fence quite clearly. Yes, it was Moon's two pups. Thorn had already scrambled beneath the high wire fence; behind her Storm could make out Beetle, clawing at the ground, flattening his back to wriggle through and join his litter-sister. Both the young dogs stood for a moment, scratching

and shaking themselves, and peering around the raw earth and new walls.

"What in the name of the Earth-Dog are they up to?" Mickey blinked and tilted his head.

"I don't know." Storm licked her jaws. "Looking for food?"

"In there? I doubt it."

So did Storm, to be truthful. "Maybe Alpha has sent them on a scouting mission?"

"I doubt that, too." Mickey frowned. "Alpha wants us to keep as far away from the longpaws as possible, doesn't she? I don't think she'd send Thorn and Beetle on such a dangerous mission. It's not as if they're familiar with longpaws and their ways."

Storm shifted, sat down, and scratched her ear. "If they're doing this without permission, and Alpha finds out, she's going to be in an even worse mood."

Mickey shot her a half-amused glance. "Well, we're the ones who put her in the bad mood to start with. But we should tell her what they're up to." Morosely he added, "Maybe she'll still be so mad at us, she'll go easier on Thorn and Beetle."

Storm licked her jaws. "Or they might end up on punishment duties too. And it's not like the Pack can afford that. It's enough of a waste leaving the two of us up here licking our paws." There

was something else, too—she'd had a perfectly good reason for breaking the Pack's rules, and as much as she regretted the lie, she didn't regret letting Fox Mist go, not one bit. What if Thorn and Beetle had a good reason too? How would they feel about the dog who reported them to Alpha?

Thorn and Beetle seemed to like Storm, to believe that she was innocent. If they were caught and punished because of her, when they weren't doing anything *bad*, would they ever forgive her?

Mickey's brow furrowed; he seemed to be thinking deeply. "Well . . . perhaps we shouldn't tell Alpha right now, then—but we should mention it to Moon in the morning. I'm sure she'd want to know."

Storm squinted to stare down at the longpaw settlement. She could just make out Thorn and Beetle, now creeping in and out of the shadows, sniffing at sleeping loudcages, standing up on their hindpaws to investigate what lay behind the new walls. Thorn gestured with her head to Beetle, and the two litter-siblings vanished around a corner.

"I know what it's like to have dogs watching you, talking about your mistakes," Storm told Mickey. "Thorn and Beetle are grown dogs, with their own Pack names. We shouldn't be reporting back

to Alpha, or their Mother-Dog, on what they're up to. In fact, telling Moon might be even worse. It doesn't look like they're working against the Pack, and I don't believe they ever would."

Mickey sighed. "I don't know, Storm. We're supposed to be watching for unusual activity, and that's *very* unusual activity. And the idea of keeping anything from Alpha, now of all times—"

"Mickey, listen," said Storm, remembering what Alpha had told her before, in a friendlier moment. "Thorn and Beetle—well, they've been struggling with the way Fiery died. And they're a bit obsessed with longpaws. So maybe sneaking off to that place is just their way of finding out more about them. It's natural, don't you think?"

"I suppose so." Mickey's eyes softened. "We all miss Fiery, so I can imagine how hard it is for those two. Fine, Storm: I won't mention it to Alpha. Or to Moon."

"Thanks, Mickey. I really do think that's wise."

"But," he added sternly, "I'm going to have a talk with Beetle and Thorn tomorrow. Longpaw settlements are dangerous. I know better than any dog that some longpaws have good intentions—but a lot of them don't." He shuddered. "And even the places where they live and work can have hidden dangers. Loud-cages, machinery—I'm going to have to impress on those two

what a risk they're taking."

Storm nodded. "That's fair, Mickey."

He licked her ear. "I'm going to go and see if there are any floatcages around." He turned away and padded over to the edge of the cliff, then sat down, curled his tail around him, and gazed out across the Endless Lake. Storm wondered if she too should watch for the giant floating vessels that carried longpaws on the water, but her time would be better spent, she supposed, keeping an eye out in the other direction.

At the edge of her vision was the huge boulder that had concealed Bruno's body. She couldn't help her gaze slanting toward it. In her mind's eye, she relived the scene again: the brutal injury, Bruno's body covered in so much blood. *Could a small dog really have done that to him? Was I crazy to think it could have been Chase?*

The fox said the killer might be no bigger than Daisy. But that creature admitted herself that she isn't good at judging a dog's size or appearance. "The same size as Daisy" could mean any dog from Sunshine to Mickey, for all Storm knew. *And that's if she is even telling the truth.*

There was a sudden scratch of claws on dry rock, and Storm jumped, her heart thrashing. But the dog who came into view at the top of the steep cliff path was only little Sunshine, followed by Moon. Moon was still limping slightly, Storm noticed; the

Farm Dog was using her wounded paw with great caution. Storm was glad they had decided not to mention Thorn's and Beetle's movements—if Moon knew they'd sneaked off, she would only go rushing after them, and her paw was still weak and sore from her fall.

"How is that paw doing?" Mickey, walking over, cocked a concerned ear at Moon.

"It's a little better, thank you. Still sore, though." Moon licked at it, looking faintly annoyed.

"And how are things in camp?" Mickey went on, a look of longing in his eyes.

"It's all right," Sunshine told him. "Quite quiet, really. Oh! I have to tell you what happened with the pups. Yesterday, they asked the Patrol Dogs to bring back any feathers they found, and no dog knew why. They were in their den for ages and ages this morning, and every dog thought they must be taking a nap." She gave a high yelp of laughter. "We should have known better! When the pups came out, they'd stuck the feathers into Fluff's fur, all over—because she'd decided she wanted to be a Sky-Dog! Beta had to tell her the feathers wouldn't make her fly, and she was *so* disappointed—but oh, Sky-Dogs, it was funny." Sunshine's tongue lolled. "It took Breeze forever to get the feathers out, but

when she was finished, Lucky gave Fluff a ride around the glade on his back, to make her feel as if she was flying. And then of course all the pups wanted a turn—" Sunshine ran out of breath, and at the same time seemed to register Storm's and Mickey's bleak stares. "Well, anyway, that kept the pups busy for a while," she finished lamely.

I never thought I'd feel so miserable about missing an ordinary day in camp, Storm thought. *I wish I'd seen that, even if it was only silly pup antics.*

She had a suspicion Mickey felt the same way. He cleared his throat. "That sounds fun, Sunshine. And, Moon, how are Beetle and Thorn doing?"

Storm shot him a warning glance, but Moon didn't seem to pick up on the edge in Mickey's voice. "They've been volunteering for a lot of patrols," she told them. "I worry that they aren't getting enough rest, but I have to admit, it's been helpful. The Pack has needed all paws working, especially in the last few days. . . ." She licked her jaws, seeming to realize her words were a little tactless.

But Storm wasn't worried about that. *It was Alpha's decision to send two of us into exile up here; I'm not going to feel guilty that the Pack is shortpawed.*

What worried her more was Thorn and Beetle, and their nighttime expeditions. *That must be how they've been sneaking out:*

pretending that they're on a legitimate patrol.

A shiver of anxiety rippled through her fur. *If Moon had any idea that they're not patrolling at all, she would run right off High Watch and go running after them—and that's the last thing she, or the Pack, needs right now.*

Those two had better prove me right. . . .

Storm had the distinct feeling that Alpha regretted putting two of her most capable Pack members out of action—not that she'd ever admit it. The swift-dog sat on her haunches, giving Storm and Mickey her most severe gaze, tapping her tail briskly against the ground. Her eyes were tired and her fur looked dull. *Well,* thought Storm, *every dog must have had extra duties for the last three nights and days—and I guess that included Alpha herself.*

"You may have finished your sentence at High Watch," Alpha told them, "but that does not mean you're forgiven, either of you. You are back among the Pack because we need you as hunt-dogs."

"Of course, Alpha." Mickey nodded, subdued.

Storm said nothing. The Moon-Dog, half turned away, was already high in the dark-blue sky; prey-sharing had been over by the time she and Mickey descended wearily from High Watch. At least they would get a night's sleep in their comfortable dens, but they wouldn't get a proper meal till the following evening. After

the last few days of scant pickings on High Watch, that seemed harsh to Storm.

"You'll continue to eat last when we share the prey," added Alpha, as if she were digging in a claw. "That is, until you each prove to me that you're capable of being true Pack Dogs again. I hope you realize how disappointed I remain in you both."

That's been made more than clear, thought Storm bitterly as she and Mickey turned to plod toward their dens. *I wish I could feel more penitent about what we did. I know it was wrong.*

But Alpha is making it hard to be sorry.

Mickey didn't seem to feel the same way; he looked genuinely remorseful as he padded at Storm's side, his ears low and his tail tucked between his legs. But he lifted his head with sudden curiosity as Beetle and Thorn trotted past them, heading for the woods.

"There they go on patrol again," he said softly. "Or maybe not."

He and Storm exchanged a look of misgiving.

"There's nothing we can do," she told him with a hunch of her shoulders. "I really don't think it's wise to interfere. They're both smart enough to stay safe."

Mickey nodded doubtfully and turned toward his own den. *He's still planning to give them a lecture when he gets the chance,* realized

Storm. *That's fine by me. They deserve it.*

But I think they'll be all right for now. What I told Mickey is true: Fiery's pups aren't stupid.

With a sigh she squeezed into her den and trod a circle on her sleeping-place. The camp was quiet, but after the long time with only Mickey for company, it was reassuring to hear the sounds of other dogs, shifting and scratching and occasionally growling in their sleep. From a little way away, she could even hear Lucky's distinctive snoring. It was a combination of deep snorts and high squeaks that she'd always found secretly funny, but for the moment, she'd lost her sense of humor. Storm glowered at the den walls.

One of her ears pricked up. There was another sound now, one that didn't come from a sleeping dog. She could hear cautious steps; they sounded hesitant, and the dog was placing its paws as lightly as it could on the grass. Storm's brow furrowed. She raised herself up on her forepaws and cocked her head.

That's not a dog going out to make dirt. That's a dog who does not want to be heard.

Standing up, Storm pushed her head out of the den opening. It took only moments for her eyes to adjust, and she was in time to see a familiar rump and tail vanish into the trees.

Chase!

All her suspicions, all her fears came flooding back. *Where is Chase going at this time of night? She can't be up to anything good—not sneaking around like that.*

It certainly wasn't something Storm could ignore. Quietly she emerged from her den and slunk after Chase, trying not to disturb any other dog. *Whatever it is, I can deal with it myself. And with my reputation the way it is at the moment, I'm going to need hard proof before I accuse her of being up to something.*

Chase's scent was clear on the night air, and it didn't take Storm long to catch sight of her. Just as she'd suspected, the little dog didn't go only far enough to make dirt; she was pressing on through the undergrowth, leaving the camp boundary far behind her. Determined not to alert Chase till she'd found out what she was up to, Storm followed as closely as she dared.

Clouds scudded across the half-obscured Moon-Dog, and there were few stars; Storm had to focus hard to keep Chase in view. She had expected the little dog to stop beyond the boundary of the Pack's territory, but still she trotted on, giving an occasional nervous glance to her side or over her shoulder. *She looks shifty,* Storm decided. *What will I do if I catch her in the act of some bad deed? Will I have time to go back to alert the Pack, or should I deal with it myself?*

Will the Pack even believe me?

She picked up her pace, exasperated and increasingly worried.

In the name of the Forest-Dog, how far is Chase planning to go?

Just as she thought it, her question was answered. Ahead of Chase, a second shadow appeared through the trees: a scruffy-looking dog of around the same size, who bounded up to her with friendly woofs.

The shattering of the nervous silence took Storm by surprise, and she came to an abrupt halt, blinking. More dogs were emerging from the shadows now, and they looked familiar. Crouching low, Storm slunk closer.

Their smells . . . I know these dogs!

Now she could see and smell them all clearly. That dog who was nuzzling Chase was Rake, her old friend from Terror's Pack. The scruffy dog's companions were familiar, too: Storm recognized Woody and Ruff—and there was Dart, the skinny hunt-dog who had originally been part of the half wolf's Pack, before Sweet had taken over as Alpha and Terror's former Pack members had joined with them to make one big Pack.

But these dogs had never been truly happy in the Pack. They didn't like the way Alpha dealt with the awful things that were happening and felt that she favored the dogs she had known the longest. So they'd left to form their own group.

This must be where they're living now, Storm realized. *They haven't gotten very far from our camp, have they?*

She lowered herself closer to the ground—keeping the cheerful reunion in view, but herself out of sight. A terrible thought was racing across her mind.

If they're living so close to us, I wonder . . . could the bad dogs be from outside the Pack after all?

She craned her ears. *I have to know what they're planning.*

"It's been difficult," she heard Chase say, and Storm narrowed her eyes. *What's been difficult, Chase? Concealing your plans from Alpha? Hiding your treachery?*

"I'm sure it has." That was Rake. "I'm sorry we had to leave, but you can understand why, can't you?"

"Oh yes," said Chase softly, "and I don't blame you. Holding that territory with so few dogs is tough—and there's a lot more tension now."

"Still," broke in Dart, "the pups must be fun, and I guess they hold the Pack together. They must be growing up fast!"

"They're sweet," agreed Chase. "Breeze and Sunshine are both as crazy about them as their parent-dogs are. They do a lot of the pup-minding, which is helpful. But what about you four? How have you been doing?"

Oh, come on! thought Storm impatiently. *Enough with the chatter—I want to know about the conspiracy!*

"Well, we found this place for our camp," Woody was saying, "and it's worked really well. The only competition was a couple of raccoons. They were tougher opposition than I thought they'd be, but we chased them away eventually. See, Chase, there's a fresh-water stream across this dip—can you hear it? The prey situation isn't bad, either."

"It's not as good as your camp," said Ruff, "but it suits us just fine. Tell me, how's Moon? And Thorn and Beetle?"

"I want to hear more about Breeze and her pup-minding," said Woody. "And about what you've been doing, too, Chase."

What? Storm pinned back her ears, frustrated. *This is just the kind of chat Lucky and I had with Bella and Arrow, when we visited them. It's all small dog-talk.*

For the first time, she felt a niggle of doubt in her belly. *Is that all Chase is doing? Catching up with her old friends?*

They'd soon get to talking about their plans, Storm reassured herself. She'd find out what their next attack would be, and when it would happen, and where. *All I have to do is wait. . . .*

She had to wait an interminable time. Once or twice she nearly dozed off as she listened to the five dogs gossip about their past

Packs and the dogs they had known. The snippets of news were the most tedious Storm had ever heard; no dog spoke of murder, or poison, or sabotage.

When Chase sprang to her paws, Storm thought she was finally about to reveal her plot. But all she did was share more friendly licks with her former comrades.

"It's been so good to see you all," she was saying. "And kind of relaxing, after all the trouble and stress in the Pack. I'll come again as soon as I can."

And with that, Chase turned and trotted back the way she'd come.

Storm almost yelped in surprise; she had to choke it back. It took her a moment to recover her wits, and with Chase quickly out of sight and earshot, she realized she'd have to hurry to catch up. *Was that all completely innocent? Really?*

It was too hard for Storm to believe. Picking up her paws, she began to run, determined not to let Chase out of her sight for longer than possible. *She could be doing anything while I can't see her. She could double back and talk quietly to her friends again. She could dodge me and get up to some terrible mischief—*

Panic rose in Storm's chest, making her heart thunder, and she forgot to be careful. Just as Chase's haunches came into view,

both Storm's forepaws landed hard on a drift of dry leaves in a hollow, and as she lurched forward, she hit a twig. It snapped with a crack.

Chase spun around, her paws skidding on the earth. The small dog's eyes popped wide; Storm could see the whites of them in the dimness. She heard Chase's gasp, too, and saw her hackles spring up.

"Storm!" The small dog was breathing hard, and not from exertion. She backed slowly away, her legs trembling, but her rump banged against a pine trunk and she stifled a yelp. But she didn't take her eyes off Storm.

She looks terrified.

For a moment they gazed at each other in tense silence; then Chase whimpered, "Don't hurt me! *Please!*"

For a moment, Storm was too flummoxed to move or speak. Chase's whole body was shaking now; her fur was erect all over her hide.

Chase really *thinks I'm the bad dog!*

Storm licked her jaws; the simple act made Chase flinch and cower.

And if she truly believes I'm the traitor, Storm realized with thumping certainty, *it's not possible that she is.*

Chase couldn't be faking her abject terror; no dog could do that.

Oh, Sky-Dogs, thought Storm, with a sickening sensation in her gut. *I've been on the wrong trail. All this time I've wasted. It can't be Chase: I can see that she truly thinks it's* me.

But if not Chase, then who *had* killed Bruno and Whisper? The answer seemed to be further away from Storm than ever. *Right now it would be easier to catch the Golden Deer than to discover the traitor.*

"Chase! Chase, please." Storm stepped forward very carefully, feeling her own paws tremble. Chase had pressed herself hard against the trees that were blocking her escape; her lips were curled back from her teeth, but her eyes were still frenzied with fear. "I'm not going to hurt you, Chase, I promise. I'm not the traitor!"

"So you say. Stay back! Stay back, I warn you!"

"Chase, I'm not the bad dog." Storm dipped her head and pricked her ears, trying to look unthreatening. "I thought it was *you*! That's why I followed you in the first place!"

At last Chase's shaking began to subside. She narrowed her eyes, pinned back her ears, and gave a low, quivering growl. "You thought what? Storm, how *could* you?"

"I'm sorry. I can see now you're not guilty, or you wouldn't be so afraid of me." Storm risked another paw-pace toward the small dog, and this time Chase didn't wince; she looked more offended than scared.

"I'm not afraid! I—don't come any closer!" Chase's flanks heaved.

"I promise I won't hurt you. I swear on—on the Forest-Dog!" Storm pleaded.

Chase's eyes narrowed even farther. "All right," she said slowly. "All right, I'll believe that oath."

You're just not sure you believe me about anything else . . . realized Storm sadly. "We'll walk back to camp together. I won't even touch you. Come on."

Chase hesitated briefly, then gave a sharp nod. Keeping a dog-length between her flank and Storm's, she set off in the direction of the camp, one wary eye still flicking frequently toward Storm.

I'd best keep my word and my distance, thought Storm with a heavy heart. Carefully she made her way without letting even her tail swat Chase's rump by mistake. The silence as they walked together was the most awkward she'd ever experienced.

As they paused to scramble up a rocky slope, Chase flicked an ear at her and gave a low, warning snarl. "You'd better not tell any

dog where Rake's camp is. I don't want them getting attacked by the bad dog too."

"All right," agreed Storm, as reassuringly as she could. "I won't tell. I've visited friends I miss, too."

Even confiding that secret didn't seem to affect Chase's attitude one bit; she still looked wary as she sprang up the slope, then turned very quickly to keep her eyes on Storm. She slunk on through the forest, halting to sniff the air as they drew nearer to the glade.

"I don't smell any Patrol Dogs," she growled.

"Maybe they're on the other side of the clearing," suggested Storm quickly. *Beetle and Thorn are supposed to be on patrol, but I'm not telling Chase that. They must have gone off by themselves again!*

The sky was already lightening, as the Sun-Dog yawned and stretched, when the two wanderers crept back into camp. They didn't exchange a word as they parted to go to their respective dens; Storm felt guilty and resentful all at once. *Chase was sneaking off in the middle of the night! What was I supposed to think? Of course I suspected her!*

There wasn't much time left to snatch some sleep, and uneasy dreams made Storm restless. Jumbled, horrible images kept startling her awake.

Chase, cornered and at bay, her rump against the tree; that fearful snarl widening and widening until suddenly the vicious, resentful face wasn't Chase's at all, but Terror's. The mad dog's eyes filling with blood; his jaws opening in a violent, shrieking howl. The savage brute lunging at Storm's throat. . . .

Storm woke so abruptly she was already springing to her paws. Dizzy, she trembled, blinking. *That howl is real! It's real!*

But it wasn't Terror's voice, or even Chase's, she realized as her senses returned. *It's Moon!*

The white-and-black Farm Dog was running into the glade as Storm wriggled out of her den. Lucky appeared from his own sleeping-place, and Sunshine, and Daisy too. Moon skidded to a halt on the grass, her eyes wide.

"I can't find Thorn and Beetle!" she yelped.

"What do you mean?" barked Lucky as the rest of the Pack began to scramble from their dens.

Moon's tail was as still as a tree trunk. "They never returned from patrol last night. . . . What if . . ." Now, her flanks began quivering. Storm could imagine the awful thoughts that were charging through her mind. "What if something's happened to them? What if they've met the traitor?"

CHAPTER FIFTEEN

The silence was so heavy, it was as though the Moon-Dog had placed her whole jaw on the head of every dog.

Storm's belly prickled with unease. *Was I wrong to keep my muzzle shut? Should I have told Moon, and Alpha, as soon as I saw what Beetle and Thorn were doing?*

Then she shook herself. Either way, there was nothing for it but to speak up now.

Storm took an abrupt pace forward. "Alpha . . . I might know where they are."

"What?" Alpha's expression was rigid with anger and disbelief as she stared at Storm.

Moon's face was even harder to look at as she echoed Alpha: "*What, Storm?*" There was a tremor of rage in her voice. "What do you know?"

Every dog's head had turned to watch. Storm swallowed hard. "We—Mickey and I—we saw Beetle and Thorn before—while we were on High Watch. They were prowling around the place where the longpaws are digging and building. I'm sure they're all right; they must have—"

"You *saw them*? What was the point of being on High Watch if you didn't report this?" Alpha's bark was dangerously high-pitched.

Moon bounded in front of Alpha to face Storm, her shoulders stiff with fear, her muzzle curled with aggression. "*Why didn't you say something?* Either of you?"

"I—Moon, it's my fault," stammered Storm. "Mickey wanted to tell you, but I said no. I thought they'd be fine, they're such capable dogs, and they know the dangers—"

"That was *not* your decision to make!" howled Moon. "I could have stopped them!"

Storm felt the heat of shame rising in her chest. "I just didn't want to get them in trouble, not if they weren't doing anything bad. . . ." She saw Alpha give her an angry look and went on quickly. "I didn't want you all to go dashing after them if they had a good reason for—"

"*Of course* I would have gone after them! *They're my pups!*" Moon's

face was right in Storm's now, her eyes showing the whites, her fangs bared. "You've learned nothing! You made a decision that wasn't yours to make! And Thorn and Beetle *clearly aren't fine!*"

Storm swallowed again, dipping her head. What could she say? *Moon's right.* She forced herself to glance at Alpha, but the swift-dog's expression remained coldly furious. She had obviously decided to let Moon's fury do the barking, and she clearly agreed with every word her lead Patrol Dog was saying.

Storm opened her jaws to apologize, but the words wouldn't come. *What can I say? I was so wrong. I've committed the same crime twice, proved Alpha was right not to trust me....*

"Packmates." It was Lucky who stepped forward, his face stern. "We can discuss the rights and wrongs of this later." From the look he shot Storm, though, it was clear where he thought the wrongs lay. "Right now we need to go after Beetle and Thorn. No more delays!"

"You're right, Beta," said Alpha. Her voice was too level and cold, as if she was repressing a need to bite some dog.

"I'll take out a party to search for them, and rescue them if necessary." Lucky raised his head to look around at the closest dogs.

"I'm coming, of course." Moon shot a venomous glare at Storm. "They are *my pups*."

"And I'll come," said Storm, averting her eyes from Moon's.

"Me too." Mickey sounded subdued, but his shoulders quivered with determination.

"And me." Breeze padded into the circle.

Lucky nodded. "That will have to do. There's no time to waste."

"The rest of us will search the other side of our territory, closer to the Endless Lake," said Alpha. "Just in case they went that way instead. Good luck, my Beta."

Lucky sprang into a run, and the other dogs of the party followed at his heels as he raced into the forest. Storm could barely feel the snap of twigs and the crackle of leaves beneath her paws; her head swam with horror at the thought of what she might have done. She could only focus on Lucky's golden haunches, and keep running, and try not to think. She was aware of Mickey close behind her, and she couldn't help wondering how he was feeling now. *Terrible, I guess. And that's my fault too.* Breeze and Moon were farther back, the gentle brown dog staying close to the anxious, wounded Mother-Dog. Guilt made Storm gather speed, keeping

her well ahead of them; maybe it was as much fear of Moon as desperation to get to Beetle and Thorn.

"I can't imagine how worried Moon is," muttered Lucky as Storm bounded abreast of him. "I never really understood the bond parent-dogs have with their pups until I had a litter of my own. There's nothing more important than your pups, nothing. If anything happened to mine—" He fell silent and ran even faster.

Despite the heat of her shame, Storm felt a deeper stab of sadness that made her catch her breath. *His own pups are far more important to Lucky than I ever was,* she realized. *Is that what he's telling me? Of course they are. It's natural.*

But it still hurts.

As the search party broke out of the final line of trees, Lucky slowed the pace, lowering his body so that the long meadow grass would give him cover. Beside him, Storm followed his lead; she heard the others' pawsteps slow, and the rustle of the undergrowth as they slunk across the meadow.

Something tickled the sensitive flesh inside Storm's nostrils: something familiar. *That's Thorn's scent!* Close behind it, she detected Beetle's, too.

"Lucky," she murmured, pausing to sniff at the air. "Lucky, I smell them both. They did come this way."

Lucky retraced his steps and lowered his muzzle to the ground at Storm's paws. "Yes," he agreed, "and the trail's heading for the longpaw site, just as you said." He shot Storm a disapproving look but said no more. That didn't reassure Storm. *He's only holding back until Thorn and Beetle are found.*

As Moon and Breeze caught up to them, Moon's eyes widened at her pups' scent, and her ears pricked and trembled.

"Thorn . . ." she whispered. "Beetle."

Lucky gave her a reassuring nuzzle. "We're close to them. Come on," he said softly. "Every dog behind me. We'll approach the site in single file, so we disturb the grass as little as possible. We'll have your pups back in no time, Moon. I promise."

Hunching himself low, Lucky turned and slunk with cautious pawsteps toward the first gash of raw earth and a line of new-looking tall metal stakes. Storm fell in behind, feeling her heart begin to race with what seemed like unreasonable, tearing anxiety.

I know what it is, she realized abruptly. *I know why this feels even more terrible than it should. It reminds me of the day we set out to rescue Fiery. We were just this full of hope, just as confident we could rescue him and get him to safety.* Cold fear shuddered down her spine. *I hope we're luckier this time. . . .*

As they drew closer to the shiny metal poles, Storm could see

a net of crisscrossed wire between them; it was a complete barrier that blocked their way. But the trail of Beetle and Thorn didn't stop at the fence, so the searching dogs couldn't either.

"I saw a hole . . ." Storm told Lucky as she snuffled at the base of the wire. "Here."

Lucky came to her shoulder, and both dogs studied the turned earth. It was rawer and darker even than the paths of the great loudcages: The soil had been clawed out very recently. At the base of the fence, the wire was slightly twisted and warped, as if a sizable dog had squirmed beneath it.

"This is where they went through," murmured Lucky.

"Then so will we." At his shoulder, Moon looked tense and determined. Before Lucky could so much as growl a warning, the white-and-black Farm Dog had pushed past him and plunged into the hole. Her haunches wriggled briefly, and she emerged on the other side of the wire, shaking earth from her coat.

"All right," said Lucky softly. "Let's follow Moon."

One by one the rest of the party squeezed through the tight gap, shook off the loose mud, then paused to look around for dangers. Storm came last, following Breeze; she couldn't help flinching as she spotted a giant loudcage not a rabbit-chase away.

Every dog held their breath, but the massive yellow creature

was as still as death; no growl or breath came from it. Behind and beside it were others of its kind; every single one was motionless, lifeless.

"Don't let that fool you," growled Lucky. "They're not dead. And they wake up fast. Let's be very careful—just because we can't hear longpaws doesn't mean they're not close."

Storm's hide prickled beneath her fur as the dogs picked their way between the slumbering yellow beasts and the great piles of gravel and sand the longpaws had left. The stink of the longpaws was very strong and their traces were everywhere: paw prints, loudcage-tracks, great gouged holes that made astonishingly straight and level lines in the earth. Breeze stretched her neck to sniff at a pile of metal rods; she leaped back almost at once with a suppressed yelp of alarm.

"The stink of all this stuff," she growled in frustration. "What in the Earth-Dog's name is it all for? It's so hard to pick up Beetle and Thorn's trail."

"No, it isn't," whispered Storm, treading nervously closer to a loudcage. Her paws shook, but she had to get closer. There was something . . .

"Storm," Breeze murmured, "what are you doing? You shouldn't get too close to it."

"I think it's okay," Lucky told her. "Loudcages don't move if their longpaws don't make them."

"Weird . . ." Breeze sounded no more confident, but Storm ignored her. She got right up next to the loudcage.

"Yes!" she exclaimed, a rasp of fear in her throat. "Smell this loudcage's paws!"

The paws were huge, round, and black, softer than the loudcages' metal bodies, and they alone were taller than any of the dogs. Storm risked a glance up at the beast; it didn't stir, even when she touched her trembling nose to its paw. The stench of it was strong, mixed up with scents of earth and mud, but there was something else, unmistakable.

Beside Storm, Moon gave a low snarl, her hackles rising. "Beetle. He hasn't just touched this. *He marked it.*"

Storm's eyes widened. Moon was right. Sniffing again, she found Thorn's scent beneath her brother's.

Moon scampered to the next loudcage and put her nostrils to its giant feet. "And this one!" she growled. "They've marked all these loudcages, deliberately. Reckless young *fools!*"

Moon's voice was full of fear as well as fury. "When I find you two, you're in for the scolding of your lives!"

"Then let's find them, Moon, and get them out of here." Lucky

was calm and resolute, but there was an undercurrent of anger in his voice, too.

I may have been an idiot to keep it to myself, thought Storm. *But really—those two should have known much better than to come here at all, let alone mark it as their territory.*

Now that the search dogs had found the markings, the trail was easy to follow, in spite of the powerful longpaw scents that pervaded everything. They crept on through the site, sniffing at fences and piles of wood and upturned buckets, finding evidence of Beetle's and Thorn's markings everywhere they went. Although Moon was limping quite badly now, she was moving ahead of the others, her nose more certain of her pups' trail than any dog's.

Moon came to a standstill beneath yet another sleeping loudcage. She stared up at it, seeming unafraid, yet the whites showed around her blue eyes. Her shoulders trembled as the others joined her.

"The trail: It stops here," she growled. Her voice rose on a tide of panic till it was a frenzied yelp. "I can't smell anything but longpaws. *Where are my pups?*"

Every dog froze. "Moon, no!" growled Lucky. "We have to be quiet!"

But Moon could contain herself no longer. *"Where are they?!"*

For a horrible moment every dog stood rigid with fear, waiting for the trampling, rushing tread of longpaws. But there was nothing. Into the silence came a sound that made Storm's hackles rise; then she recognized it.

Barking. Desperate, muffled barking. *Beetle! Thorn!*

"This way!" exclaimed Storm, and bounded toward the sound with the others at her heels.

She skidded to a halt on a patch of drier, dusty earth. Before her was a squat, square longpaw den on wheels. As Storm hesitated, Moon lurched past her, then halted, eyeing the small den with fear.

"Beetle!" she barked. "Thorn!"

Another volley of familiar barks came from inside the den's metal walls. "We're here! In here!"

Moon gasped, terrified, as did Breeze beside her, but Lucky and Mickey bounded confidently up to the den. Lucky even rose onto his hind legs and placed his forepaws on the metal wall.

Of course, thought Storm, *he was a Lone Dog, and Mickey was a Leashed Dog. They might know just how to get inside this den.* Storm tilted her head, staring in perplexity at the weird hybrid thing. *No shining clear-stone eyes, like a loudcage has, but it definitely has loudcage-paws. Maybe its head has been chopped off by the longpaws. Why would they do that?*

But there was no time to think about why longpaws would need a headless loudcage. Moon seemed to know that, too; she crept up to the beast's belly, terror in her eyes. *She's thinking of Fiery*, realized Storm.

"Are you all right, pups?" she whined anxiously. "Have they hurt you?"

"We're fine, fine!" Thorn's voice was muffled by the walls, but her bark sounded strong. "The longpaws shut us in here, but they haven't harmed us yet!"

Moon closed her eyes, looking shaky with relief. But she quickly opened them again. "How will we get them out?" she muttered to Lucky.

Storm paced up and down, examining the walls of the den and sniffing at the metal. "We could try to break a hole in the wall? If we all ran at it together, we might get through."

Lucky shook his head. "No, that won't work, Storm. But I know what to do."

He padded to a hatch in the wall, one with straight sides; there was some kind of silver-colored stick attached to it. Every dog watched, dumbfounded, as Lucky reared up on his hind legs again, stretching high. He scrabbled with his paws at the jutting silver thing, finally catching it.

And he tugged.

It clicked down easily, rotating on its end. As if the Sky-Dogs had run at it from the inside, the hatch swung wide open sideways, banging against the wall.

Lucky jumped back, grinning, but Moon was already racing past him. Despite her injured paw, she sprang up into the den with a yelp of joy.

Storm caught a glimpse of what was inside: Beetle and Thorn, straining toward their Mother-Dog, but held by ropes around their necks. There was barely time to register this new problem, though. An earsplitting shriek tore the air, a terrible wailing sound that no dog could have made. Every dog flinched and froze in terror, crouching low to the ground, but the deafening noise didn't stop. On and on it went, an appalling howl that could scramble a dog's brain.

The headless loudcage was calling the longpaws!

CHAPTER SIXTEEN

I want to run. I need to run. It was all Storm could think through the screeching sound that was battering her skull. She shut her eyes tightly and clenched her jaws.

But I must not run!

She forced herself to stay in her place, digging her claws into the ground, every muscle rigid and taut. *I must not run! Beetle and Thorn are still tied up in there—they can't run!*

Through the shrieking wail, something else was in her ears, a reassuring sound. *Lucky's voice.*

"Don't be scared." He was barking now, calm but insistent. "That sound can't hurt you, and neither can the den-thing. It's calling for its longpaws, that's all. It's what they do when you disturb them. Don't panic."

Storm felt her heart begin to slow; she was able to think again,

though her brain still hammered with the ongoing, wailing racket. Breeze too seemed less terror-struck, and Mickey looked wide-eyed but steady.

"But it does mean the longpaws will come soon," Lucky went on. "We need to get Beetle and Thorn out of here, and fast!" He leaped up into the den hatch, vanishing inside just as Moon had.

It went against all Storm's instincts to follow him in there, but she fought against them. Tensing every muscle, clenching her jaw till it hurt, she crouched and sprang up into the belly of the beast.

It took a moment for her eyes to adjust to the dimness, but she quickly made out Beetle and Thorn. The two stood against the far wall, eagerly facing their rescuers, their tails quivering. Both dogs strained against the rope collars that fastened them to round metal hooks in the wall. Before them, on the ground, sat bowls of water and dry pieces of food that looked untouched. Moon stood by them, tugging helplessly on Thorn's rope with her teeth.

"Storm!" barked Beetle. "Lucky! You came!"

"Breeze and Mickey!" yelped Thorn with joy.

"We came, but we'll have to be quick," growled Lucky. "The longpaws are already on their way."

Thorn shook her head violently, snarling at the bite of the rope. "We tried to get loose, but these are too tight."

"I can't do anything," whined Moon. "They don't yield to teeth."

"And we can't break the ropes," added Beetle in frustration. "They're too strong."

"Backward," barked Lucky sharply.

Moon gave a snarl of belated realization. "Of course! Try that, my pups. You have to wriggle backward, like Lucky says." She fastened her teeth around the loop of rope on Beetle's neck. "Pull back now."

She lowered her hindquarters, straining hard with stiff forelegs as Beetle struggled and writhed. The rope slipped a little toward his jaw.

"Pull harder!" Moon demanded, urgency overcoming the fear in her voice.

Clenching his jaw, Beetle dragged his head backward, twisting and yanking. The rope moved slowly, jerkily, toward his ear. Moon gave a low growl and hauled harder on the collar, her paws slipping.

Lucky was already doing the same thing for Thorn, his teeth sunk into the rope collar as she strained backward. As Storm turned anxiously to watch him, she heard a thump and a clatter. When she spun back, Moon was spitting out the rope collar, and

Beetle was dancing in a circle, as well as he could in the small space. "You did it, Moon!"

Lucky was still fighting with the rope on Thorn's neck; Thorn's eyes were wide and white-rimmed as she wrenched herself backward, claws scrabbling. Nervously Storm twisted to peer out of the door. "We have to hurry!" she growled.

"What's in the bowls?" Mickey was sniffing at the dry food. "It smells good—didn't you want to eat?"

Moon shot him a look of disbelief; Storm raised her brows. Beetle gave a yelp of disgust. "We don't touch longpaw food!"

Thorn gasped and snarled as she struggled. "Longpaws—killed—poisoned our—Father-Dog!"

Mickey hesitated for a moment, then cocked an ear in the direction of the bowls. He gave them another sniff, then hunched his shoulders and began to wolf down the nuggets of food.

Thorn's rope snapped away, whipping her muzzle, and she staggered backward, shaking her head. At just that moment, through the hatch entrance, Storm saw two pairs of gleaming bright-white eyes, jolting across the ground toward them. They flooded the muddy ground with light.

"Longpaws! They're here!"

All of the dogs spun toward the entry hatch. Mickey gulped

down the last mouthful of food and growled. Then, at the same moment, they all sprang for the way out, bumping one another's flanks as they hurried to escape.

Storm emerged first from the chaos, her forepaws landing hard on the earth, and she bounded forward, leading the way toward the ragged hole in the fence. She could hear the pounding paws of the others as they ran behind her; *we're going to make it!*

Her ears twitched and swiveled as she ran. It was hard to count the pawsteps running behind her, but she didn't dare pause to glance over her shoulder. The glowing eyes of the loudcages were bumping and weaving toward them, but the fence was nearly in reach.

Then, horribly, she heard another sound: a hollow thud, and a yelp of distress.

Storm skidded to a halt, her claws sending up a shower of loose earth. All her companions were still behind her, slowing in confusion—

But not Breeze!

Storm turned and raced back between her comrades. She saw the dark pool of shadow in the ground almost immediately: a deep hole that she—and they—had only avoided by blind luck. Storm crept to its edge. Breeze was a slightly paler shadow in the

bottom of the pit, her eyes staring up at Storm in panic, the whites showing. The brown dog stood up on her hindpaws and scrabbled frantically at the earth walls.

"Help me! Storm, help!"

The rest of the party had turned back now and were gathered around Storm, yelping in dismay.

"Hold on, Breeze," Storm growled. "Don't panic. It's not too deep at all." *Just too deep for a dog Breeze's size to climb out . . .* "We'll help you!"

Taking a deep breath, trying not to think about the approaching loudcages and their increasing roar, Storm jumped down into the hole next to Breeze. She nuzzled the smaller dog's neck, trying to reassure her panicking friend.

"Keep calm. I'll push you up." Storm raised her head and barked to Lucky and Mickey, who were peering over the edge. "Be ready to pull her!"

The two dogs crouched at the edge of the drop. Storm lowered her head and pushed at Breeze's shaking hindquarters, shoving as hard as she could as Breeze clawed desperately at the sheer sides. Earth crumbled and Breeze whimpered, but gradually she was scrambling higher.

"The longpaws," came Thorn's whimper from beyond the edge of the hole. "They're nearly here!"

"Hurry, hurry!" yelped Beetle.

I will, thought Storm irritably, *if you'll all just shut up!* Gritting her teeth, she heaved again, harder, jolting Breeze up another few worm-lengths. Breeze's hindquarters were in her face, and her lashing tail almost blinded Storm.

Then, abruptly, her weight was lifted away. Lucky had the brown dog by the scruff of her neck and was hauling hard, with Mickey's help. Breeze was pulled up and away, and Storm heard her land with a soft thump on safe ground.

Panting, turning a full circle, Storm glanced around the hole. There was no room for a running start; she would just have to spring for it.

"Come on, Storm," barked Lucky. "I'll pull you up, too."

"Oh, *hurry!*" yelped Moon.

Crouching, coiling herself tightly, Storm clenched her jaws. When every muscle was bunched tight, she pushed away with her hindquarters and sprang toward safety.

Lucky bared his jaws and opened them, ready to catch her by the scruff, but his help wasn't necessary. She was clear of the hole

by a tail-length as she landed on all four paws.

"Thank you, Storm," panted Breeze, her sides heaving. "Thank you!"

"Never mind that now—let's *go!*" Storm bounded toward the fence but stood back as the others dived for the hole and scrabbled through. Moon was last, after her rescued pups, except for Lucky. He waited, nodding impatiently at Storm.

"Go on, Storm! As Beta, I should take the rear."

There were barks from the longpaws now, and the screeching noise of loudcages drawing to a halt. As pounding longpaw feet ran toward the fence, Storm twisted and shoved herself through the hole in the wire.

When she emerged on the other side she turned, looking desperately for Lucky, but he was already halfway through the gap. He hauled himself out, barking, *"Run!"*

The longpaws were running now, too, but they were on the other side of the fence and they carried no loudsticks. Dizzy with relief, Storm spun and raced at her Beta's flank, back toward the safety of their camp.

CHAPTER SEVENTEEN

The pale golden, early light of the Sun-Dog glowed between the pine trunks as the dogs crashed through the undergrowth and back into the clearing. Panting, they all came to a halt as they blinked at Alpha. She was standing on all four paws, worry still etched on her face as her pups gamboled between her slender legs. Watching her eyes, Storm could tell she was counting the members of the rescue party, over and over again. At last Alpha nodded, her expression one of satisfaction and deep relief, and all her muscles seemed to relax. She sat back on her haunches.

"You did it," she said quietly. "Well done, all of you. And welcome back, Thorn and Beetle." Her greeting to the two wanderers was tinged with the promise, Storm thought, of further stern words to come later. But for now, their Alpha was clearly too happy to have her Pack back together—whole; no dog lost.

The rest of the Pack was gathering, yelping with delight. "What happened?" asked Daisy.

"Where did you find them?" yapped Sunshine. "Oh, it's so good to have you *all* back!"

It was Moon who stepped forward, her stiff tail quivering, her eyes flashing with anger. "My pups—*my offspring*—decided it would be a clever idea to go to the place where the longpaws are building. They thought it showed intelligence to go and mess up that place, as some kind of ridiculous revenge." The growl in her voice grew louder, more threatening. "And they did all this *after I had told them* to stay away from there—to stay away from *all* long-paws. And I apologize to the whole Pack on behalf of my stupid, irresponsible litter!"

The Pack stood silent, shuffling and blinking in shock and slight embarrassment. It was so unlike Moon to criticize her pups, thought Storm—especially with such savage words. *She must be really furious. It's clear they terrified her with this escapade of theirs.*

"Moon! That's not fair!" protested Beetle. "All we wanted to do was make the longpaws leave! We thought if we made a mess at their building-place, they'd go away!"

"And we deserve revenge," barked Thorn grumpily. "The longpaws killed our Father-Dog and they should pay."

"That is exactly my point, you foolish pups!" Moon turned on the pair of them. "They killed your Father-Dog, the strongest, smartest, *best* dog I ever knew. Fiery was the most powerful fighter our Pack ever had. What did you two think *you* could achieve? What was the point of putting yourselves in such needless danger? You're still young! You don't have the strength your Father-Dog had—and you're certainly not as smart, judging by your antics today!"

Thorn and Beetle stared moodily at the ground, their tails clamped to their haunches, their ears drooping. There was sullen resentment in their posture, but it was clear they were cowed by their Mother-Dog's words.

They know what they did was wrong, Storm thought. *They may not ever admit it, but Moon's made it pretty clear how stupid and reckless they've been. They know.*

"Tell me exactly what happened," said Alpha, her voice level. She seemed to have decided that for the moment at least, no more scolding was needed from her, after the tongue-lashing the two had had from Moon.

"We just wanted to mess things up a bit," mumbled Beetle. "But two longpaws caught us. They grabbed Thorn, and I was furious and I went to help her—but they were cunning and

strong and they grabbed me too."

"That was always going to happen," snapped Moon.

Thorn tucked her ears back, looking ashamed. "And they tied us up, with rope around our necks so we couldn't get away."

There were gasps from the Pack, especially from the dogs who had never been Leashed in their lives. "Tied you up?" barked Snap in horror.

"Lucky knew what to do," said Mickey, nodding respectfully at his Beta.

"It wasn't hard, once we knew where Beetle and Thorn were." Lucky paced forward. "It was the kind of den I knew how to open. And ropes can be wriggled out of, if a dog has help and can keep its nerve. The worst part was getting away from there, once the den sounded the alarm and the longpaws came running."

"Yes." Breeze nodded vigorously. "That was frightening. I fell into a hole while I was running, and Storm had to get me out." She wagged her tail gratefully at Storm.

Gradually the muttering and the shocked explanations died away, as Alpha remained silent. At last she stepped forward, waving her tail slowly and thoughtfully. Her face was stern.

"I agree with Moon," she told them all. She shot Beetle and Thorn a disapproving glance. "These two pups of hers ran

willingly into a perilous situation, and by doing so they put the whole Pack in danger. And that danger has not gone away; what if the longpaws come looking for them now?"

That did not seem to have occurred to Beetle and Thorn. They exchanged a look of dawning horror, and their heads hung low.

There was movement at Alpha's paws; the pups had abandoned their halfhearted game, clearly sensing the seriousness of the adult dogs around them. Storm could see Tiny, cowering behind her Mother-Dog's legs, her eyes huge. The pups surely did not understand the gravity of the Pack's situation, but she could tell they knew that the older dogs were on edge—nervous.

It would be so tough on all the pups if we have to leave this camp now, she thought. *And it would be especially hard on Tiny. She's the most vulnerable of the four of them. . . . And they'd be even more vulnerable if we didn't have a camp. . . .*

Alpha's loud bark broke into her thoughts. She glared at Thorn and Beetle. "You two were irresponsible and stupid to go to the longpaw place."

Neither of the litter-siblings said a word, but they crouched low, clearly knowing that their only choice was humble submission.

"What's more," Alpha went on, "it was equally irresponsible and stupid for Storm and Mickey to conceal what they knew about your no-sun jaunts. All four of you will be punished."

Again, thought Storm, gloomily and rather resentfully. *Always, I get punished. When I'm just trying to do the right thing . . .*

Alpha was still talking in that severe, disapproving voice; Storm wished that she would just get on with the punishment. "Mickey and Beetle will take High Watch together. When their watch is finished, Storm and Thorn can take over. You can all use the time to reflect on how irresponsible you are. And maybe, if you have older dogs close by, you won't be so eager to run off and put the whole Pack at risk!"

The earth between her claws was raw and moist . . . the stench of loudcages clung to her nose like a vicious claw. All around her was darkness, except for where those strange longpaw-lights shone down in pools of glaring whiteness. Strips of metal, pale planks of freshly cut wood, and shining longpaw tools lay all around, in heaps and stacks; she flinched away from them in fear. And there, right in her line of vision, was the metal den on wheels where Beetle and Thorn had been caged. It looked bigger and more intimidating than it had before, and the longpaw-lights bathed it in a sinister white glow.

How can I be back at the longpaw camp? *Storm wondered.* Oh,

Sky-Dogs, Alpha will be so furious with me. . . .

With shaking paws, she trod toward the light of the den, feeling herself slip in the damp, turned mud. The hatch was there in the wall, with its silver lever; as Storm stared at it, she could hear the barks of the dogs imprisoned within. But they didn't sound like Beetle and Thorn; the yelps were high-pitched and terrified, the squeaking cries of tiny helpless creatures. . . .

It's the pups! They've been captured!

Storm lunged for the hatch, scrabbling at the lever. But the trick that had worked instantly for Lucky proved impossible for her. The silver thing slipped from beneath her paws, or stuck fast, however hard she tried to grab and turn it. Her teeth slid off its surface, making her stumble and bang her skull against the metal side of the den. Once again she scratched wildly at the lever with her claws, but it would not turn. She bit down on it, pulling with her jaws—but succeeded only in tearing out her own teeth.

It's no good. I can't open it. I can't help the pups!

There was a roaring sound behind her. Wild-eyed, Storm turned to see the glaring eyes of the longpaws' loudcages, bumping across the ground toward her. It's too late!

Then she realized the loudcages weren't bumping at all. They were flying across the ground, faster and faster. She'd never seen loudcages move so swiftly. They raced toward her as if they had wings. . . .

And then she saw. They were not loudcages at all; there was only one pair of

glowing eyes, and those belonged to a dog. A great, black, terrifying creature that thundered toward her and the imprisoned pups. It was almost upon her, a hulking beast made of shadow and terror.

The Fear-Dog.

Storm could not move, could not bark. She was as powerless as the pups that she could not save. Frozen, helpless, she watched the Fear-Dog loom over her, its jaws falling open to reveal deadly fangs and an endless, gaping throat. . . .

She woke, shuddering, her racing heart pumping blood through her veins that felt like ice water.

The Fear-Dog.

The longpaw site.

And one of them, at least, was real.

Staggering to her paws, Storm stared around her. Against a gray sky, pale at the horizon with the promise of the waking Sun-Dog, she saw the walls and trenches and loudcages of the longpaws' building-place. Storm swallowed hard, suppressing a whine.

I walked in my sleep again. And this place is wide awake!

The longpaw site was a chaos of activity. The giant yellow loudcages growled and rumbled and screeched, digging deep grooves in the earth, or shoving piles of mud and stones. Longpaws barked

and yelled to one another, and hammered metal spikes with great clubs of iron. Even more of those huge square pits had been dug in the earth; vast piles of excavated soil dotted the ground like small, newborn mountains. Turning, Storm saw more loudcages approaching from her own side of the wire fence; they looked purposeful and determined, grumbling and growling toward the site.

Alpha was right. More longpaws are coming! They want this place for themselves, and they'll keep it no matter what we do. How could Beetle and Thorn ever have believed they could stop them?

A loudcage roared to life, barely a rabbit-chase from her flank, and Storm leaped into the air in fright. She had been too disoriented to notice it lying there in wait, and now it was attacking her!

Camp! I have to get back to the camp! Spinning, she fled, but the ground was uneven and her head was still dizzy, and she stumbled. She had barely gotten back to her paws when the loudcage was upon her.

With a bark of pure terror, she tried to leap to freedom and safety, but there was no escape. Storm felt herself engulfed by a great metal maw. She slithered back, whining with terror.

Metal bars were in front of her, and at both her flanks. Something thudded onto her back and she struggled wildly. *No! This can't be happening!* The growling of the hungry loudcage filled her ears,

throbbed inside her head. *It's eating me!*

From somewhere in her addled, terror-stricken brain, a memory came to her. Moon's urgent voice, barking an instruction to help free Beetle and Thorn: *You have to wriggle backward!*

Would it work for a ravenous loudcage the way it did for a rope? *I have to try!*

Desperately she struggled and writhed backward, claws raking the base of the cage, haunches straining. She flattened herself as the cage constricted around her. She kicked back, fighting it, shoving herself with her forepaws now. Her hindclaws found purchase on a hard edge, and she gave a final massive wrench of her muscles, scraping her spine against metal.

She was flung backward into free space and crashed to the earth with an ungainly thump, showering herself in loose soil. *I'm out!*

There was no time to glory in her escape. Rolling over, scrambling upright, she sprang past a barking longpaw, dodged another that lunged for her, then bolted for the forest and for freedom.

CHAPTER EIGHTEEN

The Sun-Dog was a low, golden dazzle between the trees as Storm dragged her aching paws into the camp. She let herself feel a shiver of relief at being home and safe and unseen; the feeling lasted until a stern voice growled her name.

Storm's heart plummeted. *Lucky.*

He stood on the grass of the clearing, watching her, and he did not look happy. His ears were low, his tail still, and his eyes were dark and displeased.

"Beta." She decided the respect of formality was her best option.

"Where have you been?" When she didn't answer, he stalked forward, studying her from nose to tailtip. "What do you think you're up to, wandering about during no-sun when you're not on patrol? Do you have any idea how bad this looks for you?"

Despite her exhaustion, Storm felt her hackles bristle. "I don't

care how it *looks*. I went to the longpaw site. And there are *lots* more longpaws around than before."

"*What?*" Lucky's eyes widened. "You deliberately went to the longpaw place again?"

"No," Storm murmured. "Well, not exactly. I—"

She had no time to think of a way to explain it; Lucky's yelp of disbelief had woken some of the other Pack members, and they were crawling from their dens, shaking themselves, yapping and growling to one another in confusion.

"What's going on?" Snap blinked. "Did I hear right?"

Daisy shook herself as if she was trying to rid herself of sleepiness. "Storm went back to the longpaw place?"

"Wait, no! I—I didn't disobey orders or anything." Storm glanced guiltily around at her Packmates. "It wasn't delib— I mean, I didn't plan to—" She swallowed hard. "Look, it doesn't matter why I went there! What matters is that there are *lots* more longpaws now! Everything we worried about, everything we feared—it's happening!"

They all stared at her, but not as if they were interested in heeding her warning. There was disbelief in their eyes, and shock, and more than a little disapproval. In the middle of the awkward

silence, Alpha stalked from her den and came to a halt in front of Storm.

"What do I have to do, Storm?" she growled. "What do I have to say to you to get you to stay in line? You are a Pack Dog! And Pack Dogs respect Pack orders!"

"But, Alpha—"

"Quiet!" Alpha's lip curled back from her teeth. "You are walking on very thin ice. And you have not heard the end of this, Storm—Beta, Third Dog, and I will be discussing your attitude. In the meantime, make yourself useful. Get up to High Watch and relieve Mickey and Beetle, *as you've been ordered.*"

Storm's tail and ears drooped, and she stared at the ground, torn between shame, embarrassment, and pure, hot rage. *I should explain. Maybe now is the time to tell them all about my sleepwalking. How else can I convince them that I didn't mean to do this?*

But what would I say? That I wander around during no-sun, while I'm fast asleep, with no idea of where I'm going and what I'm up to? That will only make things much worse.

Defeated, miserable, and resentful, she turned without another word and plodded out of the glade and onto the path that led to High Watch. She heard another dog run to her side and knew

from her scent that it was her fellow sentry, Thorn, but she didn't turn to look at her.

She heard the bark that followed Thorn, though. It was Moon, calling a warning to her daughter:

"Be *careful*, Thorn. Keep your eyes and your nose open!"

Storm's breath caught in her throat, and her heart turned over. Even after all that had happened since she'd gotten back to camp, she still felt hurt. Moon didn't warn them *both* to be careful—she was telling Thorn to be wary of one threat only: Storm herself.

I saved Thorn, thought Storm, as grief and loneliness settled in her belly like a stone. *Not only that, I saved Alpha's pups—I saved the whole future of this Pack.*

And they still don't trust me.

"I don't understand why *you* would go back to the longpaws' place," Thorn was saying as she walked at Storm's side. "After Beetle and I got into such trouble? It was *our* idea to go and threaten the long-paws, and we got the tongue-whipping from Alpha, and then *you* think it's a good idea to go and do the same?"

Storm said nothing; she was too busy trying to control her temper.

"And you did it *right afterward!* It's not like you have a bigger

right to go there than me and Beetle. It was *our* Father-Dog the longpaws killed. What were you thinking?"

I am going to turn around and bite her in a moment, thought Storm grimly. *Yet that's the one thing I absolutely can't do.* She clamped her jaws together tightly and stalked on up the cliff path, every sinew taut and trembling with the strain of keeping control.

"*We're* the ones who should be attacking them, not you!" Thorn's petulant voice was like a buzzing mosquito in her ears; Storm would have loved to swat her off the cliff with a paw. "The longpaws aren't *your* problem, and now you've made Alpha even angrier, and it will be even harder for us to get revenge for our Father-Dog."

Even through the heat of her anger, Storm realized one thing very clearly: All of Alpha's scolding, all the punishment she'd inflicted on Beetle and Thorn, was for nothing. Thorn was plainly still determined to do something about the longpaws, and that must mean Beetle was too. They hadn't been warned off at all. *Those two aren't even a little bit grateful that I helped rescue them,* thought Storm angrily and with a horrible undercurrent of dread. *They just see me as some dog who thwarted their plans. They're idiots, both of them!*

Thorn still hadn't shut up by the time they reached High Watch and settled down to keep guard. *I'd have thought ignoring her*

would put her off, but she's too fanatical about the whole longpaw problem, Storm realized with a roll of her eyes.

"You watch the Endless Lake," she snapped at last, when Thorn paused for breath. "I'll keep watch on the land side."

With Thorn's complaints still battering her ears, Storm tried to turn away and stare determinedly inland. It was hard to ignore the nagging, but she could try.

The trouble was, if she'd wanted to take her mind off things, Storm had chosen the wrong direction. Far below, the longpaws' building-place was bustling with activity. The fence had been opened at one side, and a stream of small loudcages poured in, while the much bigger, noisier yellow loudcages plowed and grooved the earth inside. The longpaws on foot looked like a swarm of insects; they wore yellow fur, and even brighter yellow coverings on their heads. It all reminded Storm of the relentless busyness of bees around a hive. Even at this distance she could hear their purposeful barks.

They know exactly what they want and what they're doing, thought Storm. *I wish I did. It's so vital to the Pack and our future that we find out what these longpaws are up to.*

Why couldn't Lucky have listened? Storm lay down, her head on her paws, and sighed deeply as she watched the site. *He used to*

listen to me. He used to trust my instincts. He used to trust me. *And all that wasn't so long ago. What happened?*

She was ignoring Thorn's muttering, to the point where it was as incomprehensible as the distant barking of the longpaws. It was an apparently endless whine about *Beetle and me* and *Father-Dog* and *longpaws* and *vengeance* and *it's not fair.*

"How was that supposed to help any dog? 'Ooh, we're all in terrible danger.'" Thorn's voice was high and indignant, scraping on the inside of Storm's skull. "Were you *trying* to sound like you were making threats?"

Storm didn't even know what happened then, only that the last thin rope that was holding her fury in place snapped. She was suddenly up on all four paws, her sluggish misery shattered, snarling viciously into Thorn's face.

"What's that? How was I helping? You mean, how dare I care about the Pack? How dare I try to keep every dog safe? You tell me, Thorn. *You tell me.* Tell me about the last time I hurt any dog in our Pack! When was it? *When did I hurt any of the Pack Dogs?*"

Thorn wasn't answering. Through the red mist of her rage, Storm became aware that Thorn was cowering, quivering, her wide eyes locked on Storm's and filled with terror. She lay flat, crouched tight against the ground; Storm herself was standing

over her, forepaws splayed on either side of her head. Something dripped onto Thorn's petrified face; Storm realized it was slaver from her own snarling jaws.

What am I doing?!

Blinking, Storm drew back—though for all the will of the Forest-Dog, she could not uncurl her muzzle. Her eyes stayed locked on Thorn as the smaller dog shivered, crept a little closer, then rolled to show her belly. Thorn's tongue hung sideways from her dry mouth, and the whites were visible all around her dark eyes as she whimpered, "I'm sorry. Sorry, Storm."

"No." Storm licked her jaws, forcing herself to cover her fangs. "No, *I'm* sorry. I wasn't attacking you, Thorn."

"I—I know, Storm." Thorn's voice trembled as she rolled back onto her belly and crawled clear. "It's fine. No offense taken. Sorry." Her eyes did not once leave Storm.

"I didn't mean to scare you—"

"No! No, I know! It's all right. I went too far. I'm sorry." Thorn was gabbling now as she sat up, her tail tucked tightly around her haunches. *"Sorry."*

And even as she wriggled around to face the Endless Lake once more, Thorn was *still* eyeing Storm sidelong, her expression full of nervous fear.

Storm shook herself. *I must not lose control like that! I must not. . . .*

She sat on her haunches, staring down at the building-place, but she could hardly focus enough to take in the longpaws' movements anymore. Her heart felt heavy in her rib cage.

How did that happen? How could I let myself do that?

She could not shake the image of Thorn's terrified eyes; they were burned into her vision. And she was haunted by the memory of such a tough, stubborn, stupidly courageous dog, lying trembling and submissive at her paws. *And all I had to do was growl at her.*

I would never have bitten her. Surely she knew that? Yes, I was angry and I lost my temper and I barked, but I wasn't going to bite!

But would the Pack ever believe that?

The thought hit her like that cage had done, slamming down onto her back. It was a horrible weight of misery and frustration and despair. *It doesn't matter what I do, and it doesn't matter how often I help the Pack or save any dogs. They are always watching me from the corner of their eyes, just the way Thorn did just now.*

They think there's a vicious monster inside me, just waiting to break out. They think it's only a matter of time.

And they will never, ever trust me. . . .

CHAPTER NINETEEN

It was even more of a relief than usual when Storm's time at High Watch came to an end for the day. She trudged ahead of her companion down the cliff path, and Thorn made no attempt to catch up. The black-and-white dog had an air of utter dejection, and not a word had passed between her and Storm since their argument.

Something prey-sized rustled in the dry grass to Storm's flank, but she had neither the energy nor the enthusiasm to lunge for it. Instead, she plodded on down the cliff, thinking hard. *At least I have some peace to gnaw over things in my head. And at least I finally put an end to Thorn's stupid ranting. I guess there are some advantages to being a scary Fierce Dog.*

One by one, and only to herself, Storm counted off her list of suspects. She'd been thinking some more about the dogs who had already left the Pack. Chase had managed to visit her old friends

quite easily in a single no-sun; she hadn't had to travel all that far. And that meant that, in turn, Rake, Ruff, Woody, and Dart were close enough to sabotage the camp and attack their former Pack-mates, if they wanted to.

Woody is quite a big dog, she remembered, *and he was always wild. He's a survivor, and pretty ferocious. Could he have sneaked back here and killed Bruno?*

I can't think of any reason Woody would have to attack the Pack, but then I never knew him very well. And I have to bear in mind—the fox said that it was a small *dog who killed Bruno.*

But that's so hard to believe! And even if that fox had a reasonable idea of the different sizes of dogs, can I trust what she says? Every dog knows foxes can't be trusted, and they've certainly harmed our Pack before.

One thing was for sure: Storm had reached the limit of what she could work out by herself. She would never solve the mystery if she didn't actively look for more information, more clues. *I need to talk to the dogs who knew the other dogs, the ones who left. That's the only way I'll ever get anywhere.*

By the time she reached the camp, a morose Thorn still trailing a rabbit-chase behind her, Storm knew what she had to do. *I could talk to Chase*—she shivered at the thought of trying—*but I doubt very much Chase would want to talk to me. It's not as if she'd give me any useful*

information about the defectors. She's their friend. No; I can't find out more about the dogs who left the Pack without asking Breeze.

Luckily Breeze was easy to find; she was sprawled in the middle of the glade, soaking up the late-afternoon rays of the Sun-Dog. Storm padded over to her, grateful to be able to slump down on the grass and relax. Breeze raised her head and gave a small *woof* of greeting. For a moment Storm basked happily in the warmth, rolling onto her back and forgetting her troubles; but it couldn't be more than a moment. Sighing, she rolled back onto her belly and touched her nose to Breeze's neck.

"Breeze, can I ask you a question?"

Breeze looked amused as she opened one eye and gazed fondly at Storm. "You have a lot of questions, Storm. But of course I don't mind. Go ahead!"

"This is going to sound like I can't let go of a bone, but . . ." Storm hesitated, licking her jaws. "What did Woody think of being in this Pack?"

Breeze pricked up her ears in surprise. "Woody?"

"Yes. I mean, there were many dogs who seemed to just go along with the two Packs merging. It wasn't their actual *decision*, but I guess they just accepted it at the time. I never really heard Woody's opinion."

"Well." Breeze tilted her head, thinking. "He was fine with it to begin with, obviously. I don't think any dog would have joined the united Pack if they *hadn't* been. But then, he wasn't all right with it by the end. If he had been, he wouldn't have left, would he?" Breeze raised her brows at Storm, rather as if she thought the answer was too obvious for words.

Storm felt rather silly now, but she knew she had to press on. "Did he—did Woody get along all right with Whisper?"

Breeze looked even more astonished, if that was possible. "Why do you want to know that?"

Storm sighed, and closed her eyes briefly. "I don't know, it just seems to me that the bad dog doesn't *have* to be one who's still in the Pack. It might be one of the dogs who left. What do you think, Breeze? The night of Bruno's death, rain was pouring down. An outsider could easily have slipped into the camp and back out, and even if they'd left a trace, it would have been washed away in no time. Don't you think so?"

Breeze's lower jaw fell. "Why in the name of the Earth-Dog are you asking me, Storm?" Her voice was rising with her obvious shock. "How would I know how a dog would get in and out of camp unnoticed? I wouldn't have the first clue!"

Storm winced. She rather wished she hadn't asked. No wonder

Breeze sounded offended—she'd obviously had no clue why Storm would quiz her about Woody in the first place, and then to ask her how a dog might sneak in and out? *I should have stopped talking, about two questions ago. . . .*

But she did wish that Breeze would keep her voice down. Other dogs were turning their heads now, swiveling their ears toward Storm and Breeze. "Breeze, can you talk more quietly?" said Storm.

"Oh! I'm sorry." Breeze looked embarrassed. She dropped her voice. "Sorry, Storm. Look, I know you're finding it really hard at the moment. You seem to be on the wrong end of a lot of suspicion from the others, and that must be horrible for you. I know you want to find out who's responsible for all these awful things, but . . . but, Storm, can't you leave it alone for a bit?"

"I just can't do that," growled Storm in frustration. "It's so difficult, being with the Pack all day, and always watching, always wondering . . . never knowing which of these dogs is a traitor. I can hardly sleep at night."

Breeze was very quiet for a moment, gazing intently at a patch of grass. She scraped her claw across it, then raised her head and looked Storm full in the eyes.

"Storm," she said quietly, "maybe that's the answer. Maybe

being with the Pack, day in and day out, is just too hard for you."

"What?" Storm blinked.

"You can't let it go," Breeze went on, her voice urgent and sympathetic. "You're not getting a moment's peace while you're surrounded by the Pack, while any dog might be the culprit. And in the meantime, every dog seems to suspect *you*."

Storm licked her chops. "What are you saying?"

"I'm saying, maybe you should give things a chance to calm down. Give yourself a chance, too." Breeze's soft voice lowered still further. "You need to take a break from all this viciousness. Perhaps it's best if you leave the Pack for a while."

Storm started, her ears shooting up. Her heart beat hard in shock—yet somewhere deep down in her gut, she realized this was not a new idea to her. *Maybe I've been thinking this. Maybe I've been considering it for a long time, and I just didn't know.*

Maybe I've been denying it to myself. . . .

"Storm, *listen to me*." Gently Breeze touched Storm's nose with her own. "Let things die down. *Prove* it isn't you. If you're not here and—and Sky-Dogs forbid, something else happens—it will prove beyond doubt that you're not the guilty dog. Then they won't just welcome you back—they'll *beg* for you to come back. . . . They'll look to you to protect them. You'll be a hero to the whole Pack, Storm."

"I don't know, I . . ." The image Breeze presented had its attractions, she had to admit. *They'd beg for me to come back and protect them, would they . . . ?*

"I think you need to do this, Storm." Breeze nuzzled her unhappily. "I'd miss you so much—more than you know—but I honestly think it's the only way. And I'm saying this out of friendship. I don't *want* you to go, but I think you *have* to."

"I would miss the Pack." Storm's voice was huskier than she'd expected; she realized she could hardly get the words out. "I'll be lonely without all of you." And with those words, she realized with shock that she'd already moved on from *I would* to *I will*.

"I think every dog will miss you too," said Breeze, with a sudden anger in her eyes. "I think they will realize very quickly just how much they depend on you. How much you do, every day, for this Pack."

"Thank you, Breeze," croaked Storm. "That means a lot."

"And let's face it," Breeze said, nudging her gently. "When the supply of rabbits dries up, they'll soon understand what they're missing." She raised her voice again, quite deliberately. "You're the best hunter in the Pack, Storm, and every dog knows it."

Storm felt another twinge of embarrassment—*will Breeze never learn to talk quietly?*—but at the same time, she couldn't help

feeling grateful and a little pleased. *She wants every dog to know what she thinks—that I'm a worthy member of this Pack. And I've no doubt she wants them to feel bad if I'm not around. . . .*

When *I'm not around . . .*

It felt good to have some dog on her side, even though it was almost too late. Storm had forgotten again how good that felt. And even if Breeze was only trying to cheer her up, she'd known exactly how to do it.

The smaller brown dog leaped suddenly to her paws, letting her tongue loll and bowing her shoulders in an invitation to play. "Come on, then, Storm. Catch me if you can!"

With a yip of delight, Storm sprang after her. Breeze dodged and rolled, nipping Storm's tail playfully. Storm doubled back and pounced, but let Breeze wriggle free again and dash in a circle.

It's only for a moment, but this is fun. Storm felt her worries slip away as she played and romped with Breeze in the glade. They were still waiting for her, all her horrible fears and anxieties—she could almost see them, like dark shadows waiting at the edge of the camp—but just for a little while, she could ignore them. Barking with excitement, Storm leaped for Breeze, and the two dogs tumbled over and over, wriggling and yapping and play-biting. Once more, Storm drew back to let Breeze slither out from between her

forepaws and race away in a teasing circle.

I can't remember the last time I just played . . .

Breeze was pausing, wagging her tail in a taunting, tempting gesture, her head tilted as she grinned. Storm gave a mischievous bark and sprang for her.

Her forepaws thumped onto Breeze's back, and again the two of them crashed down in a heap. The brown dog was helpless beneath her paws—hah! Standing over her, Storm took Breeze's ear softly in her mouth and worried it. Her paws slipped on the grass and she planted one firmly on Breeze's leg for balance.

It was only when Snap barked, "Stop, Storm!" that she became aware something had changed. Blinking, she let go of Breeze's ear. Breeze's yelps weren't playful anymore. . . .

She was barking in pain.

Storm leaped away from her, horrified, and Breeze scrambled awkwardly to her paws. Storm took a cautious pace forward and nuzzled her friend.

"Are you all right?"

"I'm fine, I'm fine!" Breeze was breathless and her voice was a little shaky. She glanced around, looking embarrassed, at the Pack members who had rushed over when they heard her yelps. "I'm all right, for Earth-Dog's sake. Storm was only playing."

"What happened?" asked Mickey anxiously.

"Absolutely *nothing*," said Breeze firmly. "It was a game, and Storm landed a bit hard on my paw, that's all. There's nothing to worry about." She took a step toward Storm, as if in solidarity, but winced as she put down her paw.

"Breeze, you *are* hurt! I'm sorry." Storm licked her nose remorsefully.

"Oh, Sky-Dogs, don't worry! There's no need to apologize." Breeze sat down close to her. "It's my own fault. You're a big dog, and you don't know your own strength."

The Pack began to disperse, muttering and growling among themselves. Snap and Chase shot disapproving looks at Storm; Mickey shook his head a little sadly. Trying to ignore them, Storm lay down, head on her paws, and watched Breeze as she began to lick carefully at her hurt paw.

It was an accident. Breeze knows that, and she doesn't blame me.

But the Pack . . . I know how they'll see it. How they saw it. They've already made up their minds what happened: The Fierce Dog lost control. Again.

Storm gave a huge, miserable sigh.

And if I can hurt Breeze without even trying, without even knowing I was hurting her . . .

Maybe they're right.

* * *

She was running, running hard. It had never been more important to race as if Lightning himself were chasing her. Her paws pounded, her heart thrashed, her chest ached with the effort. But she had to run faster, and faster, bolting through the utter darkness.

She had to reach her quarry in time! He was ahead, just barely ahead. . . .

The Fear-Dog. The shadowy, menacing Spirit Dog flew before her, huge and terrifying. But why was he running away from her? Why should he flee? Why didn't he just turn, and snarl, and gulp her down his ravenous throat?

And suddenly Storm knew.

She knew why she was chasing the Fear-Dog. Gripped in those dark jaws, whimpering and mewling, was a golden pup.

It was Tumble—small, helpless, and vulnerable. And the Fear-Dog was carrying him away.

Straining every muscle and sinew, Storm sprinted after the horrific shadow. His giant haunches were always at the limit of her vision, dashing between the trees, and however fast she ran, she could not catch up. The Fear-Dog was silent, but she could hear Tumble's desperate, terrified cries. The Fear-Dog halted, turning to stare mockingly at Storm; Lucky and Alpha's pup dangled from his jaws.

"Help me, Storm," Tumble yelped. "Save me!"

Still she could not reach him. The Fear-Dog turned his rump on her once more, contemptuous, and bounded on.

Storm's breath burned in her throat and chest. She flew through the trees and burst out suddenly onto the beach that fringed the Endless Lake. Ahead of her the Fear-Dog raced; its massive paws left no marks in the sand, while Storm's sank and slithered on the shifting ground. The Fear-Dog and its terrified captive were drawing farther away! They were heading straight for the thundering white waves. Storm gave a desperate, wailing howl with her remaining breath.

The Fear-Dog was going to drown Tumble!

Storm's eyes snapped open and she gasped in a lungful of air. But with the air came cold, salty water, and she coughed and staggered to her paws. She sneezed, blinking in shock, and looked down. Her paws were submerged in the foaming waves of the Endless Lake.

No!

Snorting again, shaking her head and then her entire body, Storm snuffed at the bitter, salty air. She bounded onto dry sand. There was a scent she was half expecting, though she had thought it was only a dream. She sniffed again, to be sure, and her heart turned over in her chest.

Tumble. Tumble has been here!

She spun on her paws, tail stiff, her nostrils flaring wide and her eyes searching all around. There was no sign of the pup in

the dim predawn light, though she was certain now that she had smelled him. *Yes, Tumble was here. But he isn't anymore. . . .*

Terrified, she turned again, staring out at the crashing waves of the lake. It could have swallowed him without a trace. *I would never know!*

Her eyes ached from scanning the bright surface in search of Tumble's golden coat, but she could see nothing. *Not that that means anything. The Endless Lake could eat a pup whole and barely even notice.*

Has Tumble gone in there? Has he drowned?

With a howl of frantic terror, Storm spun and raced back up the beach, heading for the Pack, terrible thoughts tussling in her mind. She'd dreamed about the pups in danger from the Fear-Dog before—but then she'd gone to the longpaw place, and there had been no scent of them, they had all been safe with the Pack. . . .

Whisper warned me that there would be a death in my dreams, and that came true.

What if she'd ignored her Fear-Dog dreams, but they were warnings too? What if something terrible had happened, because of her?

Where is Tumble?

CHAPTER TWENTY

Storm barely paused for breath as she leaped the thorny scrub at the edge of the camp, not bothering to find the easier entrance. Barks and howls rang in her ears; the Pack was already awake, and they knew something was wrong. Their voices collided, rising and falling, echoing into the forest till Storm couldn't tell which dog was barking.

"Where's Tumble?"

"TUMBLE! Tumble, where are you?"

"Has any dog seen Storm? She's missing, too!"

Lucky's panicked voice rose above the uproar. "Tumble! Tumble, my pup, answer me! Please!" He buried his nose in a tussock of grass, then abandoned it to race across to an old stump. *"Tumble!"*

As Storm burst out of the trees, every dog spun around, startled, and the volley of barks that met her felt like an incoming

wave of the lake. Mickey and Snap dashed toward her, Chase in hot pursuit.

"Storm, where have you been?" yelped Mickey.

"What have you been doing?" barked Snap. "Tumble is missing!"

Daisy bolted between the two bigger dogs, her eyes pleading. "Storm, do you know where Tumble is? Have you seen him?" Behind her, Sunshine was yelping, too, but her cries were too full of distress to make any sense. Breeze, too, was howling incomprehensibly.

Alpha, though, was not howling or whining. She was silent, her face drawn with worry, but she stalked through the throng of dogs toward Storm with her teeth bared.

She was right in Storm's face when she stopped and barked, *"Where have you been? Where is my pup?"* Her dark eyes blazed. "You must have something to do with this, Storm! Where is Tumble?"

Storm felt a wrench of hurt, deep inside her chest. She opened her jaws to deny all knowledge, but the words would not come.

Maybe she's right. I did dream of Tumble. And I sleepwalked. I was at the Endless Lake.

And Tumble. He was there too, though I didn't see him.

Storm's heart turned over. *Did something happen to him while I was sleepwalking? Or . . . could the Fear-Dog really have taken him?*

"I was . . ." Her voice caught, as if there were a thorn in her throat. Every dog fell abruptly silent and stared at her.

"Yes, Storm . . . ?" Alpha's prompt held a growl of warning. "Speak!"

"I was at the lake." The admission rushed out of her, hot and shameful. "I went down there, because I . . . I couldn't sleep, and I . . ."

"You were at the lake?" Alpha's voice was cold and dangerous. She looked as if she was holding back terrible fear and anger, and there was no room for any other emotion right now. "And Tumble? Was he there, too?"

"He was—yes," croaked Storm.

A gasp went up from the Pack members, along with growls and exclamations of disbelief.

"Tumble had *been* there," she corrected herself, glancing from face to face. None of her Packmates looked sympathetic; they seemed only angry, and anxious, and confused. "I could smell him, I . . . but I couldn't *see* him. I couldn't see him anywhere. I did look, Alpha—I knew something was wrong, but he was nowhere

in sight! And that's why I ran back just now—to tell you all . . ." Her voice faltered. *I sound as if I'm lying. I sound like a dog with something to hide.*

And I am. But how can I tell them about my sleepwalking?

Every dog stared at her, their eyes narrowed. Snap exchanged a glance with Mickey. Sunshine looked miserable and a little suspicious. Twitch looked disappointed. Chase's eyes were downright hostile.

As for Alpha, Storm still didn't dare even look at her.

Chase snapped, "What were you doing there? At the lake?"

Storm turned toward the little dog, lowering her shoulders, pleading. "That doesn't matter right now. We have to get back to the lake and find Tumble!"

"Oh, but it *is* important," cut in Moon. She was standing farther back, looking thoughtful, but her eyes were hard. "You're often where you're not supposed to be. Where do you go, Storm? You're always sneaking around, turning up in odd places at odd times. What are we supposed to think?"

Dogs were nodding, murmuring agreement.

"It's true," muttered Snap to Mickey, loud enough for Storm to hear. "Even you can't deny that."

To Storm's horror, Mickey didn't. He said nothing, but he

didn't contradict his mate. And he wouldn't meet Storm's eyes.

"Wait a minute." The voice was Daisy's. The little white dog padded to Moon's side and stared up at her. "Storm's done nothing wrong," she barked.

"You don't know that—" began Moon, but Daisy shook her head.

"I do." Daisy turned to look at the rest of the Pack. "I know something the rest of you don't." She then turned her gaze on Storm, her black eyes apologetic. "Storm walks in her sleep."

"What?" barked Alpha.

Storm's rib cage felt heavy with dread and shame. *Oh, Daisy.* The little dog was trying to help her, she knew—but she wasn't sure this would make things better. *My secret. It's out. And I have a feeling it is only going to make things worse.*

"I've known for a while," Daisy admitted, padding up to Alpha and crouching in apology. "It's completely harmless. Storm didn't want you to know, so I kept quiet, but she doesn't do anything sinister."

"What *does* she do?" barked Chase. Other dogs yelped in echo of her question.

"She just walks." Daisy nodded at Storm. "That's all. She wanders around and she wakes up in odd places. There's nothing bad

about sleepwalking. She can't help it."

For an instant, there was shocked silence. Then the Pack erupted in a cacophony of barking.

"This makes her *more* dangerous!" yelped Snap.

"Daisy, how could you keep this from us?" howled Chase. "You're the one who said we had to be honest with each other!"

"Storm walks around in her sleep and doesn't know what she's doing?" barked Moon in disbelief. "How can that possibly be innocent?"

"It may not be her fault," muttered Mickey, with a sideways apologetic look at Storm, "but it certainly does raise some questions."

"She could have been doing all the terrible things that have happened around here," yapped Chase, "and she wouldn't even know she was doing it!"

"No," whined Storm, trying desperately to make herself heard. "No, that's not possible. I couldn't have—"

"*Quiet!*" Alpha's sharp bark silenced every dog. She glared around at the Pack, finally letting her eyes come to rest on Storm. "This is something we can—*and will*—discuss later. For now, we have something much more important to do. Storm! You say you smelled Tumble, down at the Endless Lake?"

Storm nodded, relieved that, at least for now, she had a respite from their questions and accusations. "Yes, Alpha. His scent was there, and it was fresh. I'm sure of it."

"But he was nowhere in sight?"

"No! Or I'd have gotten him, no matter what, and brought him back to you!" Storm's eyes pleaded with her leader. *You have to believe me, Alpha.*

"Very well." Alpha nodded to Lucky, who looked somber and fearful. "Every dog to the beach, now—except for Sunshine. She will stay and watch the rest of the pups."

Sunshine nodded and scurried over to guard the three remaining pups. At once, with a summoning bark, Alpha leaped and bolted away into the forest, as fleet as the wind. Lucky was hard on her heels. The rest of the Pack fell in behind them, and Storm joined them, pounding through the trees as fast as she had in her terrible dream. *Faster.* A rising panic threatened to make her trip and stumble. *I don't understand any of this. How could I have dreamed such a vivid dream of Tumble, the very night he went missing?*

Her breath ached in her chest, just as it had in her dream. Her muscles stung with the effort. *It's as if I've run this route before.* She felt sick.

And just as she hadn't been able to catch the Fear-Dog, there

was no way Storm could keep up with Alpha. She had never seen the swift-dog run so fast. Only when she reached the beach did Alpha finally slow to a halt, casting around with her raised muzzle for any trace of her pup.

"Spread out," she called, as one by one her Pack emerged panting from the trees behind her. "Look for any trace of Tumble. If Storm is correct, and he's been here, we should be able to find his trail easily enough."

Daisy, though last to arrive on her short legs, gave an immediate yelp. Every dog turned to her; she stood, tail quivering, beneath a small dune just next to the trees. "I have his scent over here!"

The dogs raced over, plunging through the soft, dry sand. Storm snuffled with the others, trying to follow Tumble's scent—but it petered out after only a rabbit-chase.

"That doesn't make sense." Mickey stood stiffly, his nostrils snuffling at the breeze. "How can his scent just vanish?"

"I've found it again!" barked Breeze. She was some way down the beach; sure enough, when the others ran to her side, they could smell the pup's distinctive scent once more. But yet again, it disappeared within a few paces.

It's as if he was carried, and set down now and again, thought Storm. *Carried in a big dog's jaws . . .* A thrill of horror went through her bones.

The Fear-Dog in my dream carried him like that!

"Here!" called Snap, who was farther down the beach, near the wet sand where the lake-tide reached.

This time only Mickey and Lucky ran to investigate; the other Pack members continued sniffing for Tumble in a wide arc across the sand. An occasional yelp signaled that a dog had picked up the scent again, but no dog managed to follow it for long. Alpha was lashing her tail in frustration, gazing around the beach in increasing desperation. Storm saw that her eyes were more and more frequently drawn to the crashing waves of the lake itself, and then they would fill with terror.

If Tumble's gone, Storm thought, *I can't imagine Alpha's and Lucky's grief. . . .*

Hesitantly Storm padded toward the water. It was hard to pick up any kind of scent on the sodden sand, beyond the smells of water grasses and crabs and salt, but she felt she had to try. *But if Tumble did go into the Endless Lake, what can I do? There will be nothing any dog can do.*

A memory came to her: Spring's limp body, floating in the lake after that terrible storm, one ear flopped over her dead eye. *Even the River-Dog couldn't have brought Spring back. If Tumble went into the water, there's no hope for him. . . .*

Wrapped in horrible thoughts, she barely heard the howling at first. Then it penetrated her thoughts: a piercing, summoning cry. "My Pack! My Pack!"

Alpha!

Storm's heart turned over in her rib cage, and she raced up the beach toward the sound. Other dogs were running too, from their searches across the wide bay, and they exchanged glances of fear as they converged on their leader.

The howl was coming from the bottom of the cliff, where two great slabs of gray stone had split and collapsed against each other. In the tiny gap between them, hidden by yellow grasses and scrubby brush, was a dark, cool cave. The echo of howling came from inside; Storm wriggled through into murky half-light, her Packmates behind her.

There stood Alpha, still howling her summons—in between frantic, furious licks to a cowering Tumble.

Storm felt dizzy; her heart raced and pounded with relief. The little pup's golden coat was sodden and dark, and he was trembling—but he was alive, and he seemed unharmed.

Lucky shoved past Storm to his mate's side, and he too fell to licking warmth back into his pup, his tongue almost knocking the little dog onto his side. "Tumble. *Tumble.* You're all right."

"We'll get you home," Alpha was murmuring as she licked the top of Tumble's golden head. She had stopped howling; the whole Pack was crammed into the cave. "We'll take you back to your sisters. We missed you so much, Tumble. Thank the Sky-Dogs we found you." She closed her eyes briefly, tilting her face toward the unseen sky.

"What happened to you, pup?" Mickey asked, his brown eyes huge.

Tumble opened his little jaws, but he was still shaking too much to speak. It took a lot more licking and nuzzling from his parent-dogs before he calmed down; the whole Pack waited patiently, tails wagging with relief and happiness.

"What happened, little one?" Alpha repeated at last, gently. "Why did you come here?"

He still quivered, and his voice shook. "I had to hide, Sweet. I had to hide!" He sounded small and terrified in the echoing darkness of the cave.

"Why, pup?" coaxed Lucky, licking his ears gently. "Why did you have to hide?"

"I don't know," he whimpered. "I don't know. She told me I had to hide."

Alpha and Lucky, startled, stared at each other over the pup's

head. Then Alpha nuzzled him again. "Who, Tumble? Who told you to hide?"

In the silence, the little golden pup raised his trembling head. His whimper was barely audible.

"Storm did," he whispered. "Storm told me I had to hide."

"*What?*" Lucky's head snapped up, and he glared at Storm. Alpha lifted hers more slowly; again she gave Storm that cold, furious look.

Storm stammered, "Tumble, I—what—I don't unders—"

She took a pace toward him; he flinched back between his Father-Dog's paws, recoiling, pressing himself close to the ground.

Lucky looked down at him. Very softly, he asked, "Did Storm bring you here, pup?"

Tumble swallowed and nodded, quickly and frantically. "Yes," he whispered. "Storm picked me up and brought me. Storm was scary, Lucky!"

For a moment, Storm thought she was going to faint. There was no light of cunning in Tumble's eyes, no hint that he was lying or playing some strange pup-joke. He was scared, and shaking; and he was telling the truth. Storm's head whirled even as her heart plummeted in her chest.

"Lucky, I didn't. You have to believe me," she pleaded. "I can't have—I didn't—"

It's hopeless. And it isn't true. I obviously did.

But I never meant to do it.

"Lucky!" she blurted again. "I must have done it in my sleep. I—I didn't know! I didn't mean to. I would never hurt Tumble, you know that!"

Lucky didn't answer. If anything, he drew his protective paws closer around his trembling pup. Glancing up at her Packmates, Storm saw that, one by one, they were stepping back from her, drawing away. Their eyes were bright with fear and anger and mistrust. Even Daisy's . . .

Alpha spoke at last. "Pack," she said, and her voice was chillier than the water of the Endless Lake. "We must get Tumble back to the camp, and to his den. We cannot stay here. . . ." She glanced at Storm, then deliberately averted her eyes.

"We will talk about this later, as a Pack. The matter demands a proper gathering, and a Howl. But first, we must look after Tumble. The most important thing right now is that he's safe."

Lifting him gently in her jaws, Alpha carried her pup out of the cave and into the warm light of the Sun-Dog. Lucky followed

her, and the rest of the Pack went behind him; not one of them looked back at Storm. She stood in the cold darkness of the cave and watched them all turn away.

The worst thing of all was that Storm couldn't blame them. They had every right to turn their rumps on her. Even Mickey and Daisy. *Especially* Lucky.

Oh, Sky-Dogs. The full horror of it rushed through her blood, swamping her, threatening to crush her.

What have I done?

CHAPTER TWENTY-ONE

Storm lay on her belly in the center of the camp. Her paws were in front of her and her head was raised; she didn't want to lower it to rest. Every member of her Pack sat in a circle around her, and despite her shame at what she had done, she did not want to look humiliated and beaten.

What I did was terrible. But I didn't mean to do it.

The late-afternoon Sun-Dog breathed warmth on her back, but her blood felt cold. *I'll never be truly warm again.*

She blinked, gazing into the eyes of her Packmates. They were all quiet—some sullen, some hostile, some just miserable—as they waited for Alpha and Beta to emerge from their den. The two of them had vanished in there to settle Tumble back with his litter-sisters, but every dog knew they had also gone to discuss the way forward for the Pack. Twitch, the Third Dog, had been

summoned inside after a while, and he had not yet reappeared.

Now the Pack awaited their leader dogs' decision in an unnatural, heavy silence.

Storm twitched an ear. She thought that even the birds must have caught the mood in the glade, for there was no singing. Somewhere, distantly, there was a crack of undergrowth as a group of deer moved through the forest, but no Pack Dog was thinking of prey right now.

Storm watched each dog's face, studying their expressions one by one. Not one of them would meet her eyes. *That's not good. . . .*

She could smell the mistrust on the air: the sharpness of suspicion and hostility. Some looked sadder than others—Mickey, Daisy, Sunshine, and Breeze—but still, they didn't dare look straight at her. Thorn and Beetle stared gloomily at the ground. As for Moon and Snap and Chase, their dislike was almost tangible.

They're all just waiting for Alpha's judgment, Storm thought. *They're waiting for her word before they tell me what they think. . . .*

But Storm realized, with a sudden clarity, that *she* didn't have to.

What am I waiting for? I know what I have to do.

I've known for a while now. It's something I should have done long ago.

The shadows crept across the glade, growing longer as the

Sun-Dog yawned and stretched and settled to his rest. Stars began to wink in the darkening sky. Beetles scurried in the grass and a lizard darted beneath a stone; Storm could hear the tiny creatures very clearly, as if all her senses were suddenly much sharper than they had ever been.

Maybe that's because I'm going to need them. Now more than ever.

At last there was movement at the entrance to Alpha's den; there was an audible sigh of relief throughout the Pack. Every dog seemed to tense in expectation, fur prickling and tails trembling.

Storm did not feel the general ripple of apprehension. She felt calmer than she had in a very long time as Alpha, Lucky, and Twitch emerged from the mouth of the den.

Their faces were very serious as they paced into the center of the glade. Storm rose to her paws and faced them squarely. Before Alpha could even open her jaws to speak, Storm took a single step forward.

"You don't need to say anything." Storm was glad that her voice sounded so level. "I know what you've talked about; well, it wasn't necessary."

Lucky sat back on his haunches, watching her nervously, but Alpha remained standing, listening intently as Storm spoke.

"*None* of you trust me now. Some of you never did, and

others . . . you trusted me when I helped find the pups, before, but ever since . . ." She cleared her throat and licked her jaws. Perhaps she shouldn't have mentioned the pups—Alpha's expression turned hard, and several of the others were staring at her as if they couldn't believe they had felt so kindly toward her. "And after what happened with Tumble, I can't blame you. I don't deserve your trust."

Some of the dogs shuffled uncomfortably and shared awkward glances; others gaped at her, but all remained silent.

"There's something I want to say, Alpha." Storm looked levelly at her leader. "With my waking mind and body, I would never, ever do anything to harm this Pack. I'm sorry I kept my sleepwalking a secret; that was a mistake, and I'm sorry. I know I don't have it in me to harm any of you—least of all the pups. But *you* don't know that. You have no way of knowing it, and I can't prove it. So I understand why all of this makes you so nervous."

Alpha gave a single, slow nod.

"I also want to say," Storm went on, her gaze roaming over each Pack member, "that I still think there's an enemy dog walking among you. And it isn't me, however bad this situation might look. Telling a pup to hide, putting him in danger without knowing I was doing it—that looks terrible. I'm sorry that I scared

Tumble; I never meant to cause him harm. But picking up a pup in your sleep is one thing. Murdering a Packmate is another thing altogether."

Alpha and Lucky shared a look, Storm noticed. They both looked unconvinced, and that hurt Storm like broken clear-stone in her belly.

She drew a heavy breath. "But even though I didn't mean to, I did put Tumble in danger. And that's why I can't stay in this Pack any longer." Storm raised her head, blinking hard. "I'm leaving. It's the only way."

She closed her eyes briefly in the silence that followed. Her calm was beginning to crumble now. *Hold it together, Storm, just a little longer. . . .*

She suppressed a shudder and gazed around the Pack. Mickey and Daisy still looked sad, Sunshine had lain down on her belly, her face resting miserably on her forepaws. Beetle and Thorn looked a little shocked. But no dog protested; no dog moved or barked out that she should stay. Storm felt as if her heart were twisting and wrenching inside her, as if it were being bitten by a hungry fox.

I know I have to leave. Everything I've said is true.

But it hurts that none of them want me to stay.

Alpha still said nothing, and neither did Lucky. The two leaders, with Twitch, stood and watched as Storm backed up a few paces. At last, taking a deep, ragged breath, she turned her rump on the Pack. One pace, then two, then a third: Storm strode determinedly out of the glade and across the camp boundary.

She could still hear no whines or barks behind her; the Pack was watching her leave in complete silence. She carried on placing one paw in front of the other. Storm realized she wasn't even aware what direction she was going; she simply kept padding on, putting a rabbit-chase between her and her former Packmates, then another, and another. With each step it became a little easier to keep walking, despite the terrible ache in her rib cage and belly.

I hate leaving. But I have to leave.

They don't trust me, and it hurts. But they have good reason.

Keep walking, Storm. Just keep going.

Images came into her head, making her gut twist with pain: Daisy's cheerful face, Mickey's wagging tail as he bounded ahead of her on a hunt. Moon's exasperated expression as she heard of more antics from Beetle and Thorn. Breeze, curled around the pups, protecting them as they slept; and Sunshine, waving her raggedy plume of a tail for Tiny to chase.

There are lots of dogs I will miss. Even the ones who didn't trust me. They were my Pack, and I may never see them again. . . .

Storm came to a halt and shook herself violently. She gave a ferocious growl, curling her muzzle.

Be strong, Storm! These thoughts aren't helping.

The Pack would be better off without her; she had to believe that, despite what Breeze had said about her being the best hunter. And she would certainly be better off without the Pack. It had become impossible: the wary glances, the muttered remarks. Life as a Lone Dog would be simpler, more relaxing; she wouldn't always have to watch her words, she wouldn't have to pad so carefully around the anxieties of her Packmates. If she wanted to snarl with rage and bite her own tail in frustration, she could do it without striking terror into every dog in earshot.

Lucky survived for a long time as a Lone Dog. He was happy, and he hunted alone. I can do the same. I can be happy too.

She had walked a long way already, it struck her as she came out of the trees onto a long, grassy slope. The Sun-Dog lit the landscape with his last, slanting rays; he was a bright point of dazzling gold on the far horizon. Every leaf and blade of grass glowed with the great Spirit Dog's light.

And then, abruptly, there was another, separate flash of gold.

It sprang up from nowhere and stood poised before her, bright and magnificent:

The Golden Deer!

Storm halted and stared, awestruck by its beauty. It was standing so close to her, she could see straight into its bright liquid-bronze eyes. The tines of its antlers sparkled with points of light and its hide shone like the Sun-Dog himself.

Storm's aching heart pounded, and her throat felt dry and tight. The beauty and solemnity of the creature was overwhelming, and for long moments she could only gape at it, dazzled.

It looked back at her, unafraid, challenging.

One leap. One good spring is all it would take. I could bring down the Golden Deer right here, right now; it's as if the Wind-Dogs have sent it to me.

If I take the Golden Deer, the Pack will have good fortune at last. The pups will be safe, and happy, and that will be down to me. Tumble, Fluff, Nibble, and Tiny: They'll thrive and be truly lucky.

If I catch the Golden Deer for my Pack . . .

For the Pack.

Storm and the Golden Deer just gazed into each other's eyes, as the last rays of the Sun-Dog faded. The glowing light died from the landscape, and shadows crept across the grass and the trees.

But still the Golden Deer remained radiant, as if a part of the Sun-Dog had stayed here with it.

It blinked at her, slowly. Storm dipped her head, once, in awed respect.

And then she turned away.

She padded across the dew-damp grass without looking back. She walked on, away from the Golden Deer, and felt no regret at all. She walked until she knew that even that beautiful, shining Spirit Deer had faded from view and disappeared in the shadows of the night.

It isn't my duty anymore. I'm a Lone Dog now. I can't bring good fortune to a Pack that is no longer mine.

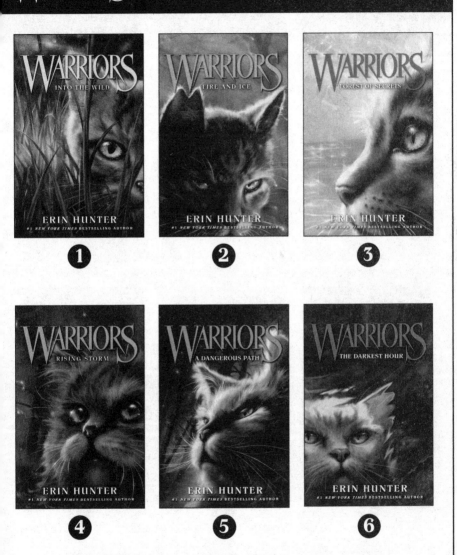

In the first series, sinister perils threaten the four warrior Clans. Into the midst of this turmoil comes Rusty, an ordinary housecat, who may just be the bravest of them all.

WARRIORS: THE NEW PROPHECY

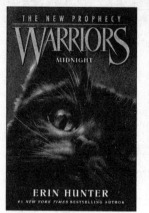
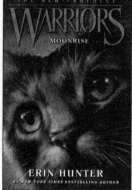

In the second series, follow the next generation of heroic cats as they set off on a quest to save the Clans from destruction.

HARPER
An Imprint of HarperCollinsPublishers

www.warriorcats.com

WARRIORS: POWER OF THREE

1. POWER OF THREE — WARRIORS — THE SIGHT — ERIN HUNTER — #1 NEW YORK TIMES BESTSELLING AUTHOR
2. POWER OF THREE — WARRIORS — DARK RIVER — ERIN HUNTER — #1 NEW YORK TIMES BESTSELLING AUTHOR
3. POWER OF THREE — WARRIORS — OUTCAST — ERIN HUNTER — #1 NEW YORK TIMES BESTSELLING AUTHOR
4. POWER OF THREE — WARRIORS — ECLIPSE — ERIN HUNTER — #1 NEW YORK TIMES BESTSELLING AUTHOR
5. POWER OF THREE — WARRIORS — LONG SHADOWS — ERIN HUNTER — #1 NEW YORK TIMES BESTSELLING AUTHOR
6. POWER OF THREE — WARRIORS — SUNRISE — ERIN HUNTER — #1 NEW YORK TIMES BESTSELLING AUTHOR

In the third series, Firestar's grandchildren begin their training as warrior cats. Prophecy foretells that they will hold more power than any cats before them.

HARPER
An Imprint of HarperCollins*Publishers*

WARRIORS: DAWN OF THE CLANS

In this prequel series,
discover how the warrior Clans came to be.

WARRIORS : BONUS STORIES

Discover the untold stories of the warrior cats and Clans
when you download the separate ebook novellas—or read
them in four paperback bind-ups!

HARPER
An Imprint of HarperCollinsPublishers

www.warriorcats.com

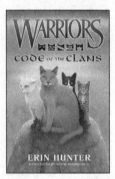

READ EVERY
SEEKERS
BOOK

Seekers: The Original Series

Three young bears . . . one destiny.
Discover the fate that awaits them on their adventure.

Seekers: Return to the Wild

     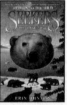

The stakes are higher than ever as the bears search for a way home.

Seekers: Manga

The bears come to life in manga!

HARPER
An Imprint of HarperCollinsPublishers

www.seekerbears.com